Sec
Jewel

PARADISE

This time the dream seemed so real . . .

There was a big, warm body next to hers, one so firm and hard. She could feel this dreamy man's hard breath on her neck.

Altogether, the knight was a magnificent man.

They were so close one could not get a cat's hair between the pair of them. They fit together like pieces of something that had been apart and were now back together where they belonged. One, as they should be.

Two halves make a whole.

"Kiss me, Maiden," he whispered huskily. "A maiden's kiss is all I ask."

His lips touched hers and Autumn shivered.

Raine drew her closer to his hardened body. Her warmth and soft loveliness started his heart to beating a rapid song, the feel of her young body setting his male flesh afire.

Never had a dream been more vivid. Like a tumult, the light contact of his lips shivered through her as he now kissed her eyes, the softness at the nape of her neck. He bent to kiss the corner of her tempting mouth. Her whole body seemed to melt into his, while his lips continued to possess her in a passionate kiss.

Autumn wished never to awaken from this paradise that was more true than reality itself. A completion and a wholeness . . . a meeting of souls and minds.

SONYA T. PELTON

Secret Jewel

ZEBRA BOOKS
KENSINGTON PUBLISHING CORP.

ZEBRA BOOKS are published by

Kensington Publishing Corp.
475 Park Avenue South
New York, NY 10016

First Printing: April, 1994

Printed in the United States of America

In memory of "Oreo."
We thank you for four wonderful, love-filled,
fun-filled years, our beloved purr-son.

While we look not at the things which are seen, but at the things which are not seen: for the things which *are* seen are temporal; but the things which are not seen *are* eternal.

2 Cor. 4:18

Prologue

"You have to kill her . . . You *have to* kill her."

The words, the haunting words, they stayed with the young man well into the forest as he trailed after the girl he had been ordered to exterminate.

She is so very young, he thought as he kept to the shadows, watching, biding his time. He did not think he could bear to see the look of horror in the innocent lamb's eyes as he sent her plunging to her death.

He kept following the girl with the red hair. She hadn't covered her head with the cowl of her cloak. He just kept following the hair that seemed as if flames of fire lived in each separate strand as it danced and rippled to a tiny waist.

She looked so innocent, so very damned innocent. He could not see her face. He had only been told he would know her by the plum color of her cloak and the flames of hair.

Pulling a long jeweled dagger he moved faster now. She had begun to move quickly, tossing a glance over her shoulder following every ten or twelve steps. She remained just out of reach, pulling away every time he was prepared to pounce and stab.

He was desperate.

Then he heard the dogs. Hunters. He could tell by the baying sounds.

She was gasping now, looking into the shadows more often. And he moved faster, coming closer to her. So close he could see the dark red lashes that were thick and long. She had no idea if he were man or beast.

But she knew, knew something was there.

She had been picking flowers. They dropped now, scattering color across the forest floor. Her slim legs pumped swiftly and her cloak swirled behind her in her flight, coiling with the red helixes of hair.

The dogs leaped into the clearing. His prey was lost, for he heard the sound of men searching in the under-brush.

A richly dressed man stepped out, narrowed his eyes, and the young assassin melted into the shadows.

The girl was gone, having skipped way up ahead, no doubt gone back to her wildflower picking. Such was the way of the very young.

The blackness of the assassin's chausses and cloak fed themselves into the blackness of the forest, leaving no shape for the eye to catch. There was only the shine of captured light from his naked dagger as he meant to sheath the thing, dropped it, darted to fetch it up, fumbled and fled.

One

1422, England

She was not aware of the blood trickling down her wrist as she squeezed the pointed jewel suspended from her neck.

Suddenly the beautiful baroness spoke to her husband.
"I'm not sure why, but I feel that Autumn is in danger, or moving toward danger." She kept gazing out the solar room window.

Orion Sutherland came up behind his wife and, brushing aside her jet-black hair, kissed her neck softly. "Why is this, my love?"

"A feeling." Turning her head slightly, she stared mistily toward the tawny greyhound, and a second black-spotted one, both lying at the foot of a huge carved-oak chair, upholstered in a sunny golden apple print.

Orion pressed her arm. He loved the satiny feel of her in her deep blue dressing gown. "Hmm. A woman-feeling. I know about those, firsthand from my beautiful lady wife."

Elizabeth finally stirred and took her husband's hand, bringing it to press to her cheek. "A woman," she said. "Autumn is a woman now."

"Autumn is still a maiden at twenty-one."

"Twenty," Elizabeth said, then her brows lifted. "However, I cannot be sure of accuracy. Just like Dawn, my sister-in-law, no one can be certain of Autumn's true age. What does age matter anyway." She sighed, looking down at the tan hand caressing her arm. "Does not the spring sun feel good and warm coming in the many windows?"

Orion wanted to discuss their newest project, lay out the drawings and show her what he was renovating in the old castle next; he'd just finished making the addition of the newer, larger solar as well as another wing. "I, too, worry about Autumn." He knew what was foremost in Elizabeth's mind yet did not broach it. "But you worry about every sickness and sorrow on the castle grounds; even the village folk hold your concern and compassion. Yet, I, too, worry about our next child."

"Why?" she asked with a throaty chuckle.

"That he does not turn out as wild as our two-year old Maryse Nicole!"

"He?" she said exuberantly; even while in the back of her mind lingered the worry of Autumn Meaux.

"If the child's another "she," you'll worry your pretty little head right off your shoulders having two Sutherland daughters in the manor." Orion paused and kissed Elizabeth's smooth cheek. "Autumn is not our daughter. She is one of so many orphaned children come to our castle, under your wing."

"Though twenty, Autumn is a just-emerging butterfly.

10

She knows nothing of men and what they can . . . you know."

"Aye, yet my knights have noticed her. An exquisite creation barely aware of her power to dazzle and charm. Much like you when you first came here." With a familiar gesture he stroked her sleek hair with the back of his hand.

"Autumn Meaux is gently bred. Remember when she came to us at fourteen in that torn but finely made gown? Sad to lose your whole family like that." She frowned and her clear eyes darkened. "Scardon's men, they are evil, what remains of the band. They had killed Autumn's parents when the family had been visiting relatives in the English town of Brighton. Autumn and her sisters traveled to Herst in hopes of escaping the madmen, but they had been there waiting. Autumn still does not know what befell her sisters."

"Aye," Orion said. "They had always been together, all their life, four girls born at a single birth. Almost seven years gone. Where could the Meaux sisters be?"

"No doubt Scardon's men scattered them to the winds." She hated to think they were dead; refused to. "Now I hear Scardon's nasty young cousin Drogo is raping and terrorizing the countryside with his band of outlaws . . . Oh, Lord," Elizabeth went on as if to herself, "I'm becoming very worried about Autumn . . . she went off alone on her search for her lost sisters."

There was an immediate explosion.

"She . . . What! When?"

"She had been dreaming, remembering . . . she is not completely alone; last week they left from here. She's grown now and she's with the"—she hid her eyes from her husband—"uhmm, village idiot."

"What idiot?" asked Orion, his brows menacing.

"The one I found work for here at the castle. His name is Barry Jeraux. Actually, he is quite capable and not so simpleminded. You did not know because you have just returned from Brighton."

Noticing for the first time the blood on her hand, Elizabeth frowned, touched the jewel below her throat, then wiped the blood from her palm and the gold-encrusted ruby.

Pacing, Orion gritted his teeth and growled as he swung toward the door.

"I can see your feelings are very strong in this matter," Elizabeth said.

"Yes, madame. That is true." He walked over to wrench open the heavy door in the north wall.

Elizabeth sat down heavily next to her tapestry frame as the door swung closed. Oh no . . . she had promised Autumn. Now she had done it. Orion would put some knights out at once. Perhaps it was better this way, since she somehow knew that Autumn was moving toward danger.

Her hair was a flame following her. Gray mist wreathed the woods as Autumn darted through a long tunnel of trees. She held a crossbow in the crook of her arm and she had scratches from branches hanging low and wide. She stopped now and then to cast quick glances behind her. Closer they came on the unbeaten path. She inhaled sharply and bolted down the green tunnel. The dirt plumed out beneath her hammering feet as she put every last ounce of energy into running fast. She angled wildly to her right, only to have a dark horse angle in to cut off her escape. The riders, four of them, were surrounding her. Hot breath rippled on her nape, her shoulders, horses' foam flecking her as she gave a yell that produced renewed energy in her limbs. Up ahead a woman on a white horse crossed the path in front of her. *Winter . . . Ghost!* The pounding of the white's hooves was now like thunder from the hills and there at the end of the tunnel was a jewel shining mauve-white; it was her own family jewel. And her sister Winter, with a circlet of daisies braided into her blond hair, was holding it. No, now a man was holding it . . . and suddenly he tossed it to someone else. A very good-looking young man wearing odd clothes.

"Maiden, rise," a deep voice said.

She looked up, seeing a man, finding herself staring into a dark shape framed by the forest moon. He wore a green cloak, black tunic, brown leather vest. Below that she couldn't see. Didn't want to . . . because . . . because, he seemed to be devoid of clothing in that area. Softly, there was the call of a night bird. Autumn watched the man melt away.

She realized she was dreaming.

Autumn awoke and looked about the tent in search of someone. "Barry. I've had a dream of . . . of— Where are you?"

Slouched low, the village idiot entered. She looked at the hair plastered to his skull and greasy strands hanging in his eyes. He lumbered when he walked, but she smiled up at him. This just made him more endearing to her, all his faults, bad manners, even his filthiness. Dirt, she kept reminding herself, was only dirt. But sometimes she had to shudder.

"I'm here, princess," Barry mumbled. "You had another dream; I heard you talking in it." A broad grin etched white crinkles across his dirty face. "Just went and fetched wood." He sounded like he had a chunk of lamb's wool wadded up in his mouth when he spoke.

The dream was already fading. "Barry, thank you. I will have to make that soup and the wood will keep the fire going. Where is my mount?"

"Uh, Ghost is doing well. She and the pack-asses are at the stream being watered. I hobbled 'em."

"One thing, you must remember." She saw Barry look up at her with a sheepish pout. "I am not a princess. You mustn't call me that."

He blinked as he looked at her adoringly. "You sure sound like one. There's an air about you that's almost, uh, regal."

Autumn blinked and shook her head with a little jerk. "And you," she said laughing, "you don't sound like the village idiot when you talk like that."

Barry hung his head and shifted big clumsy feet. Looking at him, Autumn's mouth hung open and she was at once ashamed. "Oh, Barry. Forgive me, I didn't mean it like it sounded. Truly."

"Yes you did, pr—I mean, Mistress Autumn. I know everybody thinks I'm just a stupid lummox and a dumb dunce and—"

Autumn chuckled. "They mean the same thing, Barry." When she saw him drop his heavy head lower, she rushed over, made to touch him on the shoulder. But he flinched away and pressed his lips together. "Barry . . . you do have feelings about your looks and lack of"—she left out the word "intelligence"—"and I'm so insensitive at times. You are very special."

14

"I am?" He looked over at her with bright gray eyes, before his bushy brows crashed together again over a long, wide, dirty nose. "Special to you?" His voice lifted and he snuffled. "Mistress Autumn?"

"Well . . . yes." Autumn thought about this.

She had met Barry in the village of Herst several weeks back. The villagers said he had been begging food in the streets and the baker had taken him in. Barry had helped make pies, and then the baker had kicked him out for his clumsiness. Barry had tripped and dumped a pannier of strawberry-rhubarb pies into the street. Autumn had been in the village with her maid to shop when she saw the man sitting on a low wall eating a dirty piece of pie. She had asked what had happened and gotten the whole story. The only thing Barry wouldn't entirely tell was where his home was.

"I got no home now," he'd said, bending to wipe his nose across his tattered sleeve.

"But you must have lived somewhere before?" She spread her hands.

"North from London. Used to work in a manor there in Nottinghamshire, but they kicked me out for my clumsiness. Just like today."

"No family? You have nowhere to go then?"

"No. Nowhere." He had peered up at her with such loneliness in his gray eyes; she couldn't tell if they were really truly gray, or dull green, maybe both having much dirt around them.

She told him about Sutherland castle, where she lived. There were many orphans living there; she was one of them in fact. "Would you like to come and live there? We could find something for you to do. My lady,

15

the baroness Sutherland—I call her Elizabeth because she demands it—she is kindly and will find a job for you."

"I have heard that Sutherland is a place like that, where they take in strays."

"Yes. What is your last name, Barry?"

"Uh. Barry Jeraux." He scratched his ear. "I guess I've got a little French in me."

Autumn frowned in thought for a moment, then let it pass. "I, too, have French blood. I am Autumn Meaux. My mother was English but—she is dead now, as my father is. My sisters—" She sighed heavily, unable to finish, thinking it wouldn't matter to tell.

Barry had only nodded and grinned as he got up, wiped sticky hands on his pants and followed her to Sutherland, out of the village, and up into the green hills and crystal blue sky. That had taken place several weeks ago.

Now they were together, at the edge of the greenwood where Barry had pitched the small tent they had borrowed from the weapon-stores of Sutherland. One of the blond, blue-eyed knights by the name of Howell Armstrong had dropped his jaw upon seeing Barry as though he wanted to speak to the idiot. Puzzled, Autumn had whirled to look at Barry. It had been an odd exchange, but both men had gone back to what they were doing before the knight had looked up into Barry's face and froze.

They had camped in a beautiful clearing. The morning wreaths of mist had been dispelled and the long grass looked almost blue. The short hills and heath beyond the forest were a rich blending of colors, gray and mauve and purple, even a hint of red. Silence was complete, as it should be at such an early hour.

"I just want to get my sisters back. The sooner the better. It's been too long. I am very lonesome without my kin."

Autumn hadn't realized as she stood alone that she'd spoken out loud the words most often in her mind. Barry came closer and he spoke softly.

"Sisters?" He tipped his greasy head. "Thought you only had the one, Mistress Autumn?"

"I—" She did not want to lie. She would not mention all *three*. Then Barry may not wish to help look for them as he'd first agreed to on that sunny Sunday when he'd asked what was troubling her. Confessing to him had been the start of their journey; now they were almost to London, so Autumn said, "I have to get her back." Well, that was not a lie, she thought. She'd start with one sister at a time.

"What's her name?" Barry asked over his shoulder as she followed him back to camp where he'd already folded the tent onto the two-wheeled cart.

Autumn chose at random. "Hmmm. Winter."

"Uh. That's a nice name. Too bad your parents didn't have time for Summer and Spr—"

"Oh look! The cakes are burning!" Autumn ran to their breakfast, indeed burning, over the campfire. With her back to Barry she flapped the black barley cake in the air, thinking, Saved by Barry's high flame! "I shall cook more," she called in a singsong voice over her shoulder. "You just finish your packing."

Barry grinned and set about his task, whistling a merry bawdy tune under his breath.

On the road again, Barry walked beside the huge

white horse that had been a gift from the baroness to Autumn; in that season she had given it to the girl, as a "birthday" present. With a familiar gesture Ghost bumped Barry's shoulder often with her velvet muzzle as they trod the dusty road; Autumn's musical laughter was heard above them as she chattered gaily about the charming country sights before falling silent for a spell.

It was Barry who broke the silence. "Why did you not go after your sister before this?"

Autumn blinked. "Why, I was too young. I had done some serious thinking about it over the years. Seven, I think. Steadily the feeling that I must do something became stronger. I had to find them . . . her."

But how in the world was she to know where to look, to go? Sutherland's knights had searched the countryside for years, with no luck. Yet they could not just have vanished from the earth without a trace; someone had to know something. Barry had said they should start in London. She had asked why, and he had answered that that was where most pretty young women were "brought to be bought"; and she had a good idea just what the nasty kidnappers had in mind! Barry hadn't said. But she was not naive. Young women were taken there to become painted doxies, harlots. Well, Barry said "Whores" so loud Autumn thought the whole castle had heard.

She just prayed she wasn't too late for Winter. *Or* the others.

That night, camped under the English starry skies, Autumn dreamed about the Windrush jewel again and the beautiful man who had entered her dreams and set her heart to trembling. She had dreamed of him for three nights in a row and when she awoke Barry's gray eyes were above hers, questioning.

"Did you dream again?" Barry asked, moving back against the cart as she walked from the tent yawning and stretching.

Autumn grinned as Barry whirled from her to duck his head, and she looked down at herself, her bare ankles beneath her long white, heavy nightgown, her toes tickled by the grass. The brisk morning air made her breasts stand against the coarse material, and she blushed, not for herself, but for Barry's embarrassment.

All that day she fantasized about the gorgeous man in her dreams. Who was he? Why had he just all of a sudden appeared in her dreams? What did his presence mean?

"I had a dream about the Windrush jewel again," Autumn said to Barry as they camped for a second night, in order for Barry to hunt some fresh meat.

Barry popped a juicy morsel of rabbit into his mouth, chewed, and said, "Your family jewel, this Windrush name?"

Autumn frowned and blinked at Barry's words. Then she sighed, saying, "Yes. It is most beautiful, our family's lost heirloom, dating back to the days of the Black Prince. I must find it, another reason for setting out from Sutherland. Without it, I can prove nothing of my family's rich and royal heritage."

Gulping a chunk of meat, Barry gasped, "Royal?" He blinked. "See. I knew you were a princess." He pictured her wearing an imperial purple gown with gold embroidery.

"Oh." She laughed. "Not that royal, I'm afraid. Before my parents were slain by Scardon's men, they talked about the jewel, saying they must locate it, else all would be lost. Before they could search further, they were murdered in Brighton. That is when I became separated from my sister."

"Scardon's cousin is Drogo. He and his band of younger robber-knights, that is, much younger than—" Barry looked at her suddenly wide eyes and his meat froze in its path to his mouth. "What is it?"

"When you're tired," she murmured, staring at him.

"Oh yes." He laughed. "I am tired, Mistress Autumn." He licked his lips and looked away. "The horse is tired, too; we needed this extra rest."

"No. No." Autumn stood and paced the campfire, staring into the orange flames. "When you're tired—" Coming to a halt, she stared down at him. "Your guard is not up then. I noticed this." Her voice grew hard as she bent closer, whispering, "Who are you really, Barry? Why do you sound not like the dunce you are supposed to be when you are tired from a hard day's hunting? And what happened to the wool in your mouth?"

Rocking back on his haunches, the blue-black sky behind him, Barry laughed up at her. "I am the man of your dreams, princess." He stopped suddenly and looked at her seriously. "You do dream about me, do you not?"

"No. Not you. You are my friend; I think." She moved back several inches as he rocked to his heels. "What is wrong with you, Barry?" Then she gasped as her hand slapped over her mouth. "You have deceived me . . . who are you?"

Then he sat back down and began to cry, with much moaning and groaning, his hands covering his face.

Autumn did not dare touch him. "Barry? What is wrong?" Daring to step closer, she timidly tapped his shoulder. "What are you doing? Can you tell me why you cry?"

"Well," he sniffed, "I lost a close kin, see."

"You, too?" Her violet eyes held surprise as she gawked at his flame-tinted features in the firelight.

"Yup. He"—*gulp*—"My twin. Sometimes the . . . twin comes out of me, you see."

"Oh." Autumn frowned. "I'm not sure that I do. But I shall try to understand. You're my friend, Barry." She remembered that Elizabeth said he had a "problem of the mind" and could be helped. She just did not know how.

"Hold my hand."

"What?" Autumn stood there, wondering what to do. "You want me to—"

"Yeah. Sit down here and hold my hand. I'll feel so much better, Mistress Autumn. Will you do that?"

"Well—of course." When she sat down and moved closer, she took his hand in hers—actually, his paw was so huge that she felt her hand was being swallowed by his. After a while she asked, "Feeling better?"

"So much. I'm going to get some sleep, Mistress Autumn."

"Yes. And so am I."

The morning was sunny and clear, and the song of the forest birds mocked Autumn's worries of the previous night. Barry was his old self once again. They ate some dried meat from Barry's pouch, drank and she bathed in a small stream; Barry himself did not wash or watch.

Later that day they entered Lincoln Forest and Barry stood and watched her while she had no idea he was studying her in the bluish light of the woods. Astride the big white, deep green and ash-brown surrounding, she was like a lost princess, with her tattered velvet cloak of heliotrope falling gracefully over the back of the horse. As night descended and it grew darker, he watched her ghostly image beside him, her pale loveliness as the moon glowed down over her head, a loveliness so simple and charming she reminded him of a disheveled princess. He told himself he would have to be more careful, yet she was so enchanting that he often forgot himself, forgot he was supposed to be Barry Jeraux, the village idiot. It was a difficult task, when all he wanted to do was court her, kiss her, take her in his arms. What was he thinking? This he could not do.

When, he wondered, would she see through his disguise? He was good at disguises; he'd worn many different ones for various "projects" he'd been working on at court and in the duchess's manor—and in the forest. He'd have to be more careful, however, otherwise Autumn was going to catch on. And that he did not need—not this early in the game.

First he had to unearth Autumn's secrets, and he was sure she was holding out, not telling him everything even though he was only the village idiot and could be trusted. So she thought.

Two

The brook that rippled over mossy stones not ten feet from where Barry and Autumn sat offered a cool break following the long, hot ride. Often they dismounted and walked the animals to give them a break, and Barry would then once again mount and ride the jennet, Autumn riding Ghost.

"Oh, look!" Autumn picked herself up and headed away from the water's edge and through the wildflowers up the hill. "It is lovely. Come and see, Barry."

A tall stone house stood at the edge of the forest, abandoned, looking as if it dated from the fifth or sixth century. A great marshy hollow dipped into the side of the large hill to the north and east.

"It looks abandoned," Barry said, unshouldering his bow and setting arrow to string. "One can never—"

"No." She put a hand on his arm. "There is no one here but scurrying creatures seeking food. It is abandoned. Oh"—she laughed and picked up her skirts—"it's all to ourselves!"

In the garden she plowed through she saw writings, from centuries before, scrawled on a sundial. Making

23

no sense of the greenish writings, she strolled on. She paused to look at everything, walking in the tall, weedy ryegrass as Barry followed close behind and into the tall house.

Barry said nothing as he readied his weapon again, his eyes sweeping the dark doorways and window openings with flapping oilcloths. A thin wind sprang up, gnawing around corners, sending tiny twisting streamers of dust scurrying among the pave stones.

Autumn stood in the largest room, looking up at the old stone walls. "I wonder where that stairway leads?"

Barry shrugged, hiding a grin as he stashed his weapon. "Don't know myself. But I know you. You'll be going up those narrow, winding stone stairs before long." He turned to look at piles of junk in the corner, at the heavy ring in the huge door. He then looked around, then up, saying, "Never saw a woman move so faa—"

Her head hung over the stairwell. "I'm already up here," she called down in a singsongy voice. "Come on up. It's enchanting, I can see all over the country from this height, oh, and the verdure and azure colors are beautiful."

Barry scratched his head. "I'll be right up," he yelled, humming as he went around and around the narrow stone stairs. "You are right. We can see all over from this high." He stood close behind her, staring down at her lovely arms and hands. Her hands were creamy and delicate, but strong. He liked her independence; she was like no other maiden he'd ever met before.

She's utterly enchanting, he told himself as he trailed after watching her poke into this and that. With each

24

step, old rushes and herbs rustled underfoot and the skirts of her plum floor-length inner tunic folded against the worn umber wool cloth of the undertunic. Her skin was like alabaster against the deep tones of her clothing. . . .

Suddenly she turned to the simpleton. "We shall sleep here." She walked slowly up the length of the hall.

"Here?" He made himself look as cloddy as possible, as he looked around the cold stone rooms, up and down the gray walls. He saw her eyes trained on a large oaken tub, so old it had turned coppery. "Now my work is cut out for me."

Her laugh was playful. "A bath, a real bath. I cannot wait."

"Neither can I." Barry went outside, flexing his muscles and looking for the nearest stream to begin hauling the water for the maiden. He saw a celestial stream conveniently within reach.

After a long, wonderful bath, Autumn curled up on a pallet with linens she aired that she had found stored in a low, broken drawer; what mattered a few moth holes, she thought as she snuggled in the bed and waited for Barry to finish with the supper things.

But she fell fast asleep and before long Barry came to stand over her, his head bent, his fingers near hers with only a cat's hair between them.

While poring over some drawings from old manuscripts inside the main room—the great hall—where she'd had him drag the rickety daybed, Barry looked up to see her staring at the stone wall where dusty tapestries hung and would, with one touch, fall apart in one's hands. He noticed a black speck.

He grinned and shrugged. "It's a spider."

"I know." She sighed, rustling some old pages, yellow as parchment, that fell apart at the corners and littered the folds of her plum skirts. "It is not what I am wondering about."

He came to sit on the edge of the bed. "What is it?"

"Barry, this is not helping me find my sister. These manuscripts belong to others, as far away from my family as the moon is from my face." Her head slanted as she watched the spider without care. "We will return to Sutherland. My mind is decided on this."

"We have only just begun, mistress."

She nodded, liking him calling her that instead of princess or some other royal name. There was nothing royal about her life at all. She had no idea where her family truly came from, too young back then to have cared. Her father took care of all; he was like a king to her and her sisters. Now he and her mother had perished by outlaw's hands. Her sisters had vanished. And the jewel, if one existed, would never be discovered; all was lost.

She shook her head, her long braids brushing her shoulders in a feminine dance. She heard the hounds again, in her head . . . it was as if they were hot on someone's scent. Again she shook her head to clear it.

"The world is so big," she told him. "Where will we look? Where will we start?"

His own troubled frown cleared. "Ah, mistress. Fret not. We have already begun the long journey."

That night she had a dream, again of the man in

foresting clothes, then transformed into royal garb. All her sisters were walking toward her; they were smiling with joy, without fear. Tears of happiness pooled upon her lids. She dreamed on and on. In it she heard a voice telling her she must not go to London but Nottinghamshire; there she would find her sister, but which one? Winter?

Winter had been in her dream. Someone had been chasing her and Autumn heard the hounds again. They were hot on the scent. There! There, she could see her sister Winter. She was gilded by afternoon sun and she stood still, in an arrested attitude of listening. Autumn's heart pounded for her sister's safety. The pack, in full cry, passed near Winter and out of Autumn's dreaming vision.

Autumn awoke, breathing heavily, her mind tripping over fragments of her dream. She had been back at home and had seen the green woods and tawny fields of Windrush Castle. But where was home? How far would she have to travel to get there? Why had the Sutherland knights not been able to find the place? Was it even in England? Did the place only exist in her imagination? And "Stepfather"? Why did that name come to her in her dream?

"We have rested enough," Autumn told Barry in the morning sunlight peeking around the narrow openings in stone. The oilcloth permeated a golden glow that gilded and likened them to ancient statues brought back with the Crusaders.

"You had another dream, mistress."

A soft gasp came from Autumn. "How did you

27

know?" She turned to look back at him from her bag-packing task.

"You talked again. I believe you mentioned Notting-hamshire." He looked at all her bags; she had packed enough for a royal retinue to haul along.

She blinked at his words. "I did?" For a moment she frowned. "You are right, yes, I believe it was Notting-hamshire. That is where we will go and find my sister I think. Perhaps even my castle is there."

"It is far, far away to the north this Nottinghamshire."

She smiled, her eyes made even more pixyish. "I know. Still, we will go. We are rested and the journey should be pleasant now that we have our strength back and have fished from the stream." She shooed him out of the room in order to finish her toilette.

Barry turned away, looking very pleased with him-self, looking back once, catching her alone in sudden thought as she paused to decide what to do next. She was enchanting again, a princess from long ago, as though infused with ancient sunlight.

I must go, he told himself.

Alone in the chilly stone room Autumn dressed swiftly into something warmer. Her fingertips brushed her skin, making her wonder why it tingled, even more so a few moments ago when Barry had been staring at her in the soft, golden glow that had crept around the edges of the oilcloth.

It means nothing. He is but a warm friend, she told herself.

She stood, her fingers flying as she shook her long hair loose—hair all said was red as fire—then combed it smooth with her fingers, pulled and piled it high in the air, and began to braid the many strands from the top of her head, starting with a fat braid and tapering down to a two-inch hank.

Quickly, Autumn gathered her things, looked around the ancient room she had occupied the last few days and went out. Her feet flew down the steps, her leather slippers barely touching the cold stones. Fat braid bouncing on her back, huge bags slung across both shoulders, she raced out the door.

Sunlight poured around her as she flew out the door, sending dust motes scattering . . . and collided right into Barry lifting his bulging bag—and many more of hers—from the weedy entrance.

He instinctively grabbed her arm to keep her from tripping and flying past him onto her face; they were so close her natural wildflower scent was in his nostrils. "How nice. We should stay this way a while," he murmured in a deep voice.

Sunlight in her eyes, Autumn looked up into his dry dirty face, inches away, the top of her red head near touching his chin. Those odd, warm tingles started again, beginning in her toes and fluttering all over as if sunshine glittered within her.

He chuckled, wanting very much to blow in her ear.

She moved away, calling over her shoulder, "You did not have to plant yourself right outside the door where you knew I would collide with you. Did you?"

"Uh—" He appeared to be thinking for a moment, then blurted, "Yes. It was nice to bump suddenly into each other. Don't you think, Mistress maiden?"

Autumn quirked her mouth. "Oh, Barry," she said with a quick laugh. "What am I going to do with you?" She walked away, going to get Ghost out from the old shed.

"Everything"—he began—"would be nice for a start." She had not heard; already she was too far away.

Hungerford was a village on the western fringes of the sparsely settled Wellingsford, a village situated at the junction of the east-west King's Road and the Post Road running north and south. It was a trading center for woods dwellers, farmers, travelers. The Unicorn Inn, with its many rooms, usually had a wayfarer or two as well as a nearby settler overnight. Occasionally there would be some of the king's knights from Henley Castle heading south, dropping in for a pint or two and a look at strangers and to hear the news from far away.

This night there was much singing and merriment as Autumn entered, her purple hood hiding her face in shadows. Only silence greeted her; all patronizers had quit making talk and noise. She moved across the common room, past the long tables and benches, then threaded through the small tables and chairs. She stopped at a table where the candle was unlit. A shiver had begun to course her spine.

I just know something unusual is going to happen, she thought.

Barry moved behind her just then, reaching to borrow a candle and using it to light their own. "Eyyy, whady'ya think yer doin'," the fellow at the next table protested the hunk leaning over him. "Get out of me way, ye big lunk."

"Lunk?" Barry chuckled. "What is this? A woman's word?"

"Barry," Autumn whispered in a fierce tone. "You will start trouble. Sit down and we will mind our own business." She frowned, noting Barry's manner of speech had changed once more.

The drunken fellow bent low to peer into Autumn's face. "Here now," he said in thick speech, "was a pretty one," and laughed his yeasty breath into her nostrils, making Autumn cringe. "What do ye hide yer woman for?" he said and guffawed at Barry. "Has she a scrawny frame under them costly rags? Or is she so buxomy ye're afraid we'll have a look at her sweet curves?"

Purposely, Barry nudged the lout in the jaw with a clumsily positioned elbow. "Oh, sorry," Barry taunted. "Had I known your face was in the way I would first have moved it."

"Barry!" Autumn hissed. "You are about to start a fight."

"Not me," Barry hissed back, louder than her. "He started what he might not be able to finish." Barry had been on the keen edge of frustration for many nights, and a fight would do him well. The lout was picking on the wrong man in the ale-room.

With a wary eye, the serving girl came to their table. "What can I get for ye," she asked, shuddering at the greasy looks of Barry. "Mayhaps a pot of soap and a rag to start?"

"That was not humorous," Barry said, looking up from beneath a lowered lid, "though you might have thought it was."

Her chin doubled as she started back, her cow-eyes glaring down at the man with the deep, sensuous voice. She was looking him over, with more depth, when the drunken lout at the next table chose that moment to grab Barry's shoulders and haul him to his feet.

"Never ye mind, Meg," he said to the serving maid. "I plan to teach this dung heap a lesson he'll never forget."

Though drunk to the gills, the man did not waver as he took one shoulder in a farmer's big mitt and hauled back his other hand to hit the stinking hunk in the face. He looked surprised when lowering his hand back to his side; his fist had never contacted with flesh.

"Eyyyy, where'd you go?"

"Leave him alone, Harvey," one of the drunk's companions yelled. "This one's fast, see, he ducked before you could say jack splat."

Barry's grinning face popped up again and Harvey grinned back. Harvey knew he was going to get a good fight and his adrenaline was beginning to flow; he was angry, Meg would not give him what he was aching for. The tart was getting herself married come next week and he now had no woman to poke.

Suddenly Harvey made a mistake as he let his eyes drop to the pretty face in the hood. He'd been wondering if she could replace Meg. He was just getting hard at the thought. And that's when Barry popped him a good one, landing a right hook onto Harvey's jutting jaw.

Autumn sent her chair back and stood just behind it, looking down at the man sprawled on the floor. She clamped a hand over her mouth to keep from laughing out loud. The drunk had been leering at her just moments before Barry let fly with his fist.

With a backward glance at the bloody Harvey, Meg hurried off to get supper and ale for the couple. They were a strange pair: like the fairy tale Beauty and the Beast. She would hurry and serve them, see if they needed a room, then send them up there as quickly as possible. Her man was coming and she had no care to have him take a peek at the maiden's hair, strands of fire peeping out of that hood, nor her odd violet-colored eyes, and heaven help her if she took off that cloak and there was a pretty body to boot beneath all.

When Meg returned to the ale-room she let out a gasp. Indeed, the girl had removed her cloak, and her body was as lovely as the rest of her. Her threads were of fine stuff, a bit worn for the wearing, and Meg began to wonder how many secrets the pretty woman was locking behind that winsome face.

Meg's eyes went to the homely man very nicely picking Harvey up off the floor and handing him to his friends. They took Harvey out and Meg kept glancing at the victor of the fight. He had secrets, too, and Meg knew they would be gone before she ever learned a thing about them.

Meg was wrong.

As she bent down to serve the unlikely pair, the ugly brute's hand covered hers and she straightened like a jolt of cobalt lightning had passed through her.

"What can I help ye with now?" Meg's worried look went to the pretty face. She prayed the red-haired beauty would still the beast if he became any bolder with his hands.

"We be looking for a comely maid—or lady—with hair like winter snow."

Meg let out a breath. "Well now—"

"Her name is Winter," Autumn's words rushed out before the harried serving girl could think twice on the matter. "She is very lovely. She is my sister and I have not seen her for several years." Autumn went on to describe her and was shocked to find she was telling about a much younger girl whose character she barely remembered at all.

"Well"—Meg said with a pause—"she *would* be your sister, seein' as you ain't hard to look at yourself." She grinned, showing one chipped tooth. "And what would your name be?"

"Autumn."

"How clever." Meg had dismissed her fear of the greasy lunk already. Dragging a chair up, she sat close to Autumn. "Tell me more." Her chin was on her hand; her elbow on the scarred tabletop. "Are there more than two seasons, then?"

Autumn pulled back at the sharpness of musky-sweet perfume. The alehouse girl reeked of the scent. Her gaze dipped into the jiggling cleavage and she drew back even further. Autumn's eyes lifted. There was something dark that slithered in the greedy eyes of Meg as the woman studied the cloth of Autumn's cloak.

"What?" Autumn said.

"I might tell you." Meg's fingers ran over the expensive cloth. "For a price."

"A . . . price?" Autumn looked up. Her voice was like white velvet.

A throat cleared roughly beside Meg. She looked up to see the gray-green eyes studying her as the hunk loomed above. "Here now!" Meg scraped to her feet. "Only my lover gapes down me blouse like that!" She tossed her oily blond curls. "Mind yer—"

Barry's voice cut her off. His eyes caressed Autumn as he spoke. "There is more charm in my charge's thumbnail than in the whole body of Meg Baggett."

Meg gasped. "How did you know me last name?"

"Never mind." Barry looked bored as a lord and just as aristocratic. "My only interest comes from aiding my charge in her search for her lost sister. That and nothing more." His eyes passed insolently over her form, her cow-eyes, the hills of her breasts that were white as udders.

Again Autumn blinked and frowned at Barry's words, the fineness of them, the timbre charged with eloquence. Her frown eased. Now she knew: the idiot was affecting airs to get what information he could from Meg. She blinked again as Meg began to spill with words, while Barry's fist spilled first coppers then gold coins.

Yet, where did he get all of them? Autumn asked herself.

By the time they took their separate rooms at the inn, Autumn had a few clues that might lead them to her sister. It *was* Winter! What other young woman would have such snow-white hair at the fresh age of twenty? Meg said some rough-looking louts had taken her north some five or six years ago, when Meg had begun work at the Unicorn Inn. This was good news and Autumn was terribly excited, knowing she would have a hard time sleeping on the crushed goose-down pillow this night.

There was only one thing missing, perhaps two things.

As Autumn entered the downy meadows of sleep, she realized Barry still had not answered her question: Where had he gotten all that money he'd spilled into Meg's greedy paws? Not twice or thrice, but fourteen coins in all Meg'd walked away with in each plump, tight-fisted hand!

The second question came to Autumn in her dream. She was at that place again, gilded by afternoon sun as she sat atop a big horse and then she'd gone for a walk in the woods to pick wildflowers. She heard the hounds once again and she could see in her dream's eye the great full-throated pack. She had been running from something, then arguing with someone; Spring and Summer were off in the herb garden; Winter had gone on before her to a shallow graveled ford by the stream. Something in the hounds' cry now drew her attention. Her reckless gallop away from the castle, letting her mare take her master as far from . . . ah, yes, Windrush as she could get, had carried her to the boundary line. Beyond that line lay the lands of . . . Baron Drogo! *Le Meurtrier*, the murderer! The devil himself!

Autumn woke, bathed in sweat. She remembered the day she'd been picking the wildflowers and someone had been tracking her, or so she'd felt; she had only been thirteen. Why could she only recall these happenings in the middle of night? Why, she asked herself, when I peel that incandescent thread I unravel the events of my life?

She cast a wild look over to Barry to see that he was sleeping soundly.

Again, she remembered. Only at night, late, dark of a moon. Remember . . . almost seven years ago—The visions came to her in a flash.

Her knees had trembled. Her peril was great. She had sent up a quick prayer, glancing down for comfort at the wildflowers in her hand. Her mother's gardens were blighted by an early frost and young Autumn knew the bouquet would please her. Her taut shoulders

36

relaxed. The hounds' cry was fading away, taking Drogo's hunt with it. She unsheathed her jewel-hilted dagger from the slender belt at her hips—or had it been someone else's dagger?—she'd been snipping a tendril of vine for binding the bouquet. Now she hurried to return; there was little time before dark. She had hitched up the skirt of her flowing bliaut, the smoky blue of the silk matching the lavender daisies she carried. She had been so furious with—someone—that she had not even paused to change into riding clothes.

She had started toward the spot where her chestnut mare was tied. She gasped as a man stepped into the clearing, dressed in a black tunic of velvet embroidered with scarlet thread. He stopped in astonishment at the sight of Autumn, letting go of his mount's bridle as thin lips twisted into a smile.

"Ah, a most delectable maiden," said the hunter, walking closer to Autumn. "Who might you be?" He was looking her over and a long, low whistle escaped him. Then another question, "Someone was following you. Do you know who?"

Autumn had seen the knowing light in his pale eyes and her heart stuck in her throat; her hand went to her flowing red hair she had not fastened back at her nape. She told herself she would not show him her fright. "If you are looking for your hounds," Autumn said as she pointed to the other side of the glade, "the poor things went that way."

"My hounds? *Poor?*" He chuckled nastily. "You'll never see a lead dog as handsome and shrewd as Stygian."

"Only one hound you value? Sir, what of the others?" the thirteen-year-old Autumn dared ask. She must keep his attention on the hounds, while she edged her way to her horse. She must be careful and not make a mistake once she was mounted. And she must ride away as quickly as possible.

Now she knew the man's identity. A big man with a slim face, with lean cheeks framing an arrogant beak of a nose. Cruel, thin pink lips that made a slash across an otherwise handsome face, and black, peaked eyebrows. A scornful and cynical man: Baron Drogo Villaine.

"You will not run, I pray," he said. "I am the Baron Drogo." His smile was cold. "I know who you are, little maiden."

"And I know who you are!" Her voice did not quaver, even when she saw a wicked gleam in his eyes. He would enjoy seeing her tremble, she thought.

"Come—let me show you that I am not as bad as rumors would have me."

Sunlight poured around her in the clearing as she stepped back. "I am Autumn Meaux, one of four sisters born at a single birth. We are called the Seasons. And my father is—"

His hand turned, palm up. "You are a beauty, but I regret that I've heard of your loveliness only of late."

"I shall have to dismiss your flattery, sir." As Autumn said this she saw an unpleasant smile flatten his bloodless lips. She had thought he'd lied.

"Ah, so you are untamed—"

"And none of your concern," Autumn shot back before he could taunt her more. She turned to flee.

He caught her before she was out of the clearing. Twisting her wrist, he brought her sharply around to face him, bending her arm cruelly behind her. As he forced her close to him she panted for breath and could feel the fine cloth of his tunic rubbing against her.

Burning eyes gazed down into hers. She could see the devil's lights in his eyes as his free hand stroked upward from her waist to cup a tiny little breast. A smile quirked the corner of his mouth.

Thrusting her backward against the trunk of a great oak, she could feel the hard bark poke her painfully. "Sweet, wild, will-o'-the-wisp, I think you'll not escape. You are in for delights never dreamed of—*Ahhh! Little bitch!*"

Autumn had kicked him with the toe of her leather shoe; the point of it had not done much. Her knee had done the most damage. He grimaced for only a moment and then his lips savagely crushed hers in what would be mistakenly called a kiss. Her head was forced back as he pressed her against the tree. She was pinned like a butterfly, writhing against his hard embrace. But he held her in an iron grip. In cruel fingers he pinched her young flesh and she cried out hotly against his wet mouth. His grip on her wrist had turned her fingers numb.

What would she do now? Autumn saw it as if it was just yesterday and she watched another person who was not herself.

She had dropped her own weapon to the forest floor. There must be another way of escape. She could knee him again. But no, that would only serve to anger him. There had to be something that would hurt him bad, something serious enough to give her an avenue to escape by. . . .

"Mistress Autumn, can't you hear me?" Barry tried to intrude on her reflections. "I asked you—"

"Please. Not now, Barry. I am trying to recall something. Please go back to sleep."

"The sun is rising."

"Good," she said with a dismissing wave of her hand. "Let it rise; let me be."

There had to have been a chance to escape. Autumn's left hand felt the baron's smooth tunic, the heavy, studded hunting belt he wore. He pressed against her hard, up to her whole body until she could feel the gold embroidery chafing her soft flesh, and the rough weave of his hunting garments against her thighs. Then, she found what she wanted. Knife! His enormous hunting knife lay heavily in her small hand. Caution had fled! Wrenching the blade from its scabbard, she held the blade high over the baron and plunged it downward into his shoulder with all her might.

Autumn felt the blade penetrate the heavy folds of the baron's tunic, and then rapidly it slid into living flesh. Now his eyes went dark with shock and pain. His grip loosening, he staggered back and shouted at her, calling her a witch.

She had shouted back, "Your treatment of me was far from gentle, sir! You forced me upon this path!"

Fury burned in his eyes, his eyes dark as Satan's cloak. He started for her again, his unhurt arm trying to grab for her. He pulled up. She still held his hunting knife, directing the point at his chest.

"I dare you," she warned, waving the bloodied blade.

"Little witch, that is my knife you hold. First you stab, now you'd steal. Fair maiden, do you wish to be hanged for a criminal?"

"You're on Meaux property, Windrush land," Autumn

warned right back. "You are more likely to hang than I when Richard, my father hears of this."

"I go," he said with a sneer. "Remember this, little lady. I shall not dismiss this injury to my person. One day, revenge will be met." His breath shuddered with pain. "Exactly from you." He turned and left the clearing.

Autumn began to shake. She told herself she must get herself home while she still had the strength. He could return; she did not trust Baron Drogo. She was halfway home, leaving the dark forest behind, when she saw the towers of the castle rising against the sky. She looked down, realizing she had not brought the flowers.

But she had one souvenir from that day. She still had held Drogo's jeweled hunting knife in her left hand. Later, Barry asked her what she had been thinking so hard upon. "Nothing," she said. *" 'Tis nothing."*

He looked at her oddly and then went back to what he had been doing after he had risen and dressed for the day.

The past events were coming to her piece by piece, like a huge puzzle. All day long Autumn tried to remember what she had done with the jeweled knife that belonged to Baron Drogo. His words, however, would always remain with her.

I shall not dismiss this injury to my person.
One day revenge will be met.

Three

Primeval moonlight filled the forest. Turning this way and that, Autumn walked, with eyes as deep violet as moonstruck amethysts as she peered into the wood. She heard a rustle here and there, wondering, hoping that it was Barry returning with their kill for supper.

"Oh!" she said with a jump as Barry emerged from darker shadows, an animal of some kind slung over his shoulder. "I was afraid it might not be you."

He laughed, coming full into the spill of moonlight. "Then why did you come to investigate, Mistress Autumn?"

"Hmm," was all she offered with a slight shrug. Why did his deep, soft voice make goose bumps rise on her flesh?

Autumn stepped out from the woods back into the clearing where they had made their camp. A small fire was crackling and snapping, filling the air with fragrant wood smoke and lifting hot stars like fireflies in the misted night.

"Watch that fire that nothing catches a light and starts a brush fire." Barry stomped a fat boot on an orange spark that had landed nearby. "We'll have to eat our food soon as it's done and put out that fire until it's but embers."

Walking about the camp area, Autumn said nothing. She was listening. His voice had made another change into something rich and strange; he was not Barry again. He was trying very hard.

"Barry." She said it so softly, she wondered if he'd heard. She sat doing her hair over, weaving strips of soft rose wool into her long braids; two for at night for slumbering. "My father had let our home go to ruin but would do any and all repairs at the dwellings of friends and relatives. Yet only his friends; not my mother's."

Her eyes flitted about the clearing as if she was trying to remember more.

"I hear you, maiden." Barry continued to prepare their meal, adding some fresh herbs she had plucked from beneath stones. He watched over his shoulder as her wool mantle lifted and swirled as she settled it over her back. Sparks flew into the air. Why was she telling him this?

"My mother never could understand her husband's methods of dealing with those closest to him. Among the girls, it was the Autumn season he favored."

"You," Barry said without turning to look at her.

"Me. But his actions lied. He was going to give me the gemstone; he never did. Perhaps he gave it to Winter for safekeeping before he was murdered." But that could not be; her parents had been searching for the jewel, she thought. She went on, "I was supposed to be his favorite." She sighed. "Why did he have to have a favorite at all? Why not all four of us equally cherished?"

"Who knows the ways of parents," Barry said in a low voice that mumbled. "Tell me more about your family. And about the jewel."

"A lord who did not protect his family was no lord at all," she murmured. Richard had not wished a wedding for her. Why? How often she had dreamed of her own wedding . . . the feasting, baking, games laid out in the lists below the curtain wall, with brightly colored tents set up for the honored guests that would come.

If she could remember all this, why could she not recall other more important events?

"Eh. What do you think so deeply about again?" Barry asked the maiden.

"If I would have been wed as my parents still lived. They would have moved among their friends, receiving congratulations on their first born daughter's fine marriage to an important heir of a large estate. Hah! My land-obsessed father returned from . . . from, I don't know; it does not matter. He came to our castle to tell my lady mother that he loved her and not the mistress he had sought. Yes, now I remember it. Some of it." The shock of seeing her parents killed caused much of her past to've been erased, but now it was now coming back to her in tiny snatches.

"What was your castle like? And your family?" Barry asked as if jealous of her home and family.

She frowned for a moment before she found the buried answer. "I remember the tower steps; I would run toward them, race up the winding stairs to my own apartment in the donjon. The rooms set aside for the Meaux daughters were comfortable, far from the main hall. We each were allowed privacy," she laughed, "and we guarded it jealously. Our maidservants were the only ones allowed to enter."

Barry leaned back. "How did the rooms look?"

She paused, then rushed on. "They were simply furnished, holding a narrow bed each, a table, a chest under the window for our clothes. Oh yes, and footstools covered in our favorite colors, each of our own; mine was green velvet. I remember my maidservant, Judith, who was our age. The girl was fresh from a village, far out at the edge of the oak forest."

"Where?" Barry asked. "England? France?" He nodded. "It really sounds like France."

"France?" Autumn lifted one deep russet eyebrow. "Hmm, that is odd. I had the feeling, too, the castle Windrush was not in England but some other green country. No, no, it must be in England. North perhaps."

"Judith?"

Autumn shook her head, her quick fingers brushing a strand of hair from her cheek. "I cannot recall her last name. Some say she was one of Scardon's misbegotten. An orphan. She lived with a man and his daughters, but there was never enough food for them all. Judith had been lucky enough to be taken into household service. Trouble was, I remember, she was too outspoken. Richard almost sent her back to her father— *her real father,* the nasty Scardon."

Now Scardon was dead, his evil life snuffed out by Orion Sutherland, aided by his wife Elizabeth who had made a special shield that had blinded Scardon when he would have ended Orion's life. Elizabeth Juel had broken the curse that had been on Sutherland, freed his mother from the tower, and brought love back into Orion's home. This Elizabeth Juel was the same woman

45

who had taken Autumn under her wing after her husband had saved the girl from being taken by Scardon's men.

Struggling with his emotions, Barry looked over at the now silent Autumn. Her hair was the color of the deepest red-orange leaves, and eyes the color of wood violets in spring. His eyes went past her to the black mule, almost as big as a horse was Dusky, the force that pulled the small two-wheeled green cart with the other jennet he sometimes rode upon to give Dusky a rest from Waddel's nipping.

Autumn made a movement that rippled her long sleeves like purple banners in a fitful breeze. His eyes held hers for one long look, as intimate as a whisper. She got up and walked into the tent without another word.

The man standing alone out in the Saxony moonlight looked down at the charred rabbit and shrugged. He sat down to tear and chew, all the while staring at the slowly moving sadness the candle flickers created on the tent's walls.

The maiden.

She was pacing and then she stopped, her profile silhouetted, then sat down heavily on the low rock he'd pitched the tent over.

He *could* tell her.

He *should* tell her.

But he dare not.

Not yet.

In Autumn's sagging pouch she carried some old coins that were beautiful and rare; needle and various-colored bright threads; as well as more odds and ends. Another pouch held herbs, ones that she plucked along the way in case they needed medicine or came upon someone who could do with a healing potion. She also had seeds in there for planting, ones she had herself gathered from her own personal kitchen-garden at Sutherland; she carried them as an ancient custom and for good luck.

They stopped late for the nooning. Barry was quiet and disappeared into the wood for longer periods each time. The woods were thinning as they neared London, more like stands of smaller trees and brushy scrub here and there. With more coins Barry had purchased some bread and cheese at a goater's hut. She took the food to a small outcropping near the side of the road. Spreading the extra mist-gray cloak she'd brought along, she sat upon the sun-warmed rock and ate alone.

She could see far from here, to the flower-dotted meadows. A narrow stream meandered through lavender-tipped watergrass. She caught a glimpse now and then of blue sky reflected in the pools, drinking in the heartrending beauty of England's countryside.

Barry returned and Autumn looked up at him, not asking where he'd been off to.

"We'll be going around London," Barry said. "Unless you want to stop there and ask some questions. Mistress?" He saw that she was listening to something, her head canted, her eyes narrowed.

"Do you hear it?"

"Aye," he said at last. "Horses, many. They're coming this way, mistress."

She shook her head. Barry was not himself again. He was a new person each day, it seemed. She had not time to dwell on that, for now the horses were riding straight for them.

"Do they see us?" Autumn asked, holding Ghost's reins after she had gotten up from the rock. "They appear to be many."

Barry laughed. "All is well, mistress. We're getting close to London, is all. More folks'll be about, you know. In fact, the traffic gets considerable going to and coming from London town."

"I will ask these men." She stepped right in front of the riders coming their way.

"Ask them *what?*" he almost screeched, watching the knights pulling up their mounts as she held up an arm to wave them down. Brave woman, he thought, wiping sweat from his brow. "What—?"

"You will see," is all she offered Barry. "I have some questions," she called up to the big knight in the front. He was grinning as if enjoying the sight of her immensely. "Have you seen a lovely woman with snow-white hair? She is rather tall . . . no, small . . . I think."

Barry rolled his eyes. The king's knights must think her daft of wit as she showed each part of her features that resembled her twin's. "She has small, dainty feet as I," Autumn announced, sticking out a leathered foot for them to see. Chuckles surrounded her but she kept on, trying, with much difficulty to describe a sister she had not seen in over six years. "She would be a woman now, perhaps taller, even more beautiful than the moon and stars."

"I have seen such a woman," one of the knights said, looking more serious than his companion knights.

"Oh! Where?" Autumn held on to the reins of his

48

mount, as she peered up with eyes that beseeched. "Where have you seen my sister?"

"In a nunnery." He tried not to laugh. "I believe she is about to take her vows. She was brought there to the abbey and from there was transferred to the Notting nunnery and then on to the, uhm, the one in Whitby." The other knights looked at him in surprise. "I would never forget such as she; she was very beautiful and shy as a freshly sprung daffodil with hair like a white satin star."

"That must be her!" Autumn could hardly keep herself from kissing the big knight. Her joy sank for a moment before surfacing again. "Why was she brought to the nunnery? Had she been abducted by some foul men at first?"

"Of course," the knight said. "She was lost, she said. There was nowhere for her to go."

"So she was taken to the convent," Barry said, making them all shift their eyes to him. "How can this be the same woman? And you seem confused about which nunnery she is really to be located at," he said, for a moment sending Autumn into renewed worry.

The informative knight answered. "The voice. It is the same as this anxious maiden's. Strong and full of volume. It's as if the two were twins, but for the difference in coloring. Oh and now I remember: It was the nunnery of Kirklees," he ended, staring at Autumn's red hair.

The other knights blinked in confusion.

Autumn's nod was firm to the poetic knight. "She has to be my sister."

After discovering that one of the knights had not overcome a recent ailment, Autumn made him a special

49

meadowsweet herb tea to drink, pressed extra leaves into his hands with instructions, and then sent them on their way.

"You were very nice to them," Barry said, looking at her oddly. "Why?"

With a shrug of one shoulder, she hurried to pack her things so that they could continue their journey to the nunnery. "They were very nice to me. They gave me information."

Sometimes, she thought, Barry was awfully daft.

"Ah." He scratched his ear, toting bags that seemed to grow weightier with each stop they made. "How does a dainty maiden as you know about herbs?" he asked her.

"I have studied the work of Dioscorides in the monastery herb gardens. Their abbeys have become the storehouse for books. They have painstakingly copied earlier books on the subject of herbals and naturally absorbed a great deal of the information along the way."

"Monastery gardens"—Barry touched his chin—"Hmmm."

"The gardens were cultivated for the benefit of the sick and suffering. All who are in need of medical aid come to the monasteries for "simples"—the herbal remedies. After reading the work of Dioscorides, I added the results of my own practical experience and experiments with herbs."

Barry suddenly said, "We need not go into London town then."

"No."

"To the forest of Nottinghamshire then!" He packed up the two-wheeled cart, patted the cart horses and turned to see Autumn staring at him hard. "What is it?"

"No," she said, and he looked at her with a questioning eyebrow. "No?" His lips were tight.

"No. To the nunnery—*first.*"

"Nunnery of Kirklees, you mean."

With a shrug, Autumn said, "The same."

Long after their supper of cheese, a knife-hewn loaf of bread, and a freshly caught and roasted rabbit, Autumn lay awake. Not until she heard the noise of Barry snoring, did she move and rise from her bed beneath the cart.

She had inched a yard away from the dying embers when she became aware of an alteration in Barry's breathing. She froze, waiting until he would lapse into sleep again. Now the breathing was subdued, regular.

She walked to the shadows for some privacy, holding her skirts up from the wet grass, carrying the extra cloak to dry herself with. A quick bath in that creek yonder would be nice, she thought.

And then he was upon her!

Wrestling and grappling her to the ground, Barry stretched his full hard length upon her with a rush, pinning her to the ground beneath him, covering her open mouth with his hand.

Surprise tore from his throat. "Mistress."

She blinked. "Barry."

The force of their fall forced Autumn's tunic away and there was nothing between her flesh and Barry's padded leather undershirt. The rough leather was cold, chilling Autumn to her bones. The shock lasted as long

51

as a full minute, holding her immobile for several heartbeats.

Barry's hot breath whispered words in her ear that she could not understand. But their import was plain enough. "Barry. Let me up."

He seemed not to have heard.

She felt the thrust of his hard body and, even in the dark, she knew he was jerking at his leather shirt, and yanking down his chausses. He fell against her, already hard and pulsing.

Autumn remained as still as stone, gasping for each breath. His arms around her, his hard breath in her ear, on her neck were bringing a rush of disturbingly new sensations.

Yet one thought was outstanding: *escape*. With the strength of one desperate motion, she twisted beneath him, then heard the tearing of cloth where his knees pinned her torn inner tunic to the ground. She clawed at him, wherever she could reach, and felt the skin rip at his back.

Recalling Drogo's attack, her knee came up to do the same.

Barry was stronger than Drogo. The cloak worked from under her, and twigs and debris pushed into her bare back. Her breath had caught in her throat and she couldn't get another one; she was so startled at Barry's attack.

Autumn swallowed. If Barry had turned beast, then she must be as alert as any prey, she told herself.

Quick as a rabbit, she grabbed and yanked a corner of her cloak over her thigh. Putting all her strength into one rippling movement, she clutched the cloak and tossed it over Barry's head.

Barry was up in a flash, pounding heavily behind her. It was so dark, Autumn thought it was like running under a blanket. She ran fast, ran and ran, clutching her cloak and fell headlong more than once. Dry sticks scraped her skin, thrusting at her body.

Barry! Barry! She could not believe her kind friend and road companion was after her.

A stitch in her side brought her to a halt. Her breath emerged in shuddering gasps. She fell over a fallen limb, and sprawled her length upon the ground, as before. He would catch her again.

She had to move. Instinct prompted her to roll into a ball; that way revealing her exposed flesh as little as possible. Anxiously, she sent up a little prayer. Barry, Barry, not him. Not like Drogo.

Barry's footsteps thudded closer and closer. Another minute and he would be at her heels. Her heart was pounding hard, shaking her body, leaping up into her throat. She could see, against the faint ruby of the distant campfire, the bulk of him. He moved like a cat, a panther, but he did not see her.

His back was turned.

Now!

She got up and ran and ran. She shivered but kept moving. She must get away from Barry. He was no better than any other man rutting for a lay. Perhaps in the morning he would come to his senses. For now, she had to get away, from *her only friend in the world just now.* It was a painful thought to be so betrayed.

The night was colder now. Shivering, she kept moving, as the wind, even gentled by the surrounding forest, was as sharp as a jeweled dagger.

Dagger! Where had she left Drogo's dagger? At Sutherland? She must not have packed it else she'd have remembered; unless it was at the bottom of the bag in the leather sheath.

Keeping the faint ruby light of the fire behind her to serve as direction, she moved carefully farther into the woods. Fear of Barry's sudden lust momentarily diminished. Other fears were crowding in. She paused often to listen. No sounds of pursuit, she thought as she stumbled over a fallen log.

She was alone.

The moon was high, touching the upper reaches of the forest with sparkles of light. And the lower regions, where she felt her way cautiously, were by contrast much darker than before.

Vivid pictures circled in her mind. *Barry had tried to force her.* She gulped, hardly believing even now.

She would have to hide in the forest until morning, then find the road back to London. Over to London, *how*ever. She would ask if she needed to, there must be a harmless person she could trust to give her a kind word. The knights. She had not been afraid of them. No, they had not the intention of raping her as Barry had had.

Or still had. Is he following even now? Would he catch up before morning light? She shuddered to think what he would do to her this time.

He had made her feel so good, so many times. Even ecstatic, to be with him, eat with him, even touch him once in a while. There had been that sudden tightening of the muscles in his arm, every time she touched him. Hurt gathered like a cold rock in the pit of her stomach. She should have been warned of his deep lusty male appetite. Fool!

I cannot go on. She slumped into a hollow, pulling her cloak all around her.

She slept.

When she awoke, the moon was in another place in the sky. Hours had passed as she slept. It was still dark, but there was a strange orange glow. No, more like deep red.

A campfire!

Rising to her feet, swirling the cloak around her, she crept on cat paws toward the campfire, knowing it was not the small one she and Barry had made. She pulled back when she could make out four men sleeping near the fire for warmth. Of course she did not know them; they were not the king's knights.

She hugged her cloak. She needed that warmth herself. Who were these men? Could they be trusted if she went to the fire? Hah. What man could be trusted, she was beginning to wonder.

One man stood away from the fire. He was tall, with weight and shape like Barry. That made five, Autumn thought. Half in shadow, he stared in her direction. The sleepers did not move.

Autumn was not cognizant of her wraithlike appearance, the pale cloak flowing like mist from her shoulders, her tangled red hair.

He was walking toward her now, away from the sleeping men, pointing a long, thick arrow in her direction. He spoke.

"Who might you be?" he asked. "The witch of the wood?"

"Nay," she said and forced her shaky legs to take another step. "I have been hunted." Her nose twitched. "Is that roasted meat?"

"Aye." He smiled, but did not let down his guard with the bow and arrow. "Who are you? Speak!"

"I am—*hungry.*"

Her voice had carried such volume that the four men awoke instantly, leaping as one back from the firelight. "Who is—" One with limp black hair looked to the man with bow and arrow, as if they had not seen him there before. Then he saw her. "God bless me, who have we here—a lily witch?"

Expressions were exchanged and subdued in the twinkling of an eye.

"I've a change of clothes, chain mail missing," the man in the shadows complained.

"Be still," a voice snapped.

Autumn sat on a stack of wood before the fire where another indicated she should sit. He handed her the food. She wolfed it down as though she had not eaten for days. The chase through the forest had made her very hungry. Her energy stores had been drawn down by the lusty betrayal of her friend.

In a hushed circle, the men stood away from her and talked in very low voices. When finished with the meat and ale, she looked up at her hosts. Here were the five she had spotted first off, and apparently no others were about.

The magnificent knight with the bow and arrow, relaxed now, looked her over. The second and third of them wore hunting attire. One wore a long brown friar's robe, and this one kept to the shadows as if uninterested; she could not make out his face. They sat in a protective half circle before her and watched with vibrant curiosity. All but the bashful one in the shadows; she thought his hair was gold. He wore the friar's robe.

They must be safe if they are recluse men.

Autumn laughed. "I'll not disappear like a wraith—or witch. By the way, what is a *lily witch?*"

"Superstition," one said. "A witch of the woods."

"Do you think you could tell us who you are?" the brown-robed friar asked.

"First," she said, hoping they were friendly—more gentle than Barry had proven to be, she prayed!— "What are your names?"

"We asked first," said the man with height and shape like Barry, but that's where the resemblance stopped. This knight was like a prince, with dark hair, and eyes . . . she couldn't make out the color at the moment.

"I am Autumn Meaux, lately from Sutherland Castle. I was traveling with a companion"—her eyes misted sadly—"but I have lost him." Which was true!

Still, they sat there watching her with that vibrant curiosity. They did not sit long, but got up to pace, then they went down again to watch her. They are trying to decide what to do with me, she thought.

"Do you suffer, little lady?"

What did the man mean? Autumn said, "Suffer? Oh, of course. Else I would not be roaming the woods this late at night." Pressing her knees, she stalled for time. "I say, someone was chasing me."

Autumn tried to think. It was late; she was weary and dirty from scurrying about in the woods. She wanted to have a good cry, too, because Barry had betrayed her. These men were a strange body of travelers, to be sure. Two hunters, a man of God, a knight, and a hooded stranger with golden hair peeping out, also a man of God.

When one of the friars had made way for her to sit

near the fire, she had caught a glimpse of metal through the slit in his woolen robe.

A mailed friar? Could this be at all possible? Something was very odd here, especially the manner in which the handsome knight studied her. She could not describe it.

She must tread carefully. They could send her back the way she came, back to Barry Jeraux. They could, yes, they might even take her to the convent themselves. Yet, she feared to reveal too much, even the fact that she wished to make her way to Nottinghamshire.

"Your story, lady?"

With an easy air, she replied, "I do not think my story would interest you."

"Try," prodded the knight.

"I am on my way to a convent—or nunnery if you will."

"We see"—the knight looked around at his fellows—"don't we." He nodded and they followed suit.

It would not help to know their names, she thought. What manner of men were they? She searched the knight's face for some clue. The man in the shadows said:

"Raine, what—?"

"Rain?" she asked puzzled, looking up at the black sky. It seemed clear.

"Hush," said the knight to the golden man in the shadows with the friar's robe. He moved restlessly, conscious of her gaze on him. His face was shadowed as he bent down, leaning his elbows on his knees, purposely preventing her from seeing into his beautiful shaped eyes to read his thoughts.

She saw one of the hunters fingering his lower lip

in a thoughtful manner. What were they planning for her? Was she out of the soup kettle and into the fire? Perhaps she should reconsider Barry. He was mercurial often; perhaps had changed his mind and decided not to lust after her, after all. She would go find him at first light. Yes, that's what she would do, take her chances with Barry than with these strange men.

"I see no reason why you roam the forest," began the knight harshly. "You are fleeing someone." His perfectly arched brows lowered. "Why?"

"He—he was not very nice to me." Oh, how she wished she had worn the jeweled dagger of Drogo on her person; if only she had discovered its whereabouts. "I believe he was about to r-ravish me." Looking right into the knight's eyes, she saw no change in him. His glance lingered on her bare leg, and quickly she covered her knees. It was too late, however, to hide the fact that she wore nothing beneath but her inner tunic.

More confidently, she continued. She told of the search for one sister and how she and Barry had come upon some clues . . . in the Unicorn Inn.

"Where is your escort?" pressed the knight. "Ah, you have already said; he betrayed you as he lusted after you. Tsk, tsk," he said with a click of his tongue.

The knight stood and walked into the shadows to speak with the mysterious man there, leaving Autumn to the others for company. "She is beautiful," said the light-haired one and went on dryly, "I believe there is some hope for you after all. I have wondered how long you would live a monk's life."

"Hush, Tyrian," said the knight with the beautiful eyes. "She will hear."

"Where in God's name have you been? We have been

up and down England looking for you. Why did you steal my—"

"Again—" the knight said. "Hush. Speak no more of your accoster now. You do not understand."

"Oh but, *forgive me,* yet it seems to me that you are indeed bewitched. *What?* Not by this lady here?"

"Have you seen the duchess?" asked the knight.

"No, Raine."

"Damn you, man, be still. Do you want to give it all away?"

"Why do you play this silly game? Is she someone special? Raine, you do not answer me. Why do you smell so foul?" He kicked at a mound. "Why were you wearing this pile of rags? Those what you wear *now* are my only spare pair of *braccae.* You put them on as I slept, did you now." He looked down at the special trousers the knight wore. "And *my chain mail—*"

Knight Raine, looking bored, walked away from his relative.

When he went over to where the young lady in tattered finery had been sitting, he now found her fast asleep beside a log near the fire. He looked down and then walked away, going to change his clothes once again.

The knight lingered and watched her sleep as the others rode away into the stygian night, taking a northern route and the change of *braccae* and chain mail with them.

Four

Autumn came awake slowly and looked around at the camp that the five men had occupied; now the ashes had turned gray and it seemed she was alone. Hauling herself up to her elbows, she peered into the trees and brought herself to sit.

There was a cough.

With a start, Autumn looked over at the overhanging oak tree to see who was there. She gave another start, this one more violent than the one before as she lifted her violet eyes to cautiously study the largest tree branch.

"Barry," she said, letting her breath out slowly and preparing her body for flight. "What are you doing up there?"

"Resting," he said, then he yawned, reclining elbow to ear as he stared down at her from the huge branch. "I searched for you all night, mistress. What happened to you?"

Autumn licked her dry lips. Barry was his old self again. But could she trust him not to set himself upon her again, as he had the night before?

She came up from the ground cautiously, shivering from the night's dampness still in her bones. One cloak was not enough cover to ward off the chill that had seeped up from the forest floor. The leaves piled there had not given her much warmth or comfort. She felt achy all over.

"My apologies, mistress," he said, coming down as easily as a cat dropping to its hind paws.

She whirled on him, her eyes blazing. "You won't attack me again, Barry?"

"Uhh-hmm." He hung his head like a naughty boy. "I sure won't do that again."

Cocking her head, accepting the simpleton's word, she asked, "What got into you? I get up to wash a bit at the creek and you rise and attack like a lusty buck in rutting season." She brushed some bark from his sleeve.

"I thought you was someone else, truth be told." He continued to study the ground and not look at her. "Thought you was an outlaw stealing up on me—uh—us. That's why I did that."

Frowning, she said, "You would be so familiar with a mere thief?"

He chuckled, "A female thief, perhaps."

She continued to study him, rubbing briskly her slim arms to shed the night's chill. "You sound strange again, Barry. Why do you always change your voice like that? Are you hiding something from me?"

"Me?" He hunched his shoulders. "You asked me before and I've said no."

"What's this?" She reached out to touch his wounded wrist. "These look like the scratches chain mail would make hastily donned." Her eyes narrowed into his face.

"What have you been doing, Barry? Did you steal that chain mail from the hunters and friars?"

"Don't you remember, mistress? You don't?" He shook his head and looked away sadly. "You scratched me, that's what you did when I came upon you like that. That's where these are from."

"Oh." She bit her lower lip. "I am sorry, Barry. You frightened me. I suppose I scratched you." She heard her horse whinny just then and looked toward the stand of oaks to see Ghost over there looking as disembodied as his name implied, tied to one of the ancient oaken sentinels, munching a bit of grass. "Rain," she said.

"What?" Barry flashed around to face her, then noticed she merely looked up at the bit of sky above the treetops. He relaxed at once. "Oh, rain. Of course. It might just do that."

"Do you have the cart with Dusky?" She stooped to gather the things he had brought to her and looked up to see the black mule waiting on the wide unbeaten path. "Oh, I see. And where is Waddel?"

"Nasty again. Left him on the other side of those trees. He won't go anywhere; he's too dumb."

"He is that." She looked aside.

He touched her hand, feeling her shiver slightly. "Please don't be afraid of me, mistress. I just got too close to you. I got to keep away from you. I am a man, after all, so don't hate me much for what I did. You are a lovely young woman. I like you very much and don't wish to hurt you. Never."

She blinked away warm compassionate tears as he walked away to fetch her clothes and horse so that they could ride out of the woods to where the moorland stretched away to the north.

Later, when it began to rain they sought some shelter, but there was not much the land could offer as they were now far north from London, no village or hamlet in sight; Barry said they had not come to Luton yet.

The trees were sparse across the open woodland and they could only see a few yards in front of the plodding beasts. Dark clouds followed them all the way, it seemed. Autumn began to shiver and Barry coughed again.

"Look," Barry called through the chilly gloom. "There's the shell of a barn. We will stop there for the night. What do you say, mistress?"

"Anything," she said with a gasp, holding her sodden cloak up against her shivering frame. She pointed, water spilling from her sleeves like rain dripping from eaves.

Indistinct shadows loomed up ahead as they headed for the gray bulk Barry had said could be a barn. The rain was slanting harder by the time they reached the shelter and slipped inside.

"How will we make a fire?" she asked. "Everything is so damp. I'm shivering and . . . and miserable." She moaned, rubbing her arms. "I have never been so wet and hungry and, what is wrong—?"

"Be still."

"What?" Autumn spun around at the sharp command in Barry's voice.

"Quiet."

She frowned as she looked at him in the murky interior of the old barn. Water dripped from his nose, his eyebrows, his chin, and his dark hair was plastered to his head. At least, she thought, some of the dirt had washed from his skin. He was a nice color, a golden tan, and his eyes . . . they were. *They were* . . .

Where had she seen those eyes before? She was exhausted from her adventures, and perhaps her mind was fuzzy yet, his lashes were black, his eyes . . . *beautiful.* His—

"Stop staring and try to think of ways we can keep warm." He tossed bags onto the floor. "Ah," he said, "I believe I see a dry spot in the corner with some old hay. Over there, yes, where the water does not drip. Mistress, I warn you to stop your staring at me as if I'm a chunk of meat you'd like to bite off." He coughed as if embarrassed. "Remember what happened last night?"

Ceasing her staring, Autumn became very busy as she rummaged through her leathern bags, coming up with some clothes that were blessedly dry. She looked at Barry, pitiful Barry, and wondered what dry clothes he could change into. After she had gone to the dark corner to slip into the cool but dry shift, she found Barry had done some changing of his own.

"Wonderful," she said slowly, wondering where he had gotten new clothes. "You have dry clothes, too." Her eyes widened at the small corner where they would have to lie down—together. "We shall do it back to back," she decided.

"Yes, mistress." Barry saw her eyes widen more when he reached behind him and brought out two blankets.

"How did they stay dry?" she asked with open mouth.

"I, too, have leathern bags, you know. I'm not all that much a peasant that I cannot afford some nice comfortable things."

"Oh Barry." She gave a tired laugh. "You always amuse me." She thrust a finger out at him. "You looked so charming when you told me that you are not poor as a church mouse, first at Sutherland, and now here. Then and at this moment, I never thought of you as so inferior."

She swallowed a laugh.

"Come to think on it, I know practically nothing about your former life. Come, let's get warm in this corner and you tell me something about yourself as I fall into dreams."

"Naw," he said. "I'm weary. I'm going to get some sleep after some food." He turned over in his blanket twice to keep warm. "Some other day, Mistress Autumn." He reached into the bag he'd dragged over to the corner with him. "Here, I forgot, you must be hungry. Bread and cheese." He chuckled. "The bread might be a little on the soggy side, but the cheese is hard as ever."

After sharing the meager fare, lounging with elbows bent and cheeks on palms—Autumn struggling not to stare at the enigmatic Barry—Autumn fell fast into a deep sleep in hay and blankets, Barry's body keeping her warm through the night.

Autumn was dreaming again. This time the dream seemed so real. There was a big warm body next to her, one so firm and hard. She could feel this dreamy man's hard breath on her neck, too.

It was a very nice dream. The man was so close now, touching her hip with one hand. She could almost make out the color of his eyes as he looked over her one shoulder. Green. Moss green. Hazel green specks, she imagined. His hair was almost black in its shade, strands with deep nutmeg shine and heavy texture. Muscles stood out on his body, arms, legs, chest, shoulders, there were long muscles, shorter ones, finger muscles, toe muscles.

Altogether the knight was a magnificent man.

He was pressing into her in the dream. The hard shape of his maleness was against her backsides. She had never felt anything like this before. She snuggled deeper into the dream—and closer to the man in it!

They were so close one could not get a cat's hair between the pair of them. His front was curled against her backsides. They fit together like pieces of something that had been apart and was now back together, where they belonged. Not missing, but one, as they should be.

Two halves make a whole.

What sort of dream can this be? Autumn dreamily considered the physical intimacy even as she enjoyed the pleasurable fantasy-tingles at the same time.

Then his low voice invaded her dream. "Turn to me, Autumn. I will warm you like a gentle summer wind. Like the golden kiss of the sun against a wildflower's upturned face."

What a deep and wonderful voice!

She did as the dream man commanded. The chill that had been in her bones was rapidly diminishing, being replaced by something nice and warm and lovely. She had never felt this wonderful, this peaceful, this secure. And she sighed, for 'twas only a dream. She wanted to stay here forever. Was this what it was like to fall asleep and never awaken?

This was so lovely.

Sweet golden suns were in her blood as she snuggled in the man's arms, feeling the hardness of his thighs between her own. She would speak and see if he would answer.

Who? Who . . . are . . . you?

Raine had heard Autumn begin to mumble in her sleep. At first he could not understand her words and then she repeated the question, awaiting his answer.

"Who? Who? Are you the handsome knight who invaded my dreams once before?"

His answer was soft and gentle. "More than once, fair maiden." Should he wake her, he asked himself, remind her of his presence?

She sighed and felt her slim arm meet a solid bicep. "Dream . . ." she said softly. "What would you have me do?"

"Kiss me, maiden."

"Kiss?" she asked. "Will I like this kiss?" she mumbled.

"Of course. As much as you want, I can give. Now, a maiden's kiss is all I ask."

His lips touched hers and Autumn shivered with intense pleasure.

What the touch of her lips did to Raine was more earth-shattering than he would have ever believed possible. They kissed lightly. Then again. And again, soft not fierce. "More," he said. *"Ah yes, more."*

Raine drew her nearer to his hardened body. Her warmth and soft loveliness started his heart to beating a rapid song, the feel of her young body setting his male flesh afire. He could feel the tips of her breasts grow hot and erect.

Passion slammed through his body like a bolt of thunder.

Unresisting to his caress and kisses, Autumn's breath escaped her body and she seemed to be afloat on air. Never had a dream been so vivid. Like a tumult the light contact of his lips shivered through her as he now kissed her eyes, the softness at the nape of her neck, then pressed her back into the hay. He bent over her to kiss the sweet corner of her tempting mouth. She arched upward from the sweet touch of male lips. The nectar of their lips joining again and again, slipping, sliding, sucking, they flowed together like a hot whirling surge of life's blood and reckless sensation. Her whole body seemed to melt into his, like hot wax, while his lips continued to possess in a passionate kiss.

Her body was likened to wildfire. In her dream, his male scent was driving her wild. She never wished to awaken from this paradise that was more true than reality itself. Tides of energy swept back and forth. She stood in a world of pure desire that stretched off in all directions; and there was a completion and a wholeness to what she was doing in her dream: a meeting of souls and minds. It stood in sharp contrast to the tenuousness of reality. Then again, her conscious mind argued, if her dream was nothing else, *it was real.*

Real!

When Autumn awoke she screeched at finding herself in Barry's arms. "Barry! Get away!" He mumbled something incoherent. She frowned. He was fast asleep.

Everything had seemed to be real.

Only a dream, a very disturbing one, she thought as she turned over and stared at the gray and misty drizzle in the moonlight of the old barn. Water dissolved into

69

mist that rose up in wraithlike clouds. Ancient wood creaked in the night wind; a loose board somewhere. A dog howled in the distance and Autumn tried to get back to sleep. Chilly drafts squeezed between the cracks. Finally her eyes closed slowly, blocking out the sight of the lonely old barn in night shadow and damp.

But *he* lay awake, aching, and staring at her back, wishing he could tell her who he was and why indeed he was with her, why he *could not expose himself as her guardian.*

The irony of that: Guardian. Twice now he had thought that very same thing. How new and novel this time to have only one, *her,* to look after.

Soon there would be the *others* . . . also. They were nearing the ancient Forest of Nottingham.

For now, the longing for completion within her virginal sheath was a physical pain that ate at his chest and loins like an unspoken grief.

Just at dawn, they topped a rise that gave them a clear view of their destination. The great forest lay ahead one day and one night.

Barry gave a hoot and a yell and Autumn followed suit, laughing as she spurred Ghost onward and over the hill. Barry ran with Dusky, Waddel, and the bumping, trailing cart. Riding down the rocky hilltop, the cart bouncing and wheels twirling fast, they came to a momentary halt. They were like insensible children at play, looking toward one another, laughing, chuckling, giggling, and shouting at the bright new day. The jennets brayed and the horse whinnied. Even the flowers over the hill danced and sang.

It was not raining. They were alive, young, real.

They set off once again.

The sun cast its yellow light across Autumn and Barry. Shadows fled before the sun, and the land was fresh, green and golden.

Barry pitched a tent, and hastened from the maiden, leaving her and walking away. "Where do you go?" she shouted after him, already unshouldering her baggage and readying a dry, tasty meal of bread and fresh-picked herbs. She had even got a few berries down from some overhanging vines, springtime's first luscious bounty.

Looking around at the bags, then frowning in indecision toward the direction Barry had taken, she bent to search one more bag. "Oh, Barry. How could you be so absentminded?" She followed his direction into the woods. "You have taken my bag and not yours."

Autumn spied a completely nude Barry through the brush, rubbing fresh mud on his face. It dried in the sun and then he brushed it off, leaving a dirty stain.

Her eyes lowered.

Lord have mercy! Barry was like a Greek statue, bold, alive on the energies that whispered down from the sun and blue sky. Lord in heaven, where did he ever get such a . . . such a manly physique?

She gulped, wanting to get away as quickly as possible. He made her think of her intimate dream of the tigerish knight and . . . and yester eve when . . . when . . . Dear Jesus, she felt so very warm.

Autumn blinked.

What was that all about? Was he mad? Mud on his

magnificent body? Autumn wondered and swallowed tightly as she whirled away from spying on him and hurried back to her tent as fast as her feet could fly. Her heart was pounding loud, like a hundred knights galloping over a drawbridge!

All day long she peeked at Barry, and even squeaked once in surprise when he happened to brush her hand with his dirty one. He looked into her eyes, deeply, then grinned as if he hadn't studied her like that. Like that? How had he looked at her?

She was bewildered. Bothered. He began to whistle a merry tune and the happy sound grated on her already bunched nerves.

"Come here," he said to her after they had finished the light meal.

"What?" Autumn whirled from the rock where she had set her comb down after grooming her hair.

"Come and sit with me. Here, I'll share this rock with you." Barry adjusted the blanket he'd wrapped around the huge standing leg of rock, over one of the protruding toes.

Autumn laughed as she drew near the rock. "It looks like a giant's lower half, does it not?"

"It does," Barry agreed. "Come, sit with me at our giant's footstool."

With a carefree laugh, Autumn lowered herself next to Barry and they shared the bit of blanket. They talked of the day, the beasts, and the fowl of the air. A conversation with an idiot, Autumn mused. He is most unusual. Propped against the rock, as if it were the most natural thing to do, Autumn reclined against Barry's chest.

She giggled as his long knobby legs stuck out along

72

the ground. "What have you in your leggings?" About to pat down his legs, she abruptly decided against the action. And she wasn't about to tell that she had seen him perfectly whole at the brushy creek!

A smudged eyebrow rose. "In my leggings?" He chuckled deeply, making the sound felt in her shoulder. "I'd best not tell else you'll run away from me." His gaze fell to the chausses he wore.

She knew his body was firm and manly, with muscular calves and thighs. She had seen him—and that was not *all* she had taken serious note of.

"You are big all over," she dared mention. "But tell me, what is that in your chausses? You are not all that knobby, I realize." A laugh escaped her curling lips. "The lumps are always in a different place after you return from a creek or a rivulet."

"Ah, so you have noticed," Barry grumbled without embarrassment.

"Yes—I have."

"I have an aching of the bones and the warmth the lengths of bunched linen yield save me from much . . . pain. Pain," he repeated, looking at her steadfastly.

"Oh," she said, not asking more.

Autumn wondered why he would wish to conceal such a magnificent body, even in the name of soothing a little ache. What could cause much pain at Barry's young age?

"How old are you, Barry?"

"Near to thirty, I would guess. In these times, does anyone tally their own age?"

His manner of speech again. Puzzling. Barry intrigued her more and more each day, so much that she

73

was almost forsaking the important mission she was undertaking.

To find her sisters, one at a time. This was what was meaningful in her life. Not a simple man's magnificent form.

Autumn laid a hand on Barry's thigh in getting up from the blanket. He jerked as if she had laid a hot piece of wood there.

"Did I hurt you?" She looked down at him, his look of anguish, and wondered if she had been wrong about the premature aching of his joints.

"Never touch me there again," he said.

"What?"

"Remember what happened before."

How could she forget?

Thoroughly bewildered, and just a little vexed, Autumn blinked as Barry walked away.

Her eyes still sparkling, she touched her mouth, wondering why and how it still burned from the kisses she had shared with the handsome knight of her dreams.

She stood in one spot dumbly gazing at nothing, her mind full of castles in the air and happy leaps in fields full of daffodils and daisies.

Five

"Are there men like Robert Hood in the forest even now?" Autumn asked Barry as they neared Nottingham-shire.

"Always," he said. "Another Robert Hood was in the wardrobe accounts of Edward the Second."

Suddenly Barry fell silent, acting as if he was saying far too much.

"Aye." Autumn went on, unaware of Barry's nervous-ness. "Hobbehod, a Yorkshire fugitive mentioned in the pipe rolls of the late 1220s." She knew much about Robert or Robin Hood, since he was her very favorite romantic character to read about or watch in plays. "He was, as an outlawed follower of Earl Thomas of Lan-caster, one of the "contrariants" pardoned by Edward the Second during his visit to the north in 1323. Further color was given by pointing to a Hood family men-tioned in the court records of the manor of Wakefield in the West Riding of Yorkshire, the area where some of the "ballad episodes" are located."

Barry could not keep silent on the subject. "It was just a century ago that the sheriff was most prominent as the local representative of law and order and that there was the greatest resentment against the laws of the forest."

Forest, yes.

Autumn looked around the deep one they had just entered. She had to alight from Ghost in some places, for the bramble and brush was very thick, and then she could mount him again when the way was clear, which was not very often.

To keep from shivering and wondering about the ghostly sounds in the wood, she went on about Robin Hood.

"The most obvious feature of Robin Hood's life is that he was"—she gazed around again—"rebel against authority. The most striking episodes show him . . . Oh, what was *that?*"

Autumn blinked, holding onto to Ghost for dear life.

"Only a rabbit. Now, where was I. Oh yes. The most striking episodes show him and his companions robbing and killing men who represented, ah, authority I mean. Their"—she started, then stopped, went on—"most frequent enemy is the sheriff of Nottingham! Oh. Barry, where are you?" Autumn peeked over her shoulder noticing Barry was making no comment. "Barry, where did you go?"

Autumn shrugged, keeping her cowardice from showing as she kept walking, thinking Barry would catch up. She kept up a stream of chatter, as if he still walked behind her.

A deep voice intruded and hung on the silent wood; it was as if a tree was speaking its thoughts.

"Ah yes. The sheriff, the principal local agent of the central government."

Autumn whirled. "Who is that? Is that you, Barry?"

Dear Lord, she hoped it was him, and not someone or something else.

"Next came the wealthy ecclesiastical landowners, of whom the most vividly portrayed is the abbot of the Benedictine monastery of St. Mary's, York."

"Who said that?" Autumn's eyes roved the trees and thick brush on either side of her. The voice was very nice, deep with a masculine growl. "Go on," she urged, with a shaky laugh, "I am listening, Sir Tree."

"The courtesy that characterizes Robin's treatment of the poor knight, of women, and of persons of humble status, disappears when he and his followers are dealing with the sheriff and his agents—" The wonderful tree cleared its throat, then went on. *"In this case he goes by the name Guardian. Here he does, at this time in Sherwood and the villain is Drogo and his agents, ah well, you will see."*

"Where *are* you?" Autumn bent low and then straightened to full height, stretching her neck a little. "I can hear you. Why will you not show yourself? And"—she whispered in a singing voice to herself—"Where is Barry?"

Sherwood Forest.

This was where they had finally come to. There was no Robin, he was only a fable. But this man in the tree—Guardian, now. Who was he? Did he live in exile, or in hiding, in disguise no doubt, in this deep and scary forest? For certain, others lived among the forest trees—Drogo and his outlaw agents were real.

At last, Autumn came to a halt. Barry was nowhere to be found. She frowned and sniffed, choosing the mossy end piece of a log to sit upon.

"Oh!" she screeched, when a furry little creature scurried out the other end of the log, gave her a big-eyed glance and waddled off. "What was that?"

Shrugging again, with her hand whirling and then propped beneath her chin, Autumn waited.

And waited.

She looked up. Sunset would soon carmine the tree-tops. Would it grow dark suddenly here?

"He took the jennets and the cart with him," Autumn told Ghost. "Wherever they went. No doubt he is off to a stream to put more mud on his face. Hmm—"

Very odd that he would do that, she told herself, rubbing her slim arms for warmth.

Does the sun not shine in any part of this deep forest?

"Barry!"

Autumn grew intensely bored in her surroundings; and she was a bit worried. She started to talk to herself again: "I will have to get out of this forest before dark if Barry does not show up soon."

Ghost nickered and brushed a velvety muzzle over Autumn's arm before nibbling around in the forest carpet for more green things to eat. To keep herself from worry she began to hum, and before long she was feeling happy, and the sights and sounds and smells of the wondrous forest were new and stimulating.

She hummed even louder.

All of a sudden her soft noise came to a halt. Someone had joined her.

A boy's voice was raised in plaintive, lonely song. Was that the sound of a flute? How lovely.

"I suppose there could be people in the forest. Of course there could. They must be traveling also."

Just where was Barry leading her? And where was he? He should have caught up with her by now.

In a low voice Autumn sang, "Where are you, Barry? Oh, where are you? Are you hiding, playing games on me?"

Barry. Barry. It was all difficult and incomprehensible. She did not want any of these new and uncomfortable feelings and did not know what she was supposed to do about them.

Barry, the Betrayer. Barry, the Magnificent (in body, that is). What had become of Barry, the Simple?

Autumn swirled the long red helixes of her hair. Her chin was in her hands again. Besides the singing, there were the innumerable small noises around her: rustlings, patterings, and the quiet movements of branches and leaves. Some of the sounds came to her as eerie, like the creaking of a high limb and distant, mysterious voices of the ancient forest. She wished she would have remained at home, with all her friends at Sutherland Castle.

Still, she had sisters she must find.

So busy was Autumn with her thoughts, that she did not hear the singing when it stopped, nor the last tune of the flute.

A faint twitch of her skirt made her spin around. A tawny-headed boy stood there. A boy with tousled hair, blade in hand . . . was making off with the purse he'd just sliced from her belt.

"Halt! Thief!"

With a yell of fury Autumn was up and after him, along the forest floor, her feet in their soft hide boots tingling on the tiny, poking branches scattered about.

The boy looked back once, judging her distance, then

79

raced on through the tangled brush. He screeched when he saw the horse, like a full-blown ghost, following with a slower pace. But the trotting horse was there just the same, giving him quite a scare with its rolling eyes and tossing mane while maneuvering through the tall trees.

Even so, Gelflin thought it was a magnificent beast.

Autumn saw that the boy must turn off up one of the tree avenues if he was to lose her, so she veered away from the stony crop of rocks and kept close to the wooded walls opposite.

Making a heart-thudding effort, Autumn gained on him before he could make his turn. "Ah! I have you now, you little thief!" she yelled.

For a split second he stopped, then feinted and would have run back the way they had come, only to sprawl headlong over the foot she had thrust in front of him. "Aha!"

Again, making full use of her advantage she tossed herself upon him and wrestled the wiggling boy.

In attempting to subdue the thief, she found her frustration and puzzlement of the last few days translated into firm physical statements. Autumn wrestled the boy until she realized she was no longer meeting with any resistance.

She stopped and sat up, astride her enemy. Victorious and triumphant she noticed the urchin was very still. *Had she killed him?*

"Speak," she demanded and, apprehensive, she examined him. He did not seem to be breathing. "Speak, I say. Lad?" She bent closer. "Are you—?"

All of a sudden Autumn was the one on her back

on the hard forest stones. Her arms were pinned to her chest and her head terribly sore where she had hit it.

"Why—you." Tears sprang but she shook them away and spat straight up into the grinning dirty face.

"Now what do ye say, middy?" he taunted, red freckles standing out playfully.

"Let go, you, you—misbegotten thief! And give back my purse or I shall holler so loud the forest will fall down!"

Whether or not she could accomplish the fate of Jericho without the aid of trumpets would never be tested.

Before the boy could answer this interesting threat he found himself torn with shocking suddenness from the body of his victim and hoisted into the air.

"Heyy!" he cried and dangled for a second, and then, from an unkind height, was dropped with a *kerplop*.

"Gelflin. What the devil are you at, attacking a little bit of fluff the likes of her?"

"Rood, Sir Tyrian! I thought you was still a'sleeping!"

Autumn sat up, rubbing her head, and stared and stared. Tyrian. She liked the name, even though a bit odd. Any rescuer was welcome, but this one presented an extra dimension that stunned her reactions for the moment.

Was it a trick of the sun or did the man really shine like that?

He was tall, this Tyrian, perhaps as tall as Orion Sutherland, and appeared to be made of gold from head to foot, as if he wore armor like Sir Lancelot or St. George. Even as these dashed across her mind, she saw that the sheen really was that of chain mail; but his look expressed amusement rather than chivalrous concern.

81

"What?" she said when he reached down.

"Here," was all he said, with his hand out.

She was helped to her feet in considerate enough manner and dusted down with a swipe of his gauntleted hand: It was a glove with an extended cuff for the wrist, a glove such as worn by an armored knight. But he wore no heavy armor that clanked; only the chain mail.

He seemed to glow. Where had she seen that glow, and this man, before? In a dream? Nay. He was not the knight who had touched her soul in her dream. The man in her dream was more like Barry, but he was *not* Barry. It was all very confusing.

The boy, crouched with his grubby paws over his ears like a bad dog, was faring not as well at the toe of an expensive green boot.

"Up, you fool. Make your apologies to the middy," Tyrian ordered the boy.

Middy? What's this language? Autumn wondered, not having heard the word before.

She got up. She stood tall and did her best imitation of her best friend, Elizabeth Juel Sutherland, who had beautiful manners.

"Thank you, sir, for your timely assistance. Your forest talk is strange. To whom have I the pleasure of addressing my gratitude?"

His manner became suddenly less angry, even toward the skinny lad.

"You have heard my name," the big golden man said.

"Oh, yes of course." Did he not have another name he went by?

He had read her thought. "My name is Tyrian Armstrong, second in authority of the, uh, Forest Brother-hood."

How disappointing. Autumn had thought him at least a baron or an earl riding shortcut through the forest.

"An outlaw, as in the fable Robin the Hood?"

He cleared his throat quietly. "Somewhat. And I am not the Guardian of the forest. That would be"—again he faltered—"someone else." He held up a gauntleted finger.

"I know an Armstrong. He is a knight at Sutherland."

"Howell," he said under his breath.

"What name did you say?" she asked, staring at his beautiful face, golden eyes, yellow hair.

"And this," he went on as if he'd not heard, taking the risen cut-purse painfully by his goblin ear, "is Gelflin the Bastard. This lad is one of my apprentices. Well, what say you, fair maiden? Shall I keep him on, or turn him out to beg his living in the slums of London?"

Standing, Autumn watched and considered. The boy's face was scarlet with discomfort but it was a nice face, all pointy and alive like a fox's. And he had light freck-les like hers. She scuffed a toe in the leaves, avoiding the lad's furious look. He must hate her. "If you turn him out of the forest," she told the bold, golden coun-tenance above her, "he will spend *all* his time stealing instead of only some of it."

Gelflin's roar of pleasure made Autumn jump.

Staring at the young woman's rowanberry mouth, Tyrian said, "There's wisdom in that. Aye, as well as kindness. Your name, mademoiselle?"

"Autumn Meaux. You'll keep him then?"

"I will. I can't have an elf of a dozen summers show

me up for a cruel taskmaster. You may grovel at Mistress Autumn's feet, Gelflin."

Gelflin looked shamefaced but openly relieved. He liked his work of cleaning and polishing armor. Thieving was only his pastime; as it was with the other folk in the Forest Brotherhood. Though when they were hungry, what about that? That was another thing entirely. And they had to fill their bellies, didn't they. It was only this young woman Tyrian had not wanted him to rob.

Nodding at Autumn, Gelflin showed slightly crooked teeth in an amiable grin. It was clear that he had forgiven her his embarrassment.

Smiling, he took her purse from his baggy trousers and handed it back to her. She exchanged a smile for it. "A mistake, maid Autumn. Won't 'appen again."

The leader spoke again. "A Meaux, you say?" he asked Autumn. "Of Sir Richard's family?"

Memory returned like little birds landing one after the other. "My father, sir." The birds flew off, leaving her brain naked again.

She blinked. *And an uncle?*

Tyrian seemed pleased. "My father was acquainted with your father and his brother."

Yes, I have an uncle. His name evaded her memory. "Please tell me all you know—"

Before she could say more, he was turning away.

Now she noticed his clothes. Tyrian, dressed oddly, she thought, wore besides the chain mail and gauntlets, mustard-colored forest clothes, huge leather jerkin, broad waistbelt for holding weapons, a long yellow leather thong with hunting horn and water skin. Last, his hair and short beard were a dusky blond.

He was, in truth, a great golden god.

Autumn gave a little laugh. "Robin Hood?" She lifted a nicely shaped eyebrow of russet hue.

With his own deeper laugh, Tyrian jested, "I'm not. And how could that be? Those are only of legends."

"There are those of us romantics who believed he lived. You might be a more recent version of him?"

He leapt to a log and posed there, with outflung arm. "I suppose you could say that. Shall I capture you like Will Scarlet captured his lady Kate? Or will you come along willingly?"

"I think I'll come along willingly." She could see all the forest-colored figures forming a partly invisible horseshoe about her in the greensward. "I see many eyes."

How long had they been watching? She saw the feathered caps bobbing in the lush undergrowth, a nose here, an ear, a white hand upon a bow strung taut.

The forest. Its great green secrets. The laws of its dark heart.

Oaks, ten centuries old, soared above with the beech trees, and mosses made a green carpet of the forest floor. The ancient forest ranged far and wide, acres beyond counting, conquering and claiming every chart and sketch of England's north region. Here, laws were cast aside, cultures and traditions left behind, and those who strayed from the paths to enter its green clasp were rarely seen again.

Sherwood was the sanctuary of a lost society, the beginning of dreams, the last retreat of the outlaw. The one refuge where no man gave chase.

Aye, she thought, no one would dare come to seek

out these outlaws, for fear of becoming lost in the forest's green embrace themselves.

"I would like to leave a message for my friend," Autumn told the leader, or second leader, of the—what had he said? Brotherhood of the Forest?

"A message? For who?" asked Tyrian.

"My friend," she repeated. "Will you allow that? He is Barry Jeraux, the village idiot."

"Which village?"

She laughed very hard. "Herstmonceaux. At least, the last village he was in."

Tyrian looked away from her and grinned at his companions all around them. "Of course," he shouted. He bowed like the gallant outlaw he was. "A message it is, herb maiden."

"Herb?" she asked. "How did you know?"

"That you carry herbs and seeds, while knowing at the same time how to heal the sick?" He shrugged one big shoulder. "I know, that is all."

She opened her mouth to ask again how he knew but she had so many questions, she could not give words to them. Instead, she set forth making arrows out of sticks, pointing the way she had gone. "There. He will follow the arrows."

"Very clever." His voice had an edge of sharpness now. "Come along and quit your dawdling. I know you are trying to escape."

She blinked up at the tall, handsome god of man. "You really do think to capture me, don't you."

"Of course. There is someone who would very much like to meet you."

She gave a curt nod and followed him, while Gelflin bowed and scraped at her heels, carrying her bags.

Ghost followed close behind, but no one seemed to notice Autumn now; they stared at the huge white horse.

Her heart beat faster. Could her sister be here? Could it truly be Winter's sanctuary from the bad people in their life?

As soon as they entered the forest stronghold, Tyrian turned and vanished into the wood, Gelflin lingering.

By now, ghostly shadows had formed beneath the moon.

Six

In the forest mist and moonlight Autumn looked up at the rope bridges that had been built between the trees. She stood below, in the rude forest camp, then looked around at all the people staring up at her. Dirty faces, hardly any clean ones, suspicious, watchful, and mistrusting faces, all wondering about her and where she had come from.

She looked around for Tyrian, but he seemed to have vanished into thin air.

"Go on up, Lady Autumn," Gelflin urged her up the rope ladder secured with slices of wood for tiny stairs.

How exciting and not a little frightening, Autumn thought as she climbed upward, higher and higher into the lofty forest air to the crude but substantial tree-hut atop the greenwood.

"I am to sleep up here?" she asked herself, glancing over her shoulder at the bonfire and the faces circling round it gawking up at her.

Gelflin heard. "That's right, m'lady. And Tyrian says I'm to grovel at your feet. Your slightest wish and I am to run and fetch. What do you want me to do, m'lady?"

The rope ladder swayed and Autumn laughed nervously, looking down at Gelflin. "I'm not sure what I want just yet, Gelflin." She bent a little to look into the hut; the door was partway open. "Perhaps a little light. It's very dark up here."

"There's a candle up there. But you got to be very careful, m'lady, else the place will go up in flames. That's been known to 'appen, m'lady. And your eyes will get used to the dark up there; it's like that, m'lady."

"Gelflin," she said, looking down from her perch. "You may call me maiden or Autumn. And I prefer that you do."

"Yes, m'lady. I mean, Autumn." He turned to go to the bonfire to get a bowl of soup. "Would you like something to eat, m'lady. Autumn. There is hot soup and a hard crust of bread for you. That's all we got—for now."

"Oh . . . Aye, yes."

After she had eaten and Gelflin had gone back down the rope ladder, Autumn curled up in the bed to sleep. The moon's silver glory peeked into the thatch and she snuggled down further into the rough sleeping blankets, grateful that they smelled nice and fresh instead of sour and soiled.

The words came to her in her dream: *I pledge to always love you.* Who was saying them? Her eyes flew open as she saw that the man mouthing them was Barry. Then they closed and her dreamworld shifted and melted away like something soft and creamy under the sun.

In the morning Autumn was startled to see a big man

emerging from the additional room. The room was small and the man was almost too large to fit in there, but that was from where he had appeared and come to stand across from her.

Autumn glanced at his clothes while pulling the roughly woven blanket up to her breasts. His clothes were even more strangely stitched than the man Tyrian's. This man was tall but she thought him heavier than Tyrian and not as good-looking as the second leader.

If Tyrian was the second, who was the first?

She did not even study this man's clothes all that much; she was so interested in the odd-colored eyes, which seemed to have all sorts of shades imbued in them. Hazel eyes, she decided.

She knew at once.

"You are the Guardian," she said, tugging the olive-colored cover closer about her linen shift. After he had nodded, still staring at her, she asked, "Where is Winter?"

He looked around her to the opening. "Winter?" he said from the shadows. "It is not even full summer."

"My sister, Winter, is she here?"

"Ho. Winter. What then is your name, fair sister?"

Autumn's eyes narrowed as he walked from the shadows. "I am Autumn of Herstmonceaux." She looked up, her eyes lifting a level higher than this area. Had he been asleep in the other room? "My lord and lady are the Baroness Elizabeth and her husband, Baron Orion Sutherland."

"Of Sutherland Castle naturally."

"Well"—she said with a shake of her head with its red braid swishing—"of course." So. He liked to play games, did he? And was that a twinkle in his eyes, or were they always this beautiful?

He was not that handsome yet she could see he was strong. His hair was shaped all about his head like a monk's, but it was much longer in back. He was just a big man in plain, dark clothes. Dark green tunic and . . . he was speaking now, rather rudely.

"Gelflin has brought food," he grunted, seating himself at a crude bench before a small table someone had no doubt hastily built. "You had better rise, wench, else you'll go without your morning repast."

Tucking the blanket about her, Autumn snatched up her clothes and ran to the cubbyhole to pull her inner tunic and outer tunic over her head. She emerged, wearing the green and blue washed-out outfit.

"You have pretty hair, shiny and red," he said as she sat across from him in the treetop thatch. "Why don't you wear it loose?"

"I shall"—she gave a nonchalant shrug—"when I feel like it." She took a bite of the blue goat cheese. "Has Barry come for me yet?"

"Barry?" He chewed the bread and cheese for a moment, then looked enlightened. "He has come and gone."

Autumn blinked. That was it? He had come and left her with these people? How long would he be away? She wanted to ask all these questions, but she had to explain herself first.

"We have to find my sister. That is the purpose of our journey to the North Country, to the nunnery of Kirklees, between Halifax and Wakefield."

"I know where the nunnery is. And I did not say he would *not* return."

She looked sad; Barry was a paradox. "He might not."

"He will. Trust me, Mistress Autumn." His eyes were the color of mossy stones and he smiled for the first time since emerging from the tiny room; he was rather handsome, if you let him grow on you. "Barry will return. He has been here before; we know him."

Barry? Here, *before?*

She continued to study the man.

Now she changed her mind again. He was *not* very handsome, no, not at all. Now then Tyrian, that man was a pretty sight to behold, unquestionably.

With a berry halfway to her mouth, Autumn turned away so he'd not see her puzzled look. She had clamped her mouth shut and found herself staring at something fastened to the hut's thatch wall. A picture, a crude drawing actually, of a real home, a castle compound with a lovely manor inside and a moated enclosure.

"Dreaming, Sir Guardian?" she ventured.

"Aye, yes. One can only wish, fair maiden." He dragged his gaze from the drawing.

This time he had not called her wench and he could see the relief on her little face. "Don't you have a hankering for a thing?"

"I do," Autumn confessed. "I would like very much to find sister, Winter."

Hearing voices, Autumn got up from the table and poked her head out the flimsy door. She could see across the swinging bridge that another thatch similar to this one, had been constructed into a similar grouping of tall, huge trees.

Tyrian was over there. He waved at her and she

blushed at the handsome bold man's morning perusal, then pulled herself back inside with a deep sigh. That man was so very handsome he almost took her breath. Almost, but not quite.

When she turned around she found herself against a solid wall of man. Warm, hard, with muscles that flexed and strained to keep her from tripping over him as he stood right there like a great big wall.

Before she knew what was happening, she found her lips beneath his, her thighs trapped between his, her breasts crushed flat in a mighty embrace. This had all happened so fast that Autumn, in her surprise, felt nothing but bewilderment and more surprise.

Was she supposed to feel something? What was he trying to do?

This was not a kiss. This was an attack and a violation to her person!

She could not breathe, and as she began to wonder if he would ever come up for air himself and leave off crushing her, she brought her knee up to his crotch.

And lifted hard!

She stood back as he fell against the table, holding his privates in pain. He blinked up at her as he lay half on the table, half on the bench. He rolled his eyes toward her.

He said, "I believe we have met before."

"What?"

Pushing himself up with his one elbow—the other was still cradling his hurt—he strode past her and out the door. She heard him groaning all the way down the rope ladder, and she gave a soft giggle when he jumped the last step down and groaned even louder.

He looked up and grinned once, quickly, part comical and part sarcastic.

With her hands clamped across her mouth, Autumn whirled and faced the crude thatch's interior, her eyes sparkling with playfulness and intrigue as they passed over the barely consumed meal.

Her smile melted. With wondering eyes, a frown quirked at her brow with gentle animation.

We have met before. The voice in the forest.

She set about to clean up the crude thatch and then sat down to dump out her baggage and check the seeds to make sure they were still secured in their tiny cloths. Her herbs were still intact. Separately she had tied many tiny little marked bags of seeds and herbs, enough to plant a whole garden.

The vegetable seeds had been carefully selected from the kitchen garden and the herbal beams at Sutherland.

She wondered if these sorry-looking folk had a garden planted already. They should have. There were many beautiful clearings in the woods with streams nearby where a garden would thrive and grow wonderful things like herbal medicine and nourishing food.

Perhaps she should plant a garden, as thanks for the hospitality and then quickly return to her search. If only Barry would get over his strange mood and emerge from hiding. Then they could go on their merry way.

Soon, she knew it, very soon she would be reunited with her sister. And she had a strong feeling that Winter wasn't very far away. Perhaps in the Kirklees convent. She had a feeling that that was where she'd find Winter. There, or in this place called Whitby.

The Guardian's kiss, when she thought about it, seemed born of a burning desire. But was that not what man's carnal appetite—his fiercest passion, which lay in his nether regions—was all about?

Staring at the spot where the Guardian had pulled her against him for that exotic kiss, she thought . . . *What did she think?*

Abstractedly Autumn thought, almost any woman would do at a time when a man has a fierce ache in his privates, when he thought not with his brains but his bold lower half.

Which reminded her of Barry, the Betrayer.

She brushed her hair with a grooming tool until it shone, then braided and wound it around her head in a regal crown. Realizing she would look too much like Barry's "princess," she took it back down but left in the braids.

Where was plain and simple Barry? When would he return?

That night Autumn had a dream. Of stories that had no origins, jewels that held no glitter, lands that dropped off into nothingness, a past she did not remember.

Below, on the cool forest ground, Barry could not sleep. He had restless waking dreams of Autumn Meaux in which she was kissing him. This kiss seemed to last forever. He was in a fever. He wanted to have her here beside him, to hold her, caress her and tell her . . . What? What did he wish to tell her?

It was too soon to be in love with her.

Or was it, the Guardian asked himself as he ripped off his tunic and stuffed it beneath his head and, after a time he moved closer to the campfire, trying to get warmer. He wanted to take her so much that his body shook with his intense need.

He knew what would happen if he went up that rope ladder. Autumn Meaux would be a virgin no longer. He would have to take her and make her his forever. He wanted her, more than he had ever wanted the Duchess Rowena.

Seven

"Tyrian makes you blush. Do you like him?"

With her mouth open, Autumn looked at the Guardian, wondering about his name. "You mean do I prefer him over you? *No.*"

Watching children as they ran back and forth, the Guardian asked, "Then I am the one man of your most tender dreams?"

"Hardly."

"Really," he said, making her frown delicately.

Her eyes widened as she took note of the clothes he was wearing today. Just like the man of her dreams, he was dressed in chain mail and chausses, high boots, logan green gloves. Had he been working or fighting? Practicing as Sutherland's knights did?

He was a mystery, this man. "Who are you, really?" she asked, feeling strange and tingling when he was near, as if she had felt these same sensations years ago. So near, as if . . . as if she could have touched him. Long ago, like some awful secret from her past. A feeling of fear.

Yet, *she had never known him in her past. Or had she? What else would she remember?*

"I am just this: A man without lands or title. They were taken, ah, stolen from me by the duc's agents."

"How could—?" Then she frowned as she thought of something else. "By Stephen, the new cardinal legate? The king himself, did he order this?"

"Neither," he said, aware of how swiftly she caught on. "With Henry at war so much, English politics are dominated by the rivalry between Duke Humphrey and the king's great uncle, Henry Beaufort."

She was puzzled. "Who then?"

"Beaufort's agents, one in particular," he said, watching her closely and testing her.

She gasped as the Guardian's meaning struck her. "You mean Duc Stephan? He is not a thief and he is not one of Henry's agents. Is he?" When he looked away as if bored, she said, "You talk in riddles." Did he mean to? she asked herself.

Guardian leaned against the thatch, watching her go back to sorting out some linen-wrapped bags, small ones mostly. His eyes went to the two women emerging from the forest carrying wood for the fires and then back to her again.

He said, "Listen to this then: His wealth is legendary. The administration's fees are multiplied by his judicious financing of a bankrupt government. His generous financing of the state was therefore not wholly disinterested patriotism. And his largest loans are made either for financial and political gain or from political necessity."

Shrewdly Autumn said, "Before 'therefore' you left something out. The most intriguing part. What was it?"

He grinned. "You are swift and astute, aren't you."

Her gaze returned from wandering about the woodsmen's camp. "I have been told this."

"What do you know?" There was laughter in his eyes, quirking at his mouth.

"You cannot tangle me in riddles. They are in fact Beaufort *and* Duc Stephan. Yet, what about it? There is more you conceal from me."

With a lopsided smile he wagged a finger at her, saying, "Stick to your garden and the plans you make for discovering your sister's whereabouts."

One finely feathered eyebrow lifted. "Else I might find out too much about you and your past political history?"

He narrowed hazel eyes at her. "Be what you are, Autumn."

Looking him straight in the eye, she asked, "And what is that?"

"A simple maiden."

Then he walked away.

Beaufort's agents. Duc Stephan's agents. Aha, she thought to herself as she was left to her own pursuits. Drogo and his Riflers must be involved in this deception somehow. How did the Guardian fit in? And Barry, somehow she was forming the idea that Barry had led her into a trap. Why was it she was never left alone for very long?

The forest seemed to have eyes as she walked along a meandering leaf-strewn trail, picking her way below the cathedral of giant trees.

Barry . . . Barry . . .

Jewels, jewels, the crown jewels. The Jewel of Jeraux.

A light flowed into her mind. She smiled a secret smile. Perhaps it was the jewels. An unredeemed loan? Jewels much undervalued?

Perhaps even the mauve-white Star of Africa? Her family's own?

Jeraux? *Barry?*

How could a simpleton like Barry have anything to do with the Jewel of Jeraux?

Impossible.

The Snot's people were trailing Autumn. They were called Snots or Notts, because they were outcasts from Nottingham, Notts being the newer version. She looked over her shoulder every so often to find them still with her, the dyes and hues of their clothing blending with the forest. The Guardian and Tyrian called the rest of the tough men wearing "Sherwood green" the Thatchers. And then there were the women who stayed with the band and provided for their many needs. And food, of course, there was always a stewpot gurgling over a fire after a hunting party had returned from the deep forest with fresh game.

Autumn was checking the soil where she had found a good place for a garden, easy watering from the stream nearby, trees standing far back, no bothersome roots in the area.

Guardian was seated on a giant tree trunk polishing bits of armor when he saw her enter the clearing. He didn't stand, but kept on with his work.

"What do you think?" the Guardian asked her as she stood there with a clump of dirt in her hand, making it into a ball and letting it fall in a stream of peatmoss and black loam. The rest filtered through her fingers like sand in an hourglass.

Dusting off her hands, she said, "The forest soil is gravel and sand. This is good. There is a rich vegetable mold here, very suitable for crops, even corn, barley or bere, turnips and swedes, vetches, and herbs."

He looked over his shoulder and shooed everyone away that had been gawking suspiciously at the woman with red hair wearing green and russet clothes; some of the poor folk had begun to call her witch.

Guardian said, "You never asked why you are able to do this."

"This?" Autumn looked around at the perfect spot for a huge garden; there was even sun slanting down through the younger trees. "Oh, why I am able to come here and look at the soil and plan the planting of a garden?"

"You don't wonder about anything very much, do you. You just go ahead and do it."

"Why waste precious time." She looked over at the massive ancient oak at the edge of the clearing. "I will have to leave soon."

With his rag, he gave a lick and a promise to his helm and set it aside. "You can stay." He picked up a yew longbow, tested it with an arrow alongside, sighted the tip, stopped and looked at her.

Autumn's mouth twitched. "So we can become friends?" She paused before she said softly, "Or lovers."

"Both," he said with a chuckle.

"You are very strange. First you attack me and now you are all but begging me to stay with you and your forest friends. How long will you be here?"

101

"As long as it takes for me to, er, do what must be done."

"And that is clear your name?"

"For now. Like you, I have a mission, to discover the whereabouts of certain objects. Once I have these . . . things back in order I will win back my ancestral holdings."

"What? Castles?" She was impressed. "More than one?"

"One in France. One in England."

"And you have to get something back," she said with a blink. "What is it?"

"More than 'it'. Them."

"You are interesting, sir, and your mission intrigues me. But I will go now. I have to see if Barry has returned. I will tell him my plans and then we will leave Sherwood and continue the search for my sister."

"Stay. Barry won't miss you."

"Stay? What do you mean? Here?"

"Of course. We will plan your garden and take a walk."

"You are more dangerous when you are out in the open, Sir Guardian. And I have already planned the garden; it won't take long for the Notts to plant the seeds with my help."

"As I said, Barry won't miss you. Even now he drinks with some of my, the men."

Autumn frowned. "He has returned?"

"Aye. And he might find himself a bit of entertainment before the night is out. If you know what I mean." He wiggled a nice set of brown eyebrows.

Autumn shook her head. "Not Barry."

Guardian chuckled. "Why not Barry? Is he too old or too ugly for some comely maid to dally with?"

"Barry is . . . just Barry," ended Autumn quickly. She thought for a moment when he seemed to be waiting. "He is not very pleasing to the eye or the nose."

"His face is ugly? He smells bad?"

"He washes at times. Do not get me wrong." There was an edge to her voice. "He is very nice to be with when he behaves himself."

"Has he behaved badly?"

"Only a little. I have forgiven him." Her eyes grew misted. "In fact, we shared some very pleasant times. Nice conversation as we shared a resting spot beneath a big oak, or a meal before a low campfire. Aye, he can be gentle and warmhearted. I would go to him now, if you don't mind."

"But I do. I want you here with me. I enjoy your company very much also, even though you speak as though you clip hedges instead of make conversation."

Autumn smiled but would not admit the truth in front of the Guardian. Yes, she found this man's company almost as pleasant as Barry's. And a bit more exciting. In fact, she was loath to be alone with the Guardian. Afraid and jumpy, much more so than being alone with the golden Tyrian who was so handsome and bold, everything a woman would want in a man.

Guardian's stolen kisses haunted and still burned her lips. What was it about him? Why did he make her feel . . . almost the way Barry made her feel? That in itself was strange; he and Barry had to be as different as horse dung and sweet cakes.

The dark-haired man held out his hand. "Come. We will walk and enjoy the forest."

What was it about this gentle outlaw who hid from some secret in his past? And what was that secret? Had he murdered someone in a high place of authority, like a royal subject? Was there a woman involved with him and his secrets? Would she learn more about him before she had to abandon Sherwood with Barry to go in search of her sister?

"Why so tense?" Guardian asked. "You jumped as high as a doe just now when I touched your arm ever so lightly."

"I did?"

"Aye. You did. I'll not bite. I might nip a little and steal a few kisses now and then. Do you mind?"

She whirled away from him. "Of course I mind. You have no right. I'm not even sure I like you"—she saw his wounded look—"not in that way, especially."

"In what way?"

"The way of a woman in love."

He chuckled deep in his chest. "Who said anything about amour?"

Men, she thought. Are they all the same? Love and lust had to be two moons apart in their world. They continued to walk until coming to a slightly darker part of the forest.

The Guardian and Autumn came to a halt. The forest concealed them in her leafy boughs, in the lividness of her shadows. Here, the sunlight came down in dusty shafts and was confusing and played tricks on unaccustomed eyes. Autumn looked up to find herself staring at Guardian's full sensuous mouth and found him blurring handsomely before her eyes.

She looked away, but remembered what she had filled her gaze with. His nose was long and had a slight flare in the nostrils, distinguishing his profile. His eyes were a remarkable shade, or shades of green, with brown, gray, even yellow in them. Hmm, sort of like Barry's eyes. His face was clean where Barry's was always dirty.

"Are you related to Barry Jeraux?" she blurted.

"No," he said at once. "No. Not at all."

Autumn looked aside, thinking the Guardian was an incongruity here, among thieves. He didn't seem to fit in and yet, part of him seemed to belong also. She was about to ask this paradox if he owned a first name, when he spoke up breaking into her musings.

He asked, "Would you like to bathe?"

"What? *Here?*" She looked around but saw no stream nearby.

"Come here."

She followed into the first bit of deep blue-green forest. "I have a crude shower of sorts. See—"He pulled aside a weedy curtain and a huge rainbarrel became visible. "The water is released from up there"— he watched her look up—"when you pull the rope and it splashes down on your"—he blinked beautiful eyes, cleared his throat—"body as you wash."

"How clever!" she exclaimed, eager to try it out.

Grinning, he took up a wooden cup and dipped in, rising with a drink of water, which he drank from, turned, then offered her the rest. "For you."

"It's very cold and refreshing." She handed the cup back, hugging her slim arms at once. "I shall freeze to death in that shower!"

"Not so. Look up. Halfway down there is another holding tank. That one is crude metals, melted down from old ruined swords."

She looked up and saw what he spoke of, then up farther to where the bowers of the oaks provided a perfect ceiling. Not much blue of sky showed up there. This was an eerie and mysterious section of the Greenwood.

He stopped to explain something belatedly: "I have a friend who is an armorer." He did not say where. "That tank is heated, again cleverly, as you say, then water runs down and onto your . . . body."

"Hmm. How long will it take to heat?"

"Awhile," he said and smiled. "I'll have Jacques make the fire now."

"I will undress in the woods. Do not look when I come out."

He bowed. "Of course, Mistress Autumn."

After the water had been heated and Autumn had taken the most wonderful "shower" of her life—with a sliver of scented soap to boot—she turned to him when she was dressed.

He was propped against a tree, a long weed sticking from his mouth; and when he saw her, with her hair wet, looking so fresh of skin and moist, sparkly eyes, dark spiky lashes, he stiffened and straightened away from the tree.

For an instant, for time never-ending, the world stood still. She looked at him. He looked at her.

Nothing moved until, at last, her gaze dropped.

Shaking her head, rubbing her hair briskly, drops flying about, she stopped her feminine movements and asked him a question out of the blue as she quickly went on to fastening her bodice strings.

"How many people share this shower of yours?"

"Only my sister. And now you."

Autumn blinked. "Your . . . sister?" *Where was she?*

"Aye. My twin. You may meet her tomorrow."

"Tom—"

As usual, Autumn was watching the mysterious Guardian walk away. She was left alone, blinking in puzzlement.

A twin. How interesting this forest was becoming. By the hour.

Three mounted figures, hidden under heavy cloaks and dark hoods, rode away from the concealment of thick trees beside the clearing. They had witnessed all they had wanted to. Now the trio rode away, taking the narrow meandering path through the giant cathedral of trees, shadow, and little dusky light.

They were making their way back to their mistress, knowing she would relish hearing this bit of news there was a certainty of: *Raine Guardian is falling in love with Autumn Meaux.*

Eight

Autumn found Barry. But the Guardian was nowhere to be seen; he had made his bed elsewhere the night before and did not come up the rope ladder into the thatch. She liked not having to share her quarters with a male. And such a big male who made her feel small and helpless and cramped into one little place. A woman needed space to move about. Especially after living inside the grounds of such a huge castle as Sutherland and having free run to go anywhere she liked.

"Drank too much, did you?" Autumn looked down at Barry where he was stretched out at the foot of a huge oak. "Where have you been?"

He was moaning and holding his head; children nearby looked down at the ragged and dirty man, some giggling, some frowning as others ran back and forth, getting underfoot.

"The children think it is hilarious that you have a big head this morning."

One girl around age three, yanked her thumb from her mouth, yelling, "Barry? . . . *Raine!*"

"No," a little girl hushed the toddler with a pat of her hand. "He is really sick now I think."

"Raine!" echoed Nicole. Then she pointed a finger at him and added, "Barry!"

"Uh-uh, he's Raine," shouted Shawn with a husky lad's vigor.

A woman rushed over. She was very pretty, with long brown hair worn in a braid and her skirts were long and dun colored. "Run along, children. Take Shawn with you, Guinevere. Uh, Barry is trying to sleep."

"Barry?" Geoffrey said with a snort of disbelief following.

Nine-year-old Guinevere said, "As you say, Lady Tiercel."

"Tiercel, Guinevere. Just Tiercel."

"Yes, m'lady." Guinevere bobbed as if Tiercel still was royalty, then took the children's hands. "Come on, Nicole, Billy-John, Geoffrey, and Shawn." She giggled as the children broke away and trailed after her in stairs, the smallest who was tiny blond Nicole bringing up the rear.

The bigger children, Suzanne Marie and Lisa Jane, covered squeals and giggles with their hands and joined the other raggedy children as they ran off to play, work, or just get into trouble.

With her head inclined, Autumn looked at Tiercel questioningly. "What was that all about? I could not make a thing out of it."

"Children's talk. Best that you didn't," Tiercel gave an excuse.

Glancing at Barry as he rolled over and moaned, Autumn trailed after Tiercel. "You must really have a monumental task looking after all those children."

"They are not mine," Tiercel remarked with a shrug. "They belong to the Notts and the Snots."

"What is the difference between the two?"

With a wickedly sweet smile over her shoulder directed at something Autumn could not see, Tiercel offered, "The Anglo-Saxons who occupied the site of Nottingham in the sixth century gave the settlement the name of Snotingaham—the ham or village of Snot's people."

Autumn asked, "Snoting—*a?*—ham?"

"Yes. A—ham."

"Ahem. Go on."

Tiercel continued. "Occupied by the Danes in the ninth century it was one of five towns of the Danelaw, and in pre-Conquest times was known as a city." She barely took a breath as she went on quickly. "After the Conquest the Normans founded the Norman borough, which existed side by side with the older Saxon borough. Both had separate administrations until about 1300. One side was Snots; the other Notts."

"Oh . . . I see." Autumn nodded, trailing close by Tiercel's side. Some children were petting Ghost and wanted to get rides on the horse but Autumn wished to speak more with Tiercel. "Who are you? I mean, where do you come from? I'm sorry," she said when Tiercel briskly faced Autumn. "It's just that you don't seem to belong among these people."

Tiercel lifted her shoulders, saying, "Neither do you."

"I am here because . . ." Autumn looked over her shoulder back at Barry who was crunched against the tree hugging his waist. "He must have really hung one on."

Over her shoulder Tiercel laughed; she looked back at Autumn. Leaning toward the redhead, she offered, "I am Tiercel Guardian."

Guardian? Autumn wondered . . . Guardian? She looked around for that man called The Guardian.

"Do the people here call their leader "The Guardian," or was I simply dreaming?" Autumn asked, watching Tiercel fold some wet rags over a crudely fashioned drying frame.

But they were not rags! They were entire sets of clothing, those of human beings sequestered in this quaint but amazing forest community. How did they stay alive the whole year?

"Raine Guardian is my brother," Tiercel said, laughing.

"Your brother's first name is Raine? And the people call him Raine *and* The Guardian?" Autumn blinked. "That is strange."

With a casual shrug, Tiercel remarked, "No stranger than Autumn *and* Winter."

Autumn's eyes sparkled with laughter and humility. "I see what you mean."

"Do not be embarrassed," Tiercel said. "My brother goes by *many* names. You never know who he is going to be next. He is so very secretive; or he would like people to believe as much." She laughed. "I'm not sure any longer what his real name is."

Autumn pressed her lips. "The children mentioned *Raine* as they stood over Barry's aching head."

"Yes." Tiercel suddenly walked away. Just like her brother. That was it. End of conversation.

Strange people, these Guardians.

Not to mention Tyrian. And Barry, he seemed to be one of them. Now Ghost was off playing with the chil-

111

dren, letting them take rides on his back. She grinned wryly. Would her horse become strange to her also?

She wouldn't find out since she was not staying much longer.

Autumn shook her head; her hair undulated in red waves to her waist. She hugged her slim arms as she walked and looked around, up into the aerial fortress of huts, platforms, and bridges, below at crude huts and hovels here and there tucked secretly into the trees as if part of the Greenwood.

Dirty faces. Suspicious faces. Happy faces, of children. Hungry babes. Moaning old men. Groaning younger ones who had drunk too much the night before. Where did their supply of ale come from? Some hapless friar on his way to the next abbey? Was it just as it had been in the days of Robin/Robert Hood? Does Nottingham still rob from the poor, and then these woodsmen rob Nottingham and give it back to the poor? But there was no Prince John or King Richard with enemies rising up against him. There was King Henry, but he was off fighting to claim a bit more of France.

Gelflin was the only normal-acting person. But to Autumn, even he, too, seemed to be holding something inside.

These people must believe Guardian to be a saint, something like their tribal protector. Who, she wondered with a smile, could their spiritual mentor be?

She remembered the friar with the chain mail; or had that been the golden one, Tyrian. But, of course, she had stumbled upon The Guardian and his men the night Barry had chased her into their campfire's embrace.

Where is the good friar? Autumn wondered with a sharp-witted sense of perception.

It seemed the mystery of this Greenwood was only thickening.

What was the secret they were all keeping? She had a good idea it had to do with Raine, or The Guardian, and all his many names. How many more did he go by? How many sneaky disguises did he don?

Aha, she thought. She would have to get a closer look at Barry. The puzzle was beginning to fall into place. At least in part.

"She has already discovered clues," Raine was telling his cousin and friend, Russell Courtenay.

"Why do you wear your hair so simple? It's most unattractive." No answer came. "So, tell me." Russell asked, pointing at Raine's head. "Ah, let me answer. One of your many façades is my guess. And perhaps you are trying to hide your identity from the lass?"

"Your guess is correct. The less she knows the safer she will be. Tell me, Russ, why do you don such tattered and stained armor? Don't you even have a suit that's black armor? Are you one of Henry's knights, or not?" Raine jested.

"You know as well as I about the black armor, Raine." Russell could see the woodsmen's distant campfire through the trees. "With your hair horribly plastered down like that, you almost look as bad as *your* Barry."

"Uhmm." Raine said nothing more.

"So, why don't you drop the name Barry, and what

do you need it for anyway? Why are you hiding or *what*—from the little red-haired lass?"

"My, so many questions. You remind me of a woman chattering all the time, wanting to know everything."

"Answer me, friend. You are hiding something from us all. What's the secret?" Russell glanced over the log, then back to the small fire they had made to warm their fronts and backsides. They were very careful about keeping from starting a damaging fire in the forest.

"I wish I knew the secret myself," Raine said truthfully, hiding part of what Russell was trying to get out of him.

"Come on," Russell begged in a sarcastic tone.

"Ha. Jewels. Many jewels, Russ. One in particular needs to be kept secret. I can't be telling everyone in the forest."

"You can trust me, Raine."

"Ha again! I can trust you about as far as I can toss you."

"You've done that. We have thrown each other across the room. Remember the time we got drunk together and ended up at Rowena's London manor?"

"Never mind." Raine groaned. "My head remembers the musty scent of stone."

"When you grimace like that you make me think of Barry Jeraux." Russell moved his thick eyebrows together, making himself look very fierce. "My God. What a smell of mud and sweat. Where did you dream that one up? And where have you been for the past four months?"

"There you go again, Russ. I'm helping the lass try to find one of her sisters. If you want to talk about

114

secrets, that one's got them up each sleeve—even her legs if she wore pants!"

Russell chuckled. "Besides herbs and seeds and all odds and ends? The women and the Thatchers are thinking the lass might be a witch."

"Not a witch, not Autumn Meaux. I've been traveling with her for these past weeks and before that I knew her a little at Sutherland. By the way, where is your friar's robe?"

"I have it still."

"And Tyrian?"

"Him, too."

Raine smirked. "Nice disguise. Only you should not allow your chain mail to show like that in front. I believe Autumn Meaux was wondering about that."

"How did you ever get her to come to us that night?" Russell asked, more than a little interested in the red-haired vixen.

"Barry got a little obnoxious." Raine sighed. "He almost did not quit once he got a taste of being so close to her on the ground."

"That nice, hmm?"

"Never mind," Raine snapped, remembering the feel of Autumn, not liking the fact that he had made her fear Barry.

"Can I get in on this discussion?" Tyrian asked as he walked into the forest glade where Russell and Raine were sitting companionably upon a log. "Sounds interesting, as much as I heard while sneaking up. I could have slit both your throats, for all the notice you gave my presence," he added with an aristocratic sneer.

"You are very stealthful, Ty," said Raine.

"Sit down and shut up, Tyrian," Russell said. "I

knew all the time you were creeping up on us. We three should combine our stealth and might and go after our manors and castles."

"Don't think I haven't tried," Raine said with a snort. "Drogo's men are too many, as we well know."

"And now Duc Stephan has joined him again. Say," Tyrian said brightly, "why don't we all don disguises, like Raine here—you know—we could glean something from him, and go after the nasty bastards. We could enlist the help of the Thatchers and perhaps even let our little lady Autumn speak to Sutherland about giving us a hand—like a few hundred knights say?"

Raine looked disgusted. He should have never mentioned Sutherland.

"Why so dark and glum, friend?" Tyrian asked Raine.

"My fight with them goes deeper than you both will ever know," Raine said. "And you seem to think it's a game we would play."

"With *who?*" Russell wondered.

"Drogo and his, er, relatives."

"Ah," Tyrian said jestingly, "we two know who that other relative might be." He nudged Russell. "The duchess, Russ's bitch cousin."

Raine warned, "Don't say her name. She's our cousin, too, you know."

Tyrian said, "Please, never remind me again. I hate that witch."

"Has she still got her claws in you so deep?" Russell asked Raine, a lock of red hair falling across his brow. She had taken Raine and already had him in her talon grip when he was a much younger man. "She's toyed with you. She's getting on in her years by now, though, isn't she?"

Now Raine looked angry enough to strike someone. "You would know that better than I, Russ. You go to her often these days, I hear. Are you—"

Russell hissed deeply and Raine left off teasing.

Tyrian moved close and whispered, "How many did you kill for her?"

Raine shot up off the log and ran his fingers through his long dark hair. "Damnit, don't talk about that! I almost—" he bit off.

"You almost what?" Tyrian wanted to know, getting up to walk to a tree. He was there for a moment before he returned; he had wanted to give Raine time to cool off. "Well?" he pressed now, with a finger in the waist-band of his chausses.

"I almost killed someone for her."

"For the duchess?"

"Yes," Raine hissed. The sensation in his chest was more of an agonizing pain than a mere ache. It was too physical, too strong, what he felt about the sin he had almost committed all those years ago. "I am not a murderer. A knight, yes, to fight in battle—"

"But you would have done this nasty deed for our *dear sweet duchess* if you had gotten the chance? Someone or something must have stopped you?"

"Yes!" Raine cried with gnarled lip. "I almost did it." His voice was low, agonized.

"So, you have gotten to know some *one* and now regret what you had almost accomplished. Could I ask: Is it a he? Or a she?" Tyrian wondered though he thought he knew very well who.

"Get him off me, Russell. Tell Tyrian I wish to forget."

Russell turned stiffly to Tyrian. "Raine wishes to forget all about it, Ty. You would do well to drop the issue. Already I believe Raine thinks he's said too much."

Tyrian snorted. "I'd never kill such a beauty."

"Aha," said Raine, whirling on Tyrian. "You are jealous. That is it. You like her. I can see it in your face. That's why you press me."

"I am jealous and I like *who?*" asked Tyrian, sparring with Raine.

"She has the name of that glorious season that falls before winter," Russell said playfully, bending over, whittling on a stick.

"She is very nice," said Tyrian. "If only she had yellow hair, then she would truly be beautiful. Does she have a sister? Ah, you said as much. Is she fair of skin and hair?"

"We are speaking of the one with fire in her hair," Raine said, then stopped himself, looking at both his friends. "I—I've sworn to protect her."

"What?" both Russell and Tyrian asked.

"Yes. Now. I've said too much."

"You see. He does have secrets." Tyrian wouldn't leave it be. "You've sworn to protect the one who you almost—"

"No more," Raine cut in quietly.

"My God." Russell looked uneasy. "You don't *kill* lovely young women. Do you, Raine? I would have never—"

"Enough I say."

"Where are these jewels you speak of?" Russell asked.

"What jewels? Did I miss something?" Tyrian's eyes lit up to a brighter golden hue, if possible. "Now there are jewels? Crown jewels, I hope. They are always more valuable. Then you both can get your lands back. Me, I really don't care and rather like it here in the forest."

"I have to get the ruby back for King Henry."

"Ah." Tyrian stroked his chin. "That jewel. The one that goes back to the time of the Black Prince. Costly gem, that. How would you ever manage to—"

"I'm afraid I'm going to have to use Autumn Meaux. The only problem is, I fear I'm falling for the girl." Raine sighed.

"Jaysus," Russell exclaimed, flipping the olive-drab cowl over his head as if to hide himself.

"Mother of God," Tyrian exclaimed more softly. "Knights don't fall in love. They fight and fornicate—"

"I am not a knight anymore, Ty. Duc Stephan has Henry believing I am disloyal." Again Raine sighed.

"Knights are not to be disloyal," Tyrian said, then looked down at the chain mail vest he wore. "At least we did not use to be." He looked very serious. "The duc and Drogo hate us because we tried to uncover their evil deeds. How is it that they remain in power?"

"Yes," Russell said. "Why does evil always get the upper hand."

"*Seems* to get it—for a time," Raine said, his jaw hard. "I have to think of Autumn, too. She has only to prove her rich and royal heritage. She must first discover the whereabouts of her family heirloom—the mauve-white Star of Africa."

No one saw Russell flinch in the shadowed side of his face as if he'd been struck.

Tyrian gave a deep gulp. "The . . . *What?*"

"That whoremonger Drogo would like to get his hands on our little huntress."

"What is she hunting?" Russell asked, trying to avoid appearing as restless as he felt.

"Her sister. Winter."

"Is she blond?" Tyrian blurted the question, looking sly.

"As I was saying," Raine went on as if Tyrian hadn't made a near-fool of himself. "Drogo would like to wed the redhead and take her jewel and her ancestral holdings."

Not if the duchess gets to her first, Russell kept to himself.

The golden knight stood up to speak as he paced like a caged lion. He halted in front of Raine suddenly.

"Oh, I see. He can't have her and the castle without the jewel?" Tyrian said. "How is he to get the king's ear, too?"

Again, Raine went on as if he'd not heard. "She has to find her sister Winter. I believe she has other sisters. I tried to get the maids at Sutherland to let me in on Autumn's secrets, but they were too loyal to the redhead."

"How nice," Russell said. "So, where is *the* jewel?" He licked his lips. "Or should I say—*jewels?*"

Raine's eyebrows were like dark brown slashes across his forehead.

"I've yet to find them all and return them to their rightful owners," he said.

Then Raine walked away, leaving the mellow circle of light; he was shaking his head and chuckling softly.

Tyrian nudged Russell, saying, "I believe I have figured some of it out. Raine wants to wed the girl and get his hands on the ancestral holdings." He shrugged. "It's obvious; and perhaps he's already got the one jewel in his possession. It will only get Raine closer to his enemies, not farther away as he should be—if he does have it." Tyrian now frowned. "The only thing I haven't yet ciphered is: Why does he have to keep up the charade and help Autumn find her sister? Of what good can the blond sister possibly be?"

Russell wiggled his auburn eyebrows at that last question.

Tyrian frowned. "Forget it. I asked about Winter first."

Nine

A mist lay upon the marl and wove itself in cobwebby tendrils among the dark green of trees. The dawn had kissed the mist with pink, and now, the encroaching sun touched it with ancient gold.

Barry was on one knee in the black loam, planting the seedlings and herbs as sunlight began to streak downward and butter his dirty face. He was working beside the plants of broom and alehoof, the alexanders and salsify, Autumn had gathered from forest and roadside.

The garden was set a small distance from the woodsmen's camp. Autumn stood by, smiling, watching him help take over the remainder of the planting task. She rested for a moment and the angle of mellow sun colored her more with a reddish glow where she paused on the other side of the huge garden plot.

Autumn looked at the trees in the outer circles, scanning the Greenwood for signs of any of the Snots and Nots who had been helping with the planting of the garden. Tiercel and the older girls had awoken while it was still dark to walk with Autumn to the freshly turned

122

earth while moonlight splashed through the trees making pale puddles for their passage. Barry had come along a bit later as the sky above the forest cathedral had begun to lighten with twilight; standing there he had yawned and scratched his belly and smacked his lips loudly.

A bit overdone, Autumn had thought to herself.

She stopped looking into the trees now for the men and women who decorated themselves with leaves and branches, even mud—this must be where Barry got the idea—and saw that they must have returned to the camp where the stewpot would be gurgling in readiness for the afternoon meal.

Sometimes the smell wafted the way of the garden. Venison stew. At times with wild vegetables, others not. She had given the cook a pocket of herbs for the stew. She could smell them now. Rosemary and thyme.

She looked over at Barry again. They were alone.

Wiping her hands on her already soiled tunic, Autumn walked over to Barry. Her bare feet sank deliciously in the forest loam and she felt the wonderful caress of the earth warming her soul.

She felt at one with the day and God.

"Do not be stepping on plants now," Barry grumbled, brushing against the skin of her ankle.

She laughed down at him. "Listen to you. Just yesterday I was telling you the same. You have become quite the gardener now."

"Thanks to you, Mistress. This is really enjoyable."

"When are we going to the nunnery, Barry?" She patted down loose dirt around a wild angelica herb she had transplanted. "I am eager to leave as soon as the planting is done. The Snots, the Nots, and the Thatchers will have their bounty of foods and medicines in a few months. Some of the herb seeds and plants will take longer."

"This is a swell idea you had to plant here, Mistress. The forest folk are beholden to you."

"Fine way they show it." She sniffed, tamping the angelica in a partially shady, damp spot. The plants would grow taller, with beautiful green-divided leaves. Flowers would be white and tiny, in a large composite head on very long stems. "I hardly ever get a smile. If not for the children, you'd think I was invisible."

"I smile at you." His eyes looked big and dark, matching the deepest green of the surrounding forest.

"You grin." She laughed down at him.

"Raine Guardian smiles at you real big."

With her lashes slanted downward, shielding her eyes, Autumn glanced away as Barry looked up at her. "Yes," she agreed. "He does."

Now she looked down into his dirty face. He was still staring up at her, but he showed no emotion whatsoever. Her mouth curled in satisfaction as he looked back down to the thyme seeds he was poking into the tiny holes she had made in the rich dark earth. He was quite good at not showing his inner emotions and now he was being very careful not to stare at her for too long.

"What did you say the thyme is good for?" he asked over his shoulder.

"This is *thymus vulgaris*. It strengthens the lungs, cures gout and hangovers, and some consider thyme a symbol of strength and courage. Tea made of thyme is drunk to cure shyness." She sighed and brushed her hands against her skirts. "Before we set off again, you will have to find one of the women to take care of the plants; it needs a little wood ashes from time to time, and a light covering of compost in the late fall. The flowers of this herb have flavor and fragrance that are useful in cooking, so the herb should be harvested during the flowering period. After cutting the stems you tie them in small bunches to dry in a warm place in the hut."

Instantaneously, Autumn stepped on a sticker and as she was preoccupied with hopping about, Barry's moss-colored eyes sought the low square neck of her bodice where a fine sheen of sweat glistened like dew above it. His line of vision took in the full curve of her breasts as she twisted about to have a look.

"Ouch! Another sticker!" she yelped. "I hate stickers. Come, quit gawking and pull this out for me, Barry. They get stuck on my fingertips."

He walked the few steps to her and lifted her ankle, looking at the nasty stickers. "These fellows seem to be giving you a hard time today, Mistress."

"Yes, yes. I know. This is a big one, though." She shifted to keep her balance and came in closer contact with his ropy arms and thigh tendons. She laughed lightly, nervously. "What happened to all your padding or swaddling?"

"My limbs feel better lately," he said. "Haven't wrapped my legs in weeks."

"We have been here too long." She braced her shoulder against his strong upper arm as he bent to the foot with the mean sticker. He dropped more of his sorry disguise as the days passed. She was beginning to suspect who was behind all the magnificent muscle, like the beautiful biceps, stony thighs, ropy calves; she could go on and on. "We all have secrets, don't we?" She looked into his dark moss eyes as she spoke the words.

Swiftly, he looked back to his work, this one had gone deep, and many sharp needles had stuck into her tender flesh. "I'm getting it out, little by little."

She gazed at the deep tan of his neck, and his hair, which was dark brown with a hint of red, so dark the strands were almost magenta. He wore his chausses, leather boots, and a linen shirt. At the moment, the boots were at the end of the garden. She'd noticed that his bare feet were also muscled and nicely shaped.

"How does it feel?"

She shook her head. "It does not hurt a bit." Not when this preoccupied, it didn't.

"You lie. I hear your breath pull in each time I pull one out."

"Mostly I am holding my breath," she said, laughing, her eyes on his manly profile, her emotions and responses held under rigid control, "and not letting it go."

It took a moment for her to swallow and bring her eyes to his face as he looked up at her.

Her muscles were becoming strained by holding this position and her hand now braced on his shoulder was feeling much warmer than the sunlight on their heads. Or was it something more than warmth she felt? Something more, yes. Warmth and . . . Her leg was bent across her front, the sole of her foot up in the air and across his bent knee, his other leg firmly planted on the ground.

He tugged her leg higher and she winced.

"Here, you are uncomfortable," he said. "Sit on my

leg and I'll work on your foot to pluck these last few thornies out."

Shifting her weight and coming around his knee, hopping a bit, Autumn braced herself until she was gingerly seated upon his bent leg. He grimaced at some exquisite hurt, but she didn't see the look of painful ecstasy on his face.

"Cock your leg up again and I'll have a last look," he said, his breath warm and spicy on her cheek.

"You smell of cider," she told him.

He laughed.

Now they were closer, even more so, mouth close to mouth. Breaths intermingling. She could feel the hardness of his large-muscled thigh pressing up into her privates and as her arm slipped lower on his back, she also felt the hard stretch of muscle and tendon there.

His dirty face was so near her own.

"Ah, that's it, I think." He brushed his fingers over her sole to see if any prickles remained.

"Ouch. I think I feel one more. It is very small."

Looking into her eyes, he said, "I'll suck it out."

She blinked. *What?*

"Never mind." He lifted his head and brushed her foot one last time. "There. That's it, maiden."

As he began to rise, Autumn let go but lost her balance. Tumbling backward onto the soft earth, she inadvertently brought him down with her. At least, this was how it seemed to happen.

Instinctively, Autumn's arms lifted as she held them out for him.

Unhesitatingly, he grabbed her with a violence that startled her.

Catching handfuls of his forearms—also well-developed—she kept him from falling all the way on top of her. Then she let them slip, inch by inch.

His eyes were intense. "What are you thinking?" he asked quietly, letting his body inch downward.

She murmured and blushed and could not meet his eyes. She let go of his arms more, feeling him slide.

He lowered a bit more onto her. "Were you trying to break my fall? Or were you perchance holding your arms out to me like a lover?"

Autumn felt him sinking into her lower half, his arms braced on either side of her face, his chest bare inches above her own.

"Kiss me," she told him.

"What?"

"I want you to kiss me."

"My face is very dirty," he complained.

"I am also dirty."

"Ah," he said. "If I kiss you, then you'll know it all. Right?"

"I only ask you to kiss me, *Barry.*"

"Very clever."

His mouth came down to meet the lips she was already offering up to him. He kissed her with sensuous violence and she shivered all the way down to her bare toes, ones that were curled deeply into the rich loam and lifting toefuls of it.

The stimulating currents of awareness that had flashed into life the instant she had first seen him became stronger as the kiss inexorably deepened.

Her hips lifted to meet harder ones that were pressing and lifting rhythmically. Heat flared in the pit of her stomach. His male outline was hard as he moved over her. His tongue went into her mouth at the same time.

"Barry!" Autumn gasped, breaking her mouth away. "You grow too bold." There was laughter and mischief in her voice.

He smiled down at her. "You asked, mistress. I am only a man."

"What a man!" she squealed, fastening her lips onto his and rolling him over in the dirt. She blew in his ear.

"Woman—*you* are the bold one!"

She crawled all over him, experiencing, laughing, feeling as if she were brand new, encountering the same exhilaration they had shared while rolling down the hill with the cart, the horse, and the mules, that glorious day after the rain had quit.

This was the same. *The very same.*

"You'll crush the wild plants," he yelped when she kept coming after him and rolling with him, her skirts tangled in his tunic.

When they came to a halt, he was on top again. He let his breath out in a hot whoosh. "Maiden. You had better cease this play. I am prepared to make love to you this very moment. You don't have to heat me up anymore."

"So, I do not. I can see that."

She stood up in a snap.

"What is wrong with you?" He looked up at her sardonically.

"You are the clever one, sir. *Think you are.* You were never good at disguising your voice, Raine Guardian. You let go of Barry more often than not."

So, he was Raine again.

Raine blinked as she picked up her gear, looked down at him and began to walk away. She swiped the rough sweetness of his kiss from her mouth and made a play of sputtering.

Falling on his back, spread-eagled in the midst of plants and herbs and tiny seed sacks, Raine chuckled and smiled a tiny secret smile of his own.

She loved it. Loved the taste and feel of my kiss as much as I did.

With his arms outflung, his smile grew until it was victorious and lusty. It was short-lived, however. When the duchess came suddenly to mind, he sat up abruptly, his look savage and dangerous.

Her taste was still on his mouth, her hunger still racing full speed in his blood.

In one fluid motion, he was on his feet, reaching for his boots and the plain, vicious-looking dagger he had left at the edge of the garden.

Ten

Autumn marched right up to Tiercel's hut. "I would like to speak with you, please."

Tiercel's sweet voice bade Autumn enter. "Sit down there on the bench," she said when Autumn stood stiffly at the entrance. "I'll bet this has to do with my big stupid brother."

There was a twinkle in Tiercel's eyes.

Autumn's brow lifted. "Which one? Barry? Raine? Or should I say *The* Guardian?"

"Really, Autumn, you should not let him get to you this way." She sat across from Autumn, choosing a stool and picking up the shirt she had been mending; her needle moved quickly as she spoke. "Raine has that effect on women. He knows when he's got you going and he will stretch his luck."

"He is out of luck." Autumn stiffened her back even more.

"He has always been that," Tiercel remarked, poking her needle into a seam.

"Which one? Barry or Raine?"

131

"Really"—Tiercel laughed—"I don't know who he's going to become next or what he will say or do."

"You are beating around the mulberry bush. Is Raine really Barry, or not?"

"Is *Barry* really *Raine?*" Tiercel countered, her voice full of laughter, her brown braid swishing across her shoulders in her animation. "You tell me, Autumn, and we shall both know."

"Please tell me," Autumn begged fiercely, "where are you and your brother from? Are you wealthy? Do you own castles, land, *what?* And what happened in your lives that you both must hide away in this forest among thieves and beggars?"

"No beggars, maiden. Thieves, outlaws perhaps, and just as our legendary Robin of Locksley, they steal from the very rich and"—she shrugged—"give to themselves, their families, hungry children. You saw them all here. If not for the Thatchers doing their work, they would all starve."

Autumn lifted a hunk of bread and Tiercel nodded that she could go ahead and eat. Taking a bite and chewing, she swallowed, then asked, "Ah, so that was all a play, when Gelflin took my purse and ran. Tyrian comes along and acts as if he's angry for the lad stealing my purse. Gelflin plays the sorry boy and even gets cuffed on the cheek."

Tiercel laughed. "Is that what happened?"

"Something like that," Autumn said, frowning at the subterfuge and illusionary mischief the folks practiced here.

Between bites of bread and sips of cider, Autumn kept up her questions. She was not going to walk out of this hut until she had some questions answered and puzzles resolved. If only Tiercel were not so very clever and quick to volley and circumvent the conversation.

"Why are you and your brother here?"

"You do not give in, do you?" Tiercel laid down her work and took a sip of the bitter cider. "I cannot speak for Raine. Nor for Barry. Whomever he might be at the moment. I will say for myself that I am here because I would rather not be mauled by lusty men or cheated out of something. There is safety here with so many surrounding me. And I like it here, as I said."

She was making no mistakes in her explanations, Autumn noticed, and went on to listen closely to see if she could detect any secret or flaw in what Tiercel was telling her.

"I love helping these people. Aye, they are bitter and angry most of the time, but there is love, too. The children need someone who is like a teacher to them. I like to believe that I am that teacher. I can give them all the knowledge I have obtained in my very short nine and ten years. It is not much and yet I believe truly that it is enough for them. That is what counts, Autumn, that and the love."

When Autumn finally walked out of the hut, she was no closer to the truth of the Barry/Raine mystery and what had happened to him and Tiercel in the past. Who was it that Tiercel did not wish to have maul her? Many men? Could the sharp and cruel talons of Drogo and his robber knights have reached them also? Who were these men she did not want to go near? Duc Stephan?

Here I am, supposed to be searching for my own sister, and now I find myself trying to solve the mysteries surrounding others. Where can all this lead me?

Why do I wish to learn all about Raine and his sister? What hold does he have on me?

Later, after she had washed herself and her clothes and found the secret beautiful waterfall Tiercel had told her about, she didn't have much to do. She had already eaten a little with Tiercel and the stew did not look very appetizing this night.

She was walking with her head down, not watching where she was going when she bumped right into the one person she would rather not see or have any conversation with at the moment.

Then again . . . he was just the man she'd *like* to talk with.

He was holding her arms. "In a daze, are you?" He looked down at her, those mysterious green lights moving in his eyes. "Should watch where you are going, you might bump into a lecherous chap out for an evening hunt."

None other than Raine.

"You'll do," Autumn said.

"That serious, hmm?" Raine folded his arms across his chest.

That wide, wonderful, fully muscled chest.

"Well?" he persisted.

"You could say that." Autumn lifted her shoulder and then let it drop as she skirted around him. "Or you could not." She could play Tiercel's game, too. "I would like to be about my mission in the morning."

"You mean you would like to be out of here?"

"Precisely."

"I will have to speak with Barry."

He made to walk around her. This time she was not to be evaded.

At that moment, Autumn reached up and brushed Raine's hair away from his face, pushing it back over his shoulders.

He caught her hands and held them high. "Just what do you think you are doing?" he asked, staring at her in the orange glow of the low, wide campfire. "What are you doing, mistress? Why are you looking at me like that?"

"I just want to see something. Hmm. Yes. You do look familiar," she said innocently.

"I should say. You have seen me often enough in the past several weeks."

Back, back in time. Scenes flashed before her eyes, in her side vision something ominous moved just barely out of reach. It flashed and was gone. One year later, the massacre of her parents. Her eyes enlarged as she looked up at Raine and somewhere in the recesses of her mind she was seeing, feeling, experiencing the same emotion as back then.

He . . . *Raine had been there!*

"What is it?" Raine's jaw was taut and tense, a hard muscle jerking along it. "Just what do you see, Autumn?"

He was gripping her by the shoulders. Inexplicable uneasiness coursed through her as she stared up at him. "You—"

"Mistress Autumn." His eyes went dark and dangerous lights shifted in them. "What? *What?*"

"You." She backed away. He had let go and she paused on the ball of her foot. "Why have you been keeping your true features hidden from me? What is it

135

you hide? You were there. Tell me. Did you have something to do with my parents' murder?"

He looked at her with a cool gleam in his eyes. "I have no idea what you speak of."

"Yes. You do. Did someone give you the jewel when my parents were slain? Do you have our family heirloom in your possession? I have dreams; I see and know things."

Raine clutched the hilt of the sword at his hip. "God's blood, woman. Have you gone stir mad and lost your mind?"

"No." She spun away from him. "I have just recovered part of it."

God help me, Raine thought as he watched her walk to her horse. She put the reins to Ghost and headed for the tree thatch.

From behind thick trees and brush, Tyrian spied on Raine and Autumn, trying to hear what they were saying. He stepped on a fallen branch and gritted his teeth. If he wanted to hear what they were planning, he'd have to step more carefully and keep himself out of sight. He flinched every time Autumn raised her voice, trying to sound louder and mightier than Raine Guardian.

What a woman, he thought, wondering if Winter Meaux was as fiery and beautiful as her sister. Raine already had his hooks into this one. Or was it the other way around? Tyrian wondered as he began to step back.

He decided to follow them for a few days and gather some information he would need to further the plans already forming in his head.

The blackness of Tyrian's plumed cap and cloak fed

themselves into the blackness of the forest, leaving no shape for the eye to catch.

Raine caught up with Autumn on the Cart Road. She had the suspicion he would follow and when she felt him nearing, she kept Ghost's head straight before her. Raine was angling toward the side of her and she could hardly ride with her neck twisted sideways in order to ignore him. When she finally looked up and a bit over, she saw him riding toward her; he was mounted on a huge war-horse, a muscular red with a black tail and mane.

"You are traveling in the wrong direction," he told her. "You are going east; you must go west."

Autumn tossed her bright red head. "I will. When I come to the fork in the road. I can hardly go the way the crow flies."

"Why not?"

"It is too swampy that way."

"It is only moorland. Not swampy at all."

With that, she angled off the Cart Road and headed west. "Thank you," she tossed over her shoulder, watching that the jennet followed directly behind Ghost. "I do not know what I would have done without your advice," she said sarcastically and waved her hand. "You may go."

He did not go, but stayed right beside her, his huge horse clomping beside the slightly smaller Ghost. He chuckled.

"Are you dismissing me? I thought you were a maiden, not a stuck-up princess."

"I am not *stuck up*." With that, her chin rose a level higher in the air.

"It's dangerous to travel alone, you know."

"I am not a believer in the devils and demons thought to haunt the forests and moors."

"I do not speak of that," Raine said. "Likewise, devils and demons worry me not. But there are flesh-and-blood men abroad, with blades as keen as mine, highwaymen and creatures of the night who lie waiting for any chance traveler who might come riding alone. To his or her death, if they but had their will."

"Hah!" She tossed her bright head. "Yet we move upon our hidden ways, in darkness or in light, knowing each small sound for what it is. Nor had wandering in the forests of Nottingham among the Snots and Nots allowed my senses to grow dull. I am fine, Sir Guardian."

Momentarily dumbstruck by what she had said, Raine considered this for a moment, then said, "Ah, you are a wary one, maiden, and I like that in a man as much as a woman. Still, it is dangerous for an unescorted woman to travel alone."

"So tell me again."

"It is dangerous to—" He sighed and clamped his mouth tight.

"Hush; forget it." She could not and would not forgive *him* for abusing her, however, and said so now. "You abandoned me enough that I should realize that . . . *Barry*."

He spoke as if she hadn't. "Do you know, Whitby is miles out of the way?"

"Out of the way of what?"

Raine smiled tensely. "Always the clever maiden,

aren't you? You know of which I meant, Autumn. You should be traveling to the nunnery of Kirklees. This is what the road knight told you. He said he had seen her, your sister, being taken there. Or do you believe he was only trying to brush you off and be rid of you?"

"Perhaps he was humoring me." She looked the other way, her chin riding above her shoulder.

"Perhaps," he mimicked, making his voice sound like an old crone's. "What are you so persnickety about?" She gave no answer. "You are a damsel in distress and you need my help. And don't tell me you do not."

"I do not."

He sighed in exasperation.

Autumn's head swung around as she brought Ghost to a sudden halt. "Wait. How do you know I am going to Whitby? I never told you." Her eyes narrowed. "More of your tricks, m'lord Guardian? What are you, a baron or a duke?"

"That is a very odd question."

"I wish to know. Who are you? Speak up, Sir Guardian. Why are you following me? And why do you have my jewel? I saw you in my dream holding it. Why won't you give it to me? It is mine, is it not?"

"My jewel." His eyes glittered darkly, possessively. "Your beloved uncle first stole it from *our* family jewels years ago, the Guardian jewels . . . not to mention the jewel of Jeraux." So the Duchess Rowena had informed him.

"Ah. So that is how you come by the name for your village idiot. Barry Jeraux. How clever of you."

He grinned at her with beautiful white teeth. "We are both clever, are we not?"

"Not." She kept riding.

He grinned.

For a time she was silent, then she spoke again. "Now you say it is your family jewel. How can you twist—"

He ignored her and tossed out the question, "Where are you going now?"

"To the abbey in Whitby. I spoke to someone in camp, one of the Nots. He said to try the abbey there first." A corner of her mouth smirked. "Of course, you already discovered this for yourself before you ever set out to trail after me. What a sneak-thief you are. In more ways than one."

"I am protecting you." He saw her look at him quickly. "Your guardian."

"Guardian? Hah. You swipe my family jewel, say it is *your* own, that my uncle stole it from *your* family, and now *you* wish to protect *me*." Her snort was one of disgust. "I believe otherwise, more like you have it in mind to keep my jewel and ravish me, marry me, and keep me locked in a round tower the remainder of my days."

He grinned into her face. "I like that one about ravishing you."

"You may forget it, Sir Guardian."

"Sir, hmm." He rubbed his chin.

"Well," she flashed him a curious glance, "are you a knight or are you not? Did you ride with King Henry at the Battle of Agincourt? Did you fight? Are you only a carpet knight? Or are you a plain and simple coward?"

Raine let out a long howl. "You are, by far, the most quick-tempered and quarrelsome woman to come along in a century, Mistress Autumn. I will wager you could

140

have gotten into a better and bigger brawl than the one—"

This time, she would not let him finish. "—*you* started at that inn, *Barry*."

"Stop calling me that. I am Raine now, you know that. Or do you love taunting me with your knowledge of all my secrets? You have no idea the extent of them, woman."

Suddenly he was gloomy, brooding again of what he'd almost done to her. It made him ill to remind himself of that almost fateful day. For Rowena. Almost.

Her eyes snapped over to him. "What about the jewel?"

"Ever persistent. When do you think I will give it to you?" he whispered and his voice seemed to penetrate her.

She shot a glance to him, curious as to why he spoke low and with foreboding. "Something tells me that it will be soon," she said.

"Woman's intuition?" Suppressing a grin, his eyebrows rose in earnest gravity. "A man cannot argue with that."

"What about the jewel?"

"Damnit woman! I shall give it to you when I am damn good and ready."

She slashed a look to him. "Without me, what good is the jewel to you? You will seek to wed me and steal our lands."

"Our?" He blinked as she nodded firmly. "Bull. *What* lands?" He tried to lean to see her, but she flinched away. Still, he had seen her face.

Myriad emotions had played in her expressive eyes before she shuttered her look.

"Winter's and mine. I just know we have castle and lands." She was not going to tell this man that she had two other sisters besides. And who knew? She might never see the others again in this life.

Perfect scenes of untamed moorland and rolling hills dotted with grazing sheep and an occasional stone farmhouse arose throughout the moors. Raine and Autumn plodded alongside each other, too hungry and tired at times to lift their voices to argue.

"Why didn't you remember to bring along some food?" she asked him, irritated as she came down from her horse to rest her aching muscles.

Raine dismounted Vermilion and went over to plop himself against a rock. "I thought for sure you would have done that yourself. Women think of these things. Men do not always. Food is the last thing in mind."

"In *your* mind!"

"Aye."

There was a certain dark arrogance about him she was just beginning to see.

Standing with her arms cocked over her hips, Autumn stood over him. "And how do you suppose I would have managed to tuck away some of that tasty soup your sister was making? *Soup;* do they never eat nothing but *that* and dark moldy bread?"

"Meat. You could have brought along some meat. It is easy enough to wrap in a cloth and stuff into all that baggage you carry. Ah, look. There is a stream nearby. At least we can drink."

"You are the man. You go out and catch something

for us to eat." She looked at the granite determination stamped along his jaw and chin. "Go," she ordered.

"Now you give me orders again, woman?" He tossed back a small leaf he'd chewed as he jumped to his feet. "I will hunt, if you will cook the little beastie that I bring back." Over his shoulder he said, "Have a fire going in the crook of those rocks."

No answer came. When he turned to look again, to see if she was doing his bidding, he saw that she was talking to a lone traveler. Raine blinked and rolled his eyes to heaven.

The man was gesturing wildly as Raine drew near.

"In the autumn months the heather will bloom purple and reddish gray." The traveler began to walk again, looking quite weary and run down at the heels. He held up a bony finger and twirled it in the air. "If a great and sudden storm should rise out of the darkening, seek a pub's glowing light and raise a toast for me."

"Who was *that?*" Raine asked, coming to stand beside her as she watched the man in rags walk away to the fork in the road.

She shrugged, saying, "I have no idea. Did *you* know him?"

Astonishment registered in Raine's expression as he snarled, "If I did, why would I have asked you?" He bent to jerk his head in her face.

Shoving his arrogant face aside, Autumn gave herself up onto Ghost's back again. "I am going to this inn he talks about. Perhaps I can get a room for the night."

Mouth open, Raine stared after her. Again she was walking away as if she could survive any danger. This did not say much for him as an escort or knight.

Vermilion was mounted as Raine jumped on his

back. Recovering his composure, he rode beside Autumn's horse again. "I will come with you. I have a few coins."

"Wonderful," she said with a flip of red hair as she took a shortcut through the horse path to a cart road. "Why did you not say so before? I am nigh unto starvation."

"Aye, me, too." While he said this he looked at the shapely curve of her as Vermilion took up the rear on the narrower trail flanked by a verdant countryside.

They were waiting for their food. It was going to be ham in a sweet, tasty sauce, with boiled vegetables, crusty dark bread, and plum pudding.

Seated in the pub room of the inn, Autumn took up where she had left off in their conversation. "Why did you disguise yourself as Barry? And, why did you attack me in the woods when I believed you slept as I meant to go to the stream?"

She sat back, waiting.

After taking a bite of bread lavished with creamy butter, Raine sat back with a deep sigh, wiped his mouth with a cloth, and looked into her eyes as he spoke.

"The reason I disguised myself is plain enough: I did not want you to recognize me. You might have thought I was one of Drogo's men and would not have allowed me to go on your sister-hunt with you." He stared at her lips that were the color of wild spring roses. "I wanted to go with you because I was commissioned to protect you. Richard did wish the best for you and this was why he appointed me in a hurry." He did not say Elizabeth, too, asked for him to protect Autumn.

She didn't believe him.

He looked at her, pressed his lips, and went on. "He was being, or just about to be, murdered."

"And the other reasons?" She sat up straighter to look him squarely in the face and watch his eyes for signs of deceit.

"That one is a bit more difficult to explain. I attacked you, very gently I might add, to get you away from the camp. I made you flee toward 'safety in numbers,' you see, because—"

"Yes?"

"Because the villains had been snooping around our camp that night."

She blinked. *"The villains?"* The food came and she saw Raine was watching the curvaceous serving girl lay platters down. Autumn frowned. "And why were they snooping, and who might *they* be?" She took a bite of the tasty pink ham and rolled her eyes heavenward.

"Drogo and his men. I wanted you out of there. Quickly." He, too, took a bite of the ham that melted instantly in his mouth. "Very good." He took another bite. "Excellent, in fact."

Autumn stopped chewing. She was staring at Raine's muscles again. His hard, rugged contours. And the handsome, boldly masculine face. She gulped the portion she had placed into her mouth.

Raine looked up from his food. "What is wrong?" His eyes sparked ominously. "Why are you looking at me as if you—" He dropped his gaze to the arm she had been gaping at, noticing that his muscles flexed when he brought his hand to his mouth to eat. "Do you see something that you like?" Now his eyes were warmer, gentler.

"I—" She swallowed. Her eyes were very big, very round as she took in the etched lines at the corners of his fabulous eyes. His mouth was sensuous and bold.

Reaching out he picked up the flagon of wine. "What is it now?"

She licked her lips and shrugged. "I would like to see the jewel, Raine. As soon as possible."

"That, I believe I've told you, is impossible. I am not carrying it on my person." He smiled at that and a misty look entered his eyes.

Licking a string of pink ham from her mouth, she dismissed his faraway look and said, "I see. Well then, when?"

Leaving his castle in the air, he answered. "We have to find your sister first. Then I will bring you to see the jewel. You must remember, the jewel is not yours. It is mine."

"I do not believe you; we do not have to find my sister first. You have stolen the jewel. I want it back."

He grinned. "You are going to have to fight me for it."

She looked down at her cup of cider and then back up to his face, his narrowed eyes, his strong chin. She nodded.

"Then that is what I shall do."

Ragged mists hovered around the inn and tangled in the trees like unruly angel hair. Raine was taking care of some business as Autumn waited for him outside. She had walked downstairs and through the hushed tap-room, going outside into the early-morning gloom while the occupants of the inn were still asleep. Strange men lurked in shadows, she saw.

She waited for him now, mounted on Ghost, the jennet waiting behind with all her bags on his wide back. As Raine approached, she found herself studying the way he walked with his long-legged stride, the soft mist just touching his hair with a glorious morning caress. The hard muscles and tendons of his strong body got an especially thorough going over as she devoured each and every bulge and stretch with her hungry gaze.

Raine was all man and she began to wonder if any one woman would ever be enough for such a virile being.

"Raine," she said as he approached, "you say that there are men after you, wily villains to be exact. I think you had better get back into your disguise."

He looked up at her and wiggled his dark eyebrows. "You like me like that, hmm?"

"As Barry?" She shrugged, smiling a little. "I suppose you could say he is fun to be with. He is a gentle man. And I especially grew fond of his legs." A laugh spilled from her. "Do you have the wraps?"

He was already rummaging in his bags. When he turned, showing her them, she hissed. "Liar."

"What?" He blinked up at her, quirking his mouth on one side. "Liar you say?"

"Exactly: Barry's legs pain him. Barry has a twin."

"I do have a twin. Tiercel and I are twins. Couldn't you tell?"

Autumn laughed again. "Hardly. She is much lovelier than you, and she does not have all those bulging muscles."

His eyes twinkled up at her. "Like them, do you?" He flexed one now and her eyes flashed for an instant.

"Go on with you. Get your homely disguise donned and come back to me. Do not take all day. I shall be waiting."

When Raine returned from the stream out back of the inn, he was all dirty, caked with mud, his hair plastered down in the homely fashion she knew by now too well. Too, he had brought the bumpy padding along and he wore it now. His legs appeared very lumpy, more than the last time he had created bumps in those beautifully muscled legs.

He was Barry once again.

Eleven

In addition to church ruins and castles, the area surrounding Whitby took in rugged coastline, lonely moorland farms, and gray-stone villages tucked into the folds of pastoral green valleys.

On the east bank of Whitby, the granite façade of Streangeshalch Abbey rose out of a promontory overlooking the North Sea. Here also were the ancient remains of the ruined part of the abbey.

A walk of these old abbey grounds, with the wind sweeping through the ruins, stealing away the ancient remains bit by bit, conveyed a somber, elegiac beauty and spiritual otherworldliness.

The tiny woman in black who walked there had also a look of heaven about her.

Gwendolyn stood still, looking out from a high outcropping of rock. The graveyard stood on the same hilltop, full of mossy, leeward-leaning tombstones, and it spread right over the village, with a full view of the harbor and all up the bay.

She turned and walked slowly, her hands folded and tucked into the deep folds of her loose full sleeves. Her eyes were lowered as she watched where she stepped, looking out for rocks and protruding gravestones, even wild grasses that had grown at the corners in thick bunches.

Gwendolyn looked up just as the reverend abbess, Amanda Mirande, was walking toward her. The older woman's face was red and she appeared as if she had been exerting herself. It was indeed quite a walk from the still standing abbey over to the ruined one, for it required trudging up and down hills, skirting rocks and mosses.

"Here you are," Mother Amanda Mirande said, huffing and puffing, her fleshy face red. Stopping where she was, Amanda took a deep breath, swallowed hard, before she spoke another word. "Someone has come for you again, Gwendolyn. We must take you to one of the cotter's huts. You have to hide. I believe this man with the golden hair and eyes might be one of your enemies." To Gwendolyn's silence, the mother superior continued, "I say this because he would not tell me what he really wanted to see you about. He was secretive and therefore not to be trusted. We must hide you again."

The abbess's veiny hand reached to Gwendolyn's veil, which draped along the sides of her face and over her shoulders. She touched once, briefly, then dropped her hand.

Gwendolyn looked up, her blue eyes intense. She understood. Her dainty hand lifted to the white veil and tucked back inside a strand of hair that was like silver and sunlight.

"You must be more careful," the abbess warned. "Please," she said to the young novice, "do not look so sad. We must hide you. It is the only way. Otherwise they might come and take you. Worse, they might kill you. This golden man seems to be the dangerous sort. His soft-spoken kind has come before and we discovered the bad men that sent his kind hiding out in the trees. But this man has come alone, there are no others hiding in wait to join him; this does not make the golden one any less dangerous. Do you understand?" After the young woman shook her head, Amanda said, "We will go now. The sooner the better and the safer."

The novice in black nodded and followed after the abbess who moved determinedly and quickly now that she had rested. Walking downhill, it did not take long to get to the cotter's hut at the edge of the village.

Gwendolyn and the abbess stepped inside and the door quickly closed as soon as they had disappeared into the room. A short time later, the abbess in concealing white habit emerged.

She was alone.

And no one in the village or outside noticed that the older woman had shed several pounds inside her voluminous habit, nor that her face, concealed inside her wimple and veil, was many years younger.

No one noticed excepting the golden eyes of a brown-robed friar.

She met the inconspicuous cart in the road, glanced over her shoulder, stepped up, covering a slim ankle hastily, then slipped inside and lay beneath the tarpaulin cover.

Gwendolyn was shuffled back once again, this time on her way to the nunnery of Kirklees.

She cried very softly to herself. Only tears. No sounds did she make.

Sleepily she saw a wedge of hazy sunlight pry apart the dark. It was the cart driver himself; they had stopped moving and stood still amid a green glade. After being on the road for hours, Gwen and the driver were ready to stop and eat something and walk a bit.

She stood by a river, resting when she noticed a man standing nearby. He was bent over, adjusting something shiny fastened to his ankle, and then he came alert noticing something and whirled to face her.

He made out only the white veil flying behind her.

Gwendolyn fled to the cart; the driver quickly looked around and covered her after she slipped inside. He had not seen anyone but he could tell by Gwen's actions that something had frightened her.

He trailed after them, keeping out of sight. They stopped to rest again, this time for a repast of bread, cheese, watered wine. He concealed his horse in some bushes and kept watching the nun and the huge man.

Tyrian took his own bread and cheese, and watched the little novice. Or was she a nun, he couldn't be certain, there was no telling by him if she'd taken her vows. Her wimple was like a veil of mist, draped along the side of her angelic face and over the slender shoulders. She said not a word to the cart driver, which told him she may very well have taken a vow of silence. He rubbed his chin, "Hmm. Very interesting indeed. They seem to be fleeing from someone."

Gwendolyn noticed the lone traveler. Who was he? she wondered. Her eyes went to Thorolf and she waited for the time when the cart driver himself would notice the stranger.

The brown-robed friar. How odd he seems, she thought.

Gwendolyn blinked at the tall, handsome friar as his hood came away. She scrubbed her eyes, unable to believe what she was seeing. When she was done rubbing, she looked at the tall man again. Blond wavy hair. Strong features. She thought he would look more suitable as a knight than any old friar. How could such a magnificent man become a recluse?

The man exuded danger; she could feel it coming her way. Was he after her? One of Drogo's men? Duc Stephan's?

Yes, she decided, this man was one of them. Why else would he be wearing a disguise? It had to be one; he just did not fit the appearance of an authentic, homely, recluse friar.

She tugged on the driver's arm, alerting him to the danger of the man dressed as a friar. Her eyes went to the blond man and Thorolf understood at once.

"We will have to think of something, Gwen." He knew her well by now; he had hidden her in his cart often enough and traversed the moors and woods with her to get her to the next safest abbey or sanctuary from harm.

She nodded furiously, fear shining in her eyes. At the same time her hand clutched the material of Thorolf's soiled sleeve, the blond friar started in their direction.

Her blue eyes went round and huge; she was begging Thorolf to protect her. The old man looked at her, this dainty blonde and pitied her. She knew nothing of the world; as far as he knew she was like a child still. There was no anger in her, she was only fearful, withdrawn, and reserved. She had been sheltered by the nuns and abbess for the past six or seven years, and no one could tell her age for certain. The novice had been sequestered, knowing but nuns and old folk, believing that only bad people lurked in the shadows, ready to pounce and remove her from her sanctuary.

And Gwendolyn was so weary of being set upon that she was prepared to give up and let Drogo's men capture her. For years she had hidden in the nunnery at Whitby, Kirklees, castle dungeons, and other secret places only the abbot John and abbess Amanda Mirande knew about.

Gwendolyn had lived apart from the other novices, almost a secluded life. Her days had been filled with walking through a maze of long, cool halls, columned vestibules, cloisters, and more passageways. Tall windows filtering the sun to the softest milky white. The abbey was silent as the grave. Cowled figures writing at long tables, no sounds louder than the slapping sandal, a swishing robe, quills scratching all through the night. Whispered prayers.

He was coming.

She was clutching Thorolf's arm harder now. The tall fair-haired friar stood before them, his unusual golden eyes staring down at Gwendolyn.

Her lashes lowered at once, then lifted, but not to his face; she was gazing at something off to the side. His horse. A huge black with wildly flowing mane. Strange again, she thought, that he would ride this horse, dressed as a friar. Who was he really?

"Are you in need of escort, sir?" he asked Thorolf.

"We're doing all right by ourselves, good friar." Thorolf felt Gwendolyn's fingers relaxing on his arm as the golden eyes had gone there and read her anxious mood.

"Then why, might I ask, is the little nun riding in the back of the cart as if being concealed?" He looked into the gorgeous round eyes that lifted; he couldn't go on. He felt swallowed up by the blue that was as clear and limpid as a summer sky.

Thorolf put his hand over Gwendolyn's, squeezed, and dropped her hand accidentally onto the friar's sleeve. She jumped back as if she'd been bitten by a mad dog.

Tyrian blinked as he heard her squeak like a kitten.

Frowning, Tyrian took the driver aside, walking over to a stream. Thorolf kept a keen eye trained on the white-robed female.

"I know you," said Tyrian.

"You do?" Thorolf looked worried.

Every man has a secret, Tyrian was thinking.

"You would not be the man who"—Tyrian glanced at the two horses pulling the big cart—"went to London recently?"

Quirking his mouth, Thorolf looked over at his strong cart horses. How did this man, this friar, know how he had come to own his most recent horse?

Thorolf growled, "What are you trying to pull, good friar? You know about my horses; rather, my horse. How?"

"Well, my friend, the harness is new, purchased from London lately, and so, I determined that the horse must be a recent purchase also?" He stared into the man's bloodshot eyes. "No? The horse was not a legitimate purchase? Tsk, tsk."

Tyrian rubbed his chin as he mulled this matter over. "What is the trouble with the little nun?" he asked suddenly.

"Trouble?" Thorolf grunted. "Who mentioned trouble, good friar?"

"Why both of you did. It is written all over your face and the lovely nun's."

"She's not a nun. Gwendolyn has not taken her final vows. She's a novice."

"Gwendolyn, hmm?"

"What's your game, friar?" Thorolf growled, wanting only to protect Gwendolyn, with his life if need be.

"Why does she not speak?"

"She has no voice."

Tyrian's head jerked in the direction of the novice, she who looked about as frightened as a little mouse. She made him think of a mournful, melancholy, or plaintive poem; but not an elegy, no, never a lament for the dead. He knew she was not that timid nor dead, however, for he had seen the hidden fire within those eyes of summer blue. She was very much alive, though she was not yet aware of it.

"Who might you be?" Thorolf asked. "You look like no friar I've ever seen. Are you . . . mayhaps working for *someone?*" A bushy eyebrow rose into the wrinkled forehead.

"I?" Tyrian said, lifting his chest. "I work for no one, er, but God, of course."

"Of course," said Thorolf. "I can't understand why. But I find myself liking and trusting you, good friar. Travel with us?"

"As escort?" Tyrian said with a wink.

"Why not?"

Safely tucked in a belt beneath his tunic, Thorolf carried a long, nasty blade. He knew how to use it, too.

There was a hunter's moon that night. Beneath her blankets and straw, Gwendolyn shivered and shifted in the cart. It was not all that uncomfortable; she was used to a hard bed by now. It was the night chill she would never get used to and often she wondered if her body would ever warm up in her lifetime. If this had something to do with her past, she would never know. In her mind her past was dimly lit by shrouded candles. It seemed unlikely she'd been born as a babe, since she often felt her life began when she was in her teens.

Mother Amanda told her she had shut the door to the past. Maybe she'd never know if she had parents, a sister, a brother, uncles, aunts.

And then there were the nightmares.

Earlier she had heard Thorolf and the odd friar talking around the campfire. More like whispers in the night. She thought they had been discussing her, and she worried about the reason why. Who was this man? What did he want? Why was he traveling with them? She could not put these questions to words. She could print some letters and make some sentences, thanks to Mother Amanda's tutoring, but Thorolf could not read.

Thorolf had not explained the reason for the man's presence in their camp. He had only patted her shoulder and nodded vigorously. What? In reassurance? She could not know. Only the abbess understood her written notes and sign language.

Tyrian could not sleep. Each time he closed his eyes, he saw crystal blue ones swimming with unshed tears and loveliness in the extreme. His heart was twisting in anguish as never before. What was wrong with him? Was he coming down with an ailment? Ho, that was a laugh; he was never sick.

Some things puzzled and intrigued him. Like why Thorolf was taking the little novice to the nunnery in Kirklees; that was quite a distance to travel. The cart driver would offer no explanation. Only that he must take Gwendolyn there, for the abbess at Whitby had ordered him to do it.

Someone had inquired after the little novice.

"Why do you have to?" Tyrian had asked Thorolf. "The abbess must have a reason for having you cart her there."

"I have brought Gwendolyn to Kirklees before. We have gone back and forth, me and Gwendolyn, many times in the past several years. We get along good. She never gives me trouble like other women do. Do you understand?"

"That's easy." Tyrian shrugged. "She cannot speak."

Thorolf chuckled. Then he turned serious. "I guard this little one with my life." His bloodshot eyes narrowed in a dangerous warning. "I sleep with one eye open and a hand on my weapon."

"I would guard her myself," Tyrian said. "She is tiny, helpless, and precious as a small glass doll I saw, er, once before."

"Where do you come from, friar?"

"Curious?" Tyrian watched the man nod. "The woods."

"Nottingham?"

"Aye."

Right then Thorolf fell silent. As he came to stand, a look of understanding passed between himself and the other big, but slimmer, and much younger man.

All day long the cart bumped along. During the day, it was warmer, and the clear sky and good weather brought out many to travel the rutted roads. The roads carried an endless flow of pilgrims and peddlers, bishops making visitations, merchants with their pack trains, royal officials and tax collectors, friars and pardoners, jongleurs and preachers, wandering scholars, messengers and couriers who wove the network of communication from village to village. Especially to the larger cities did they travel.

Travelers stopped before nightfall, those of the nobility taking shelter in some nearby castle or monastery where they would be admitted indoors, while the mass of ordinary travelers on foot, including pilgrims or folks of the holy order, were housed and fed in a guest house outside the gate. They were entitled to one night's lodging at any monastery and could not be turned away unless they asked for a second or third night. Inns were available to merchants and others, though they were likely to be crowded, squalid, and flea-ridden, with several beds to a room and two travelers to a bed.

The party of three stopped at rivers and streams to fish and Gwendolyn would quietly sit upon a rock or stare with a melancholy gaze off into the distance. She had the Books of Hours in her lap. The "Books" was made to order with personal prayers inserted among the day's devotions and penitential psalms; the books were richly illustrated, and not only with Bible stories and saints' lives. In the margins Gwendolyn had drawn flowers, birds, castles, and a knight climbing a tower to kiss and capture an apple-cheeked damsel in distress. She had even drawn a handsome noble climbing a tree to a beautiful woman with long, flowing, wavy hair. This other maiden in the forest-drawing had made Gwendolyn smile and stare at her own art curiously.

"What is she seeing?" Tyrian asked as Thorolf speared a big, fat fish to break the fast; perhaps more than one fish. "She stares like that for hours sometimes."

"Ah. You are keeping your eyes on our precious Gwendolyn, are you?" Thorolf's jaw hardened as his mouth moved. "You wouldn't be getting ideas about what's beneath that holy habit?"

Tyrian saw the man's look and grimaced. He sighed deeply. "No. I have none such ideas. She touches my heart as no other maiden or gorgeous bit of artwork has done before. I lust for no woman. Truth be, I've had my fill of them."

"Hmm." The big man's bushy brows went up. "Had your fill, have you?" Then why was he still gaping at his sweet little Gwendolyn! "Well, what say you?"

"Oh, aye. That I have. I'm no saint and pretend not to be one." Grabbing the second fish for the man, he slapped it onto the riverbank, slicing it open with a swiftness and deftness that made Thorolf blink. "Suddenly my mission is to aid my friends in seeking out a lost young woman who disappeared six years ago from Herstmonceaux village. In fact, Autumn Meaux says her sister is fair of locks and quite beautiful."

"Gwendolyn is blond."

Tyrian halted in gutting the fish. He looked up at Thorolf and then over at the woodenlike novice seated upon a rock staring out across the water. Time was insignificant to her, it seemed. She was a picture of enchantment, sweetness, purity. She made him believe in *forever*.

"Does she have a last name?" Tyrian asked, finishing his task of cleaning and gutting the fishes.

"Nay. No one knows if she does have one."

"That is enough," Tyrian shouted as another wriggling fish slapped him in the chest. "They will go to rot if you catch any more."

"I salt 'em," Thorolf said with a huge grin.

Tyrian caught the movement of white at an angle from where they'd been busy catching food. "Where is she going?" he asked, feeling alerted at her sudden motion.

"Into the bushes. She won't be long. Gwendolyn is cautious, alert, and watchful. She does have some simple thoughts, you know."

Tyrian thought: Possibly more complicated and intriguing than you will ever know, big man.

Gwendolyn had been staring across the water when a movement from the good friar made her look that way. She watched the play of muscles in his shoulders and arms. He is a very big man, she was thinking. Mischief entered her blue eyes. He is much like a knight. The sun dropped lower and played on his golden hair. She had seen his eyes. They, too, had a golden cast. She had not stared when he had stood close. She

161

had felt like doing so, but it was just not something a novice would do. She did not feel like a woman of the holy order. What she really wanted out of life was to discover her past, perhaps recover some of that life she had lost. She wished to know where she was from, what her people, her family, were like. Where did they live? Were they still living? How many sisters? Any brothers? Questions like these plagued her and worried her day in and day out.

Now this man had come along. He with the golden hair and eyes. What did he want? Did he pose a threat to her? Was he one of Drogo's men?

Gwendolyn had asked the abbess who Drogo was, and the abbess had told her the man was a robber baron. Why did that villain's name stick in her mind like a repeating nightmare? What did he, this Drogo, want from her? Why was he trying to get to her and take her away? Was he involved with the reason why she could not remember? Mother Amanda believed this was so, that Drogo had done away with some of her family and the scene had been so shocking that she had lost her voice, her identity, and her spirit.

No, Gwendolyn told herself. I have not lost my spirit. I must not think that way. And she should not have listened to Sister Fiametta either. The sister told her that "Woman" was, or could be *if not careful of one's natural narcissism,* a distraction, an obstacle to holiness, a temptress. In the *Speculum* of Vincent de Beauvais, a great encyclopedist, woman was supposed to be the "confusion of man", a continuous anxiety, a daily ruin, a house of tempest, an insatiable beast, and, of course said Sister Fiametta—a hindrance to devotion are some women.

The Church denounced women on the one hand for being the slaves of vanity and fashion, for the lascivious wearing of their garments, then on the other hand for being too busy with children and housework, too earth-bound to give due thought to sacred things.

Gwendolyn thought, What would it be like to wear beautiful clothes? She had seen some of the visiting clergy gorgeously clad. Like linings of fur or silk; jeweled girdles hung with gilt purses; large hoods and long tippets. In some monastic orders the monks had themselves pocket money, a gallon of ale a day, wore jewels and fur-trimmed gowns, ate meat, and employed servants who in wealthy convents at times outnumbered the members.

A deep sigh slipped from Gwendolyn's lips. Sister Fiametta spoke of nobles of multiple fiefs and castles, who wore tunics embroidered with their family crest, their hanging sleeves scalloped and with colorful linings. Breathlessly Gwendolyn had asked what the women wore. Sister Fiametta had answered that it was too sinful to tell about.

Gwendolyn's blood turned to glowing warmth as she watched the friar stand with the catch of fish. For a moment his eyes met hers. Gwendolyn saw his image change. He was garbed in colorful, resplendent clothing from head to foot. Now he was a knight in shining armor. Next he was entirely . . . She blushed terribly. She blinked again and shook the image from her brain. He was once again the brown-robed friar . . . yet she could have sworn he, too, was looking at her as if she were a princess or something equally wonderful.

Later, finishing up a supper of fried fish, watered

verjuice, *rissoles,* and dried oat cakes, Thorolf looked over at Tyrian. "What is your other mission, friar?"

They both looked at each other and then turned away, back to their food.

Thorolf waited.

Tyrian bit into the rye pastry and glanced over at the sleeping novice. Though she functioned like a melancholy child, she had filled his day with brilliant, lovely, fluttering flame. As he stared, he felt a little thrill pass across his chest.

Tyrian said, "That is *my* secret, old man."

Twelve

"How interesting; how quaint," Autumn said as she stared at the old town clustered on the slopes of East Cliff. Below, fragile houses and shops of every imaginable kind were wrapped in mazes of hedge, not yet stirring to the day. All curves and gentle slopes were covered with vines, imitating the verdant land itself.

Raine said, "Streangeshalch."

"What?"

"The Saxon name for Whitby."

The tangy atmosphere retained an unpretentious appeal, with fishing cobbles bobbing at their moorings, gulls circling above thatch-roofed harbor homes.

Autumn glanced back the way they had come, at the greens and dusky reds of the rolling forest land. She stared ahead once again. Immense knobs of gray rock pushed up through the trees like thick, stubby fingers. Houses clung precariously to the brooding gray and lovely green moss.

"It's beautiful here," said Autumn, as she held Ghost beneath the huge white face. The horse nuzzled her back lovingly and Autumn smiled at Ghost's affection. "What else do you know, Sir Guardian?"

"It is the seat of a religious house founded on the site of the abbey in 656. Caedmon, the cowherd who became a lay brother and the father of English sacred song, died here in 680, the same year as Saint Hilda." Raine looked down at her from his high red horse.

"Saint *Who?*"

"Nuns of the Benedictine order. Its abbess Hilda, opposed the claims of Rome at the synod in 664. Whitby owes its name to the Danes, who sacked the town in the ninth century. It was refounded as a Danish colony. After it had become the most prosperous town in the district, William the Conqueror destroyed it again. Thereafter came many grants, bribes, and the struggle continued until the beginning of the last century."

She remounted Ghost now. "Did it not have something to do with tolls?"

Raine's eyebrow rose at her question as her face came up to meet his. "Aye. Sir Alexander Percy claimed the hereditary right of buying and selling in Whitby without payment of toll." He was about to look away when some mood brought his gaze back to her face. "What is it? Have you suddenly remembered something else?"

Autumn blew out the breath she'd been holding, saying, "Yes. Winter breaks out if she eats strawberries."

"Oh? Is that all?" This did not seem significant to him.

"Come, Barry," Autumn said, looking away from his dirty face. "We must go see if my sister is here or not."

"Tell me," Raine said as he rode his magnificent red

beside her white—packed jackass trailing behind—and they rode toward the abbey, "how did you know your sister might be here and not in Kirklees?"

"I told you. The people of the forest informed me. And I had a dream. I dreamt I walked into a long, narrow room. It was very dim in there. There was this light that lifted and swirled. It looked like very fine, silver dust. I saw high-backed wooden benches . . . the place gave the impression as being cold and empty, like a graveyard. I glimpsed Winter through the gloom and silver dust, saw her make a little gesture with her hand. I stepped forward and could make out a silky gleam in that dim, smoky light. It was *her,* Winter. I tried to catch her eye, but in that shadowy room, where every beam of light seemed reflected from somewhere else, it was hard to tell.

"She came closer then, with a soft swishing of white robes. The light swirled around her like a silent whirlpool. Like a misty dawn reflected on the water, her light swirled and eddied; and then a distant smile spread over her face. She spoke, saying, 'Come to me, my sister. As you draw near, you will hear the whisper of prayers, the gentle swishing of robes, the slap of sandals; and the river as it flows into the harbor. Come where shipwrecks and drownings are commonplace just beyond the harbor's safety.' And then," Autumn finished, "like shadows folding into shadows, she was gone."

Raine cocked a mud-caked brow at her. "How did you know where this would be, this place of shipwrecks and drownings?"

She laughed at his dirty face as he sat astride his magnificent war-horse. "I told you: the Snots told me. Not the Nots," she said, giggling, "the Snots."

167

He laughed with her. "Ah, no, you said it was the Snots also who told you."

They stopped laughing suddenly. As they neared the abbey, it was like the ancient dust of tombs, settled all around them.

"Did you feel that?"

She looked up to the hilltop with the ruined abbey and the overgrown cemetery. "Aye."

They turned from that sight to stare out to the far, flat glitter of the sea. Low, knotted clouds dragged across the abbey, weeping over it like a keening widow by a grave.

Raine shivered. "Damn me, I feel as if someone just now walked over my mother's grave."

She looked at him curiously. "How about your father's grave?"

"His, too," Raine answered, absently stroking Vermilion's neck.

Silence. Autumn did not look back at him. She looked up at the sky where clouds passed like emotions across the fleeting blue. A smile touched her mouth.

She had just learned one of his secrets.

Raine's parents were dead.

Thirteen

Autumn gave in to the emotion and cried.

"Here now," Raine said, handing her a small square of cloth. "You really don't have to cry. We shall try again. Now, maiden, take the cloth."

Sniffing, Autumn took the cloth from him and dabbed at her eyes. He leaned toward her, kissed the tear-streaked corner of her mouth, leaving mud on her face, and she smiled. "Thank you, Barry."

"You really like Barry, don't you?"

"Hmm—yes." Her voice was low and melancholy.

They had walked in the puddled alleyways and crooked, cobblestone streets, looking to the east bank, where the abbey and opposite ruins faded in the day's last light. They had been turned away at the nunnery, and the abbess Amanda Mirande would not even hold audience with them. In fact, Raine had emerged to tell her this. She had been too afraid to go inside and discover that Winter had passed away, or was not there anymore.

The late afternoon fog stole in and mantled the town

in gray vapors as Raine hugged Autumn, asking, "Are you ready to go inside the inn now?"

She laughed shortly. "With you looking the way you do?"

"Why not?" He shrugged. "I did so before while in your company. Do you find Barry suddenly repulsive to be in the company of others?"

"No."

"Well then, let's go inside and get some food."

At the base of East Cliff, cottages huddled in the old village. In the Black Horse Inn, old salts told tales of a punishing life at sea, where shipwrecks and drownings were commonplace just beyond the harbor's safety.

"How interesting," Autumn said as she ate her food and looked around.

Raine chuckled. "You said that before." He only received a noncommittal shrug.

Suddenly he said, "I talked more with the abbess while you waited outside."

"You what? Why did you not tell me this before?" she snapped, drawing his eyes from his food back to her.

"I told the abbess you were Winter's sister and that your name was Autumn."

"Oh. And what did she say to that?" Autumn sipped the tangy brew, waiting.

"She actually snorted and said: 'That is a good story if I ever heard one!' "

"What happened next?"

"She walked away from me and I watched through the triangles in that black iron grillwork until she was a distant speck of black. Or white—" He shook his head. "There were black-and-white habits everywhere;

one could not tell this nun from that nun. She went the way of that long white glistening hall and disappeared into the green shrubbery of the gardens."

"Oh," Autumn said heavily, tearing her gaze away.

"Don't cry and look sad, Autumn. Please do not." He took her hand, then got to his feet suddenly. "Come, let's go for a walk. I will wash first and you rest in the room we have taken."

"Have you seen to the horses?"

"All taken care of, m'lady."

"Wait," she said just as he was about to mount the narrow stairs. "What will everyone think if you wash and I am seen in the presence of a *much* different man?"

He grinned. "They will think you a *much* sought-after woman."

"Ah Barry. You are always more fun to be with than Raine." She looked up into his grime-rimmed, moss-green eyes. "You will tell me about the jewel then?"

"Soon, Autumn. *When* I am good and ready. I will even bring you to her." He laughed nervously. "I mean—*it.*"

Following him up the stairs, Autumn reminded herself she was supposed to be vexed with Raine. How could she, when he was the sweetest, most wonderful man in the world? She meant Barry, naturally.

After Barry/Raine had washed he looked very handsome and fresh. Especially *fresh.* He couldn't seem to keep his hands from straying to her back, the small of her waist, the nape of her neck, but when he moved to

171

cup her chin Autumn read his intent and pushed him aside.

Her back was very straight as she marched away.

For several moments he stood smiling to himself, shaking his head. Wondering if he'd ever really get to know the real Autumn Meaux.

He caught up with her as she was nearing the beach. "You are going too far. What do you think you are doing?"

"Going for a walk. It's a gorgeous evening and I wish to walk," was all she'd answer.

"Haven't you walked enough?"

"This is a pleasure walk, Sir Knight."

"How do you know that I am a knight?"

She stopped to stare at him in the twilight blue. "It is written all over you. I have seen plenty of knights at Sutherland. Where are your golden spurs, Raine? Did you not say you rode with King Henry and his knights?"

Raine rubbed his chin, marveling at how she knew this. "I might have." Did he talk in his sleep?

"Might have said that or might have ridden with him? Do you own golden spurs or not?"

He shrugged languidly.

"Ever evasive." Autumn cocked her head up at him and then resumed her walk. "You may come with me or you may not," she tossed over her shoulder, flipping her red hair.

He hurried after her unusually long stride. "I'd better accompany you else you'll fall into the wrong company."

"Bad company?" Her snort was unladylike. "I shall not have to search far for that, I'm afraid."

"You search for bad company?" he said, sounding aghast. "Are you so bored then?"

Saying absolutely nothing to his terribly insincere question, she kept walking.

"Autumn." Gripping her by the shoulder, he swung her around. "You are nice to Barry and nasty to Raine." He let go and turned. "I'm going to go and get dirty again. Then you will like my company once more."

She stared at the shoulder he put to her gaze. "You are disgusting." She resumed her walk.

Coming to a nice, lonely stretch of sand and bunch grass, Autumn put her bare feet in a tidal pool as she sat on a huge, fat, gray rock. She jumped as Raine came beside her and said something in a grumpy mutter. Autumn turned suddenly.

"What?"

His face came very close and Autumn jerked again. He almost grinned. "I said—"

"Yes? What was the grumpy sound for?"

"I meant to say: You are so lovely." He gazed into her eyes. His face was mere inches away. "Would you mind if I kissed you again? I really can't resist the temptation of you. Just the look of you makes me insane with lust."

"Lust!"

"You are so very desirable, Autumn. You are like a jewel. Precious, sweet, colorful, lovely"—he smiled—"unyielding, like a rock." He grinned then.

"And desirable." She moved to the other side of the rock with a *humph!*

Now he took off his long boots and put his feet into the sand. At once his black hose became wet. She inched her way back to his side and looked out to the black, diamond-studded sea.

And sighed.

"What was that for?" he asked, lifting the sand with his toes.

"For Winter. I believe she is lost to me." She bit her lower lip; her eyes lit up and she turned with a jerk to look up at Raine. "The abbess, what did you say her name was?"

"Amanda Mirande. Why?"

"Mother Amanda—I have the idea she knows where Winter is. Only Winter does not go by that name anymore. You told the abbess that Winter's sister was searching for her. Did you not?"

"Well—yes."

"Her name, you said, is Autumn. What did she say to that?"

"I told you before but you must not have listened. Again, she said: 'That is a good story if I've ever heard one.'"

Autumn gasped. "Yes, I did recall but the words only set me to deeply thinking. *That* could mean only one thing."

"What?"

"The abbess knows where Winter is . . . because otherwise she would have looked at you as if you were crazed."

"She *did*."

Autumn's excitement waned. "Oh."

Taking her hand, Raine brought her attention around until she was staring into his face. "You might have something there, maiden." He saw her flinch but went on. "I mean it. Mother Amanda seemed to acknowledge the name of Winter—if only for a moment."

"Oh Raine." Autumn tossed her arms about his neck. "Do you really believe this is so?" She saw him nod, his nose inches from hers. "Then we should get to bed at once—"

"I am all for it." His eyes glittered with excitement.

"I meant—in order to rise early and return to the abb—"

His mouth covered hers. Autumn's eyes flew wide and then closed as his kiss went deeper. Her toes curled into the sand as she thought how beautiful this moment was. His kiss was thrilling and she felt her blood begin to heat until it was close to the boiling point. Her cheeks and ears burned. She came up on her toes to fit herself more snugly against him. She felt his male muscle and almost swooned.

As he continued to kiss her, she peeked up at the round golden moon from one eye. Then she closed her eyes and felt the thrilling kiss progress to extraordinary sensation as he explored with his tongue. Now she was yanking him closer to her body.

Raine heard drums pounding in his blood.

Autumn heard angels singing.

He ran his powerful hands across her shoulders and through her hair. With each caress, excitement grew. She stepped back. He pulled her firmly back toward him and again kissed her face and eyes, her neck, and, finally, her mouth again. She put up her arms and clasped him about the neck and opened her mouth to receive him.

Raine now pushed her up to a tumble of rocks and sparse undergrowth. She could feel every part of him, and him her. She could taste, touch, and smell him. His manly scent drove her nearly wild. She slid her hands inside his tunic. Beneath her fingertips, she felt his muscles grown taut and hard.

She raked her fingernails across his flesh, but did not hurt him.

What a perfect physique, she thought.

Raine could feel her long finely muscled legs as he brought her knees together in a clinch between his. His lusty physical urges were running rampant.

Her muscles leaped reflexively, against him; she could hear his soft laughter.

"You take my breath away," he said.

She laughed in a sweetly husky rumble. "I should say those words to you, Sir Knight."

"Say them," he growled against her throat.

"You take my breath away."

"Aye," he laughed, "the feeling is mutual."

"You already said that."

"I mean it. I have grown so hard I feel like a finger of rock."

"Understandably," she said with a feminine giggle. "We have been quite close, gotten to know each other *much* better."

"I love it when you laugh."

Her palm pressed his cheek. "You are sweet, Barry."

"Raine."

"Oh—I am sorry."

Moonlight poured around them as they stopped kissing and fondling. They were both breathless. She had felt the dagger at his waist and a sword on his hip.

"Do not be embarrassed, Autumn."

She tipped her head and smiled softly, curiously. "Why do you whisper? What is—?"

For a moment she was paralyzed, hypnotized by his stare.

"You give me courage and strength," he whispered again. He saw her delicate wonder and frowning brow. "Much more comfort and support than my mother ever did."

"I do?"

With a curious frown, Autumn looked down at her feet. Her eyes swept the surrounding area. Strange speech this, she thought to herself. What was he up to? Why did he appear to be listening, waiting, tightening with a new alertness.

"With all the weapons you wear this night, I believe, sir, you would not be in need of a woman's help to give you courage and"—she choked back a fresh spurt of laughter—"a mother's comfort?"

"Shh-hh." He snatched up her arm and squeezed. "I hear something."

"Ah," she whispered back fiercely, "I thought so."

He shook her arm. "Be still, woman!"

With her chin in the air, Autumn looked the other way, wondering what game this audacious man was playing now. They had been having a magnificently passionate time and he had brought all the kissing and caressing to a halt. She supposed this was best. They might have ended up becoming lovers. And she had no time for that. Still, it had been wonderful being close, *very* close, to this man with arousing face and form.

Raine? Handsome? When had she begun to think so? Perhaps she could even entice him to hand over her jewel.

Slowly Autumn turned to see what Raine was doing. He had moved a few feet away and now his arm shot out, holding her from stepping out from behind the huge rock. "What is it?" She tried to see but he blocked her view. "Who is it?"

He growled back to her, "How do I know? Your guess is as good as mine."

"Let me see."

He jerked, dropping her arm and reaching for his sword. "You asked for it," he told her. "Look."

She stepped out from behind the rock, her jaw dropping as she stiffened with anger. "My horse! That is my horse. Where do they think they are going with my Ghost?"

He shrugged against her chest as she stood on tiptoe to see better. "My guess is that they are stealing your . . . Ghost. Stay here. I will take care of them."

"What are you going to do? There are . . . three of them. I am going to demand that they give back my horse."

As she stepped to go around him, Raine swatted her back behind him. "Stay. Do you want to get us both killed?"

"Ohh. You are not worried about yourself. You are sweet, Raine, you worry only of my safety. And I," she shoved him back, "I am going to get my horse back!"

He slapped her back against the rock again, his chest all the way across her, his elbow up against her chin. "They have seen us! I told you to stay. I will take care of these horse thieves."

"Mummy's little boy," she taunted in a singsong voice. Her voice went hard. "Let me go, Raine. That is my horse and I mean to get him back." Her knee came up and threatened his vulnerable parts.

He caught her leg and held it like that, in the air, while he pushed toward her and gave her the most unbelievably beautiful kiss. He dropped her leg, leaving her in a daze.

Autumn had swooned up against the rock, touching her lips dreamily before she realized he had left her!

"Damn that simple wayward knight."

Looking up at the moon and waiting until it was eclipsed by a floating cloud, she then shoved away from the rock. She ran from bush to building, fled from cottage to cottage, scurried from gate to gate, always keeping to the deepest shadows. She was like a shadow herself.

She trailed the men—and Raine—to the . . . she almost hooted riotously . . . the White Horse Inn.

They were giving her money. She said, "That is not nearly enough. My mount is very special. He comes from the distant sands of Arabia."

"Your horse is a mare," one of the insolent thieves said sarcastically.

"No, he is not," she argued. Then she flippantly asked, "Have you even *bothered* to look?"

"Listen, stupid bitch." The man saw her flinch and took satisfaction in that, if nothing else. "You take what we say"—he jerked his head in the direction of the corner—"or else your gallant knight gets it in the ribs again."

She frowned until she appeared like a ferocious tigress. "You will not kick him again. He is . . . my servant. My knight, as I told you."

"He killed one of my men, *lady.*" He bowed tauntingly. "I apologize for thinking you a bitch."

"Why that's very kind of you," she said, her voice dripping with sarcasm. The frown had not left her face. "How many men do you have?" She looked around the back room of the inn. "I thought perhaps there were only four, now there are . . . seven." She gulped. "Are there any more of you thieves?"

He ignored her question. "How much do you want for the horse?"

She shook her head. "I still can't believe you ask me what I want for my horse. You are thieves and you give me money?"

"I like you," he said with a toothless grin, "even though you sounded the bitch before. You remind me of my sister, and well, I'd never cheat her. I do call her a bitch sometimes, too." He laughed to his friends. "But you are more like a princess with your long dark red hair and jeweled eyes."

"You are very strange thieves." With tongue in cheek, Autumn looked around, named her price, hearing them gasp. "That's it. Do you have the coins?"

"Aye," he growled. Pouring them into her hand, which she kept putting into her cloak and coming back with, he finally threw the sack down on the floor and said, "Keep it. The horse is worth it."

Falling greedily to the floor, Autumn spilled the coins from inside the secret lining of her cloak back into the heavy sack. The thieves looked over their shoulders, shaking their heads and giving the man in the corner a kick or two as they filed out.

As soon as she heard them ride away she forgot the coins and ran to Raine, untied him, and crooned over the bruised washboard ribs. "You saved me." She heard him groan up at her as she looked him over for other injuries. "They could have killed you. Why did you not just let them go? And why did you have to go and kill that big man?"

"He . . . was coming at me . . . with a knife even bigger than he was. Didn't you see it?"

"I don't care about that." She hovered over him. "Where else do you hurt?"

"My brain."

"What?"

"Aye. For agreeing to become your lord protector . . . and"—Raine laughed hurtingly—"practically your servant, *Princess* Autumn."

"You are the wealthy one, Sir Knight." She helped him to sit straighter against the wall. "Where is your castle located?"

"What castle?" He jerked his head aside to spit blood onto the floor. He swiped an arm across his mouth. "Damn bloke almost knocked my teeth out. Wouldn't I have been a pretty sight then?" He laughed mockingly. *"Princess."*

"Well." She stood in a huff. "I save your life and what do you do? You call me names."

He looked up at her looming over him like a Valkyrian maiden. "Names? Princess Autumn. That is most lovely, if I do say so myself." He groaned loudly and grimaced.

She dropped down beside him again. "I am sorry, Raine. You must be hurting very badly. I could not even look at times when they were beating you. One man held you and another came at you, and then another, they struck you here, there, in the stomach, with blows about the head, kicked you in the ribs . . . Oh, I am sorry. Come, let me get you up and take you back to the inn. We shall get you into bed, tend your wounds, feed you hot stew for your aches and—"

"Is this not our inn?" he asked with an aching chuckle.

"No. We are at the Black Horse Inn. This is . . . well, you'll not believe it, so I will not say."

That night, as Autumn hovered over a hurting Raine, she paced back and forth beside the bed. He caught her hand as she made the hundredth pass. "You are worried about Ghost."

"I just hope she does not kill them all."

"What?" he almost choked out. "You are worried that she will kill them? What kind of horse do you own?"

"Oh!"

"What is it?" he asked, sitting up in the badly sagging bed with a grimace as he saw her snatch up her cloak. "Where are you going? You might be in danger, Autumn."

"Not in any more than I have already been in this day," she flung over her shoulder as she raced out the door, cloak flying out behind and almost guttering the fat candle on the table.

When she returned, she sat down on the creaky bed, her shoulders slumped, her look dejected and depressed. He laid a hand on her shoulder, asking, "What is it?"

"They've taken your horse," she told Raine. "I am—"

"They . . . *What?*"

Raine shot up out of bed reaching for his clothes, and with great loud groans, he dressed as quickly as he could under his wretchedly bruised condition. He felt a hand on his shoulder and looked up as he was about to pull on his boots.

"Those thieves are long gone by now." She looked toward the window, as if gazing far away. "Vermilion and Ghost are lost to us I'm afraid."

"I loved that horse." He wrapped his arms about her waist, flicking a glance up at her, then groaning miserably into her skirts.

She stroked his dark head. "Shush. I know," she whispered. "It will be all right. We can walk."

"Walk," he croaked against her belly. "Do you know how far it is to the next nunnery?"

She grinned. "I've a pocketful of coin and we can purchase all we'll need to travel with. Now, don't be so gloomy. Let us be to bed and get on the road by early morning. Oh, I forgot, your sorely bruised state. We shall have to linger a few days, won't we?" She walked away.

Grimacing, Raine helped himself up and stripped again while she looked the other way. He was back in bed and when he looked across the room Autumn was sound asleep on a pile of old furs and pelts she had heaped onto the hard cot.

He groaned again, yanking the one threadbare blanket over him as he tried to get to sleep. This was a most difficult task when his body was both hard and sore at the same time. He suppressed a feeling of desperation, groaned and bit into his hard pillow, and squeezed his eyes closed.

Two days later they were on the cart road again. They were searching for the best purchase of horse-flesh they could find. But there did not seem to be much available in the way of good mounts or cart horses or even jennets.

Raine still ached; not as bad as the first day of his recovery, however.

They were trudging down the road, Raine pulling the jackass by hand since Dusky did not want to travel without her companions. "I shall ride," Autumn said, climbing on top of the jackass; but soon she was getting back off. " 'Tis too much of a load for Dusky. She will be tired before long and we would have to stop too often. We continue to walk then."

"He. Dusky is a he, Autumn." He grinned, shaking his head as he looked over at her walking again beside him. "Can't you tell male from female?"

Autumn looked down at Dusky and cracked out laughing, Raine joining her, and they laughed and laughed till Autumn's stomach ached and tears were flowing down her face.

Raine shook his head. "You are more entertaining than a tourney, Autumn Meaux. I use to think jousts and tilts, knocking the other knight off his horse especially was a barrel of fun. You beat any sport I've ever known and been good at, woman."

So, Autumn thought, he had been in tourneys. He was indeed a knight and he's had many forms of entertainment. His parents were deceased. He had a sister . . .

"Do you have any brothers?" she asked him suddenly, seeing that he'd gone stone-cold silent.

He was quiet for so long that she thought she had touched on a tender subject. He appeared to be on the edge of a precipice all of a sudden and she thought it better to let the possibility of any male siblings drop. She was right, for he said nothing more for a long time.

"Look!" Autumn shouted as two horses burst from the trees and thundered at an angle toward them. "It is Ghost and Vermilion! They have let them go, Raine. Look, Raine, our beautiful beasts have come back to us." She turned around and around. "Raine?"

Then she saw him, sitting on a rock at the edge of the road. He held his chin in his hands and glanced up with something approaching boredom as his horse ran up and nuzzled his shoulder.

He stood up as Autumn approached wearing a curious frown. "What is it? Why were you sitting there like that? Are you not excited that our beasts have been sent back to us?"

In a flash his hands were upon her shoulders, pulling her savagely against him for a hug. After he had hugged her, he let her go. She blinked, wondering what that was all about.

"I lied," he said, looking Vermilion over for any signs of abuse. He looked up at Autumn from the hindquarters of his horse. "He always comes back to me. It was your horse I was mainly concerned about."

"What?"

"Vermilion has been stolen before. He is a good, strong, war-horse. Many a man would love to own him." Saying this, he simply shrugged.

Autumn's eyes narrowed into slits. "You mean you let those thieves beat you up for my horse, *only* mine? You knew they'd stolen yours and . . . *of course*. Why would they just steal Ghost and not Vermilion." She pursed her lips. "Yet you knew you'd get your horse back. But what about mine? How could you have been certain they would return together?"

He dropped back down to the rock, looking up at her. "I killed a man, Autumn. I did it so the others would not ravish you."

"What?"

"Sit down. You look ready to kill someone yourself. I'll explain." He put his hand over her knee and rubbed back and forth as he spoke. "The thieves wanted one of the men taken out. I did the nasty task for them. Do you know there were fifteen men in all? No? I did not at first know this myself. They would have ripped you apart. The leaders, two of them, huge nasty fellows, wanted it to look like a real fight."

"But you said he pulled a knife on you, a great big one." She looked into his eyes, liking the feel of his huge hand rubbing on her knee.

"He did. And he made killing him easy for me. He said he wanted to . . . well, I shall not repeat what he said he was going to do to you once he had me out of the way."

She gasped. "Then you allowed those men to beat you so horribly . . . all for my sake?"

"Aye . . ."

"Oh Raine." She hugged him fiercely about the head. "You are a wonderful hero. And I *love* you!" she cried innocently.

Rising, she went over to her horse where it stood

186

nipping grass, checked to see if Ghost was all right, just as Raine had done with Vermilion. She felt a light tap on her shoulder.

When she turned around, Raine was right there.

He whispered, *"What did you say?"*

Fourteen

Autumn seemed to search for the lost words.

"I love you?" he supplied.

"Oh." She paused to look around. "Is that what I said?"

Clenching his jaw very tight, Raine turned away and tromped over to his horse. Mounting, he rode away. He never looked back.

"My Lord," said Autumn, holding Ghost beneath the long white face. "What *did I say?*"

Ghost nickered and Autumn laughed. "Maybe it was what I did not say." Then she grew quite solemn and worried, watching the back of Raine getting smaller by the second. She blinked and drew an arm across her brow. "He was perhaps serious?" she muttered to both Dusky and Ghost.

This time the jennet tended to nature's calling, nonchalantly in the middle of the cart road and Autumn jumped aside to avoid being soiled. Big men, she thought, they are supposed to be noble, well-mannered, generous, and courteous. Not unchivalrous. Perhaps he was not so noble after all. Knights did not act as he had, not the ones she had been acquainted with at Sutherland, anyway.

Autumn shook her head with the braying jackass. "You are right, Dusky. Men are never serious. And sometimes I believe they are too fierce and demanding."

But he *will* come back.

Several hours later Autumn was still traveling down the road, hoping she was going in the right direction. Then she saw a tilting wooden sign at the fork pointing the way to Kirklees, and she took a left. On and on they went along the road. Autumn was starting to get worried, wondering where Raine could be.

The air, fragrant with the scents of wild thyme and honeysuckle, caressed Autumn gently. Butterflies flitted past. Spurring Ghost to a trot, she joined the main road leading north. Dusky trotted right behind. Only a few merchants, their carts heavy with trade goods for the various villages, were moving in the same direction as Autumn. The hours passed by slowly. She stopped twice to rest and water the animals, but each time she was too anxious to pause very long.

Was he very angry with her?

He would not just go ahead and desert her, would he?

She was very much alone. As the road ahead grew empty again of merchants and travelers, a new fear joined her dread of outlaws. Without escort, she was vulnerable to robbers or even worse. Raine was right about that.

Regretfully, she wished she had stayed her hurried pace and remained within the shelter of travelers. Surrounded by other people, she would at least have some protection. Alone, when night approached, she would have none. Bravely she told herself that England's roads were safe under the king's peace.

Autumn forced herself onward. Accustomed though she was to long periods in the saddle, the tension of worry and being alone for many hours began to weary her. A copse of trees appeared around the next bend and Autumn drew rein, the jennet following right along. In the rapidly deepening afternoon, she relished the peaceful sense of solitude. Only a few birds fluttered their wings in the arching oak trees. The ground beneath her was soft and inviting.

A small spring gurgled nearby. Her horse whinnied longingly, spurring Autumn to a decision. She would halt her journey for a few hours, continuing when the moon came out and was high enough to light the road.

Leading the animals to a particularly verdant clump of grass, she lowered her own exhausted body beside the stream. Cupping cool water in her hands, Autumn drank eagerly and bathed her face. Her stomach growled hungrily. Realizing that it would be some time before she ate again, Autumn took comfort from the fact that recent rainfall had filled the many streams and rivulets.

At least she would not go thirsty.

Stretching out full length beneath one of the massive oaks, she stared up at the sky. In the sheltered glen, it was possible to forget there was anyone else in the world. The confusing sensations Raine aroused in her faded before the serenity of fragrant moss and the distant chirping of night birds.

Sighing softly, Autumn slept.

Ghost's snorting woke her. She sat up quickly, uncertain how much time had passed. A swift glance at the moon riding high above the oak branches told her she had slept much longer than intended.

Disoriented, Autumn's eyes flew wide open and her heart, which had been barely beating, began to hammer as she lifted soundlessly to her feet.

She swallowed hard. Moving among the ancient oaks she could see the shadowy silhouettes of men. Steel clanked in the still night air as the men glanced around warily, as if waiting for something to happen.

She could hear their low conversation. They were looking for her! She had made out the words: *A woman. She came this way. We will get her.*

In the bright moonlight Autumn could clearly make them out. Tattered tunics and well-cared-for weapons. Odd, she thought. Were they outlaws? Baron Drogo's men? Duc Stephan's thegns?

Praying silently that her animals would keep still, she looked around desperately for some way of escape. They were coming closer, and soon they would be upon Ghost and Dusky.

Keep still, please . . .

Out of the darkness of the oaks rode a warrior astride an immense black stallion. Across the knight's massive arms and chest, chain mail gleamed dully. Autumn had a moment to wonder at the strange twist her nightmare was taking. She was alone and unprotected.

Then all thought fled as moonlight bathed a naked shaft of steel and death galloped into full view. The men had seen her. The knight had seen her.

With her nightmare visions coming to life around her, she watched as one moment the men were standing

191

before her, ready to take her into the bushes, the next they were dead. Both heads were severed as the men continued to stand right where they'd been ready to attack her. One swipe of the warrior's sword and blood, hot and sticky, gushed forth.

Autumn felt faint as the horrible scene continued to unfold before her eyes. The remaining renegades, realizing it was hopeless to try to get to her, or to try fighting for their lives, dashed for their horses. Whirling his stallion, the warrior tracked them with dreaded skill. More of her would-be assailants fell before the others managed to mount and try to flee. Briefly the clash of steel rang out and the last of her attackers toppled lifeless from their mounts.

All of those who would have attacked her and taken her God knows where, lay unmoving on the bloody ground.

The knight whirled his black and approached her. It was impossible for her to run to a hiding place. He knew she was there. Her eyes, wide and unconsciously pleading, stared up at the black knight as he halted just inches from her.

Autumn waited to learn her fate.

The Black Knight looked down as he reined his charger in. Her red tresses cascaded over shoulders and breasts. In the moonlight, her skin glowed like alabaster. The womanly curves of her soft body were clearly outlined in the gentle wind blowing her tunic against her.

Surely, Autumn thought, I am having a nightmare. Soon she would awaken from this terrible drama. She had dreamed vividly before. But this detailed?

He was very close now. The black's lathered breathing mingled with the sound of her own erratic pulses and hard heartbeat as she waited for the death blow.

Autumn flinched as a steel-gloved hand reached down to flick away a silken strand of hair blurring the ripe curve of her breasts. A mailed finger, hard and cold as death itself, lingered against her skin.

"Beautiful," the Black Knight muttered.

Dazed, she whispered, "Who are you?"

"Beware," he said.

"But—" She gulped as he moved.

Fear stood in her eyes.

Pressing a finger to his mouth, somewhere beneath the black helmet, he shook his head. But he did not lift the visor of his helmet so she could see into his eyes.

A warning.

Turning his horse, he rode away, like a dark nightmare.

All strength went out of Autumn's legs. She sank to the ground, shaking in profound relief. He had saved her from the gang of renegades. She flinched away from the smell of blood and stood shakily to her feet.

She could have been attacked by all of them. She tried hard not to look at the surrounding carnage.

On legs that felt as though they had turned to lead, Autumn moved slowly toward her animals. She shook her head as she took hold of Ghost's face. This could not have happened, she told herself.

The knight had left her a warning. She could not speak of what had happened this night.

Beware.

* * *

193

For the remainder of the night, the hours before dawn, Autumn rode hard, too afraid and tense to find a spot and go back to sleep. She rode and rode, praying that the Black Knight was not following.

The sun came up.

Around the bend was another stand of mighty oaks. And there was Raine. The Guardian. Her Guardian. Waiting for her. As she knew he'd be, sooner or later. But why wasn't he smiling?

You'd think he would be happy to see me.

No matter; she had never felt safer or more thrilled to see a man in her life.

Gwendolyn put her hand to her face and felt how very hot it had become.

She'd been watching Tyrian, but he had no idea she'd spied on him for over a quarter of an hour now.

Now he had her worried. What sort of man carried such a wicked weapon on his person? Only a knight, as far as she knew. She would have to write a note and ask Thorolf, yet, how could she? The big man could not read one word of a brief written comment or instruction.

Besides, she had not taken quill and ink along; she could always scratch in the dirt with a stick. If Thorolf could only read. She had only those items hastily tossed into a bag by one of the nuns—no doubt Fiametta—and given to Thorolf. She sighed forlornly. If only she had learned better communication with the cart driver, like sign language, then she could be telling him the situation, all of what she'd seen.

Well, perhaps *not* all.

Gwendolyn blushed to think of it even now. She could not help keep herself from coloring with a warm flush. The friar, whom she'd heard Thorolf calling Tyrian, was probably not a friar at all but a robber knight. And why, she especially wondered, was he trailing along with them? Did he not have better things to do, like go somewhere and fight a battle or win some beautiful damsel's hand, perhaps even rescue one from distress? What was his game? Did he know her situation? Who was he? She blanched as she thought of the terrible possibility again, of Tyrian being one of Drogo's men.

Coming into the firelight, Gwendolyn rushed over to where Thorolf was skinning a rabbit. She smiled and helped him with the spit, had it ready by the time he turned to her with the skinned and dressed rabbit.

"So, little novice," he said. "You know how to do something else besides read your psalter and stare off into the distance, eh?"

She nodded vigorously. Then she showed him with lissome body movements how she'd watched him prepare a meal for them before out in the open. She pointed at his chest, grabbed his hands, and made all the motions of dressing a rabbit and building a spit over the fire.

"You surprise me, Gwendolyn." He chuckled warmly. "When did you become so talkative?"

She grinned, showing beautiful pearls of white teeth as her shoulders hunched and dropped. Now she became more serious, however, making the motions of a knight and building a great long wide sword with her fast-moving gestures.

Thorolf's eyes narrowed. "What are you trying to

show me, little lady? You look awful serious about something. Looks like a sword." He watched for more as she continued to pantomime with swift and efficient motions. "A knight? Where? Here?" His eyes squinched then flew wide. "You're pointing over your shoulder. Someone is bathing? Ah. The good friar? Oh no. You didn't watch him at the water's edge, did you?"

She nodded more vigorously than before.

The big man moved her closer to the fire as the night grew darker. "Tell me more. Something's got you excited and I know it can't be a man's body."

Her blush was covered by the ruby glow of the fire cooking their dinner. She made the motions of a man hiding something under his clothes. Then she built a sword again.

"The friar has a sword hidden under his robes?" Thorolf scratched his chin with thumb and forefinger. "Well, I don't see anything to be alarmed about with that. But I'll do some serious checking, m'lady."

Thorolf moved to walk away. She held up her hand for him to wait. She tried to show him how something would sparkle beneath the friar's robe, something with small links but she wasn't getting across to Thorolf.

Then Gwendolyn pointed at the stars and looked to be pulling them down and scattering them across her chest. But Thorolf only scratched his chin and pulled his ear some more.

"How enchanting. She speaks. However quietly."

Both Thorolf and Gwendolyn turned to see Tyrian move into the small circle of light. Gwendolyn was glad for the red glow of campfire, but still she could feel the intense heat scorching her cheeks, shoulders, neck. Even her ears burned.

She had seen this magnificent man almost nude!

Tyrian reached for Gwendolyn's hand but she snatched it away. "I do not lie. Whatever you said with sign language, it was enchanting. Something about taking the moon and stars to your breast?"

If only you knew, Gwendolyn was thinking, her red face in sharp contrast to her white wimple.

Gwendolyn nodded and moved away from the disturbing man.

"What did I do to get such a silent treatment?" Tyrian asked Thorolf.

"Gwendolyn don't like to be touched. It makes her nervous."

"I would say it makes her more than nervous. She looks downright scared." Tyrian frowned at Thorolf. "Why would she be frightened of a friar? She has been around my kind plenty enough." He shook his head, watching her as she performed some feminine chore with her hair at the other side of the fire. "Here, I have brought another rabbit." He did not hand it to Thorolf but set out to skin and dress it himself. Then he put the raw food on another spit he'd made quickly and expertly.

When the meal was cooked to juicy perfection, the three of them sat down on a log to eat; Gwendolyn was down at the end. Her end.

"What is really the matter with her?" Tyrian wanted to know. "She can't speak, so something disturbing must have happened in the past."

"A ravishing, I think."

"You believe she was ravished?" Tyrian coughed and almost choked on his bite of food. "A nun? Who would do that?"

"She wasn't a nun yet." Thorolf tossed a bone into the fire. "And she's not a nun. She's a novice."

"She hasn't taken her vows yet, the final ones. Does she want to?"

Thorolf flashed wide eyes to the friar. "Why wouldn't she? Every novice wants to become a nun eventually. At least I would think."

"Do they?" Tyrian washed his food down with some cool water; suddenly he spoke up. "I had no idea. I don't know any nuns." His eyes twinkled as he thought of the "other kind" of women he had known. But that was all in the past, a woman every night, when he'd sown his wild oats. He was twenty and nine now. But he was certainly not dead!

Thorolf had looked down at Gwendolyn and saw she had suddenly frozen in the eating of a juicy leg. She still held it aloft but lowered it slowly as she stared at the friar Tyrian. Thorolf swung around to face the friar.

"What was that last thing you said? Something about nuns, I think."

"Oh." Tyrian licked a finger clean before answering. "Nuns." He nodded, aware of Gwendolyn's waiting stare. "I've known many nuns in many different abbeys. Or nunneries, take or leave a few. All quite nice ladies, I'd say."

Gwendolyn shot up from the log and tossed a portion of uneaten rabbit down in front of the gaping men. Then she picked up her white wool skirts in hand and stomped away.

"She looks quite angry," Tyrian commented.

"She is angry. Something has made her this way. You must have said a few words she didn't like; as I said, she is made nervous easily."

Thorolf made to rise and go after her. A hand came to his arm, making him look down. "What is it?" Thorolf asked the younger man. "Shouldn't I go after her?"

"No. Let her go. It's good for her to walk. I cannot imagine life with nuns and that stern-faced abbess day in and day out," Tyrian said with a wry smile.

Thorolf had been watching Gwendolyn but now he swung about like an angry bear to face the friar. "What did you say?" He received a vacant stare. "About the stern-faced abbess? You've seen her?"

"Of course," Tyrian said smoothly. "I know of Amanda Mirande. I've never spoken to her but the nuns sure do cluck about that one."

"Nuns don't cluck, good friar." Thorolf laughed with Tyrian. "They do a lot of hushed pecking about but I've never heard them cluck." He nudged the man. "Not that I know of anyways."

On the other side of the fire Gwendolyn stood fuming, listening to the men laugh. Did Thorolf not realize that the man beside him who was supposed to be a friar was a fake? Possibly one of the men looking to take her away?

If only she could speak.

A few more hours passed and then they readied for the night's sleep.

Suddenly a commotion broke out and the area around the campfire was filled with fierce-looking visages, men who appeared to be highwaymen. One of them swung Gwendolyn into his grasp and began hauling her away. One was behind Thorolf in a flash, holding a knife to his throat. There was nothing he could do with that weapon resting on a jugular vein.

With a gasp, Gwendolyn watched as Tyrian tossed wide his robe, flung the belt to the ground and leapt onto a log. He brought up the great sword she'd seen earlier, and swung it to and fro; as its wicked light gleamed in the campfire, many fell back, not wishing to have a fight with *that*.

"Come," Tyrian beckoned, wiggling his fingertips. "You asked for some sport. So, who'll be first to taste my blade?"

Hearing a bloody gurgle behind him, a faint scream in front, Tyrian glanced down to see that one of the outlaws had slit Thorolf's throat from ear to ear, even before the big man could use the wicked blade he held in his hand. That one was picked up and added to the belt of one of the bad men.

Tyrian swung his gaze back to the silent novice, marking that the tiny explosion of sound had come from her.

These were all warriors, seasoned men, sneaking outlaws.

One leaped onto Tyrian's back, but he shook the man off as if an ant, and dispatched him with ease. The outlaw's head went rolling across the ground, severed by a single swipe of Tyrian's sword, the hair sizzling as it contacted the fire.

Gwendolyn's eyes rolled heavenward but she did not weaken and faint. The night was pierced with a blood-chilling roar. She realized it was Tyrian and quickly decided it must be a battle cry.

In no time at all, Tyrian had killed off six men and the others were fleeing the glade. There was one more—the black-haired devil who would not release Gwendolyn but tried dragging her into the dark, where a horse waited. "I'll soon spread you on the ground and get on with it," he whispered in her ear as he grinned wolfishly. "Plenty of brothels in London will pay good for you."

Gwendolyn hardly heard him. She was sinking further and further into an abyss of pure terror. Her skin was icy cold and her breath no more than shallow pants as she prayed for unconsciousness.

Tyrian could hear the dark outlaw tell Gwendolyn he'd always wanted to have himself a nun.

She squeaked like a mouse. For a moment the outlaw appeared puzzled, then kept tugging and pulling and dragging. In the next instant, Gwendolyn was abruptly thrust back to awareness.

Gwendolyn dug in her heels as the last outlaw tried to carry her away. Miraculously her veil and wimple stayed in place and with all the scuffing and kicking in the dirt, her white habit hardly got any dirt on it at all.

The outlaw smiled unpleasantly when Tyrian had his drawn sword pointing at his chest. "I got this little nun here and there's nothing you can do unless you want to see the pretty lady dead." He was still several feet from the knight with the deadly sword. "I'm taking her with me. She'll come in handy for all the things I've in mind for her."

Tension-filled seconds passed. Gwendolyn could only stare at the heavily polished glittering suit of stars Tyrian wore. Now she recognized it: chain mail. So, he *was* a knight. She had never seen a man fight quite like that. In fact, she had never witnessed a sword fight at all, and not one in which heads went rolling.

Gwendolyn felt sick and faint; she would have eaten

all her food had she known this was going to happen. Certainly, if ever she'd needed her energy reserves up, it was now. The fat-bellied man behind her must have eaten a whole hog before attacking their camp.

The dagger that the outlaw held at Gwendolyn's throat was tiny and narrow; at first Tyrian had not seen it. He stared at the gleaming blade, at the tiny flecks of blood on Gwendolyn's chin and staining her pure white wimple.

Tyrian's eyes lifted to the outlaw's face and Tyrian read greed and hunger in the man's eyes. In fact, all the deadly sins were there in his face to see: pride, covetousness, lust, anger, gluttony (evidenced by his protruding stomach), envy, and sloth. He hoped he was right, that the man was prone to indolence and would avoid too much exertion this night, all the easier and quicker to execute him and save Gwendolyn.

Gwendolyn realized she would rather go with Tyrian than this man who held her so ungodly tight she could not take in the proper breaths she needed to gain strength and daring. She glanced round the campfire. She swallowed. There was a great deal of blood everywhere; the smell of it hung heavy in the air, making her tremble.

"Kick, Gwen, damnit, kick the bastard!" Tyrian yelled as the outlaw came up against the huge horse he meant to force her to climb upon.

Tyrian realized his mistake. Another drop of spiteful blood appeared on Gwendolyn's wimple, but she had not made a sound, not a whimper since she had witnessed the cruel death of her friend, the cart driver.

Tossing her up onto the horse, the outlaw readied to jump up behind her, but just then Gwendolyn drew back her leg, let go, kicked out with her hard service-able shoes. The outlaw's arms did cartwheels as he tripped over a big rock, then went flying backward until he lay in the dirt.

He looked up with murder in his eyes.

Gwendolyn snatched up the reins, handling the war-horse like an expert equestrienne. For a moment, Tyrian watched her with awe as she spurred forth the mount, breathed in its ear, whirled about and from a rearing position, performed a curvet.

She headed for the knight. His eyes widened, wondering at her game.

Just as Gwendolyn was about to reach Tyrian, she turned the horse so that its side swept close to Tyrian. He understood her maneuver perfectly and bunched his muscles in readiness.

The outlaw had retrieved his wicked little dagger and was charging toward his horse with a bloodcurdling war-yell.

Tyrian sprang up behind Gwendolyn and, swinging his sword as she brought the horse around, he swept in a wide arc and lopped off the surprised man's head, and it bounced dully down a hillock.

"Look, Gwendolyn, his eyes!" Tyrian shouted with a warrior's bloodlust and glee. "Have you ever seen such a look as that."

No, she hadn't. Gwendolyn slumped forward; Tyrian reached around taking the reins from her, and they galloped away from the carnage.

Tyrian pulled Gwendolyn back against his chain-mailed chest as he slowed the horse. "How are you?" he asked. "You have not fainted, I pray."

Whimpering at that last word, she began to attack

him with her elbows, pumping like an enraged falcon, raining blow after blow backward into his ribs.

"Here now, novice Gwen," he said into her ear. "What have I said or done to make you this angry? You should be thanking me for saving you from a fate worse than death."

She gave a weak squeal.

"Poor dove," he murmured against her veil-wimple. "Why do you dislike me so? Have I deceived you? Are you afeared because I have killed so many for you?"

She nodded so vigorously that Tyrian was certain she was going to lose her wimple; she was angry because he'd fooled her and the cart driver perhaps? That must be—

"Dear God, I've forgotten about Thorolf. How unpleasant for you."

Hearing that, she sobbed as the tears flowed down unchecked onto the breast of her habit.

"At times I'm such an insensible idiot."

Again she nodded, but this time without as much vigor. "Poor little nun," He felt her shake her head. "I'm sorry, novice," he corrected.

Helping Gwendolyn down from the horse, Tyrian felt her sobs worsen and taking her into his arms, he found that beneath the starched linen and heavy white wool she was very soft and womanly. Perhaps a bit slim in the backsides. Her arms did not come around him, they just hung at her sides, quivering.

As Tyrian began brushing the side of her head with his fingertips, she snatched herself back, apparently thinking he had the idea to remove her wimple.

"I am sorry, novice. I won't touch you again. If that's

what you want. Or what you don't want, I should say. I know you can't talk to me. Can you write brief letters?"

She sniffed and nodded.

"Good. We shall talk in the morning. Right now, we have to go back and find the cart. Are you up to it? No? Fine. Here, upon your wish, we shall spend the night then."

Weary beyond words, Gwendolyn went directly to sleep in the bed he had fashioned of leaves, big horse blanket, small logs, feathery branches. It was warm and cozy in the little sanctuary. She went to sleep, just like a tired babe.

Tyrian stayed awake, staring at her, noting how he liked how Gwen sounded on his lips.

Wondering about the undoubted shock that had robbed her of speech.

And now again.

Fifteen

It was gray daylight; not yet sunrise. But it was fully light enough to see. Lying still, Gwendolyn listened, stiffly intent, trying to ascertain whether Tyrian was asleep or not.

Slowly lifting, she looked down, saw he was not beside her, then glanced around the glade to see him standing at the far side. How handsome he is in the morning light, she thought. How strong. How gallant and bold. How . . . dependable. Could she come to depend on him? It seems she already had had to.

Tyrian turned when he felt Gwendolyn staring at his back. He knew her eyes were on him. He felt it as if she were actually touching his body. He shivered with that thought and put his leg back up on the rock, continued cleaning his blade, not watching her as she began to move about.

Feeling uncomfortable, Gwendolyn sat for a few moments, then climbed from her bed and raked her hands through her . . . veil. No wonder she was uncomfortable. She had slept in her headpiece and she hadn't removed the wool outer dress. When she had bedded down in the cart, she had removed the white habit on the warmer nights.

Last night had been particularly warm and now she felt scratchy, almost faint as she came to her feet and swayed.

"We will stay at an inn tonight, if you would like."

Tyrian's voice cut across to her like a blade and she responded to him by nodding. She would love to spend the night in a real bed . . . but could she trust this man? She barely knew him except for the fact that he had saved her life and had felt bad concerning Thorolf's death. He was also dependable.

"I buried him," Tyrian said.

She blinked, wondering when and how. Had he left her during the night? She had slept out in the open, alone?

"At first light I returned to the camp and buried him beneath rocks." He shrugged. "Said a few words, too, I did."

He prays? she thought. She stared at the huge rock and back up at him with a question in her eyes.

"No," he said with a wry laugh. "I buried him with smaller rocks and stones that I piled in a mound. Even fashioned a cross of sorts on top."

Her eyes told him she was thanking him and a tentative smile peeked out. Who are you? her eyes asked him next. The question was all over her face, filling her features with enchanted wonder.

She is beautiful, he thought. Even with the soiled veil floating about her waist, wimple askew at her forehead. And the eyes, they were even more beautiful than anything he had ever seen. Big, sweet, blue, wondering. Was she a little afraid of him?

"I know what you are thinking, Gwendolyn. Should I call you Gwendolyn or Gwen? Nod once for Gwen; twice for Gwendolyn."

At first she was going to shrug, and then she nodded once. Picking up a stick, she bent over at the waist, and began writing in the dirt: "No last name." She looked up at him and shrugged.

"You have no idea what your last name could be?"

She shook her head.

"What would you like to do first, Gwen—bathe or eat?"

She put the stick to the ground again and wrote, "I am very hungry."

He laughed. "I will see what we have here in this bag." Tossing all kinds of junk out of the outlaw's bag, discarding moldy bread, rotten apples, bitter roots, Tyrian said "ah" as he finally came up with two perfect crusts of dark brown bread that had been baked with some kind of seeds in it; and a handful of dates.

"The highwayman must have swiped them not too long ago." Tyrian took a bite of a date. "Not bad. I'm sorry we don't have any fresh meat, Gwen. I don't care for meat all that much in the morning but I'll eat it if there is nothing else to partake of. I shall hunt small game if you wish."

Tyrian stopped talking and looked at her as she began writing again, "Why do you ramble on so?"

Pressing a long finger to her cheek, he said, "You make me very nervous, sweet novice."

Her eyes were big and blue and perplexed as he walked to the horses and explained over his shoulder, "The cart horse and my horse, they were waiting for me when I arrived to bury the dead. I think my horse and the other cart horse became friendly and—What is it? Why are you looking like that? Am I rambling again?"

She wrote, "The *dead?*"

"Yes, Aye. I buried them all. Do not look at me in quite that way; it's haunting, enchanting, but it worries me. I bury all my dead. Now you appear aghast even more. I even say a word or two over my graves. People that is."

She stepped back in alarm.

"No. It is not what you think. I never kill women. Especially not women of God. I am a knight. Of course you've already gathered that much."

"Long ago," she wrote.

A tawny brow lifted. "As soon as we met?"

Face red, Gwendolyn shook her head, causing her veil to swish her shoulders. She'd cast her eyes downward.

"When? Where?" he pressed. "You look embarrassed, Gwen."

How could she tell him the first time she'd known of him being a knight was at the water's edge? He would know she'd been spying on him if she told him *where*. She should not have spied, she thought, looking down at the wrinkled date, but she had been entranced for the first time ever of a man's nude body. The chapel drawings showed men, male angels nude—never quite as glorious as this man, however.

"Ah, you saw my chain mail between my friar's robe?" he questioned patiently, wondering if she might faint right here.

She only turned away, said nothing.

He watched her go to the water to wash her face and hands. The water, he thought. Had she been watch-

ing him as he bathed, when he'd stripped down to his
linen braies? He could think of no other reason for the
red face and intense embarrassment she exhibited.

"Gwen."

She turned abruptly when feeling his hand rest lightly
upon her shoulder. She looked at his hand, his eyes,
his perfect mouth. Then down, farther down.

To his other hand. "You forgot your bread and dates."

"Oh" was in her head as she watched him walk back
to the horses and lead them to the water.

There would be time enough to know if she could
trust him. It would take awhile to get to where they
were going. Now that she'd met him, where was she
going?

It was early evening when Gwen and Tyrian settled
at the inn for the night. They ate a tasty supper, talked
with a few of the locals and turned in for the night.
Gwen wondered what Tyrian had told the proprietor
about her when she had lingered out back for some
prayerful privacy. Stepping back inside Gwen noticed
that the owner and his wife did not stare as openly and
curiously as when they'd first arrived. Now the pair
treated her in a friendlier fashion, with no less due respect a woman of her station.

The proprietress came upstairs herself to make sure
"the little lady" had clean starched linens, plenty of
fresh water, an emptied chamber pot, the floor swept
with clean rushes and dried wildflowers put down.

"It's all done for ye, me lady. Ye need do nothing,"
the woman cooed. "Now, maybe ye'd like to wash yer
hair. I've set up a tub for your bath and—"

Gwen shook her head.

"Ye don't wish a bath?"

Gwen nodded.

The bemused woman said, "Ah well. Ye don't wish to wash yer hair, I see. Suppose it does stay clean under all that, er, covering." The woman swept a hand across an old table to make sure the maids had dusted. "You want to take it off while you bathe"—she stuck her plump inquisitive face in Gwen's—"wouldn't ya?"

Now Gwen appeared to be stumped as she felt her veil and looked at the high copper tub. The proprietress leaned closer to Gwen as the tall knight came to lean against the doorjamb. She whispered, "They didn't shave ye bald, did they? Wasn't lice, was it?"

Gwen looked at the tub again. Two overzealous young lads had been walking in and out, filling the tub to the brim. But they'd overheard the question and walked more slowly out this last time, casting sneaky peeks over their shoulders.

Gwen nodded quite vigorously.

Three separate gasps were heard. The proprietress stepped away. Tyrian had not made a sound nor moved a muscle. Now, however, he came away from the wall and waited for the inn-folks to file out. The last curious lad was too slow and received a boot in the arse for lingering overlong and goggling the pretty nun.

When Tyrian had closed the door, he slowly walked over to Gwen, where she waited for him to approach, fear of the unknown in her eyes. There was also some mischief in those unforgettable blue orbs, something approaching humor.

"No hair, eh?" Tyrian tugged at the tendrils of hair at her temples, until in his palm lay a curl of long silken blond. It coiled about his thumb as if alive. He, too, had mischief in his golden eyes.

He asked, "And what is this?"

At first he thought she was about to smile, then she pulled her lock away from him, tucked it back inside her wimple. She now turned to show him her back. A forefinger pointed at the ties, letting him know that she wished for him to untie the fastenings of her frock.

Tyrian stared for several moments. He had never undressed a nun—much less a novice since they were not as numerous—and he didn't know if he should heed her demand. Perhaps she was overtired and didn't know her mind. She had sipped only one glass of wine. He had blinked at that, not knowing that females of the order could imbibe.

He touched the first tie. "Will I be committing a grave sin if I undo you all the way down? I already slept with you." He undid the first one. "I mean, we did not, *ahem,* we only *slept* beside the other."

She turned wondering eyes upon him.

Tyrian melted into the horizon blue before she gave her back to him once again.

"Did you not know how we slept last night?" He looked away from her creamy back and over to the bed. "Well, we shall not this night. You can take the bed and I"—he saw the uncomfortable pallet arranged tidily with blankets on the floor—"I shall sleep there." Then again, he thought of the great temptation. "I might even take my rest in the stable."

All the ties had been undone. Tyrian kept his eyes averted.

Very slowly Gwen turned to face him. She saw that he was having difficulty swallowing, his face was red, his eyes a bright golden hue. She smiled with the absolute enchantment of an angel and it was Tyrian's undoing. He went to a chair, plopped down and placed his head in his shaking hands.

Gwen could see the moisture beading his noble face. She went to him, placed a cool palm on one cheek, then the other, and at last she felt his forehead. He turned the bright eyes of a very young hound up at her and she thought perhaps he might be feverish or had come down with some serious affliction.

Making him stand, she led him over to the bed, pushed him down—and Tyrian almost snatched her down with him. He felt quite unjointed.

"You think I am ill?" Tyrian shook his head and muttered, "Nothing a dip in a very cold stream won't cure."

Her face was innocent as her eyes peered into his. She wanted to make him stay, to go to bed, believing he was really quite unwell. He looked bad, she thought, incredibly ill.

"Yes—a cold dip is what I need," he echoed his own words.

Gwen had no notion of cold baths.

As soon as she touched the fastenings of his shirt, her wrist was clamped in a strong, unrelenting hold. "Do not," he cautioned. "You have no idea, lovely Gwen." He stood, swiping up the friar's robe, wiping his sweaty face on it. "Take your bath before the water is cold," he growled and walked out of the room.

Gwen jumped as the door slammed, then she turned back to her bath. The water looked deliciously warm, clean, inviting, with just a hint of lavender and rose water. While he was gone she slipped off the wimple and veil, stepped out of her clothes and got into the bath.

Gwen stopped washing with the green soap and looked

down at her body in the water. She felt so strange and the new tugs and pulls in her body gave her cause to wonder at its intricate workings. She had never really looked at her bosoms before, she had never studied as she was now. Had other young novices bodies similar to her own? Of course, they must have, she almost laughed at herself. But, did their breasts stand at attention with buds all rosy and hard? Especially now, they were very hard and sensitive. There were other stirrings in her body. Mostly when the knight came near. She felt, well, damp, and it was as if a huge feather tickled her inside while she experienced a very strange yearning above and below.

Somehow the knight's nearness was associated with what was going on in her body. It was most shocking. But very, very deliciously shocking.

She wanted to get close to Tyrian. Very close.

Gwen bit her lip, wishing she had listened to Fiametta as she instructed new novices on what they "should not be feeling" whenever men came near; and that included the good friars who visited, and the ones who dwelt at the abbey.

She started to hum as she soaped and rinsed her hair. The humming grew louder, joyfully so. Suddenly she halted the beautiful sound.

Gwen gasped.

Hummed. *Hummed!*

She had made a deep sound!

All the next day as Gwen and her knight traveled to Kirklees she tried humming again. She could not make sound. No matter how hard she tried, no sound but squeaks emerged.

She was very blue.

Tyrian was silent as he rode and said little more when they stopped for a light meal, one of many the innkeepers had packed. They had with them jugs of cold cider, dark loaves of bread, cold chicken, scones, hardtack, butter, and all sorts of preserves, like plum, peach, berry, that had been sealed in wax.

Gwen ate very little, but licked the delicious whortle-berry jelly from her fingers, one by one, after she'd nibbled on a small portion of bread.

Tyrian was watching her lick those slim lovely fingers, saw her pink tongue as it came out, licked, swirled about each member. She stopped licking and he looked into those soulful, forlorn eyes.

He moaned deeply, as if pained.

He couldn't stand it. He stood and stomped off toward a bit of trees and did not come out for a long time.

Gwen was beginning to wonder what had become of Tyrian when he stepped back into the clearing. He came nearer and Gwen, breath held, looked up at him.

His face was like the hard stone of a forbidding fortress, under siege at that, so fierce was his countenance. Gwen felt lonelier than when she'd lived at the nunnery. At least back there she had not had a knight to dream about. All that had been on her mind was God, prayers, books, holy manuscripts, angelic and demoniac beings, and all the other daily things that nuns concern themselves with.

Her soul belonged to God.

Now there was Tyrian. The golden knight.

Gwen was horribly perplexed. And for the first time in her life, she was even a little afraid of *emotion*.

"Dress, Gwen, and I'll not bother you."

As Gwen's habit was quite soiled from the fight, traveling, sleeping in, Tyrian had stopped at the house of a wealthy merchant to purchase her a change of clothes.

She was standing in a room at the back of the house, changing into a pale aqua gown. It was scandalously tight across the bosom and Gwen blanched when she looked down, saw that its hem reached an inch above her ankles. Putting on heavy woolen hose and stout shoes, she smiled hugely and blinked at how fat her feet and ankles appeared with the woolies. At least, the bulky hose took up the space where there should have been more skirt.

As she dressed she kept scratching at her scalp and, finally, reached up with both hands, tearing the wimple and veil from her head.

Blond hair tumbled freely about her shoulders and when the merchant's wife stepped in and saw how beautiful Gwen truly was, she gasped, reached for the veil and wimple. With a finger across her lips, the woman went to the door.

The merchant's wife suddenly realized that Sister Gwendolyn must have taken a vow of silence, so there would be no conversation; she filled in the gaps very well. "I will be back soon as my maid cleans your headdress. No man, not even that handsome knight who is your escort to Kirklees, should look upon a nun's crowning glory. That is only for God to see. We shall

216

have your habit cleaned soon. You'll be back on the road in no time at all, Sister Gwendolyn."

But I am not a nun, Gwen wanted to protest. She touched the hair the Mother Superior allowed the pitiful orphan to keep until she took her final vows. Yet did she want to anymore? What had changed? Something, she thought, something had, and very drastically, and it had much to do with these strange happenings inside her body.

It would be a blaspheme to the holy order to tell what she'd been dreaming the night before, much less think on it every waking hour.

She had been dreaming of Tyrian. Raking her fingers through her hair to remove tangles, she walked to the narrow window and looked out.

There, below, in the courtyard, stood Tyrian speaking with a potbellied man.

Gwen pushed back into the room before Tyrian could see her without her wimple and veil.

Gwen sat. Soon she curled up on the comfortable daybed and fell asleep. Her fresh-washed and dried hair trailed to the floor, its shining waves making a silver blond pool on the black and yellow rug.

After knocking and receiving no answer, Tyrian entered the tiny back room. He was wondering what was taking the woman so long to clean Gwen's habit and finish helping her dress.

The merchant's wife had been somewhat reluctant to do any work since her daughter's wedding was on the morrow, but he had pressed her to get the job done. She had looked at the bag of coins, eyes gleaming at the prospect of a weighty purse for her daughter to share with her new husband.

Looking round the room with a sweeping glance, Tyrian decided the woman had vacated along with Gwen, when the color of blue and silver caught his eye.

Gwen.

He happened to look up then, seeing the holy cross of wood on the wall.

Down again to Gwen. As he stared his eyes felt as if they were burning holes in his skull.

My God, he did not know such beauty existed in the world, all in one tiny woman.

A novice. One to soon become a nun.

Up at the cross he glanced again, backed up and almost ran out the door. He crashed into a young maid just coming along the hall carrying the habit; veil and wimple went flying. One arm steadying the girl, Tyrian's other arm shot out, caught the headdress and saved it from sailing into a slop bucket.

"Whew," the girl said, sighing.

Another pretty maid winked as she walked over to her bucket, bent down. "Mighty fast work, gov'ner." Hefting her bucket she jerked her head back. "Hah. If that's a real nun in there, give me that thing and I'll eat it."

"Eat," Tyrian said, holding the wimple out. "And it's novice," he added, walking away, "not nun."

"I'll bet my best besom," said one maid to the other as they stared below as the golden-eyed knight rode away with Gwen, "that that pretty nun'll never take her final vows."

"Novice," the other corrected.

"Novice or nun," the first maid said, "she'll never make it away from *that* man with only one piece of 'er gone."

"She can't talk. She has no voice."

"A nun's vow of silence."

"I don't think so."

She swept across the floor with her besom. "Makes not one whit of difference. He's going to gobble her up whole. It's in his eyes." Now this one came back to the narrow window and rested with her chin on the scrubby handle.

The other, crunching into a deep red apple, said while chewing, "And the way *she* looks up at him."

Both maids sighed. It was a while before they could get back to work as they passed the apple back and forth while gazing into the distance.

Sixteen

The sun was coming down like warmed honey all over everything. Autumn sat in the middle of a field of heather, among steep green hills, as she braided her long red hair, finally pulling both plaits up to form a coronet round her head.

The more Autumn thought about finding her sister, the lonelier she became. Winter was out there somewhere and some day she would find her. As for her other sisters, she was afraid she might never see them again. Winter, however, was a little easier to describe, with her silver blond hair and looks of an angel. Not many young women looked as sweet and flawless of features as Winter. Then again, Autumn told herself, she had not seen her sister in years and there was the slight possibility Winter had become homely and fat.

Very slight. Autumn did not think Winter would, since she herself had stayed quite slender and supple of complexion. Aye, Winter was out there, as beautiful as when they'd been children growing together. Autumn was recalling more of her past as the days sped by. She knew for a fact that Richard Meaux had been her real father; it was Robert, his brother, that she remembered as being the one to return to the castle stating that Richard had been killed in battle. It had been a lie; Richard returned the following week. Robert was the dark nasty one, not her father, who had been good and kind. Robert had been the teller of lies. She had gotten them all jumbled up in her mind. Both brothers were very close in age, and looked almost like twins. Perhaps they were; she'd never know now.

And now Autumn knew about her uncle, that he'd existed, that was all. Who would she remember next? Her mother's face was still dim to her. She had flashes of a face in her memory, a beautiful face, but the image did not last long. "It will take a shock for you to remember all," Raine had told her the other day. "Much like the shock received when you witnessed your parents' deaths."

Raine was speaking to her now. He had been quiet for only half a day and then he had broken the silence. She would have to refrain from saying "I love you," even in jest.

How could she possibly know that she was in love with Raine? To love someone was to know him, trust him implicitly with your life, share his love, soul, mind. She did not even know who she was herself, so how could she give her love to someone else?

It was so easy for a man. All he had to do was look at a woman, decide he wanted her and that was that. He looked into her eyes, thinking she would melt at his feet, follow him to the ends of the world, and believe every word he spoke was shining truth.

Not I, Autumn told herself. It was going to take some doing before she plunked herself down in a man's bed.

He would either have to get her drunk (she'd never been juiced in her life), or make her believe the world was going to end on the morrow. He would have to go down on bended knee, tell her she was the sun, moon, stars, to him. He must profess that he could not live without her. He must tell her his world revolved around her, that he would buy her the moon, and if not that, then a unicorn. The horned, horselike, mythical animal must be easier to find than flying to the sky for the moon; man could never go to the moon; that was unheard of.

"Autumn, we must go now." Raine came up to her in the heather, holding her horse.

With the sun pouring down on him like that, Autumn thought he was gorgeous. She would have told him, had he not been so serious looking lately.

"Is it very far to Kirklees?"

"Not much farther at all. We go that way now." He squinted in the sun. "It is good. The days are growing hotter as summer is upon us in full force almost; it's only days away. You'll not freeze at night."

Autumn followed him to the road, where they mounted up. She wondered and worried as to the reason for Raine's new brooding disposition. He was not himself. He did not laugh with her. It was almost as if he was getting ready to part company with her.

"You will take me to Kirklees?"

"Aye, yes."

Surely he would converse more with her soon. She missed Barry most of all.

They traveled on the road part of the day and bought bread and cheese from a vendor going from town to town.

Up ahead was a cottage of stone and timber. Autumn and Raine stopped there, ate fish from a stream and explored the abandoned cottage, inside and out.

"Look—a bottle of wine," Raine said, standing over an old trunk.

"Could be poison by now," she told him. "That bottle is so huge it could inebriate twenty horsemen."

"Do you want some or do you not?" he growled across to her.

From the other side of the room she snapped back, "You can have it all to yourself. I am going outside to see if I've missed people who might be living here. You never know, they might come home in the middle of the night and throw us out of that"—she wrinkled her nose with distaste—"musty old bed."

"Who says we stay here this night?" Taking a sip of wine, he looked at her with a happy grin. "It is good." Another sip, then another. "Strong. Good. We just might stay. See to the horses, Mistress Autumn. Ah, yes," he said, settling back against the trunk, legs stretched out in front along the floor.

Autumn was across the room in a flash, snatching the bottle from him. "If you wish to get drunk, do it when you are not with me." She capped the jug with the stopper and tossed the rest onto the fur-covered bed. "How can you be my protector when you cannot see straight or hit your backsides with both hands? If you drink all that wine you'll be out for the night and—what was that noise?"

Raine gave her a huge smile. "What noise? I don't hear anything. It is just your woman's imagination running wild again."

"Oh?" A hand went to her hip. "There, you see. Last

223

time we heard something the noise was that of highwaymen. You were alert then. Now you have imbibed just a little and your hearing is already impaired."

"Autumn," Raine groaned. "I . . . believe I have . . . just drunk . . . something bad. Maybe . . . poison." He slumped over and before he shut his eyes, he murmured, "You were right. Poison."

"Raine!" Autumn rushed to him and tried to awaken him. "Oh no. I was only speaking in jest. Raine. Oh please, please just say something." She reached for the jug, then looking at it with a shriek, she tossed it onto the floor. "Raine, talk to me, was it poison?"

A hand reached out and grabbed her ankle. Autumn went down crashing into Raine as he pulled her beneath him and laughed into her face. "Fooled you, did I not?"

"You oaf, get off!"

"Get off, you oaf? What are you saying?" He just laughed some more. "Been nipping on that jug, have you?"

"Raine, you are too heavy."

"You did not think so when I was Barry. Why is Raine heavier? Why is Barry better?" He held her chin as he stared into her eyes. "Because you do not feel threatened with him?"

"Hardly. I remember when Barry jumped on me that night and drove me to his friends. Tyrian was one of them. He was the friar."

"No. He was the one in the shadows. I believe Russell was wearing Tyrian's friar's robe that night."

"You have it all backward. You don't even know your own roguish friends. Let me up!" She pounded on his chest. "You lying sack of bulging muscle!"

His chest rumbled as he laughed. "That is what I

224

like about you, Autumn. Never a dull moment. The man who weds you will not lack for a good time."

"What?"

"A strong man needs a strong woman. One with wit and daring."

"And you, Raine Guardian, are one way one moment and another the next. Who can ever know you?"

"You know me," he said with a rakish grin.

"Your personality changes from day to day. At times, hour by hour. Who are you really? Was Tiercel your sister at all? Or was that all a show, as well as all the costumes you wear and faces you put on?"

"Who knows," he said with a shrug against her shoulder, "I might very well be a prince from a distant country, for all you know. My name might really not be my name at all."

"I would not doubt it at all," she answered with a shaky laugh and a deep frown furrowing her pretty brow. At least, he thought it was pretty, even if she did not.

"Come on, mistress. Show me your brazen spirit again. Roll over with me and kiss me as you did in the garden that wondrous day you attacked me like a bold, shameless tart."

"You are drunk on wine."

He rolled over and put her on top of him. "No. You make me drunk, maiden. On passion. Your passion. I would make love to you now, only if you let me."

"Well, I won't. If you marry me, I shall let you." She gasped at her own words.

"What?" he thundered.

"I did not mean that—"

225

"Aye, you did. And I will, will, will marry you, sweet tart."

"Of course," she said with a crisp snap. "You would marry me and get yourself land and castle. You would not even have to reclaim your own."

"How do you know I have this what you say?"

"I know." She looked at him. "It is written all over you. You must be a titled lord, even, as you say, a prince perhaps. But the king has outlawed you from your holdings because of some crime you have committed." Her eyes were shrewd and very violet. "What did you do, Raine, steal the king's jewel, which he carried for good luck during the battle of Agincourt?"

He flipped her over and was on top again. Looking down into her face, he snarled softly, "You know all about that, do you? Believe I'm a jewel thief? No, Autumn. I seek to reclaim the king's ruby to him, not steal it. What would I want with the Black Prince's ruby?"

She blew into his face hard, then shoved at his chest. "What would you want with my family heirloom?"

Releasing her, he flattened himself on the floor, arms spread. He looked weary suddenly. "We have been through this before, Autumn. I told you. The jewel is not in my possession. I am not sure it is anymore."

He appeared worried all of a sudden.

Glaring, she asked, "What do you mean?"

"I have already told you. Someone might have gotten to the hiding place and taken it back." Although he doubted that very much himself. He was just saying this to placate her, humor her, and make her leave him alone and quit questioning as to the whereabouts of the jewel. He was growing weary of all this questioning and it was beginning to make him worry about other "people" concerned with the jewel.

Precious. She would never know how precious. Not until he was good and ready to show her.

Autumn had been musing on this for several minutes and was now ready to question him again.

"Back? You mean, the king's high sheriff, Duc Stephan or Drogo. Which man? Why do you leave the jewel out in the open where any thief—like yourself—can come along and snatch it away?"

"The king's high sheriff? Who said anything about him? And who said it is out in the open?" He narrowed his eyes at her.

Autumn looked away as she came to her feet. Thank you, Raine. Now I know you keep it in a very secret place. Perhaps in a jeweled box inside a secret wall? A concealed panel in a woman's bedroom? His mistress? Ah, yes. A very good hiding place.

"And," Raine said as he swiftly stood beside her, "why do you believe the jewel is white? Could it not be blue, red, or any other color?" His hand cupped her slim waist and smoothed the curve down to her hips and thighs.

Looking down at his hand, she said, "Why so venturesome, fair knight?"

He laughed and she pushed away his hand.

"Oh no," he said, snatching her back to him.

"Raine?" She looked into his eyes; he was face to face with her. "Surely you would not think to ravish me. You are the stronger of the two of us. You could have your way very easily." She saw his eyebrow roguishly curve upward at those words. "What are you going to do?"

227

"Kiss you. You really need to be kissed, Autumn, and kissed well."

His lips were suddenly on her mouth. And now his arms were pulling her closer, winding round her back. She could feel the male heat of him and her heart raced like a runaway horse. And then she froze.

He felt her revulsion and pushed her away from him. "What do you want from me, Autumn?"

She whispered, "The jewel."

"I cannot bring you to it now. Or bring it to you."

Whirling away, she put her back to him. Long moments passed in which she said nothing. He came round to face her again.

"Why silent suddenly, maiden? You look not so sure of yourself. Have I said or done something to upset you?" He left her hip to come up with a fingertip and tilt her chin.

"Like most men," she hissed into his face, "you are quite callous. You take only what you can get and leave."

She walked away, going toward the door.

"Wait, maiden." When she turned, he softly said, "I am *not* most men. And I have not had you yet."

Deep in the night, when both of them could not find sleep, Autumn came up on her elbow and peered across the room. "Awake, Raine?"

"Of course. This pallet is hard and with you knocking about, how can anyone get any sleep? You could be a bit more merciful and have some consideration, you know. If you let me sleep with you, perhaps we could both find the rest we need."

Her snicker was filled with skepticism.

"Laugh and doubt, do you? I could show you how to obtain a peaceful night's rest. We could have a very good time. I could fetch the jug of wine—"

"No."

He came up on his elbow. "I will go smear mud on my face, put on my disgusting change of clothes, and alas, I shall be Barry once again. We will make love, be dirty together, sleep peacefully throughout the night and—"

"No."

"What is your question then? Why have you asked if I am still awake? Do you want to have a discussion?" He laughed shortly, sarcastically. "Excuse me, maiden, I meant: I shall say something and you contradict me or call me nasty names."

"Very funny."

He sighed deeply, putting his hands beneath his head. "I thought so." He turned his head to look across to her in the dim room. "You did not?"

"Not."

"I will come over and rub your back. You will like that, will you not?"

"Not."

"Maiden, you are getting on my nerves. When you awaken in the morning, you may very well find me gone. This time for good."

"I do not believe you. You have sworn to protect me. You will not leave me. You will help me find my sister, escort us back to Sutherland, bring my jewel for Baron Orion to see, he will contact King Henry, and together you will both arrange my marriage. Without my say."

"My, my. How well you do not know me." He turned

over, putting his back to her. "Go to sleep. You will need your energy reserves when you awaken one morning and will have to fend for yourself."

"You will not leave. You want to make love to me too much. Once that is done, then perhaps you will leave me alone. I will let you after we find Winter. Then you may take your leave. I don't care if I never see your face again."

"Ah. Your virginity for the price of helping you find your sister, eh? You would give up your own precious jewel, your maidenhood?"

He was up on his elbow again, staring across to her; he could see her on her back staring not at him but the ceiling. "Is this the way it is, maiden?"

She laughed shortly. "If it is to be, then I shall not be pestered by you calling me *maiden* anymore, now will I?"

"Surely, if I have you, you will not be called that ever again."

"So sure of your prowess, aren't you. My uncle was the same way. He was so sure my mother would welcome him in her bed when my father was off to battle or ship."

"Perhaps you are not a maiden, after all. Who is this knavish uncle you speak so lowly of?"

"His name was Robert. And no, he did not ravish his precious little niece."

"Precious, hmm?"

"Yes. He thought we were all precious."

"All?"

All four sisters, she would not say.

So, Raine thought, it was not Richard who had had the jewel, but Robert Meaux. No wonder she had been confused about her father. An uncle: Robert Meaux. Only if her mother had married the uncle would he have become another father, a stepfather—that was possible. And here, all this time he'd thought it had been Richard who had given him the jewel for safekeeping. It had been Robert. Robert was her stepfather; not Richard. Richard was quite possibly deceased then. Robert must have had trouble with Drogo and Duc Stephan. Both were deceased then; there was no Robert nor Richard alive to tell him more of what he would learn. Perhaps.

Autumn turned and blinked at the cracked wall. Her eyes drifted to the dark, ragged tapestry. There was the moldy underscent of sweat in the room. Who had lived here before? Had they been a happy couple? Had they argued? Or loved fiercely until the day they parted or one died? How many years had passed since these walls surrounded and protected them? Were their ghosts in this cottage even now?

They must have been happy and very much in love, for suddenly Autumn felt a nice peaceful aura surround the bed. Raine was sleeping, she could hear. His soft snores made her feel protected and secure.

She smiled at that thought as she began to drift on a delicious cloud.

Safe . . . *Could she be so sure of that* . . . with an enticing jewel thief right across the room from her? How safe was she from her own self . . . ?

* * *

At daybreak, with stars still in the sky to the west, Autumn awakened to find herself alone in the cottage. Raine was not in sight. Not inside, not outside, no horse, no traveling gear.

He was gone.

So was Dusky. The jennet was nowhere to be seen.

She had dreamed of Raine last night. He had been making love to her. And then he had left her, was standing alone wearing sword and armor. His face was cruel, heartless, and then he had turned to her with a knife in hand. She had run; he had run quickly beside her. He now was wearing dark clothing, as dark as the woods surrounding them.

And that had been the end of the dream.

Raine had come into her life like a mysterious wind and he had left the same way.

Quickly gathering her change of clothes and herb seeds, Autumn mounted up and rode away from the cottage. She had come out of the cottage feeling happy and nervous and curious all at once.

The last few stars winked down on her as she made her way silently up the path.

Why should she feel happy? It was dangerous on the road alone; she had already experienced this. She did feel happy; she was even smiling.

Which way to Kirklees? She looked in the direction the sun was swiftly rising in the sky and headed north.

North to Kirklees. She stood still for frozen moments.

"I can do this," she whispered at last.

And now her moment of paralysis broke, she stepped across the last bridge of indecision. I could go back to the town, not all that far away. I could send for escort from Sutherland. I could be back in my old room at the castle in a fortnight. I could be in my garden gathering herbs and seeds, planting, dreaming, wishing, longing . . .

I could be a coward.

North to Kirklees.

Without a man. She needed only herself; for now. She would find Winter, bring her back to Sutherland and they would live happily ever after. They would both wed good men, strong, handsome, caring men. Her own would get her jewel back for her and he would be her hero. He would battle all the villains in her life. And win. She would never be afraid with him around, be able to trust him assiduously.

If only she could find such a man. One who would not desert her in her times of need.

A good man would be like a jewel.

Seventeen

Autumn had been riding for hours. She had gone off the trail and across a rocky outcrop to another narrow trail through alder thickets. She could see the bulging roots of an enormous oak. She stopped to eat crusts of bread, drank water from her jug. Once more, as she mounted, the forest thickened with choking briars, spurs of broken rock; there was even a swamp.

Suddenly she stopped, holding Ghost still. Had she heard a second set of stirrup chains and a bridle tinkling?

A flock of sparrows about to settle among the pines suddenly veered away, surprising Autumn for a moment.

The forest briefly opened up to admit the crossroads and the highway curled the other way toward another town. To the north, she could see the common ground belonging to a village, and a few twists of smoke from peasants' huts.

Then she was riding through the trees again where the forest was dense with dark pines. A swamp stretch with reeds and rushes. More pines, thick with boughs and concealing shadows. The land began to rise in a tumble of rock. Then the ground rose sharply into a craggy headland. After that, she rode carefully through a thicket of elm and alder.

Again she slowed Ghost to listen. She was getting better at discerning whether she was alone or not alone.

She was not alone.

As once before, and not too long ago, she saw the oddest sight: a huge figure in black armor. He just sat there staring through the great dragon helm.

Again.

Autumn's heart picked up a deep thudding, her mouth going dry, and she slipped from her horse to the ground. Before she went out, she had caught a single flash of steel.

The Black Knight was back.

When Autumn opened her eyes she was in a strange room made of stone. A turret. She looked across the thick covers to find a beautiful woman standing at the foot of the bed staring at her.

"So, you have finally opened your eyes." The woman's voice was rich and vain *and* insincere. "They are a most strange color, this violet hue."

Her hair was black, glossy, cut across the forehead like Cleopatra's. She was richly gowned and beringed. The chemise was visible at the neck above her gown, at the wrists, and on the sleeves. The neckline was low cut and Autumn stared, wondering if the woman was some wealthy man's leman.

Autumn tried to sit up but found her head was spinning madly.

"What happened to me?" Her hand slapped her forehead as she stared up at the beamed ceiling trying to remember. "Why am I here?" She struggled to sit up and at last she managed to straighten her back and lift herself up. "Who are you?"

"You really don't want to know." The voice followed with a laugh that was deep and throaty.

Autumn was not intimidated. "I asked, so therefore I must want answers. It's as simple as that."

Rowena's smile vanished instantly. "You will know soon enough. I am the Duchess Rowena."

"That's it? You have no lands, no castle?"

"I have told you my name, the rest is none of your concern, my lady. Especially not the lands, which I might add, shall soon be in my possession."

Frowning, Autumn studied the duchess. Now that she could focus better she could see that the duchess was gaining in years. There was a liberal sprinkling of gray at her temples and it looked as if someone had tried to cover the strands with a black dye.

"My cousin has brought you here. He is a cold-blooded killer, a rapist, a thief. You must not cross him in any way. Do you understand?"

Autumn shrugged. "Duchess, I'm still alive, but I have no idea who he is," she said flippantly. "All I see is a big man with a great dragon helm covering all his face. He is very fierce. He killed many men for me when first we, er, met."

"You are insolent!" the duchess shouted.

The sound of her voice was so shrill and grating that Autumn clamped hands over her ears. She moved them away slowly. The woman's voice had returned to normal and Autumn sighed in relief.

"You will meet him later."

Rowena pressed hands to her red velvet skirts and gazed at Autumn from the deepest, darkest blue eyes she had ever seen.

The image of a huge black knight filled Autumn's mind. "I fainted and that apparition of black steel brought me here? Who are you and what do you want from me? If you think to use me in some satanic ritual, you had better think twice. The Sutherland knights would come after you and have you and your men for dinner."

Rowena glared. "You have a sharp tongue: I believe your pretended boldness arrives from fear of the unknown."

You could not be more exact, Duchess. "I do not pretend," Autumn lied.

"Oh. I see."

"What are your plans for me?" Autumn asked, looking on either side of her, just in case the black knight was sitting somewhere nearby.

Rowena turned her back on the defiant redhead. "You are a sight. Haven't you looked in a looking glass lately?" She went to a huge black wood wardrobe and returned with a length of material over her arm.

Shuddering, Autumn wondered what she held. "What is it?" Autumn asked.

Rowena's eyes shone dully.

"Here is a gown. You will need it."

Rowena tossed a green and sparkling gown onto the huge bed. Autumn had never seen anything quite as rich and colorful. The green was so bright it almost hurt to look at it.

She would have thought black and scarlet more appropriate during a ritual or black mass.

A maid hurried in with water, and then hurried back out again, as if afraid of the Duchess Rowena. I do not blame her, Autumn thought.

Autumn hardly noticed what the duchess was doing now, for she was staring at the green material that looked like diamond stars had been sewn into its folds.

Autumn gasped when she held up the sparkling gown. "Where is the bodice?" She would be half naked in such a gown.

She sat down again, on the edge of the bed, in awe of this lovely creation.

"Worn as is or wear nothing at all." The duchess smirked over Autumn's slim body. "You should eat more. You have no curves."

When Autumn stood alone and shivering, holding the beautiful gown to herself, she looked up and across the room.

There stood a polished mirror.

In it Autumn could see herself. Her vision wavered in the expensive glass as Autumn stood. Her curvaceous figure made Autumn realize the duchess had spoken out of jealousy.

She blinked and shivered again.

Where are my clothes? I am stark naked.

Remembering everything that Elizabeth Sutherland and her new French maids had taught her about *proper* dress and hair arrangement, Autumn washed herself quickly and contemplated the gorgeous green gown she had no choice but to wear.

She struggled into it without the help of a servant. A maid had come up to tell her she would soon join the duchess for the evening meal, perhaps then she could find a means to escape.

She gaped at herself in the mirror. There was nothing *proper* about this gown.

Sucking in her breath as she sat to do something with her hair at the dressing table, Autumn released the breath in a whoosh as she stared at all her flesh gaping above the low neckline of the gown. She reached inside the bodice wondering where all the material had gone to, thinking it might have folded itself inside.

Nothing. She looked at herself again. Just like this? Even the ladies who had come to visit Sutherland did not expose this much skin. It was quite shocking. No. *Scandalous!*

But who was there around to realize such a scandal, that Autumn Meaux appeared at the duchess's table gowned quite nude?

Autumn sighed and set about to do her hair. When she was done, her hair was swept up in a thick coronet wound about her head and she stuck a comb from the dressing table right on top of her head. It rested on the thickness of the braid, standing up like a tiara.

Now that I am done, what am I supposed to do? Wait for someone to come fetch me to the duchess? No doubt she has little charming dogs that sit in her lap and lick her hands.

Well, I for one shall not lick her hand. She giggled, feeling quite wicked in the green gown.

Autumn stood and moved to pick an apple from a bowl, the gown sparkling all around her like diamond motes.

Seated on the bed, she sat crunching the apple, looking quite bored.

A movement at the window and she was up, tossing the half-eaten apple back into the bowl.

It had looked like a man out there on the stone balcony that half curved about the turret.

The Black Knight?

Autumn felt a little weak in the knees as she went onto the balcony and looked about, but saw no one.

When she turned she almost screamed because she was standing so close to a man.

A man who looked so much like . . .

"Raine?"

He laughed. It was then that Autumn noticed this man was even larger than Raine. The same eyes, mouth, nose. Only his hair was red, almost as red as her own. Where had she seen him before? When he was not wearing armor, that is.

"A cousin," he said. "You don't remember me."

Warily, Autumn shook her head.

"Russell Courtenay at your service, maiden." He saw her flinch at that word. "The duchess is my cousin, as is Raine Guardian. We are all cousins."

"Who? You and the duchess and Raine?"

"Yes, m'lady."

Autumn's eyes flinched wider. "You were in the outlaw camp, in Sherwood Forest. I saw you from a distance. Your bright red hair."

"Very good."

"Are you also the Black Knight?"

He said no more, walked away and left her standing there gaping after him.

Now she was thoroughly convinced he was related to the Guardians.

She looked down and couldn't help but wonder how

he had gotten up this high? Had he been hiding out on the balcony all this time?

What sort of place is this? Autumn asked herself as she hurried back inside where it was safer.

But was it really. And who were all these people? Why had she been taken here? Was she to be their prisoner?

She just didn't know. But she did have a feeling that she would not be staying long.

Trying the door to the turret, Autumn found it was not locked and slipped out into the short stone hall, looking first this way and then that. No place for anyone to conceal themselves.

Why have I dressed up? What is the occasion? She could hear no sounds of a family gathering round the table for supper.

About to step onto stone stairs leading way below, Autumn felt like St. George going down to slay the dragon.

At the bottom of the circular stairs Autumn paused to look around before she ventured from the last step. For a moment she'd had the eerie sensation that everybody had departed, left her behind, and that she was completely alone with some terrible beast. Furtively, feeling more than a little foolish, she darted a glance over her shoulder.

She couldn't explain why, except that for one awful moment she'd sensed the presence of someone else there. There was nothing, of course, merely empty corridors and smoldering hearths. And thin wreaths of smoke rose lazily into the vacant air.

A mystery house. Where are all the furnishings? No tapestries? What was this place?

Something called to her. She tilted her head, as if that sound were just beyond the range of her hearing, tantalizing but unapproachable.

Nothing.

Silence, and the sound of her own breathing.

She began to run and found most of the rooms empty of people. Only the hearths blazed. She shook her head and waited until her rapidly beating heart had slowed down before she ventured forth again.

They, whoever they might be, were trying to scare her to death. And they were doing a magnificent job.

An ember popped in one of the ever-burning hearths at the end of a long hall. "Dinner," she reminded herself. Perhaps I'm the dinner. She gulped. "Where *is* the smell of food?"

The sound of her own voice shattered whatever remnants had remained of that scary and strange thought.

It was then that someone grabbed her from behind.

Dragged to the door, a hand over her mouth to keep her from making any sound, she was brought outside to two horses waiting there.

One was Ghost.

"Get on!" the voice commanded.

When she did not comply, she was hoisted in the air and tossed onto the back of her own horse. Maybe, she thought, she could get away from him. What for? She would only be tossed back into the stone prison she'd just been carried away from when the Black Knight caught up.

They rode all night without stopping. When they finally did stop, her captor helped her down and it was pitch black as he led her to the front door of an old cottage.

"Who are you? What are you doing? What of the duchess and her man, the Black Knight? Who are you?" she asked again. "At least the Black Knight came boldly to abduct me so that I could see him. But you, you are like a shadow without even a dragon helm to cover your black face."

She was so weary of all this running about the countryside. All she'd wanted to do was find her sisters; if not all of them then at least one.

The shadowed face loomed before her. "Here. Drink this."

Autumn looked up but it was also so black inside the cottage that she could hardly see his hands with the cup thrust in front of her face.

"What is it?" Autumn sniffed and jerked back. "It smells like strong wine."

"It is."

"Short on words, are you?" she asked, fearing to take a sip of the wine. "What do I need wine for? To prepare me for something I'll not like very much?"

He said nothing.

The floor was cold and damp, and the air in the cottage was musty, smelling of mold and moss. "Do you have a name, at least?" she tried again, trying to find the dark face in the blackness.

"Raine."

The cup dropped from shocked fingers.

"Raine!" Autumn said in delayed verbal response, shooting up from the bench she'd been seated upon. "Why you, you bastard. Why didn't you tell me who you were long ago?"

"You just now asked."

"I believe I asked a long time ago."

After he had made light, Autumn took a good look at him. He looked just awful, his cloak torn, and he hadn't shaved with a sharp blade in a week.

"Growing a beard, Raine?" She gasped. "And what is all that black stuff on your face?"

"Do you like the beard?" He was sarcastic. "As for the other, it's the blackest mud I could find in all of England." He stooped to unroll the bedclothes upon the floor.

Everything went still. Raine was staring at her in the green gown, as if he had seen her for the first time just now.

Raine's eyes had lifted to her hair from his bent position on the floor. He whispered, "You are beautiful, Autumn."

Autumn felt quite wonderful.

"I speak the truth, Autumn."

"Thank you," she said, looking at his dirty face.

He asked, "Who arranged your hair?"

Autumn met Raine's eyes. "I did."

"Gorgeous," he breathed. "You should do it more often. You look like a princess with fire in her hair. You make me desire you with just a look."

Hands on her hips, Autumn questioned fiercely, "Who are you now, Raine? Playing a Nubian now? I am beginning to believe you very well may have many personalities. I begin to wonder if your name is really Raine Guardian."

He sighed tiredly, swiping an arm across his black face. "I've ridden all day. Don't give me trouble now, woman. Almost killed my horse to rescue you from my mad cousins. I've lost Dusky—"

"So—you took the jennet and most of the food with

you. How cruel. Why did you leave me alone to fend for myself?"

"I wanted to see if Russell would try to capture you. He'd been trailing us for days. He's a cousin, you know."

She could feel the smoke pouring from the flames of her temper. "You already said that. So did Russell when we spoke briefly. The duchess is your cousin . . . why didn't you tell me?" she wailed.

He glared at her. "So, you met Rowena."

"Rowena *and* Russell. Charming people." She followed with a snort.

He placed dried meat, dark bread, dates and plums on a trencher, handing the food to her. "You are lucky to be alive still."

"Why did you not rescue me sooner then?"

"I attempted to, believe me. Rowena has determined knights working for her."

"Raine. Why would she want me dead?"

Autumn set down her trencher to follow him as he cared for the horses. She bumped into him in the dark and held onto his arm.

"Answer me." She reached up to press his black face. "Why would the duchess want to kill me and why did you really leave me alone?"

Her violet eyes sparkled with anger, her hair illuminated by the flames of the torch. Raine had never seen a more tempting vision. For answer, he moaned, grabbed her by the shoulders and kissed her very hard.

She began kissing him back and found that she was quite hungry for him.

"Raine," she gasped, pulling back, "Why? Why?"

"I can't tell—" Raine shook his head, saying quickly, softly, gently, "Not yet."

"Why?" She was persistent.

"It is best you do not know."

"Raine, I—" Autumn found herself staring at his beautiful mouth.

Dirty mouth.

"Raine—wash," was all she got out.

"I am going to mess up that gorgeous hair of yours," he warned as he shoved a little against her, wanting to kiss, nibble, inhale her sweetness, caress and enter the enticing realm of her womanly paradise to spiral up and down, becoming mindlessly lost in the exploding heat of mutual ecstasy.

"Please do," she breathed into his ear.

He pushed her back against a stall, grinding his thighs into her, one leg lifting between hers. Their movements became frantic and they began to tear at each other's clothes.

They went suddenly still, waiting.

"What is it?" she asked, feeling the tension.

"Storm," he said, feeling it, too.

Just then a thundercloud burst overhead and the rain began to splash a staccato rhythm onto the thatched roof.

"Run outside in the rain, Raine," she said in a sudden teasing mood. "Have nature cleanse you for me." She laughed at how fast he moved to do her bidding.

"Where were we, sir?" Autumn asked between tiny gasps of passionate breaths as he returned to her and he wrapped her in his arms.

"Where we should be, princess. We are quite alone. Do not worry about the duchess, the jewel, the rain, my clean face or anything else. My God, you have driven me to uncontrollable passion."

"Raine, please," she whispered.

"I fear I will hurt you such is my desire. You are a virgin and I must tread carefully and gently."

"Hurt me if you must," Autumn said like a hissing tigress, attacking his shirt with bared claws.

They kept tearing until they were both naked and the green gown lay in a sparkling heap on the hay and chaff floor beneath them. He kissed her until her lips were becoming bruised and sore.

They had fallen upon the bedclothes. Raine smiled into the dark. "Ah, my beauty," he said with a kiss.

Autumn kissed him back until they were both breathless and wanting. His hands were all over her; her breasts, her thighs, between her legs, up and down her back, her sides.

They rolled about and when she contacted his swollen member, he sucked in his breath but kept her hand there. "Do you want me now, Autumn? Are you ready?"

"I think so, Raine." She almost gasped the words out; she followed with a giggle at her embarrassment. "How should I be? I've never done this before, you know."

He felt her and chuckled, removing his hand from between her legs. "You are ready as you will ever be, maiden."

"Maiden?" She sighed, feeling hot and wild and wonderful. "Not much longer."

A laugh trailed Autumn's words.

When he entered her, Autumn felt the burning heat and cried out, not with pain but with joy and wonder. Why had they not come together sooner? What had been the fear? She just now realized Raine was the only man she would ever want and need the rest of her life.

There was no sin here. They were meant for each other. She could grow old with this man by her side. Another lover would never content her and it would not be right to take another after this magnificent-muscled man of paradise had had her.

"You are hard and beautiful, Raine."

"My beautiful one." He laughed with victory. "Soft as a tight cylinder lined with velvet."

When Raine felt himself sliding deeply into her, then meeting that barrier, he had felt an instant of regret, afraid he would hurt her. But now he was pleasing her. Her sheath was so tight and wonderful, moist and readily flexible.

When Raine pumped his seed into her, Autumn was finding her own stunning release at the same time.

"You are crying," Raine murmured after they had finished and lay side by side in the hay.

"Tears of love, my handsome, magnificent knight."

"Autumn; Maiden, I love you." He heard nothing but her sniffles. "Well, why so silent? Do you believe me?"

"Of course. Why shouldn't I? You've just made me the happiest woman in the world." She leaned over and hugged him tightly. "You are remarkable, Raine. Now, one thing I request."

"What is that?" He stroked her cheek.

"You must not ever call me Maiden."

"Why—" Then he laughed as he understood. "Never again!"

* * *

In the middle of the night Raine and Autumn were snuggled close in the big fuzzy bed inside the cozy cottage. Autumn sneezed for the tenth time, for the bed coverings were very old, dusty, torn, and some were ragged furs and pelts.

It was strange, but she felt as if another couple had occupied this abandoned cottage not too long ago. The faint scent of lavender and roses still clung to the musty old bed things.

"I am weary of playing the huntress, Raine. This quest has left me feeling helpless, hopeless, and drained. I don't speak of our love together but my painful search to find my sister, that is the pursuit I mean. This exploration has brought us together, true, and yet I feel lost and hurt and wondering if my sister will ever be with me again."

"I understand," he said.

"Will you take me home?"

He looked at the tears sliding down her cheeks.

"Of course. To Sutherland?"

"I have no other home."

"Autumn." He caught two tears plunging down her cheeks.

"Yes?"

"Tomorrow I will bring you somewhere to show you something."

"I know: the jewel."

"How did you—?"

"You told me you would show me when you are ready. I told you after you made love to me you would be ready. And you are."

"You must wait until the morrow for me to show you," Raine murmured, stroking her hip.

Show her. Did that mean hand it over into her possession? Come tomorrow she would know.

And would she also learn why people like the duchess were trying to dispose of her? Or—had she been? And why was there a mysterious Black Knight involved? Cousins. What was the great big secret? And why couldn't she be let in on it?

How many more relatives were there? And: Is Rowena's last name Guardian also?

She turned to put some of these questions to the intriguing self-possessed man beside her, not really thinking she'd get many answers, and found him sound asleep.

Eighteen

"Gone like summer smoke."

"What do you mean?" Autumn asked, looking around the grounds of the old castle as they dismounted.

He was looking up at the birds that had nested there, but had now flown away. She thought he meant something else.

"Oh, I see. There are no people here anymore. Everyone is gone. It is quite silent and ghostly. I wish to see the gardens."

"Why?" He looked at her suspiciously.

"One can always tell how long the occupants have been away by looking at the state of the garden. Especially the kitchen garden. I want to see that one."

Just like a woman, he thought, looking where the birds had nested, and chuckled.

He came up behind her later as she was bending over a sadly neglected plot of earth. Weeds stuck up all over with stickers and bits of old dead vegetables and marigolds. She cracked open a pea and shook her head at the tiny shriveled corpses in the pod.

"No food here," she said and walked away. "No one

has been here in—What is that?" She went to the front of the castle courtyard. "Look. Footprints. You can see them because it has rained recently. A woman has been here." She whirled to face Raine. "I believe someone is home."

Raine stared up at the beautiful old castle. "Someone is here, Autumn."

"Why have you brought me here, Raine? Who is here? You said everyone is gone. What did you mean?"

He laughed, throwing back his head. "The birds, Autumn, the birds have flown."

"Stop fooling me, Raine."

"I am not," he said, trying to look at her seriously.

"Is my jewel hidden inside? Where?" she demanded. "Why do I have to search for it? You told me you would bring me to it."

"I have. Look at the beautiful old castle, Autumn."

"Yes, yes. I want to see the jewel, hold it in my hands."

"That will be possible." He twisted his head with a wink. "I think it will, if you are willing."

"Why do you wink at me? Are you flirting?" Autumn shouted at his head. "Not now, Raine. I want to hold my family heirloom in my hand"—she put out her palm for him to see—"right here."

He sat down and laughed and laughed until Autumn, looking down at him, thought he might become sick.

"Why are you sitting in the middle of the court-yard?"

"Because"—he laughed—"I couldn't find any place else to sit." He shook his dark head. "I had to sit down or else split my sides."

"Get up," she ordered, going in front of him.

Raine shot to his feet and walked slowly to the door.

She went quickly after him, fuming. "You are playing your games with me again, Raine. What is this great mystery you hide from me?"

Nonchalantly, he said, "You will see, Autumn."

She frowned darkly. Men, she thought. Conceited, bossy men.

He turned leaning his back against the huge door, folding his arms across his chest and doing the same with his legs, one over the other. He looked so relaxed, she was tempted to kick him in the shins.

She moved closer to him slyly pressing her sweetly curved body against him. Her eyes said Please!—and if you do not . . . with a warning . . . At that moment the door was flung wide by a small woman with slanted eyes and graying hair.

It happened so suddenly that Raine tumbled backward inside the room, onto the floor, pulling Autumn along right on top of him. "Raine!"

She screeched with surprise and wondered at this new diversion; if not for the woman staring down at them it would have been a most enjoyable moment.

"Welcome, master," a tiny Asian woman said, nodding her head with a lift of one eyebrow at Autumn.

Autumn blinked. Master? Did she say that, or something else sounding like it? No, she was sure the woman had said the word denoting authority.

Raine quickly rolled her to one side as he looked up at the curious woman and cleared his throat. "This is, er, Autumn. Ah, Autumn, this is—ah, hell—"

Raine jumped to his feet lifting Autumn and setting her on her feet, unceremoniously. The woman with the dark eyes looked at the embarrassed redhead and smiled.

Autumn relaxed, smiling back curiously. Who *is* this woman?

Autumn stared around at the beautiful interior of the castle, noting that everything was so clean, lovely, and in its place. The great hall stretched before her eyes and nothing had prepared her for what she saw inside after what she'd witnessed outside. The exterior was old and beautiful but inside was tidy and nothing neglected, not a dust speck visible on table or bench or tapestry.

Two great dogs stood at attention waiting for Raine to come up and scratch their ears; they were beautiful greyhounds. They came to Autumn trustingly, letting her do the same as Raine had done to them.

With dignity the older woman slowly closed the door, so huge and tall Autumn wondered how the dainty female could even close it.

Raine tried again. "This is my housekeeper Mai-Lee."

"Hello, Autumn. You are indeed lovely," said Mai-Lee with a gentle smile. "Come, come in, you are welcome."

Mai-Lee scurried off to the kitchen. Very bewildered by this time, Autumn watched the tiny woman walk away with even tinier steps; her clothes were most unusual. She had only seen one other Oriental woman while visitors to Sutherland had come with royal banners and servants.

"Come," Raine said. "We have to talk."

"I cannot wait," Autumn said, eager for an explanation by this time.

"Soon," he whispered. "Follow me."

Raine escorted Autumn into a smaller hall, sat her at a table and Autumn waited on pins while Mai-Lee made quite a ceremony bringing tea and tiny cakes.

"Talk," Autumn said, munching and sipping and waiting impatiently.

"How are the cakes?" he asked, fiddling with one and ignoring the tea.

"Delicious." She glared at him, wanting him to begin.

"I don't know quite how to start," Raine began. "Years ago I met a woman and—"

"How many years?" Autumn put down the rice cake, fuming again.

"Put your jealously aside, Autumn."

"Talk," Autumn pressed.

"Six or seven years ago it was. She was truly the love of my life."

"What was her name?"

"That doesn't matter," Raine said, sipping tea and grimacing; he'd rather have had something stronger, but he knew Mai-Lee.

"And now?" She eyed him, almost jumping with curiosity.

He looked at her rather sharply. "After an illness, the woman died."

"The love of your life?" Autumn asked with a stiffening of her shoulders.

He went on, "She left me alone—I thought."

"You *thought?*" Autumn shrugged. "Don't you know if she—go on. You are not making much sense."

"I had been with King Henry. Upon returning from a battle in France it saddened my heart to find her dead and be without her; then I found a secret jewel that brightened my life immensely—"

255

"My jewel? Where is it? I must see it."

"Come with me."

As he approached a door at the end of the great hall he turned to her and said, "A riddle, I might add?"

"A riddle?" she asked. *"Now?"*

"A jewel within a jewel."

As he opened the door Autumn could see the flickering flames from a great hearth on a white wall and a shadow that played within that light. He moved to one side, opening the door fully.

It was then that Autumn saw a tiny figure wearing miniature garments like Mai-Lee's and seated on bright pillows in front of the fireplace.

As she studied the tiny figure, Autumn saw a head of curly blond hair as the child turned. Hazel eyes stared up at Autumn and the cherub's face beamed with a rosy smile when she took in the man next to her.

"Papa—you're home!"

She dropped the toy she'd been playing with and jumped into Raine's arms as he approached her. He gathered the little girl into his arms and held her close. The child eyed the woman over her father's wide shoulders with wondering eyes that did not blink.

"Who is she?"

Autumn was so stunned she could not speak. The little girl looked at Autumn and exclaimed, "You are pretty. Who are you?" she asked Autumn directly in an angelic voice.

Her father set her down and held her hand and she heard him say, "This is going to be your new mother, Song."

Autumn's eyes grew wide and then softened as she looked at the child and took her other soft as velvet hand. "What's your name?" she asked, looking up at the red-haired woman.

Autumn said as gently as she could, "I am Autumn."

The six-year-old giggled happily. "I like Autumn. It's a pretty name, like you are."

Autumn bent on one knee before the child and she pulled away from her father's hand to wrap her arms around Autumn's neck. The affection the child displayed caused Autumn to choke up, tears welling in her eyes.

"My name is Song."

"Where did you get such a lovely name?" Autumn asked, touching a blond curl.

"From Mai-Lee," said the singsong voice.

Raine put in, "Song is all my bride left me. She is my joy. Mai-Lee was her mother's nanny and has taken care of Song since her birth."

Just then Mai-Lee entered and Song ran to her. "Mai-Lee, Mai-Lee! This is going to be my new mother!"

Mai-Lee looked surprised and a little suspicious as she unwrapped Song's arms from around her neck. But she said nothing.

Autumn took Raine's hand and pulled him to one side of the fireplace. "We must talk and soon." She smiled up at him and one of the tears that was welling in her eyes rolled down her cheek. "I—I don't understand."

Mai-Lee read Autumn's misty mood and led Song from the room. And Song waved at Autumn and Raine over her shoulder.

"Bye. See you later."

"Yes . . . Song," Autumn said.

Autumn stared up at Raine and reached up to kiss

him softly on his cheek. "She truly is a jewel. She will someday perhaps be my jewel also. For now, however, I must have my family heirloom to reclaim my . . . life."

Raine looked at her. "Follow me."

They walked back into the great hall and Autumn was surprised to see Song was seated at the long table. "We should talk," Autumn said.

Raine turned to Autumn. "Remember the riddle." He looked back at Song.

Autumn eyed the child with profound curiosity. As she did, she noticed the sparkle from the pendant that hung from Song's neck. Her eyes widened as she recognized and suddenly remembered the mauve-white diamond.

Autumn realized the riddle: *A jewel within a jewel.*

She tossed her arms around Raine's neck and kissed him over and over. He locked his arms around her back and whirled as if dancing.

Song came off the bench and screeched in delight, jumping and dancing with them until Mai-Lee, too, giggled with glee.

They had a party that night, just the four of them. Autumn had never eaten such delicacies as Mai-Lee prepared for them and Song sang for them in a voice the angels would envy.

Later that night as Autumn watched Raine tuck Song into bed, she heard Song end her prayers, "And God bless my new mother."

Autumn cried happily as Raine looked on with mist in his eyes.

* * *

258

As Autumn and Raine sat before the fire in the lovely bedchamber, he held up the pendant; it flashed and sparkled catching light from the fireplace. He then placed it in her palm.

"The reason I have not given the jewel to you is simple: with it went a death sentence. To own it or be seen with it meant your life."

Aghast, Autumn looked up at him. "What do you mean? You had the child wearing it. Was not Song's life in danger?"

"No one has knowledge of my daughter but I and Mai-Lee. And now you know. Therefore the pendant must remain with Song."

"True," she conceded. "But who guards Song and Mai-Lee from danger?"

He looked at her and whispered, "Who do you think?"

"I—I truly have no idea."

"One you would not suspect."

She gasped. "Not the duchess."

"Never," he said vehemently. "Not that one."

"Then who?"

He thought for a moment, playing with a strand of red hair. "That must remain a secret. For your safety and everyone involved."

"When and how will I claim my holdings then?"

"Do they even exist, my love?" He kissed her cheek. "Your castle, if you still own one, might have been confiscated—or burned to the ground. But we must wait, Autumn. There are those who must perish first."

She snuggled closer. "Secrets."

"Umm, yes." She looked at the slit windows allowing

in bars of moonlight that fell across the bed, a simple bedside table and plain wood chairs.

Autumn snuggled in the rugs and skins that were spread about the floor. "What did you mean when we came here: Gone like summer smoke?"

He laughed. "Who would believe anyone lived here but nesting birds?"

"Oh—I see."

"Do you?"

"Of course. You tricked me again. Why are you so secretive, Raine?"

"As I've told you: It's for your own good."

"Raine, let the fire go out. It is warm enough in here." She pressed against him intimately.

"I agree." He pressed right back, more boldly.

He kissed her long and lingeringly, caressing her breasts, her thighs, and back to her mouth again; and she held nothing back. After a time of soul-deep kissing and caressing, he entered her and they made passionate love.

Once, twice, and long into the night they held each other.

Falling asleep in the wee morning hours, Autumn asked, "Will we marry?"

"In time."

Golden shafts of moonlight slanted through the trees. In Song's bedchamber Mai-Lee hovered over the child, watching until she was certain Song would not awaken.

In the dark of the moon, Mai-Lee's face was almost beautiful, like the smooth, carved image of some ancient goddess and her gray hair appeared almost black.

At length she slipped out, her tiny steps taking her below to a silent figure, half hidden in the shadows.

She smiled. "I like her, Sir Knight. She knows her mind and seems to go her own way, which is never easy for a woman."

"He is in love with her?" the knight asked.

Details swelled in the shadows and Mai-Lee could see his dark face.

"He is." Mai-Lee held her tongue, her face expressionless.

"I suspect what you wish to know," said the knight. "They are my cousins, and I know both well. Yet, because the duchess is a coward without her men, her actions can never support her thoughts, so she plots and conspires ceaselessly but never strikes."

Mai-Lee laughed mirthlessly. "One day. Rowena is not the coward you believe. She hates Autumn. We must prepare. Your men hide in the shadows, but are they enough?"

"More than enough. Do not worry, Mai-Lee. Does Raine love this woman as much as he loved Song's mother?" he asked.

Mai-Lee smiled again and said, "More. He loved Song's mother and Rowena. This woman is his life, as is Song. Autumn is very remarkable."

"I am convinced."

She squeezed the knight's hand. "Be careful. Go with God."

Deep in the night, Autumn stirred, cried out and came awake.

Raine was beside her at once.

"What is it?" he asked, pulling her into his arms.

"Where did you go?" she asked with a sniff against his shoulder. "I was frightened."

"I was here, only at the window. I heard a sound, but it was only a night bird."

"My dream," she murmured. "It was so strange. Winter was not Winter, but someone else."

"That *is* strange," he said, pulling her tighter against him. "Look, it is morning. The birds begin to sing."

"She was very cold. Someone had died in the dream."

He laughed shortly. "With a name like Winter I would be cold, too."

"You jest." She sat up, pulling away from him. "What if it was *Winter* who died in my dream?"

"Only a dream, my love. Winter is alive. This you must believe. You will see her again someday. And perhaps—"

"What?" She stared up at him. "You know something you are not telling me."

He nodded. "I know you have other sisters. Very quaint."

She pounded lightly on his chest. "What are you saying? You know about the others?" She looked up at him. "You do, damn you, you always knew."

"About Spring and Summer?"

"You know."

"But that does not make me love you less for your secrecy, my dear Autumn. Remember I, too, have my secrets."

"How many more, Raine?"

"Not too many."

262

Nineteen

"Do you really want to go and hide yourself in some dull dreary nunnery again?"

Gwen watched Tyrian's mouth, loving the sounds of the words that came out of it. His voice was rich, deep, smooth, and she could feel its timbre all the way to her dainty feet.

The shake of her head was energetic.

Tyrian shot up from the log they had been sharing. "Then why was I taking you there?"

Shrugging, she cast her eyes downward, then looked back up at him with a helpless expression in her huge eyes. What did he think? Where else was she supposed to go? She had no other home but the abbeys.

"Ah. I understand. You have nowhere else to go." He saw her smile. "Thorolf was taking you to Kirklees to keep you safe . . . well, that is something I do not understand. Why would men want to capture you? What for?"

She dropped her jaw as he turned away. Perhaps he had not meant that as cruelly as it had sounded? What would men want with her?

Tyrian paced back and forth across the campfire. Gwen followed him with her eyes and was startled when, suddenly he whirled and planted himself right before her. She stared up at him unblinkingly.

How Gwen wished she could speak to this man!

"Would you like to come with me? I know someone who just might like to meet you." He didn't want to frighten her. "This person I would like to bring you to . . . her name's Autumn. Think of it as an invitation, uh, I mean a suggestion. I would protect you with my life, *Gwen-with-no-last-name*."

Gwen looked up; her heart pounded with the idea of an adventure and the more she thought about it, the more she liked not having to return to one of the stuffy abbeys with their even more gloomy nunneries out back.

Who would know? Who would even care? Surely not the nuns, they were too busy with prayers and bird-watching and digging in the gardens, making their white habits all brown with dirt. And then there had been the endless laundry that had to be done. Everything had to be so clean.

There was one question she must consider and ask herself. She was prepared to do that and dwell on his proposition a bit when Tyrian brought it up so swiftly on the heels of her thought that she was startled into gaping up at him.

"Can you trust me?"

Gwen appeared so surprised that Tyrian was almost sorry he'd asked her that.

She nodded, but slowly.

Now his voice hardened. "You must trust me with

your life now, Gwen. If you go with me you must know that I will never hurt you. Can you do that?"

A question again. As if to a female he was not certain was woman or child.

She took such a long time studying him and mulling that over that Tyrian was afraid her answer would be a flat *No*. She walked about.

Time passed.

Finally she turned to him.

She nodded, this time vigorously.

"I am glad you deeply thought this over. It is a wise move. If you had trusted me at once, without thought, *I* would have *not* trusted you."

Thoughtfully Tyrian walked away, going over to the edge of the woods to fetch the horses, jennet, and cart.

At first he had left Gwen frowning at his words. Now she understood what he had meant, fully. He was a wise, cautious, admirable man. This was good.

He was as careful and smart as she.

Gwen did not go to Kirklees. She had no messages to send anywhere, for no one would miss her, and Thorolf had not a relative in the world. Mother Amanda would believe her little novice had gone to Kirklees and when she did not hear word of her for a time, she would forget, thinking Gwen had decided to stay on there.

Gwen had been close with no one. No feelings of love, not really caring deeply for anyone.

Until now.

Now something was beginning to happen inside her. It happened when she looked at Tyrian's face. She could not even think of his tall, powerful body. But there was something behind the eyes, as if she could see deeply into his soul, and he into hers. She had never experienced such an emotion.

This was a most frightening thing to have happen, she thought as they were readying for bed, she going to bed in the cart, he tucked below it.

That night she could almost hear his breathing and it was a hard time to find sleep knowing he was merely a whisper away.

In the morning, as dawn streaked golden fingers across the sky, they were on their way to a place called Sutherland.

"First," Tyrian began as they were rising this morning, "we will stop in a huge beautiful forest called Sherwood. I have to find out if Raine and Autumn have returned there. The problem is, I believe they might have not and when they discover you are not in Kirk—"

Tyrian blinked at what he'd just said and Gwen watched him, thinking he was saying something he was not himself sure about.

Gwen shrugged, tapped her head, and spread her hands to him, wiggling her fingers. Then she nodded quite forcefully.

Tyrian watched, knowing she was telling him to keep talking. He shook his head, handed her a stick and led her to a mound of dirt between two low rocks.

He asked her, "What do you wish to know?"

She paused so long, holding the stick, trying to decide how to word it, that Tyrian took the time to watch her, to give her features a hungry assessment. His eyes took in every view and facet of her glowing face and figure. He was remembering how she had appeared to him when he had stepped into the merchant's back room and found her asleep there, long silver-blond hair trailing to the floor, the aqua gown tight against her lovely breasts.

She was simply beautiful. Even in her novice's habit. He wondered about her hair. He thought novices had to shear their crowns of vanity.

Then she had not taken vows. Or had she? Now, he thought with a powerful surge of excitement, she might never be.

Still, he found it hard to touch her. She seemed so pure and celestial. White and shining.

A virgin.

"Who searches?" she wrote in the dirt.

Taken with a jolt from his musings, Tyrian gazed into her eyes.

He said nothing.

"What?" she wrote. "Speak."

"It is just that you are so lovely." He smiled and touched her veil. Clearing his throat, pulling his hand away and sitting straighter, he went on to explain. "Autumn and Raine, they are searching for a young woman who was separated from Autumn following the gruesome death of her parents."

Gwen moaned, touching her head lightly as if it ached.

"What is it?"

She motioned for him to go on, quickly, tell her what else and why this might involve her.

"You could be the one Autumn searches for. One cannot tell; not yet. Autumn's sister was named Winter. What is it?" Tyrian bent to watch her write quickly in the dirt.

She printed, "Always I think this."

Excitement pounded through Tyrian's blood. "You think about the name Winter? Or the season winter?"

She motioned with her hands, meaning the season. Then again, she appeared quite interested about the other, the name. That intrigued her.

"How did you come by the name Gwendolyn?"

Gwen shrugged. Again the stick scratched in the dirt. "Mother named me. Perhaps—"

"You aren't sure." He watched her nod. "Mother? You mean Amanda Mirande?"

Eyes, head, hands, all said "yes."

"The holy mother."

"Yes" again.

"Dear God!" Suddenly Tyrian shot to his feet. "It's Drogo's men!"

Grinding her feet in the dirt, Gwen shot around the rocky outcropping, trying to hide, to keep them from spying her white habit.

"Gwen," he whispered. "Be still. They will see you."

Crouching down beside her, Tyrian wrapped an arm about her waist and pulled her with him, making her hurry along beside him as they raced to the horses and cart.

"There's too many of them," Tyrian hissed. "I can't fight them all. We've got to make a run for it. Take the cart, Gwen, and hurry. Get in!"

Tyrian made a running leap onto his war-horse. He leaned down, whipped the cart horse and jennet into action, and when the cart was rolling, he spurred his own mount to a greater speed.

Horse and jennet bolted forward. As they raced down the road with the band of outlaws in pursuit, Gwen snapped the reins to make the pair go faster. They responded, but Gwen felt something was terribly wrong.

There was a repeated *clunk, thump, clunk, thump.*

Gwen raised her arm in alarm as Tyrian glanced across his shoulder and in a downward sweep, taking in the spinning discs, then her face. He could read fear in her eyes and as he looked back down, he could see the cart begin to wobble in a crazy fashion.

Their pursuers were gaining, the hot breaths of pounding mounts sounding like thunder along with the sound of their hooves.

As she put out her hand Tyrian reached down and, at a full gallop, he snatched her from the cart.

Gwen swung up in back of Tyrian and onto the horse's back, holding tight with arms wrapped round Tyrian's waist.

The cart cartwheeled as the long-toothed wheel came off and smashed to pieces, strewing Gwen's and Thorolf's belongings all over the ground. Gwen looked back, as did Tyrian momentarily, but they kept riding fast and furiously.

"They still gain!" he shouted.

He spurred his mount on even faster as the powerful animal pulled farther away from the beasts that gave hot pursuit.

Her struggle not to cry nearly tore him asunder. If they got to her, he didn't know what he would do without her, knowing they would tear her apart. He would never forgive himself.

Tyrian swung his mount into a blind area of trees; pulling his mount to a sudden stop, he swung Gwen to the ground and with a single motion dismounted himself, grabbing the muzzle of the horse to silence him.

The band of pursuers passed them by and rode on, leaving them safely in their hiding place. With a deep sigh of relief, he turned to Gwen; and with a slight smile as he looked her up and down, said:

"Excuse the levity, Gwen, but you're going to have to drop this habit."

Twenty

In the twilight and mist, they rode back to the cart to pick up some belongings. Some of the cart driver's clothes were strewn all over; there was a blouse, britches, vest. The wind had picked up as Tyrian turned the horse loose and then faced Gwen.

"We will go where you can have some privacy to change into different clothes."

She nodded.

He took a blanket to throw over the back of the horse, then cut the traces shorter for reins so that she could ride the jennet. She then followed him into the woods, dismounted, and smiled at Tyrian as he helped her down but she did not notice that he was looking at her with great longing. She was too busy wondering what she would wear and how he would look at her once she had changed out of the habit.

"I'll be in the clearing," he said, then left her alone to change.

In the refuge of the trees, Gwen pulled the wimple and veil from her hair, shook the blond coils free like a fall of water, down over her shoulders and back, over

271

the muted earth colors of her simple cloak, down to her buttocks.

Would he think her hair too long? she worried. She wondered if noblewomen cut their hair to a shorter length.

As she was removing the habit and changing into blousey tunic and baggy pants, she spied some pretty white wildflowers. She could hear the Greenthorne River flowing on the side where it flanked the woods.

She stopped and faced the soothing sound of water.

Wanting to look nice for him, she plucked a few of the flowers and wound them into her unbound hair. All this she fastened with a length of leather cord.

He was sitting on a low rock when she emerged from the stand of trees into the small clearing where dry wood and flat rocks were plentiful. He had a small fire going and was roasting a bit of small game he'd caught.

He stood at once, as if a princess had entered the clearing and surprised him doing something he was not supposed to do. She was not wearing beautiful clothes but she looked enchanting in the wind and firelight.

He could only stare at her, at the fall of the longest silver-blond hair he'd ever seen, the slender girlish body the wind revealed and the soft stuff of the blouse blowing in a taut stretch across her small, high breasts. Rose lips, blue eyes. She brushed restively at a loose strand of hair, only setting more free from the fat coils of silk and wildflowers. His tongue felt all tied up inside of his mouth.

Tyrian felt the pulse begin to beat at his temple.

She could not speak. And he could not. He knew how she must feel, not being able to talk and express her feelings, wants, and desires.

At this moment Tyrian wanted to tell her he was falling in love, but the words would not come. Amazement touched him with a tingling hand as he realized this could be truth; he'd loved the cool and reserved name before seeing the woman. But was she truly Winter and not this Gwendolyn with-no-last-name? There was nothing "chilly" about this woman, as far as he could comprehend so far.

She smiled and the world stood still for Tyrian.

He cleared his throat and sounded as if he'd choked on something.

She wanted to ask what ailed him but he turned away, bent down and poked at the fire.

Gwen walked slowly to the next rock and sat down, feeling very foolish in baggy clothes. The blouse reached to her wrists, the pants she had tied at the waist with a bit of cord felt way too big. But her hair was loose and she felt quite wonderful without the wimple and veil.

Gwen looked around with a tiny sigh, knowing she had not experienced this certain brand of freedom in a long while. She knew this was a man she could trust with her life.

Over a spit Tyrian roasted a rabbit that he'd snared and now the hunk of meat was done, the skin a golden crisp and the inside juicy and delicious.

"Hungry?" was all he was able to get out.

She felt him staring at her and looked up, feeling quite shy as she nodded once.

The woods and clearing were alive with bird song and the busy chatterings of creatures coming out to hunt in the wild twilight. Tyrian fetched a skin of wine Thorolf had kept in the cart and as he passed it to her, she accepted the drink and took a hefty swig, feeling the fiery drink burn her throat and warm her stomach. But it was a nice feeling and she felt all aglow as he watched her eat some of the rabbit he had roasted.

She nodded as she ate, indicating that it was very tasty.

He ate very little, passing the choicest chunks of delicious roasted meat to her, giving her more wine to drink. She was wonderfully dizzy by the time they finished the meal and had shared the skin of wine.

"Here. You might want this . . ." His voice fell apart.

She reached out with a touch as soft as a Gypsy moth.

He gave her the last of the drink.

Tyrian got up from the rock and she watched the play of muscles beneath his clothes as he stood to stretch, facing the Greenthorne River.

They both listened to sounds as night fell. Birds in the trees, the shifting shadows, a silver slice of moon in the starry heavens while the sky was just changing to evening blue. All of nature seemed to make some music and sound.

The waxing moon with its deeper hue of ancient yellow helped lighten the setting and illuminate their faces. She looked at him and he looked at her.

In the whisper of the trees and river, he said, "Close your eyes."

She did. Relaxation began to steal over her and she felt herself floating.

And the next thing she knew his lips were on her mouth.

River and wind and forest ceased to exist. For a few moments the moon struggled to pierce the darkness.

Gwen's face was red and hot; she was grateful for the cool dark.

He was so close. His huge, solid virile body and his warm, exhaustless strength and the scent of him filled her senses until she truly was intoxicated with them.

She swayed toward him.

A door opened in her mind and closed again silently. A kaleidoscope of past images had floated in and out; now they were gone.

Gwen could not describe what had just happened to her, the emotions, the sensations, the kiss, and if she had to think of words, she would say "wildly incomprehensible."

At last he murmured, "We have to sleep now."

"Yes," her eyes whispered.

Once more she lifted her face to his. He tightened his fingers around her wrist and brought her palm to his cheek. He pressed her hand against the stubble of his beard as he dipped his head, but did nothing more than gaze at her.

His hair feels like silk feathers, she thought.

It was a night of firelight and wind; Gwen knew that in the short space of time she had come to know Tyrian, he had expanded her senses and her awareness so much in fact that she would never be content in that narrow world of nuns, repetitive prayers, tiny monotonous rooms, long white corridors.

She no longer felt the kind of yearning for the past that had once made her ache to return to the places of her childhood. She no longer had the sense that her life at the nunnery had only been a long, disturbing dream. She could not imagine her life spent in a place such as that, when she didn't feel the wind or the sun or the rain for weeks at a time.

That other world was gone for her like windblown sand; there seemed to be only the here and now. Tomorrow felt carefree.

Inside Tyrian's head he heard the voice of the river and the wind; he was on fire, and not even water or wind could quench the flame of his need.

After the kiss, they did not speak as Tyrian went to unroll the bedding gotten from the wrecked cart. They moved apart as if sleepwalkers going to their separate dreamworlds.

It was the mid of the night and Tyrian couldn't sleep. He listened to the rhythm of Gwen's quiet breathing, opened his eyes to look over at her face in the darkness of moon shadow. Her own eyes were closed and she smiled in deep sleep as she lay beside him.

The rising moon tossed shadows into every crevice and along every taller object, making physical shapes of each tree and rock.

He had almost lost control, Raine thought. He studied her sleeping features, her bright cloud of hair, gleaming where the drop of moonlight caught it. Angel from heaven, he thought. Winter Angel. Unspoiled. What was he going to do with her?

I want to be the only one with you.

All his life before this seemed as distant and gray as a bank of fog now. Nothing seemed to matter but Gwen. His life was filled with her. All the women before her were like pale ghosts, mere colorless stones against this jewel of a woman. He did not know her that well and still there was the feeling that they were meant for each other and nothing in the world was going to change that. He wanted to share all his secrets with her, trust in her, knowing that she would never betray him.

He would never betray her trust.

Tomorrow he would take her to Jasmine Thatch. No Sherwood. Nor no Sutherland. Not yet.

In the morning, just as the sun was beginning to melt the mist from the trees and grasses, a breakfast of fish was eaten with enjoyment but there could be no casual verbal interchange. Gwen carried the scraps of leftovers to the edge of the river to allow the flow to take them away naturally bit by bit. What did not get eaten by wild animals and fishes would float away or decompose.

She stood there for a moment in silence, thanking God for this beautiful golden day, for all God's creatures—and Tyrian.

Summer was in full force.

Gwen rode the jennet; Tyrian his war-horse. Belongings from the cart rode heavily on the animals' backs and Tyrian did not stop as he cast some of the items off; he worked as he rode. Gwen smiled as the baggy pieces of clothing and various items went flying.

The land rose and fell in soft feminine curves; innumerable pines had concealed the ground with their dead needles. They reached Jasmine Thatch by nightfall. They walked the horses up the flower-strewn lane to the tune of bird song. Daffodils were already giving way to summer blooms of red, blue, white, orange, yellow. Daisies with their yellow discs and white rays seemed to welcome the tired travelers.

Gwen tore her eyes from the pretty starflowers and looked over at Tyrian with a puzzled expression.

"I used to come stay here in the summer as a child," he said with a laugh.

That is all? He is not going to tell me more? Why did he come here, and who lives here now? Where were they? Gwen was even more puzzled as they neared the enchanting place.

Trailing purple blooms, tiny and delicate, framed the windows, and crept along the eaves of the overhanging thatch, up the slender pillar. A stone chimney was set at the top of the thatched and tiered roof. The entrance was a tiny arched door and as they entered Tyrian had to stoop before he could get inside and stand straight once again.

Inside the small L-shaped cottage, Gwen looked around. Everything was tiny, even the narrow ladder going up into the loft room upstairs. Square windows had real glass in them.

She wanted to ask who lived here. Turning, she faced Tyrian squarely, catching his eye as she shrugged her confusion.

"Dwarfs."

She looked around again; where were they?

"It seems they have not been here in years," he told her. He looked almost sad as he bent and picked up some funny shirts with long sleeves, then a pair of funny shoes with pointed toes. He heard her giggle.

They both went still.

Gwen's eyes flew open wide at the sound she had made.

"That is interesting," Tyrian said. "Can you make more sounds?" He looked at her narrowly. "Perhaps you really are a nun and have taken the vow of silence?"

"No" said the shake of her head.

He was beginning to wonder about this Gwen. She had made sound before, at the camp when Drogo's men had slain her old friend.

"Nuns do not lie?" Tyrian asked and again saw the shake of her head. "I'm truly sorry if I have offended you. The shock of seeing Thorolf killed like that might have started you on the road to recovering your voice. Do you think this is so, Gwen?"

She thought this over for a moment. How many more shocks would she have to receive before she had fully recovered her voice? What would it be like to converse with this man and release more than a mere giggle? Perhaps he would find her quite shallow, since he had lived in the world, no doubt with pretty women at his side, at court and abroad, and she had lived a silent, cloistered life. At least for the part of her life she *could* remember.

"What?" her eyes asked him. Why was he staring at her as he was? What could he be thinking?

"I wish you could talk," he said, motioning for her to sit at the small bench. "Then I could tell you about myself and you could—"

She had hung her head.

"Gwen." He moved closer, going down on one knee beside her. "What is it? Are you sad because you can't tell me and most of all because you can't remember what happened in your life before the nunnery?"

279

She nodded vigorously.

"I want to help you. I've already told you this. In the morning we will be on our way to Sutherland. I wanted to stop here so that you can rest. We might even stay a few days. I will tell you what to expect before we reach the forest. For now, I will get us something to eat and perhaps there is something to drink around here."

While he was doing that, Gwen walked around inside the house. She could hear him outside caring for the horses and when she peeped out the window she could see him removing food from the packs that had been in the cart.

She began to clean up the place. Finding a tiny besom, she swept the floor and he stopped in the doorway to watch her. Then he went back to what he had been doing.

As she worked to make the cottage livable for the time they would spend here, she began to wonder what it would be like to live here permanently in this cozy dwelling.

With him.

She closed her eyes to listen to the sounds of nature and the thick branches swaying softly against the thatch, brushing, scratching. Then all was still as the wind settled down and the clouds left the sky, leaving the day sunny and bright green all around.

Gwen stopped her tasks to again wonder about Tyrian. Who was he? He never talked about himself as most men were wont to do. He was secretive. Had he lived a dangerous life as a knight? King Henry's knight? She had seen the frost-colored blade at his side. He wore chain mail beneath his robe at times when he sensed danger. Why had he been disguised as a friar? He had told her very little, only saying that he had friends by the names of Raine and Autumn.

Who was this Autumn? Why was she searching for a woman named Winter? Sisters, is that what he had said?

He had slipped. Did he believe she was this sister Autumn was looking for?

Could she be?

Winter. Were they twins? Had Autumn been born only minutes, or seconds, before Winter as in the seasons? Strange names. Were there any other sisters or brothers? She had no answer.

After Gwen had shaken the bed-things out, taking them into the mellow sunshine for a bit, she laid them back on the beds, two up in the loft, one downstairs.

Now she stood studying the various bottles on the shelves with curiosity. She picked one up and as a ray of sunshine entered, she saw the green tint of the bottle in the thick glass. She shook it. Empty.

"Wondering what the bottle contained?"

She spun around, almost dropping the bottle as Tyrian came up behind her. She indicated that "yes," she was curious.

"Frida was an herbalist. She made potions to heal the sick. This is interesting."

She watched as he picked up another stoppered bottle and turned it in his hands, watching as sunlight danced round its circumference and sent quiet forest hues into the room.

"Autumn works with herbs. She planted a garden in the forest and it was finished by the time she left with

Raine Guardian. I was intrigued by her, as were the forest folks."

She looked up at him with questioning eyes.

"I believe my cousin was falling in love with her. I can see why, she is most charming, her looks breathtaking. She has red hair," he said, picking up a strand of Gwen's blond locks to study it, seeing the way the sun played in the glorious coils. "I don't see how she could be—"

My sister? Gwen looked up at him.

There was no stick and no dirt for her. She could not answer.

What do you hide? she thought. Is she my sister or not? Perhaps he did not know?

She held her breath as she turned to stare out the tiny window.

He was so close.

His hands closed around her waist and the breath left her body in surprise. A thrill of yearning coursed through her. There was an unfamiliar tightness deep inside her.

He mistook it for fear or revulsion.

His eyes turned to ice, very cold and hard. "I will not touch you again."

He walked away then.

Gwen looked out the window at the sun dropping lower. Her eyes misted over. The body she had thought she knew quite well had turned into something quite different. Something had happened. Something had begun. She was filled with a sense of dangerous longings. She could not bear it if he never touched her again.

* * *

They ate in silence, went to bed early, and arose with the first twinklings of daylight.

"Gwen, I believe we have company."

She looked at him with a question in her eyes; she had not heard what he had.

From somewhere outside came the jingling of harnesses and the disturbing creak of leather and the clank of steel as they went to the door to see ten or twelve horses gathered there.

And a band of fierce knights surrounding the thatched cottage!

Twenty-one

Tyrian pushed Gwen behind him so the knights could not see her. One of them with a voice full of authority, asked, "What are you hiding?"

Howell Armstrong, one of the Sutherland knights, called for him to bring the woman out. "Do so now, or lose your head!"

Tyrian leaned toward the familiar voice, saying, "Howell? Is that you?"

"Tyrian?" Howell said, flipping open his helm exposing his face. "It is you, cousin. What are *you* doing here?"

Howell said, "I come for the Baroness Sutherland, we are in search of Autumn Meaux. Have you seen her?"

"Of course," Tyrian said. "But she is not here with us. Come out here, Gwen, so the Sutherland knights can see you."

Gwen did as she was told, demurely stepping out into the early-morning light. She just looked at everyone, saying nothing, not even a question or a whisper to the man beside her.

"What is wrong with her?" asked Howell. "Why won't she speak?"

"Howell," Tyrian began, touching Gwen's arm, "I'd like to have a word with you, if you don't mind."

Howell chuckled and the other knights joined him. "It appears as if you'd rather have a word with the little lady in private." Then Howell noticed the charming creature's clothes. "My God, what is she wearing?"

"Howell," Tyrian said, gritting his teeth. "I said I would have a word with you."

Howell came down off his mighty destrier and another darker, larger knight who had dismounted at a word, held the destrier while Howell walked off to the side of the cottage to speak with Tyrian.

With dark, narrowed eyes, De'Beau watched the head knight go with the big golden man to a spot where they would not be overheard.

The knights were making ribald comments as Gwen stood there wondering what to do. She realized they were making fun of the clothes she wore, whispering and nodding toward her manly garb.

Gwen gritted her teeth. If I were a noblewoman standing here they would not treat me with a lack of respect. They must also think I am deaf, or merely stupid, standing here without saying a word.

Oh God, I wish I could speak.

Tears almost came to Gwen's eyes. I am not normal, she thought casting her face aside. I will never be normal and once Tyrian takes me to this castle to meet the young woman named Autumn, I will be the laughingstock of the village. He will not look at me then.

She had come to a decision in a very few moments. The bold visaged knight was becoming neglectful of his job. The destrier danced sideways and pulled at the bit; the man kept relaxing his hold.

Seeing her chance, Gwen walked boldly through the group of knights that had dismounted and were just hanging around, making jokes about the tiny cottage, Gwen's clothes, and even the length of her great mass of hair.

"The hair looks too heavy for her neck," one said with a coarse laugh.

"Maybe her neck will break," said a dark-haired knight.

The knights, watching her come toward them, turned still as stone as she approached. They were not talking about her now. She looked quite determined about what she was doing.

A few of the older knights—those who had not been as cruel with their comments—smiled among themselves. The young knight with the big mouth was going to get it, they thought. No doubt she was going to slap the tall, dark-haired De'Beau.

When Gwen was close to the "big mouth" she stopped suddenly, looked him straight in those blackest of eyes without so much as a tiny smile of greeting, then she began to walk around him.

Tyrian and his cousin were discussing something with animation, so engrossed in their conversation, which, Gwen thought, with the big laughs she was hearing, was no doubt about her, too.

The knights were tense, waiting for something to happen, as the lovely little blonde kept walking circles around young De'Beau. De'Beau was known to be a troublemaker, a cruel lover, and now he was going to get his comeuppance.

Wickedly, lustfully, De'Beau's dark brown eyes followed her and he looked ready to reach out and grab her. He might have, were the circumstances different. Like, were she not with that tall golden man with the huge muscled arms and chest, he would have thought about jumping her and taking her to the ground.

Now the tables were turned, as the knights began to make bets on how this was going to come out. Would the little lady have the nerve to slap De'Beau full in the face? Or would De'Beau—with a sharp brutal remark—send her flying to the cottage in tears?

Most placed their bets with De'Beau. There had never come along a young lass who had put De'Beau down; it was usually the other way around. He was mean and insensitive to any female charm or wiles.

With a glare from his dark eyes, De'Beau looked at the beautiful blonde, prepared to put her in her place. The little bitch was making him dizzy walking circles around him like that. He would like to have this one to add to his female collection. As soon as the tall one named Tyrian tired of this wench in manly garb, he would take her for his own and break that spirit for her.

The knights began to hoot softly, careful not to attract attention their way from Howell and Tyrian. They wanted to see who was going to be the winner in this contest of wills.

De'Beau, tired of the game, let go of the destrier's reins. He wanted to grab the blonde with both hands and set her in a straight line back to the cottage. A hard shove or two will go unrecognized by Howell and Tyrian, he thought, since the curious knights had gathered round by now to get a ringside stance. Yet he must not lose face in this game else the knights would forever make a laughingstock of him.

The ruthless knight was trying to gain the upper hand when Gwen suddenly ran behind him, shoved at him, making him go to hands and knees, then she used his back and the destrier's back for leverage, and jumped aboard the giant horse.

Hoots and hollers followed her as she spurred the mighty mount forward, jumped a huge rock in the way, and thundered out of the cottage yard and down the road.

De'Beau came up from the ground like a raging maniac, unsheathing his sword, believing there would be an attack coming from the woods. Another knight held De'Beau's shoulder to keep him from swinging too wide.

"Hold, De'Beau. 'Tis only the little lady." He tried not to chuckle. "She has Howell's mount."

De'Beau realized something was wrong with her riding away like that. "Prisoner escaped!" he yelled as he ran toward Howell and the tall, golden man.

Tyrian stood gaping as he'd watched Gwen thunder out of the yard and disappear down the road.

Now Tyrian shoved De'Beau aside and ran for his own war-horse. "You idiot. What have you done?" Tyrian hissed in the younger knight's face. "That woman is precious. She may very well be one of Autumn Meaux's lost sisters."

De'Beau fell back with that news. He felt a vague prickle of alarm. He knew of Autumn, the Sutherland's most precious orphan. There were uncountable orphans at Sutherland, but Autumn was almost like a daughter to Elizabeth and Orion. And that is why they had been sent out on this search: To find Autumn Meaux!

And here was her sister, no doubt.

He felt like a fool. But why had she been dressed like that? And what had been wrong with her voice? Why could she not speak? He shoved his sword back in its sheath. What was he worrying over? De'Beau asked himself. He had done nothing. In fact, she had used his back as a platform to mount the great destrier.

He still did not like what she had done. She had used him. He would get back at her. He would discover her name.

"Howell," Tyrian yelled. "Mount up and help me find Gwen. Hurry. We cannot let her get away."

Gwen. De'Beau noted her name.

When De'Beau turned around he saw Howell Armstrong mounting his own war-horse. Beast was special to him; he'd better not come to harm.

Or someone would have to pay. Namely a comely little woman in baggy, men's clothes.

Gwen spurred the huge destrier on. The beast veered from the thick brambles and woods into a broad green field. She didn't know how she could handle him so well. It was as if he had known her forever and had learned her every body command. The same had gone for the big horse belonging to Tyrian; she had known instinctively how to handle him.

Somewhere in her past she had worked with horses. It was exciting to think that maybe she had been a noblewoman herself, had lived in a castle, and owned a stableful of beautiful horseflesh.

Like a princess.

But where was she going? Could she find her way back to Kirklees or to Whitby? Which would be closer? How far away was she from Mother Amanda?

There was too much hurt involved trying to live in Tyrian's world, she could see that. The nuns and novices had never made fun of her; they had accepted her affliction as if it were something sent from God. Back there, everything could go wrong. The man with the dark eyes looked ready to kill her. He seemed jealous about something. Perhaps he hated Tyrian.

Tyrian and the man Howell, however, seemed to know each other very well. Tyrian had walked away, forgetting all about her. She could not expect him to protect her every day of his life from here on out. Yet she could not live in a place where people would not accept her for what she was.

No. She had to get back to what was familiar. She should have known better, that to go with Tyrian was to open herself to hurt. He might have women waiting for him back at this place called Sutherland. And if she was not this Winter, but someone else, there would be another disappointment. For both her and this other woman involved. The one called Autumn.

If she escaped now, before it was too late, she would save herself from dying of a broken heart when Tyrian cast her out later.

This was better, for everyone involved.

Once she was back at the nunnery, Mother Amanda could send those away who would come for her. Even Tyrian. She would be safe. The man's beautiful destrier would be returned to him. Her dull, daily routine would fall easily back into place for her.

Riding at a fast pace for too long would only tire the horse out faster. And she did not wish to harm him. He was so beautiful and he handled like a dream. Although, her arms were becoming tired by now. She had not handled a big horse such as this one in a long time. Only for a short space of time had she handled Tyrian's war-horse. Tyrian had looked at her as if she was something truly amazing.

That was what hurt. If Tyrian did not continue to look at her as if she was the most beautiful thing in the world, and other past loves were to come along, Gwen knew she would be devastated.

After all, nothing like this had ever happened to her. Was this feeling what the poets called love? If not, it was rapidly approaching something very close to it.

Twenty-two

Tyrian and Howell followed Gwen's trail, but signs of her passage vanished at the other side of the open field. Tyrian sat his horse and Howell reined beside him, studying the serious face of his cousin.

"We will keep searching," Howell said. "From what you have told me I believe she will come back this way. At least, let's hope so. I thought Gershwing more loyal than this. He is the most intelligent destrier I've ever owned. I would've thought he'd return with her on his back by now."

"Let's hope he is keeping my Gwen safe and letting her have her way for a time." My Gwen? Tyrian asked himself. When did I start thinking of her as such? She is so very sensitive. I must remember that. Dear God, let us find her safe.

"I would not put it past Gershwing. I swear that horse has a brain that thinks past most men's intelligence."

Howell looked to the woods flanking the other side of the open field. "She must have gone that way. You keep searching and I will go back for my men and meet you here. That is, if this mount of De'Beau's does not throw me first. Beast he calls him. I believe it."

"Howell." Tyrian looked at his cousin achingly. "We must find her."

"I know," Howell said. "If she is who you think, she will be the first of the Seasons we have found. You know Autumn is safe; she is with Raine Guardian."

"Wait," Tyrian said just as Howell would have ridden away to get his men. Howell turned back to him. "The Seasons," he said. "What do you know of them? Can you tell me what happened the day you found Autumn running from Scardon and his men?"

Howell began, "I had just returned to Sutherland and found there was trouble in the village of Herst. When we drew close, having come quietly through the trees, we came onto the wall of Herst. We intended to surprise the pilferers. We waited for what seemed like hours, when actually it was only a matter of strained and tense minutes. We rode then, bursting forth from the trees, jumping thickets and thundering between the wooden gates that had been crashed open earlier by the band of pillagers. This was where we found the boy Geoffrey Johns. His mother lay dead. We took the boy—"

"Get on with the story of Autumn Meaux," Tyrian pressed his cousin, hoping and praying that Gwen would return to this place. Time was spinning away fast. They had to find her.

"Then we came upon Autumn. She must have been only thirteen or fourteen at that time. Her long red hair was tangled, her white face dirty, her skirts torn and soiled. But she had not been ravaged, we were told later. Scardon and his cousin Drogo and their men had killed her parents in the town of Brighton. She and her

293

sisters had traveled to Herst in hopes of escaping the madmen, but Drogo had been there waiting. Autumn had been separated from her sisters. She had no idea what had happened to them, they had always been together, all their life, four girls born at a single birth.

"She had come into the clearing where we awaited Scardon's men. Her red hair was tangled to her waist. She was frightened; she was shivering. We could not take her with us at that time. Orion gave the boy Geoffrey into her keeping as we rode off to deal with Scardon's men. That is it. After the battle, in which we dispatched with many of Scardon's men, we took Autumn and the boy back to Sutherland with us. She has lived there with us until now."

"What about Gwen?" Tyrian asked. Then he realized his possible mistake. "I mean if this Gwen is truly Winter Meaux, then we have found one of the missing Seasons."

Howell's eyes went to the woods. "Found her, yes. But we have lost her again."

"True," Tyrian said. "If she is Winter and not this Gwen-with-no-last-name."

"What a tangle," Howell said as he rode away, eager to fetch his men and return to find Gwen—or Winter—and his beloved Gershwing.

Gwen traveled north slowly, for there was no reason to hurry. From her vantage point atop the green hill she could see no one following.

The weather held sunny and the rain clouds she had spotted in the north were whisked away by the cornflower-blue sky.

Gershwing cropped in the warm meadows while

Gwen gathered wild herbs for her dinner. Birds circled lazily in the clear blue sky.

It was late afternoon when she waded the destrier through the shallow waters of the river and started across the Salisbury plain. The gently rolling country-side was dotted with sheep. Many of the fields were unworked, wild, their hedges broken, their furrows un-plowed and weed-choked.

She had never been in this part of the land before.

Wandering over the land she stumbled upon the grass-covered mounds and barrows of a forgotten peo-ple. Burial grounds, she thought. Here, she felt a new closeness to that race which had once gathered here to worship and bury their dead.

It was somewhat like living at a nunnery. She knew this nothingness and nothing more. She had remembered nothing of her past. Only lately, ever since she had met Tyrian, she had felt-more-than-known something, of fleeting images, of blurred faces that came and went. A young woman with red hair. Another with golden hair. And yet another with long brown shining hair.

Now she was feeling nothing again. She felt bereft without Tyrian.

Gershwing climbed one low, broad hill, larger than the others, and Gwen looked out over the land. Finally, when the sun started to cast longer shadows, she started down from the hill, climbing over the rows of ridges that ran around the slope.

The sky grew dark and filled with stars. Weary be-yond words, Gwen slipped from the great Gershwing and slept, right where she had dismounted.

* * *

Duc Stephan and two of his knights saw the destrier cropping grass. They rode slowly and when Stephan noticed the blond hair and fair face in the moonlit grass, he held up his hand, drawing his men to a halt.

"Silence," he warned. "And let the horse go. It is the young woman I am interested in." He came down off his horse and approached the lovely creature asleep in the grass. "Can this be one of the women the duchess wants? I wonder."

He knelt beside her, noticing the odd garb she was wearing. Gently, he lifted a strand of the silken hair, rubbing it between his fingers. Soft, he thought, beautiful. As glowing as her face.

This might be her, the one they all had been searching for. The novice from the nunnery.

He had captured one of the Seasons, he was sure of it. No other woman was this fair. Except maybe Autumn Meaux.

And her other sisters.

Soon, he thought, all would be his, the land, the Jeraux castle, everything. If he could gather them all before his wicked cousin Rowena got to them first.

One was better than none; *one* must have the jewel. It was a start.

Rowena had lost the one she had thought she had captured. Namely: Autumn.

Only a little light lingered in the west as they topped a rise. Tyrian rode with Howell and the Sutherland knights. They crisscrossed the land, searching for any sign that would lead them to Gwen and the great destrier.

They were nowhere to be found. It was as if they had vanished from the woods and the fields.

Tyrian would not give up. He rode as the others rested. He went long into the night. At last, he fell exhausted from his mount, knowing he had to sleep if he was to resume the search at first morning light.

His dreams were of Gwen and his tears wetted the grass beneath him, where he lay.

Many hours had passed before Tyrian felt someone trying to awaken him. "Ty, we must ride. The men have found her."

"What?" Tyrian's heart pounded.

"Aye; Gwen and Gershwing," Howell said. "And trouble, too. Gwen is not alone. De'Beau says it looks to be Duc Stephan and his knights."

"How many?" Tyrian snapped.

"Only two, has De'Beau reported seeing."

Tyrian was up in a flash, readying his horse and then leaping onto his back. "There might be more, concealed in the wood. We will have to ride with quiet and caution."

Quickly, Tyrian fell in with Howell and the knights and they rode fast until reaching the forest. It was not a big wood. In the time it would take to sit at a light meal and rise, they would be on the other side.

However, there was no time for one bite of meat or bread.

It was dark under the trees, for the branches were laced thickly overhead, not allowing in much of the morning light. The path was narrow, and tall bracken on either side hemmed them in. They walked the horses slowly, single file, hushed by the cool stillness of the trees in the early morning calm.

There was no sound other than the soft clopping of their horses' hoofs on the mossy trail.

Suddenly Gershwing neighed and lashed out with his front hoof at a man who had seized hold of his bridle. Since she had used her ears more than her mouth the past six years, Gwen's hearing was acute. Right before the destrier had made sound, she had detected another much softer sound coming from the mossy trail in the wood alongside their camp.

Gwen looked around. No one else had heard what she had. Perhaps it was only wishful thinking, she told herself.

She had awakened to find herself staring into the angriest face she had ever seen. Even when smiling, Duc Stephan seemed to be frowning and dissatisfied with life in general. When he smiled at her, however, he appeared surprisingly gentle, though she knew he was not a gentle person at all.

She knew him from somewhere, perhaps a bad dream.

Gwen had overhead his men calling him Stephan; another called him Duc. She knew he wasn't *a* duke; that was a different matter altogether. "Duc" was this man's first name.

Stephan? What sort of man had she just been about to . . . relate to *this* man? She had heard the name often enough at the nunnery, and Mother Amanda Mirande mentioning the name of . . . Baron Drogo.

Who had held her prisoner before? This man? Or Baron Drogo and his knights?

Gwen was alerted to something again and looked to see the great destrier being held on either side by the two rugged-looking knights. She had heard one of Howell's men call out the name of the horse that had taken her away from Tyrian on her wild ride to escape.

Gershwing.

She wished she could call out the war stallion's name now and tell the men who were not handling him very gently to let him go. The horse rolled wild eyes toward her and Gwen looked back into them. Go, Gershwing. Go. Be free. Escape. She cried out these words from her mind as she stared into Gershwing's beautiful eyes.

Suddenly, both knights were thrown back as Gershwing reared, front legs slicing the air, back legs dancing, almost leaping. Now Gershwing was free, whirling, flying toward the woods.

A sword flashed in the morning light.

"We could have used that mount," Duc Stephan growled at his men. "Fools. Can you not keep a simple horse from getting away?" He frowned deeply, darkly. "Damn you both."

Gwen pressed a hand over her mouth as she looked at the bloody sword. Gershwing! Oh no!

"I sliced him before he got away, Duc!" one of Stephan's knights boasted.

"You idiot!" cried Stephan. He drew his own sword and ran toward his man, crying out and slicing the air like a maniac.

Rising slowly from the log she'd been resting upon, Gwen stared at the man. Surely he is crazed, she thought. Dear God, I should have gone on to the Kirklees nunnery, for I have never known that outside the holy sanctuary I would run into such lunacy.

Men are quite mad, she thought. Do their souls cry for the blood of others?

Gwen wondered as she watched another bloody scene unfold. Duc Stephan sliced off the knight's arm, grabbed the falling, bloodied sword then ran the knight's own sword through his heart.

With unblinking eyes Gwen watched the man die in seconds. When Stephan turned back to her he was sheathing his own sword. And grinning.

Danger emanated from every pore of this man-beast, she thought as she watched him approach. What was he going to do? she wondered, her heart beating up into her throat.

Stephan pulled her to her feet, clasped her close and kissed her on the mouth. He continued kissing her until she was quite breathless, her head reeling from the sudden attack. His lips were moist but not brutal. Was this what a kiss felt like? She thought not.

She felt nothing. He had just killed a man, sheathed his bloody sword, and come to kiss her, holding her tenderly.

This man is mad, Gwen told herself. Quite mad.

Why couldn't she hear the soft hoofbeats along the mossy trail any longer? Had Gershwing bled to death? Dear God, she prayed it was only a minor wound.

And how long was this lunatic going to kiss her? Was he planning to defile her next?

Where are you, Tyrian? You are the only sanctuary in my life at this time of madness. Come and save me before I die.

Blackness was swirling over her.

She was ready to swoon. Or was she going to perish from this devil's kiss?

Twenty-three

Rowena pressed a hand against her eyes, shutting out her reflection in the mirror. Her head ached abominably. She snatched the tight blond wig from her head and stared at her thinning thatch of black hair.

She chose another wig, this one longer, black, with bangs, in the style of Cleopatra. Yes, she favored this one. Even her lovers never knew which hair was which, she was so clever with the wearing of them, pinning them to her own hair beneath so they'd not come off in the heat of passion.

She had lost the game. Her plan, her future, all were up in smoke, on this one final miscasting of fate. Because of the interfering incompetence of Raine and his men. No. Not his men. Their cousin, the Black Knight. She thought she'd known Russell better than that. Then again, Russell swore he had known nothing of Raine's plan.

Raine: he'd turned against her. If he had known what she was planning he could not have ruined her plans more neatly.

What had Raine gone and done, fallen for that flame-haired tart, Autumn Meaux?

How had Raine learned the Black Knight had taken Autumn Meaux?

Rowena threw down her brush after tearing through her wig. "Has Courtenay also turned against me?!"

She would have to begin again, with a new scheme, and one that would have to be less subtle, less fragile. And yet, potentially more dangerous to her own position.

It would take time for her spies to search out the possibilities. Her mercenaries had already discovered much of what she wanted to know, to go by. In the meantime she could have her revenge on that sweet little nun her cousin Stephan had captured just lately.

She would whisk that piece from him before he knew what hit him. Her mercenaries were good. Apparently not good enough for Autumn Meaux, however. Rowena had sent them to Sutherland, time after time, and they had returned empty-handed. That castle was the hardest one to steal into, she had found.

Her men would find a way. They must, or she would have their heads!

Rowena stood, casting an appreciative eye on her expensive new gown in the mirror. Yes, the Cleopatra wig was the best. She danced about, sliding her hands up and down her voluptuous body, coming to rest on her full breasts.

"I am not called the duchess for nothing," she shouted proudly to her reflection. "I killed the Duke of Chichester, my husband, and after that everyone else I planned to dispatch had become easy pickings."

All but for Autumn Meaux.

Damn him, but Raine had almost assassinated her six years ago.

What had happened? He'd never told her. In fact, Raine had stayed away from her ever since that fateful mishap. He had never made love to her again. Sweet cousin. Bastard.

Whirling back to the mirror, Rowena's eyes narrowed as another plan came to her.

Why not kill two birds with one stone?

She had only just lately learned that Raine had a child and where he kept his daughter hidden. The castle of Salisbury. Why not capture Song at the same time? Her men had told he had gone to the castle with his whore.

She would have Winter and Song and Autumn all in one neat basket. Foolish names, they were. Too flowery for her liking. Then there was Spring and Summer. Just as lords called their whores, Monday, Tuesday, and so on, for each day of the week they had sex with them. How stupid.

"I am the Duchess Rowena," she bragged to the mirror. "Now there, that is a name with strength."

Rowena hurried down the castle stairs to seek out her latest lover in the stables. When she got there, however, she found the mercenary had gone. That errant knight. He was forever vanished, just when she wanted him.

De'Beau. She had a feeling that one was playing both ends against the middle.

Rowena sought out another in the stables. He was big, over six foot, a robust stud. He would do as well as another. Men, she thought as she rolled in the hay with him, they were all the same.

Twenty-four

Autumn straightened from her bent position in the garden. A shiver went clear through her. "Something is wrong. I can feel it; it is a strong premonition. Someone very close is in trouble. You can tell me nothing is amiss but I shall not believe you."

"Autumn," Raine said. "You always feel as if something is awry. It must be your dreams again. I realize you have nightmares about your missing sisters, but you can't do anything about it at this time. You have to go on living, Autumn. Go on picking the weeds, planting your herbs. Look, Song is waiting for you to play with her."

Autumn sighed. "I have played with her all morning long. I love her and feel she returns that love. But look, Raine, she is tired. Mai-Lee is taking her in for her nap. Now," she said, wiping the dirt off her hands onto the coarse overtunic Mai-Lee had swiftly stitched for gardening purposes, "we must sit down and talk. Yes, now. Talk."

Raine sat on an old stone bench, pulling a weed and

sticking it into his mouth. "All right: Who is in trouble now that worries you so?"

"*She's* in trouble. I just received this strange feeling about her again. It's as if she's so close, but I cannot see or touch her."

Autumn sighed again before she sat beside him leaving several inches between them. He looked at the open space, then smiled up at her pensive features. "The garden is coming along fine. You have planted herbs, vegetables, transplanted small fruit trees; it's beautiful. Just like you. Come here." He wrapped an arm around her as she leaned closer. "What is it now?"

"She is in *desperate* trouble, Raine. I sense that she is thinking about me, too. There is something else."

Here it comes, Raine told himself. She suspects.

"What are you waiting for, Raine? Who are all those men I saw in the hills this morning again? Are they watching us? Or perhaps these men are your own men?"

"I'll tell you in time." He wanted to properly court her, woo her, and treat her like a lady. That day was coming soon. When all his wealth had been returned to him. Just last night his men had brought part of that wealth to him. No wonder they were about to be under siege. The crown jewels his men'd stolen back from the thieves were here!

King Henry did not wish him to reveal anything, the message from him had stated. He must keep these secrets to himself for a bit longer. He could not even tell Autumn; not yet. As for King Henry, one carefully unredeemed loan had brought into Henry's possession crown jewels much undervalued; this fraudulent conversion would add much anguish to Henry's tender conscience. Against the man on whom the government's solvency depended, there was little his opponents could do: this was the secret of his resilience in politics and of part of his wealth.

He had to get the necessary and proper jewels back into Henry's possession. He had them now, here, hidden in Salisbury's turret room. No one must get to them. Someone, or many, however, were trying to do that just now. Henry's desire for power not only in England but as a prince of the Church provided armament for his enemies. He had many who would steal from him, and Henry had no idea how greedy and deceptive Baron Drogo and Duc Stephan could be. They had already proven themselves murderers.

Although never committed to the cause of peace, Henry conducted fruitless and sometimes nerve-racking negotiations during wartime. There was a rumor Henry was ill. Whether this was fact or falsehood was yet to be seen.

"Study the castle, Autumn. Look at it good." Keep it in your mind because you might live here one day soon.

"What is there to see?" she asked. " 'Tis just another castle to me. An old one at that."

He flinched at those words. He owned other castles, but this one had lately been taken back from the robber barons by his own knights. Now the damned rascals were after him again. He had to protect what was important. And Autumn and his child were only two of those.

Autumn looked round the huge castle fortification, her gaze roaming far and then below them. Through the trees the large village lay at the foothills. In a wide valley there were numerous flocks and herds to be seen grazing in it. Three other villages could be made out in the distance. A strong wall, some forty feet high, ran across the hill. Two square towers stood at different angles, but there was no gateway visible from where they sat. The wall was continued right round the top of the hill, which was crossed by two other walls, each defended by flanking towers.

The castle itself stood upon a grassy plateau and was a strong and massive-looking fortress.

"This is indeed a formidable place," Autumn said. "What is it called?" She didn't expect an answer. Every time she'd asked this question he had ignored her. And he would avoid the issue again, she knew.

"I'll tell you this," he began. "The baron who first planted himself here knew what he was doing. I should fancy from the look of it the castle at the end was built first. My ancestors—"

"Your ancestors?" she breathed. "This is getting interesting. Go on."

"Gradually the walls were added until the whole top of this hill was enclosed. This bit nearest to us is an addition made, ah, perhaps ten years ago."

"You don't know?" Autumn said. "I would have thought if this castle belonged to a relative of yours, you should have more facts."

"I was gone much of the time. Off fighting with King Henry or whoever else needed my assistance and the use of my knights."

"The helper. The Guardian." She nodded. "So like you, Raine." He was very rich, too, if this was the beginning of what he was going to show her, and tell her.

Without warning, his hand flew out and caught her at the nape of the neck; when her mouth was close to his, he kissed her. Autumn's mouth clung to his and she clutched his shoulders to steady her purling heart. He pulled her into him, bringing her breasts against the solid wall of chest, one leg of his long body crossing over hers. They sat there like that, foreheads together, his leg pinning her tenderly, unescapably.

Lord, how he loved her!

Softly Autumn said, "Raine?"

"Yes?"

"How many men do you have watching from above?"

"Not many," he told her; a white lie.

"How many are hidden from view then?" she asked again.

Suddenly his fingers found her beneath her skirts, moist and welcoming, and one member plunged within. She did not gasp. She only smiled as he began to move in and out.

"Do you have your own knights?" Her smile grew. "Do Mai-Lee and Song have their own men-at-arms?"

"Yes. They do."

"Oh, Raine, my darling, you will bring me to completion if you do not cease. Can anyone from above see what we're doing?" She sculpted his face with her hands, smiling, as the magic in his hands held her body in hostage.

"Not with us so close, with my hand hidden under your skirts, they can't, and, besides, there are the tall bushes," he said. "I have to see you. Now."

She whispered, "You shall. Hurry, Raine."

He moved to the fastenings of her bodice; there were so many clothes, he thought with near exasperation, undoing them in an instant, even the ties of her skirts. He knelt between her legs and kissed her flat belly. Then she was reaching for him, pulling him to her. He leaned his body to her, placing himself into her secret core.

Autumn lost the need for anything else but this man. He moved in her deeply, then again, and again. She picked up the mighty, throbbing cadence, the pulsating force that sent streams of joy coursing through every blood vessel in her womanly frame. They moved in the ancient rhythm imbued into their souls. The delights grew until they conjured a paradise as perfect as nature itself. He called to her, begging her to take the wondrous journey with him to the sparkling sun.

She obeyed.

She laughed joyously, he triumphantly, right into a stunning climax right there on the stone bench. "In front of God and everyone else," she murmured against his shoulder, satisfied with her wonderful release.

After a time of his continued fondling, bringing her to a gentle completion this time, she looked up at him, "Now, my lord, it is your turn."

"Ah . . . no. Too risky."

"Raine. You touched me. I want to touch you, too. 'Tis not fair that I have all the enjoyment and you merely watch," she ended with a shy giggle. "Besides, we just made love moments ago. What could be so different with my *bringing* you, too?"

"My love, we will speak of something else," he said, touching her cheek with the smell of her own secrets lingering there. "Would you like for me to court you, bring you flowers and heavy silks?"

"No."

"No?" He was surprised at that answer. All women wanted the man they loved to bring them flowers and expensive gifts. "What then, Autumn? What do you wish?"

"Are you guarding us, Raine? That is it, right? Those men are going to fight. Who is it that they would do battle with?"

"Whoever knows, Autumn. This castle has been under siege so many times . . . I have not the time to count them."

"You ever avoid my questions. Well. I have to really be going, to get back to Sutherland and see if there is news of my sisters."

"News of your sisters?" He looked at her incredulously. "Autumn, years have gone by."

"Only six, and a little more."

"There had been no news previously. They must be perished by now or living happily with new families. Did you ever stop to think that that could happen? Do you think only of yourself and your happiness?"

Standing, she swept a hand toward the bench, and said with a smirk, "If you mean what just— "

"No, Autumn. Think deeply and honestly."

"Honest? Raine, Guardian of the secrets. One who thinks of only *him*self."

"Your sisters will be lost to you now, Autumn."

"Oh, you *are* cruel, Raine Guardian."

Before he'd let her walk away, angry as a spitting cat, Raine grabbed her shoulders and swung her up in his arms. His mouth crashed down to move over hers and he kissed her most affectionately, licking and plying his tongue until she was quite breathless. He blew into her ear, taking her hand down to touch him, as she'd wanted to.

She gazed at him through the russet fringe of her lashes. Then with venom, she spat, "Oh! You speak to me so heartlessly and then fondle me, kiss and blow in my ear, *let* me touch you. Thank you, Sir High-and-Mighty. For nothing."

He laughed. "You look as if you are beside yourself."

"Yes, sir!" Jerking her hem from his grasp, she began to walk away, tossing more heated words over her shoulder. "Go to hell, Raine, completely, thoroughly, entirely . . . go to hell."

It would be best not to provoke her further, he thought. It was just enough. And the kiss was one she would remember. That, and the caresses. He hoped.

Go to hell, she'd told him.

When she was gone, striding into the great hall like an enraged knight, he said to himself, "I have already been to hell and have no wish to go there again." He shook his dark head. "That self-criticism is so old; I shall have to stop saying that. I have never been to hell and neither would I find pleasure in going there. No one in their right mind would. Hell is right here on earth at times."

The emergence of strong feelings and passions could be hell, oftentimes. He had much to be seeing to. He could not have Autumn in his way. He had already informed Mai-Lee to take the child and hide her well in case of attack from outside the castle. He would have Autumn bound and gagged if need be. When the time came, if it did, this would be the wisest and best course.

He could just see Autumn stealing some knight's armor and donning it to help in the battle.

311

* * *

Returning to the courtyard, Autumn spun about as she saw shadows fleeing swiftly, nearly colliding one with the other. As if men had been there only moments before, and then had run off.

There. Again!

Autumn stared in astonishment for several moments at the seven men who appeared so suddenly from the outer yard, and then, gaping at her for a moment, disappeared the way they had come.

She quickly followed.

There was a strong gateway in the courtyard—she had not noticed this before—beyond this a tunnel sloping steeply down, eight feet high and four feet wide, had been cut into the solid rock. The underground river flowed and she could hear water running beneath the rope bridge.

Following the path, Autumn found it led her through the gateway onto the rope bridge. She emerged upon a platform extending to the turret. Autumn paused to look around for another moment or two.

When she heard someone coming she slipped into the shadows near the path.

She could hear the water running beneath the bridge and overheard Raine talking to the men she had seen.

"Jerod, if you see Drogo's men pouring up the road, cut away the rope bridge, get inside the turret and block the entrance from inside. We have to ensure the safety of what's hidden in there."

From her hiding place, Autumn's jaw dropped. No wonder he did not want her going into the turret. She saw Raine hand a key to Jerod, who hung the key from a leather thong round his neck.

One of the younger knights spoke up. "We are all getting very hungry, m'lord. We have eaten nothing but apples this morning, and fighting sharpens the appetite."

"What fighting?" another knight, older, much larger, nudged the lad in the ribs. He gave a deep snort. "We have seen none as of yet, boy."

"I'd forgotten about food," Raine apologized. "I'll see that food is prepared at once, and will send down a portion for your lad, and the others."

"Tankards of drink?" The lad looked hopeful.

"Whatever can be found in the cellars," Raine told him. "It has been a long time since I've been here. I only arrived a week ago."

"I know that," said the lad Nicholas. "You will change things, too."

Raine began to walk away. "That I will."

Hearing him coming, Autumn ran to the courtyard and hid herself behind tall haystacks.

Returning to the courtyard, Raine told a body of men to fortify their positions. He waited for the men to return as Autumn spied on him from behind the haystack.

Jerod returned with the lad and other men.

"I will place you men in charge," Raine said. "You, Jerod. And you, Fallon. I might have to leave sometime during the next few days. Only, that is, if there's no doubt we will not be under siege. I want to make certain my daughter, Mai-Lee, and Autumn will be safe."

"Everything is as it was before, Ful—"

"Do not say it." Raine's voice went deep and full of menace. "Never say that word or the other. If you take my meaning."

"I do now, m'lord. And I'll not forget your name."

Hearing this, Autumn rolled her eyes heavenward. Why did they not just kiss his fingers one by one. Who was Raine truly?

Raine looked around with wary eyes. "Speak low. Keep low. Do not be seen. What is it, Jerod? Something is wrong. What is it?"

"The lady with the red hair."

"Autumn."

"She has seen us."

"It does not matter now. She has to know sooner or later." He narrowed his eyes toward the haystacks. "Believe me, Autumn has her own way of finding things out."

"Does she know who you—"

"Of course. She knows I am Raine Guardian."

When the men had gone Raine slipped into the shadows after he had walked several feet. He watched to see who would come out of hiding, from behind the haystacks. He hadn't long to wait.

There she was.

Raine gritted his teeth to keep from laughing aloud. Autumn. She looked fit to be tied, walking with her back straight, her chin in the air.

The moon was coming up along the edge of the castle. Torches had been lit, casting eerie shadows everywhere. From the woods and hillside, Raine called his men together and distributed them along the rear wall, while Jerod made a fresh inspection of the front defenses. He placed twenty of his men in the courtyard below, and posted another ten as sentries on the side walls. He then went down through the passage to Fallon.

"They come," one of the knights said. "There are many."

"One feels almost ashamed at being so safe," Fallon said, as Raine joined him in the gate tower. "It does not give one the chance of a decent fight."

Raine was thinking of Tyrian at that moment, wondering why his cousin had not caught up with him by now. He had told him he would be making a stop at the old Salisbury castle and Tyrian had looked at him blankly. Tyrian had had other matters on his mind. Mainly a woman. Tyrian might have gone hunting up Autumn's blond sister himself, by the way he had acted upon leaving Nottingham forest.

"You have had one good fight today, Fallon, and can do without another," Raine told his man-at-arms.

"I did so detest having to gag and bound that beauty for you, Raine," Fallon agreed, "and I should tell you about that rascal who nearly smothered me in the bog."

"What rascal?" Raine wanted to know, wondering why Fallon was smiling at something behind him.

He was about to turn when Fallon said with a deep laugh, "Why; Tyrian. Your cousin."

Raine looked around Fallon. "He's here?"

"I am," said Tyrian from behind Raine, "and when I get my hands on Duc Stephan, let it be known that that day will be the last anyone on God's earth shall ever hear of the bastard!"

Raine smiled. "What did he do?"

With a heavy heart, Tyrian sank to the floor and sprawled with long legs stretched straight before him, arms flung wide, features exhausted. His blond hair, usually neat and trimmed, was long and stuck out all over; he smoothed it back with a heavy hand.

Tyrian heaved a deep sigh, flexing his wide, muscled shoulders, then announced, "He has taken away the only thing that matters to me in this godforsaken land."

Ghostly torchlight flickered across Raine's face. "You have found her? Autumn's sister?"

"I believe she is one and the same. She goes by the name of Gwendolyn, so the nuns at Whitby called her."

"Ah yes," said Raine. "I did have a meeting with that holy mother, however briefly."

Tyrian went on, "The bastard Drogo vanished so swiftly after Howell's man De'Beau caught sight of him with Gwen and Gershwing."

"What, or who, is Gershwing?" Raine's eyes went to Fallon once, he who was watching the road intently as the conversation went on between Raine and his cousin unstoppingly.

Tyrian looked around at the men, wearing the leather jerkins of men-at-arms. Who were all these men? Had all Salisbury's men come back to him?

"What, I ask again," Raine began, "is Gershwing?"

"Howell Armstrong's war stallion. Gwen escaped on the horse. Actually, I don't understand, even now, why she ran away like that. She has hurt aplenty, true. She cannot speak, true. She is full of fear, true. Yet, I thought I'd seen a valiant maiden surfacing now and then."

Raine said, "She must have gone through hell when she had been captured, than taken again away by Henry's knights, then brought to the nunnery. Only to be whisked back and forth between Kirklees and Whitby."

Tyrian fiercely asked, "How do you know all this?"

"This is the story I garnered from Autumn. I put it all together, spoke to a few men along the road, at inns, and arrived with this supposition. We just have not caught up with her."

Tyrian looked ready to kill. *Not yet.*

"I believe it's Drogo's men who've come here. Drogo himself possibly along with them," Raine informed his cousin. "You can have his head if you want, to get the rage out of your blood."

"It is not Drogo's head I want now, but Duc Stephan's; I want his whole head on a platter, an apple stuffed in his mouth like a pig. And I shall have it. We only stop to rest, and soon must be on our way. I do not want Stephan and his men to get that far away."

"You followed them this far?" Raine watched his cousin nod; he was beginning to think something entirely different. "What if Stephan has joined up with Drogo?"

Tyrian had no time to answer, for, just then, Raine touched his cousin's arm when he would have taken his leave of the castle.

"Not so soon, cousin. You might find yourself detained."

Angrily, Tyrian looked down at the hand staying him. "Why is that?" His eyes snapped back up to Raine's watchful face.

"Look."

Tyrian's gaze left off glaring at his cousin and went below to the road. His eyes narrowed, slanting upward, and he felt sweat break out across his forehead. Dear God, he was quite detained.

"Howell Armstrong and his men are below and should

join us shortly," said Jerod. "This way, m'lord. Your things are ready for you."

Raine stepped off to the side, taking up arms and shield.

"I might never leave here alive," Tyrian said, mostly to himself since Raine was being dressed for battle. "By the time this fight is over with, Gwen might not be alive herself."

"I do not think Stephan will be that hasty," came from the shadows.

"Duc Stephan is known to be a violent lover," Tyrian said, adjusting his own chain mail. "And most times he disappears like an evil wizard, taking his captives with him, sometimes not to be seen for months at a time, years even. When he is done with a woman not much remains of body nor soul."

It was too late to get himself extra knights to go after Duc Stephan. Damn, he should have never come to Salisbury.

One hundred men were marching up the zigzag road, the banner of the Red Dragon held aloft with an approach of arrogance. Tyrian saw the lovely redhead Autumn was brought into the turret and shown to the highest tower room. Yet, he was shocked to see she was bound and gagged. Raine must know.

Twenty-five

Gwen wiped her lips again and again, hoping to erase the foul taste of the man named Duc Stephan. He had kissed her over and over until she thought surely she would pass out. For safety's sake, every time he looked her way she stopped rubbing her mouth. She was sure that by now her tender flesh was quite raw.

Her hands were bound in front of her and she had been placed near a tree. She watched everything that was going on. More men had joined the errant knights, until their numbers were great. She saw the pennants emblazoned on the trappings of their war stallions; horrible white skulls rampant on black fields. These greedy warmongers were forbidding and sinister, the worst kind of men she had ever laid eyes to. They wore their hair greasy and long; they looked as if they hadn't washed in months.

Gershwing had been caught, was tied nearby; and she knew by the wild looks of the war stallion that he was ready to break loose any time and fly to his master. She could not blame him; Duc Stephan's cruelty knew no bounds.

He was coming toward her now. She steeled her nerves, knowing he was going to touch her again.

"You did not eat," he said, looking down at the food untouched at her feet.

She only shrugged. How could she eat, bound as she was.

"Ah, I see. You cannot eat tied up like that." He bent down to relieve her of the bite of the rough ropes. "Eat, lovely maiden. You will need your strength. We go to join the Baron Drogo." He eyed her closely as she nibbled the food. "You do not eat much, do you?"

How could she answer him? Even could she, she would not wish to. He was foul, angry looking, and mean. At least he did not smell as bad as the other men who had bound her. Still, his appearance was wild and unkempt. His voice was rough, his words nasty-sounding to her gentle ears.

"What happened to you that you cannot speak?" he asked her, tasting a morsel of her food. "You are the fairest maiden I've ever laid eyes on. Are you perhaps this Winter Meaux the Duchess Rowena seeks? For Christ's sake, nod your head if the answer is aye."

Again Gwen shrugged, more slowly this time. How could she know this? Meaux? The name was somewhat familiar. That was all. Then again, Tyrian had mentioned the name of Autumn Meaux. He, too, wondered could she be this woman's kin. It was all very confusing to her and she did not know what was going to happen next. Would he rape her? Kill her? What was his plan for her?

With a harsh-sounding laugh, Stephan reached out to brush his knuckles against her cheek. "Oh. What's this?

You do not like my touch? This is hard to believe, most women welcome my favors."

Like a cat, Gwen spit out at him and the spray hit him right in the face. He grabbed her arm and, snatching her close, his lips bruised her mouth. He kissed her deeply, his tongue forcing its way, his teeth grinding against hers.

"You will learn my touch, lovely bitch." He pulled back, licking his lips as if she'd been a tasty morsel he'd fully devoured. His hand went to her breast, first one, then the other, fondling and molding her small contours to his large fist. "You are a tiny bit, aren't you. Now," he said, rising to his feet, "we have someone we needs meet. You will like him. Mayhaps you will remember him?"

Her eyes shot daggers at him.

"You shall, lovely bitch." He yanked her to her feet. "I believe your memory will return, along with your voice."

Gwen doubted his words yet she feared what remained to be seen.

While he wasn't looking, Gwen swiped her arm across her mouth. He had not tied her up again. Her eyes widened then as she saw another man join Stephan, coming down off his horse. She knew him, the one she had stolen Howell's horse from. It was the knight named De'Beau.

"I have no fear of an open attack," Raine said. "They can see for themselves that the bridge is destroyed. And I do not think they will dream of coming up that road any farther."

"As they know," said Fallon, "we can sweep with stones from above. If they attack openly at all, it will be by the wall. If they make many ladders such as we had they might think they might gain a footing."

"Ha," Raine snorted. "All they have is the archers. How can they fire on the defenders of the wall; they are too far below."

"What I am really afraid of," Fallon was saying, "is that there may be some secret passage we know not of."

"Do you think so?" asked Raine, itching in his chain mail and armor. "Where could it come from?"

Fallon's black eyes narrowed. "While we were away, as they snatched and held the castle, they may have driven a passage from some place in the wood behind and it may come up somewhere in the courtyard, perhaps in one of the little huts along the side."

"Of course, the entrance would be covered by stone, and would be hidden among the bushes at the other end. Still, I do not think this likely, for a hostile force would most certainly take up its post in that wood, and attack the place in the rear."

"If there is such a passage I think that it must open somewhere along the deepest hill, on one side or the other."

Tyrian, fit to be tied, put in, "It looks to us almost perpendicular, but there may be inequalities by which active men might ascend at some point or other. As we came, Howell and I noticed that for a considerable distance we could see there were tufts of shrubs growing here and there, and one of these may conceal a small opening. From this point a staircase may have been driven up into the castle."

Raine frowned. "That would be very awkward, if it were so. They have ceased all movement; there is no doubt they will still come. Tonight all the force except the sentries shall gather in the castle, where ten men by turns shall keep guard, one or two being placed in the lower chambers."

"In this way we shall be safe, Ful—"

"Aye; yes," Raine snapped with lowered brow. "Say it not again, I warn you."

Fallon bowed his understanding.

"I go on," Raine said. "For before more than three or four can enter we should be all on foot, and as they can but come up single file, could repulse them without difficulty. Tomorrow we will lower men down with ropes from the walls, and examine every clump of bushes growing on the hillsides."

"I was but looking forward to a good night's sleep," Fallon grumbled, "but your idea, *Raine,* has quite done away with that. If I went off I should dream that I had one of those dragons at my throat. It is a good thing that you thought of it."

"I think, my lord," one of the warriors said, "there are a number of our men spying among the Riflers. I can make out helmets and shields, and I think many are clad in leather jerkins."

Raine looked heedful of this.

"Aye, there are certainly shields and helmets," he said. "I fear there is no doubt they have more forces."

"Our men? They have made them prisoners?" Fallon said. "I realize some of the men are missing."

Raine shook his dark head. "Drogo never takes prisoners. I fear they have slain them all and possessed

323

them of their arms and clothes. In no other way can there be Salisbury shields and helmets among them."

"Damn!" Fallon exclaimed. "Why doesn't Drogo attack us instead of keeping his men gaping there at the castle?"

"Because, at present, he can do nothing, and is not fool enough to throw away one hundred men."

Later that night, under a full bright moon, a little party mounted the road until they stood on the platform from which the bridge started. One of them was a tall figure, dressed in armor, and with long black hair flowing down from under his helmet over his shoulders.

"Jaysus," said Tyrian. "It is Duc Stephan." His fingers clenched and he glanced furiously at the duc. "He is here, riding right toward us; that means . . . Gwen is with him. I cannot kill him until I find that she's safe."

The rider neared and came to a halt, forty feet from them.

"I am Fulcan of Salisbury," said Raine. "To whom have I the pleasure of speaking?"

"I am Stephan, *of Hell*," the Duc drawled with a nasty chuckle. "I don't know if I have taken your castle by treachery, yet I claim to have won it by fair fighting."

"What fighting?" yelled Raine right back. "We have not yet fought, you—" He'd almost said "bastard" but thought better not to. Something was amiss here. He had this Gwen. But he could not get to Autumn and Song.

"While you were long away with your whore, your

men went out with your force to attack me among the hills, and during your absence I attacked and once more captured your castle." He chuckled again. "Now I mean to take what's inside again. No women were hurt or insulted, save one. I believe that in your incursions into France you have not always shown the same mercy." He went on. "They are safe and well," Stephan went on. "We do not massacre lovely women in cold blood."

"Lord have me," Raine said to Tyrian, right behind him. "They have caught Autumn, Song, and Mai-Lee."

Tyrian said, "And they have Gwen also."

"It seems we have a traitor in our midst."

Could it be? No, Tyrian thought, it could not be one of Howell's best men. The dark-haired one De'Beau.

"Where is De'Beau?" Tyrian snapped to Howell who was standing close by.

"He was here," Howell said in a low voice so that Stephan could not hear. "I have not seen him for hours."

Tyrian said, "I will kill him then, just as I intend to kill Stephan."

"Leave me *someone*," said Raine with a mirthless smile.

"I'll go now," Stephan said. "But rest assured I shall get what I want. After all, gentlemen, I have what *you* want back."

Raine watched Stephan ride away, safe in the knowledge they would not attack his back. He had the women and no doubt would give orders to have them slain if anything happened to him.

Save one? Stephan had said. With sweat forming on his brow, Raine wondered who this might be. He must mean Autumn.

She would take no insult from any man. Then again, she was only a woman and she was vulnerable under such an evil force as Duc Stephan. And Drogo. Had he not spotted that devil's colors also on the hill?

Gwen looked at the women and the little girl. As much as she wanted to, she could not speak with them. They had been captured outside the castle walls just after midnight. Someone, a man who looked very much like De'Beau, had brought them. The men with them, ready to fight to get the women back, had been dispatched of quickly and easily by Stephan's men. She had not seen the leader of these new men yet, nor did she wish to. She had a feeling it was the devil himself, and he must be related to Stephan.

On his sidestepping mount, Stephan returned and his eyes went directly to Autumn Meaux. He looked first at the ravishing redhead and then at the beautiful blonde. He could find no similarities. Perhaps they were *not* related.

As Stephan dismounted he told himself he would have to study them closer together.

Autumn watched Stephan's furtive eye movements, believing she knew what the lusty devil was thinking as he shifted his gaze between her and the blond Gwen. She watched as he walked over to speak with one of his men and Autumn's eyes dropped for only a moment to the heavy black, woolen hose just above his high boots. The men laughed, as if sharing a crude joke. Autumn quickly snapped her gaze from the man. She had been looking him up and down as if she'd like to carve out his black heart, while he and his dirty-minded accomplice thought otherwise.

What sort of woman would fall at the feet of such a crude human being? No. He was not human, she thought, Duc Stephan was an animal.

What did he have in mind for them? Autumn wondered as his gaze slashed over to her again.

Again Autumn looked at the lovely young woman with the fair hair and no voice. Staring at her, Autumn felt a strange sense of time and place, as if she'd stood right here with that blond woman, the feeling that there was a kindred spirit between them.

Autumn wished she could see more of Gwen's head and features, but Gwen was wearing a very old and ragged hooded cloak, and only a small portion of the shiny hair escaped in pale spirals on either side of her partially concealed face.

Song and Mai-Lee were seated beneath a huge oak; Autumn hoped the little girl was still asleep to be spared any of the fighting she might witness. She had already been frightened by the dark arrogance of the man De'Beau who had been taking them to the tower room, then changed his course and brought them out a secret passage beneath the turret.

Her study of woman and child then fell to the face of sleeping Song again as Autumn wondered if Song was wearing the Windrush diamond. She detected a movement from Mai-Lee and as they made eye contact, Mai-Lee seemed to read what was bothering Autumn. The Oriental nodded once, slowly, and Autumn took it that the jewel was in safekeeping. All she could do was hope that Mai-Lee was right; the men were keeping them all separated to keep them from making plans of escape among themselves.

Raising a tankard, Stephan drank deeply and then handed the heavy vessel back to his man. There was a dark arrogance about the man, Autumn could see. What did he want of her and the others? First she was being taken to the turret room and then a man named De'Beau was bringing her and Song and Mai-Lee out to the enemy. This De'Beau, angry that another man had dared speak his name aloud, must be a traitor.

If only she could warn Raine that he had a traitor in his midst. Was he even in the castle himself any longer? Or had the Devil's men taken him prisoner, too? She could not know. She was out here; he was in there. Would there be fighting? What was going to happen to them? Song would never be able to escape if it came down to that. Someone would have to carry the child.

All very strange, these men and their schemes.

Why had Raine planned to make her prisoner in the turret room? To keep her out of the way? What was it he did not wish her to do? What was in the small locked room up there?

Autumn looked at Gwen again and the haunting feeling returned to her. She had no idea she was being spoken to until she turned to look into the most tormented, hellish eyes she had ever known.

"You were not listening to me," Duc Stephan was saying. He ran a finger along her fine chin. "Lovely bitch. Just like the other one," he said, indicating Gwen over his shoulder. "I always kiss my captives," he said, bending to taste Autumn's mouth. "Come. You can return a kiss better than that." He opened his mouth over hers.

Autumn was shocked at the feel of Stephan's mouth on hers. The kissing beast's lips upon hers caused a shiver of revulsion up her arms and legs; she wanted to spit his taste right back into his arrogant face. From a distance Stephan was not a bad-looking man, however, as soon as he walked closer, smiled and bared his teeth, the appearance turned hard and satanic.

Stephan dug his fingers in on either side of her face, saying, "Now. I shall tell you what it is I wish you to do."

Wish? How could such a devil as he have *wishes*? Wants, desires, demands, *lusts*. He told and one obeyed. Autumn knew should they not obey, one would no doubt be punished severely—perhaps killed. A murderer; Stephan had the face of a cold-blooded killer. A treacherous, scheming bastard, no less. His kiss had made her feel unclean, but not humiliated; no, she wouldn't let him do that to her.

He slapped her once as an angry woman would, sharply, not so hard as to make her head snap. "Hear me, pretty wench. I have a plan. Are you listening?" He tilted his head, his eyes wild and crazy looking. "Have you a voice or not? Are you like the other then, you, too, cannot speak? Let me see your tongue; do you even have one or was it cut out?"

Autumn slapped his hand away and then blanched as she heard the ooohs and ahhhs circulating among the greasy, unkempt knights. "Bastard," she hissed, only for his ears. "What do you want?"

He slapped her again harder than before. His fingers bit cruelly into her slim arms and he smiled when she grimaced, enjoying her pain. He hauled her up against him and whispered against her ear, his mouth moist and hot.

"I like my women bold." He shoved her back and away. "But, mind you, not too bold."

With eyes slanted down, Autumn blinked at him and watched him suspiciously as he moved closer, putting an arm about her shoulders. She did not trust him not to put a knife into her ribs, and he knew it.

"Do not worry so, I'll not kill you. You are too valuable. Still," he said, sighing, "I must use you."

"Use me?" Autumn swung her face to him, coming just inches from his long, sharp nose. "How?" she asked, with just as much arrogance as he'd shown her.

"Where is your grace, little lady?" He shoved his face next to her. "You are a lady, are you not?"

"P-Perhaps."

"Then listen," he hissed. "If you get them for me, I shall release you and the others."

"Them?" she asked, wrinkling her nose at his foul breath. "Who do you mean?"

"Not who," he said in a whiny, impatient voice. "Them, the jewels. You know what I mean."

"Jewels," Autumn said icily. "You have lost me, sir."

"Not *sir*," he hissed again. "Duc. *Sir* is for underlings, didn't you know?"

Lifting her chin and looking him directly in the eyes, she said, "Duc Stephan"—her voice was gracious, with just a hint of pique—"what is it you wish? You do wish something, do you not?"

"Not for you to make me look an ass before my men." He shook her again, pinching her shoulder. "Leave off with your haughty look, Lady Red, and show me that you listen and will do as I demand."

Pressing her lips together, Autumn tried to look meek and mild. It was of no use. Stephan just continued to glare at her.

"Stubborn wench." He slapped his knees, rising from where he'd sat beside her on the boards of a collapsed hut. "Just do as I command and I shall set you free. There will not be any battle."

"What?"

He swung back to her after he'd stared at the other women and the child, giving each an equally dispassionate regard. "I give my word." When she laughed shortly in his face, he snatched up her slim wrist. "Be warned, Lady Red, I have little patience. When Duc Stephan gives his word, especially to a lady, it is kept."

"Hah," Autumn said in a wispy voice.

"Such arrogance," Stephan chuckled softly to himself before he gave her a steely gaze. He leaned close to her face. "Either do as I say or watch me as I torture the child. Or perhaps I will torture and rape the fair-haired wench first? Whichever"—he slammed his foot upon the bench—"they will all be killed if you do not comply."

"With your wishes," Autumn said.

Stephan said, *"My* wish is also *my* command."

Autumn muttered, *"You are a bastard,"* as she felt a wave of helplessness come over her.

331

Twenty-six

Tufts of shrubs concealed a small opening in the hill-side; from the underground passage a staircase had been driven up into the castle. Watching over her shoulder as she went, Autumn quickly moved to the ground floor of the turret. She hesitated uneasily in the passage, listening.

Bustling up the stairs, she came to a tall, arched door. She looked at the door and knew as she tried the latch, it would be locked.

It was locked.

She had heard Raine tell Jerod to keep the key, he had it around his neck, she recalled. I must find Jerod. And then the job of trying to get the key from him.

Will I ever have peace from all this turmoil? she wondered. She hurried onward yet stopped as she tried to remember the way to the Great Hall. She had not been through all of this castle, but it could not be much different from Sutherland, could it? It was slightly older and had many twists, turns, and secret passages, she was finding out.

Turning, she picked up her skirts and began walking

quickly toward what she hoped would be the Great Hall. There was no one in there. She tried the apartments above, finding them empty also. She hurried back down into the Great Hall, slipped out, found the stables and storage area. A few men were there and she kept to the shadows, not wanting to run into Raine or any of his men; there was only one she sought—the one with the key.

Some how, some way, she had to get the key, find the tiny turret where the secrets were locked inside, get to the jewels and find a way to slip quickly back to the staircase that led down into the underground passage. Once there, Stephan's men would meet her and she would have to show them to the turret room and unlock it again.

She was going against Raine, but what else could she do? The women and Song would be put to death if she did not cooperate.

The turret room. This was where she had to get to, as soon as possible.

Lock it and unlock it, so that Raine's guards when they checked, would find everything in order. She hoped. If all went well and time was on her side.

All this was very risky. Anyone could see her in a moment, even though she moved as quickly and stealthily as possible.

She knew a feeling of panicked defeat when she found Jerod in the inner bailey just making his way to the smaller, back hall. He was very much awake; she'd hoped to find him asleep and slip the key from about his neck. He had to rest some time, they all did.

Time was awasting. She did not know how much more of it Stephan would allow her. That stinking, ugly bastard, she thought angrily. If he laid a finger on Song or the other women, she would . . . *What could she do?* She was only one woman. His forces were many.

If only she could ask Raine for help, but she knew he would not hear her out; he would only have her bound and gagged again for interfering in men's business. He might even accuse her of being a spy. One never knew what banged around in a man's mind when he was warring to keep what he deemed was his. Greedy men, would they never be content with what they had? She didn't think so.

All over, torches were being lit in the bailey and on the castle wall. Their light was eerie, resembling something close to early morning in the misted woods of Sherwood.

Cautiously, she turned the handle to a door, entering the gloomy kitchens carefully and quietly, looked inside and scowled unhappily upon noticing that Jerod had not come in here from the back hall. She kept moving, slipping in and out of shadows, melding with the darker shapes of torchlight, and keeping out of the eerie yellow flickers of illumination.

Her heart pounded up into her throat as three knights appeared suddenly around a corner, almost catching her as she stepped from the shadows of an alcove. Breathing deeply but softly, she took her hand down from where it had pressed onto her chest, waited until they were far down the passage, then went quickly to the courtyard.

Jerod moves fast, she thought. He's no blundering fool. There, there he was, talking to someone that looked from the back like the shape of Raine, but could not *be* Raine. His voice was deeper, angrier, and his movements were clipped and precise. He was dressed in chain mail with a sinister outer surcoat, and he was holding before him the longest and greatest sword she had ever seen. From the ground, where he had the tip pointed, the blade and hilt together reached to the upper part of his chest, where his hands, one above the other, clasped the jeweled hilt.

He was the most frighteningly overpowering figure she had ever beheld. It was as if he was bent on destroying everything in his path. . . .

He spoke again. Horrified, she knew it was Raine's angry form. Ah, one of his various diverse disguises perhaps?

It was as if he were a stranger.

Now one of the men was speaking to him. "Fulcan . . ."

She did not hear the rest. Fulcan? Not Fulcan of Salisbury? He sounded like Raine, yet it could not be . . .

This man could not be Raine Guardian.

Autumn slipped away like a swiftly moving wraith, following Jerod who had ended his furtive conversation with the cold and unemotional man she had seen, one who looked so much like Raine but was not Raine at all.

She discovered where Jerod went to take his rest and waited until he was asleep—his snoring thankfully covered any possible noise she made—and carefully removed the key from around his neck. Then she padded down the hall silently and slipped into the turret room.

* * *

She did not see the tall knight, with full armor and dragon helm in place, who watched her from outside the turret room, through the space as she left the door ajar.

The jewels sparkled in the dark of the moon, spilling from the chest as Autumn opened the lid. She stared in awe at so much wealth. The crown jewels. She had found them. Now all she had to do was go the way she had come and let Stephan's men inside so they could carry the chest out.

This would prove no easy task.

Looking at the splendid jewels, she reached in and picked up a beautiful ruby. Was this the Black Prince's ruby, the very same one that had been lost at the battle of Agincourt? And the Windrush jewel, where was that one? If it was among these, she could not tell, there were too many and not enough time to search through all the sparkling gems. She prayed Mai-Lee had hidden it well and not allowed Song to wear it. That would be stupid at a time like this; Raine would never have put it on the child for safekeeping. This would put Song in grave danger.

Stephan's men were many while Fulcan's were few. Why did he not just storm the castle and take them then? She knew. This Fulcan must be a formidable force. But which man was he? Surely, she thought, he is not the Black Knight? No. This Fulcan looked too much like Raine, which gave her pause.

Perhaps Raine had as many men as Stephan himself, they had been scattered about, on hills, at entrances, in secret passages, outside the castle in the woods. And Stephan had known this.

As she rummaged through the jewels, Stephan's threat

echoed in her ears: do not fail otherwise the prisoners would perish did she not return.

She was doing this for Song and Mai-Lee. She did not know who their blond prisoner was, but she had seen the sadness and horror in her eyes. Stephan had mentioned Drogo, but she had not seen him. The coward must have kept himself hidden from her sight.

A sudden chill ran down her spine and along her arms right before she picked up a jewel and turned to see the silver figure standing behind her.

"Looking for something?" he said dispassionately. "Or did you perhaps find *it?*"

Twenty-seven

"Wh-who are you?" Autumn stammered.

"What are you doing here?" the voice coming through the dragon helm was deep, muffled, firing right back at her.

"I asked you first." She backed away slowly.

He reached out for her with a mailed fist. "Come with me."

Autumn would not go anywhere willingly with this man. She did not like the way he looked, he frightened her hiding himself that way under all the steel; nor did she know if he was one of Raine's men or not. What would happen if she tried to fight him? He would surely overpower her. What was she to do? She had to get out of here, forget the treasure. All this went through her mind with the swift wings of a flying swallow.

"Come," he ordered again.

"No," she told him.

"No?" he whispered.

Stepping near, he reached out, this time catching her by her wrist.

338

She tore herself free and stared up at him, pushing her hair back with both hands. "Do not touch me."

"Again I ask, What or whom do you seek?" the knight asked.

Annoyed, Autumn shook her head. "I'll not say another word." She backed away from him. Her hair had come loose and she pushed the strands behind her ear. "Answer me now sir. Who are you?" This man could not be Drogo, could he? Had he stolen into the castle, just as she had, meaning to steal her away, from even Stephan?

He was backing her up toward a wall, slowly, inch by inch. Autumn searched for an avenue of escape frantically.

"You needn't know who I am," came the voice from deep within the helm again. "Just come, and you will not be hurt."

"I'll not be hurt anyway, because I'm going to get away—"

She hadn't seen them sneak into the room behind her, and now the two guards behind her grappled with tying her wrists together as she kicked back and then down, her skirts slowing her responses.

"Leave us."

Her arms were bound, all the way to her elbows, stretched out in back. The pain was intense and she glared at the silver-helmed man before her, bright eyes displaying her misery.

He came to her, bent to loosen the bindings, only enough to lessen her pain, then pushed her before him. "Walk," he snarled.

She walked. He was right behind her, safe in the knowledge she could not escape, bound as she was.

"Where are we going?" she tossed over her shoulder, a chill of alarm beginning to quake through her body. "If you are going to bring me to Drogo or—"

"I despise Drogo," he snapped. "Why would I bring you to him?"

"I don't know; you tell me," she parried with the deep voice. "If you think to toss me onto your bed you'd better rid yourself of some of that metal first. You'll crush me before you—"

He didn't let her finish. "I would not touch you if you were the last strumpet in London, in all the country for that matter. Don't talk," he ordered. "Just keep walking."

Raine, where are you? If this is one of your knights, you'd better teach him how to treat his captive better than this. "I know," she dared say, "Raine has found me out and now you are going to—"

"To the dungeon with you where you'll be tortured in more ways than you can imagine!"

"No," she said. "No. I have nothing more to say to you." Her gaze slid slyly downward. Ah, I have something for you, Sir Knight.

"Oh! Oh, my God! A *mouse!*"

Leaping to the side, Autumn swung her torso downward, and then as he bent to retrieve her, legs spread awkwardly, Autumn made a battering ram out of her shoulder and came up hard, slamming into his crotch with the force of her impetus-driven weight.

"Hell's bells!" he shouted, wincing as he watched her depart like the fleetest deer in the forest. Together his hands pressed over man's most vulnerable spot. He'd never, not even during a battle, been hit there before while wearing chain mail. He had often wondered what it felt like.

He groaned. *Now he knew.*

"She's gone," Jerod told the man in silver helm. "She got the key around my neck, too, took it while I slept."

"Did she get anything else?" he asked, removing the stiflingly hot headpiece, running his hands through his dark hair.

The men looked at each other, down at the Fulcan's hands again crossed over himself below and tried not to break out laughing.

One began to answer. "Well—"

"Never mind," the man in pain said in an aching voice. "I'd warn you not to remind me that I've been bested by a woman." And it was not the first time, he was thinking, his green eyes asparkle.

"She got nothing of value," one of the guards snorted, nudging another man. "At least we—"

"Shut up," the Fulcan snapped. "What now? Where are Stephan's men?"

"They are pulling out of the valley. They did not bring a siege tower, so what could they have hoped to've gained?"

Jewels, the green-eyed man kept to himself.

"She's a traitor," he said. "We'll go after them."

"I'm all for that," said Howell. "My horse has come back to me."

"What horse?"

"Gershwing."

Fulcan said, "Oh, that horse. So, what has a horse to do with going after the woman? Does it fly?"

"Almost," said Howell. "I'm going after Stephan. He'll kill the women if we don't fight him—"

"He won't kill them," Fulcan said. "They are too valuable."

"He will," Tyrian put in, grimacing with the pain of possibly losing Gwen forever.

"He won't, I say. He does not have all that he needs."

"What would that be?" Tyrian wanted to know, impatiently pacing back and forth with sword slapping his leg, worried for Gwen's safety.

"Two more sisters." The man sank heavily into a chair in the lower apartments. "And he won't hurt Song. He knows what I will do to him if he touches a hair on her head."

"He's already touched your—"

"Autumn? Don't say her name in this castle!"

"You just did, cousin." Tyrian tugged at his ear and would have grinned if Gwen did not chafe his mind so. "What are we going to do?"

"We have a duty to perform," Fulcan said, clenching his fists after removing his gloves. "I have to get the ruby to King Henry. And then there is the matter of another jewel." He shook his head. "And yet *another.*"

"If we get the jewel back to Henry, he will give us the loan of a thousand of his knights. We can slay Stephan and all his men and Drogo if need be."

"We have no idea what happened to Drogo. He's disappeared from the valley."

"That is nothing new," said Fulcan. "The man is a

known coward. He pretends to terrorize and then runs away himself. We'll get him, too."

"Along with the duchess?" Tyrian asked tauntingly.

"Her. I would not hear her name this night, along with the others." Fulcan leaned forward, placing his hands on his forehead, running long fingers through his dark hair.

"What were your plans for Autumn Meaux? I mean," Jerod said, looking around at the other men. "You did not really think to tie her in bed and murder her for her deception . . . *had* you?"

"I thought seriously about that, yes."

The knights looked at one another and swallowed.

Fulcan began, "We have to make a plan. First the jewels. Then the other more serious and dangerous plan."

"Which plan?" asked Jerod, chewing on a slab of stale bread.

"I have no idea," Fulcan said. "Not yet."

The artful, beguiling Autumn Meaux had escaped his clutches. Dear God, she is one incredibly defiant woman. And how did she manage to escape, bound as she was? She moved like the swiftest of sparrows, flying through the castle and out of his life. No, never that. Autumn was going to be surprised when he showed up at Sutherland castle.

When Fulcan of Salisbury lifted his head, Tyrian stared into the dancing, menacing, blistering green eyes and shuddered. "Send men out to capture the women and the child back from Stephan and round up as many men as you can get from the forest. Make certain they have safe passage to Sutherland. At once."

Tyrian blinked at this new scheme. The other knights followed suit.

"It's going to be *a hell of a night*," Jerod told them all.

"Well said." Fulcan nodded.

Twenty-eight

Drogo and Stephan were arguing.

"That is the jewel we need the most!" Baron Drogo shouted at Stephan's head. "Where is it?"

"None of them have it on them," Stephan flung back at Drogo, glaring at the women, especially Autumn Meaux who had returned to them, bound at the wrists and empty-handed!

"We have the Black Prince's ruby," Drogo announced. "While your stupid men were bumbling about, and Lady Meaux was arguing with Fulcan in the stone tower, my men slipped in and—"

"And this is what they got?" Stephan glanced down at the jewel, snarling, "This is all?" He threw the ruby down on the ground. "It's worthless junk."

"Worthless?" Drogo's strange eyes glowed angrily after he'd picked up the "jewel." "What do you mean? Are you daft, man? It will bring us fortune and fame for the returning of it. Henry will be ecstatic to have the ruby back in his coffers."

"Ha. You think," scoffed Stephan. "Look"—he snatched it from Drogo's hand—"it is a fake. See how loose the jewels round the setting are? I have seen drawings of the Black Prince's ruby. If this is it, I will eat it."

He threw it down again. Drogo picked it up again.

"You may be right," said Drogo, studying the thing again. "It *does* look worthless. Perhaps Fulcan of Salisbury set us up and placed a fake where the real ruby should have been."

Autumn gaped at them. True, she thought. The treasure had held a multifarious display of jewels and some useless trinkets. She almost laughed at them. The blundering idiots had grabbed the wrong jewel and this Fulcan had seen to it that they did just that. She prayed that the Windrush jewel was still safe . . . somewhere.

She felt around in the deep inner pocket of her tunic. *It was safe. . . .*

"We leave, men, taking the prisoners." Drogo whipped his black sinister cloak out in a wide arc as he turned to mount his horse.

"No you do not," Stephan argued, glaring across the clearing to Drogo. "They are my prisoners."

Drogo leaned forward, curling his lip. "Try and stop me."

"Men!" Stephan shouted. "Take them!"

Drogo laughed. "Your men won't help you, Stephan. Look at them, trembling in their boots, afeared that Fulcan of Salisbury will get them."

"I should have killed the Fulcan whilst I had the chance."

Drogo sighed. "We've all had the chance to kill him.

Yet, none of us has had the courage. That man is hard to do away with."

"Not the whole time he was with little lady Meaux over there. I do not believe he had men in the trees at that time. I think they were very alone, those two. She might even be carrying his bastard. Then what? The king will order them to wed and all will be lost to us."

"You'll not share even if you do come to be the first to get the sisters all together and get your hands on the Windrush jewel. You've always been greedy, even when we were children."

"Hush. Tell no one that you are my bastard brother. I do not wish to be so known."

Autumn listened and watched Drogo and Stephan. She recalled the man Drogo now. Yes, it was he who had near-ravished her in the woods when she'd been only three-and-ten. She had gotten the jeweled dagger from him. Now she remembered where she'd had to've left it, too; back at Sutherland.

Then there had been the other remembrance. Spring and Summer had been in the herb garden. Now she recalled who she'd been arguing with. Her uncle. He had been mean to her, had slapped her. How she'd wanted to strike him back. He had been too strong, had always been punishing her, always telling her how ugly she was with her red hair and odd-colored violet eyes.

It had been the day he'd punished her severely, taken her favorite pet, had it put to death, then laughed as Autumn buried him, transplanting pink and red wildflowers about the grave. And the punishment had been over a small thing, she'd only spilled some ale he'd wanted her to bring to him. She'd tripped and the nasty brew had spilled into his lap. He'd arisen like a roaring lion, slapping her, pulling her hair, yanking her across his knee. And then the pet. That had been the last straw.

She had taken a horse, in a reckless gallop away from the castle and let the mare take her as far from Windrush as she could get. He had carried her to the boundary line. Beyond that line lay the lands of Baron Drogo. *Le Meurtrier.* The Murderer. The Devil himself.

She knew him now. She looked at him as he still spoke with Stephan. The hounds' cry that day, she remembered the sound well, it was in her mind even now. She had been picking wildflowers for her mother. She had hitched up the skirt of the flowing bliaut she had worn, the smoky blue of the silk matching the lavender daisies she carried. He had surprised her as he stepped into the clearing, dressed in black tunic of velvet embroidered with scarlet thread. His thin lips had twisted into a sinister smile. He had questioned her. She had made out the knowing light in his pale eyes and her heart had been in her throat.

Across the clearing, past Mai-Lee and Song, past the lovely blonde woman, Autumn now stared at Drogo. A big man with a slim face, with lean cheeks that framed an arrogant nose. He had cruel, thin pink lips that made a slash across an otherwise handsome face. Black, peaked eyebrows.

That day she'd said to him, "And I know who you are!"

Again she looked at him, sunlight pouring around them as it had that day in the clearing. He hadn't changed in six years.

And now she knew something else. Robert had been there the day her mother and father had been killed. They looked so much alike. At times she had not known if her father Richard had been punishing her, or her uncle Robert. It was Robert, no doubt about it. Robert had been there with Drogo on the day her parents had been slain.

Drogo. Their lands. The duchess. They had all been eager to kill her parents and take the lands, the jewel, wed the sisters, then kill them off. Robert must have been their leader, their plotter. Where was he now? Had Drogo finished him off the same as he'd done with her parents? Or was Robert merely hiding himself somewhere? Where was the stinking, cruel, evil bastard? She'd like to drive her own dagger through his wicked soul.

"You will not run, I pray," he said. "I am the Baron Drogo."

Autumn gasped, turning to see Drogo standing behind her. How had he gotten there? She'd seen him only moments ago, across the clearing. He had moved quietly, quickly, like an ill wind.

She looked directly into Drogo's evil eyes. "Those are the same words you spoke to me seven years ago."

His hand reached out to fondle a strand of her hair. "And you said to me: 'I am Autumn Meaux, one of four sisters born at a single birth. We are called The Seasons. And my father is—' " He stared at her now, almost gently. "Who is your father, Autumn? Do you really know?"

She gaped at him. "He's dead all these six years." Autumn did not see the lovely blonde as she drifted over, hands bound behind her back, ragged skirts gathering dew.

"That is not what I asked you. What is your father's name, do you even know?"

"Of course!" Autumn said proudly. "His name is— was Richard."

His laugh was an awful sound in the clearing. "You have *two* fathers, Autumn. Richard and Robert; one after the other, they both took your mother on the same night. All were drunk. She never knew. They were so alike in looks, voice, everything, it was hard to—"

"Beast! You *lie!*" Autumn screeched at him. "You try to get your revenge. I'd hurt you that day in the woods' clearing. And then, with your own knife, I stabbed you." Fury burned in his eyes, as it had that day, eyes dark as Satan's cloak. Autumn picked up, "You said: I shall not dismiss this injury to my person. One day revenge will be met—"

"Exactly from you," Drogo repeated the words.

"And now what will you do?" she asked Drogo. She heard a thump on the ground in back of her and turned to look. It was the young, fair-haired woman.

Autumn rushed to pick up Gwen's shoulders. "Now, look, you've made her pass out. Your scandalous words must have frightened her."

"And why not?" Drogo sneered down at her. "She is a nun."

"A—nun?" Autumn looked up at Drogo, shading her eyes from the rising sun.

"A nun," he repeated unsympathetically. "You two have much in common."

Cradling the young woman against her side, Autumn said, "I have never been a nun."

"You stupid stupid girl. Do you not recognize your own flesh and blood?" He curled his mouth upward. "Or is it that she looks more like Robert than Richard?"

With that he walked to his horse.

Autumn looked down again, stiffening as shock flew through her.

Just then, wide blue eyes blinked open.

Twenty-nine

Robert had blue eyes!
Her father's eyes had been hazel.

Autumn realized this now as she stared into Gwen's pale-colored eyes. She was blonde. Winter was blonde. Drogo said she had been a nun . . . or a novice?

She must tread cautiously with her, Autumn thought. I must not tell her what I suspect. But she'd heard, *she'd heard,* and she'd fainted. She must know something, otherwise she would not have reacted as she had, Autumn told herself.

Gwen looked up at the woman holding her head up and she wanted to ask her what the evil-stinking bastard had been talking about. Robert and Richard? The names rang a bell too clearly in her mind.

"All right now?" Autumn asked, still staring at the eyes that were all too familiar.

Gwen nodded. She sat up, curling her legs, pushing and pulling at the woman, at the same time. Gwen didn't know if she wanted her near her or away from her. For now, everything seemed too painful to contemplate.

"Come, you must get up now," Autumn said. "They

352

are coming for us. We will escape with Mai-Lee and Song later, when it is dark. Will you be up to it?"

Again, Gwen nodded, struggling for words she could not say.

Drogo and his prisoners traveled for what seemed many hours and Autumn had no idea what would happen next. But the sun in the sky told her they had only been riding for perhaps several hours. She had no time to think of Raine and if he would rescue them, if he could—and why had he not by now. He must not care, she told herself. She might not see him again, ever.

It was as if Raine Guardian had disappeared from her life. At the time, she didn't know if she really cared. Nothing seemed to matter but that she try to get them all to safety. Then she could begin to think about her life.

And love.

She saw the sparkles in the hills before anyone else. It must mean knights were in the distance, coming for them. Shielding her eyes from the glare of the high yellow sun, Autumn watched, wondering when the men would take notice. She noticed something over there, where the stand of trees flanked the woodlands; Ghost, he was really there, not just a figment, and now she saw him turn running back into the deeper concealing shadows. The closest knight jerked his head in that direction, rubbed his neck, frowning, as he probably wondered if he had been seeing things. Now he turned and gave a gasp.

353

Autumn looked at what he was seeing in the distance. She had already seen. Many knights were coming.

Were they about to be rescued? She could only pray.

They had been resting near a wood-flanked stream when one of Stephan's men cried out the alarm. "Knights— they are coming!"

"What knights?" Stephan shouted, tossing down a leg of rabbit he'd been eating. "The king's? Or the bastard, Fulcan of Salisbury?"

"I would not know," cried the robber knight, shaking in his tattered hose.

"We will fight," said Stephan, brandishing his sword.

"That many?" asked Autumn, walking up to him, her arms still bound in front of her.

Mai-Lee, also bound, rushed behind her, leaving Song with Gwen. "Do not speak to him," she whispered. "You will only anger him."

"What will you do now?" Autumn asked Stephan, coming from beneath the wide oak tree.

Stephan whirled to face her, his eyes glared ice. "Cease your arrogance, woman. I should have your head chopped off now, before your defiance causes me any more trouble and grief."

"Your name means troubles and grief, Stephan the Bastard."

He backhanded her across the face and Autumn stumbled back against Mai-Lee. Gwen saw and started forward, but then remembered she held Song by the hand. Song began to cry and then sob for her father. Gwen picked up the child and held her close. Song was growing curious over Gwen's lack of speech; she touched the woman's mouth now. Looking at Song rather forlornly, Gwen shook her head, pressing two fingers over her mouth. Seeing this, Song laid her head against Gwen's shoulder, blinking up into Gwen's eyes as if in complete understanding of Gwen's affliction.

Mai-Lee and Autumn stood close beneath the arms of a spreading oak, watching, waiting, as Gwen came to stand closer, with Song now holding her hand and staring up at the beautiful blonde.

A sudden smile spread across Mai-Lee's face. Her eyes were sparkling, her shoulders squared. "It is him. The Black Knight comes. Now we will be rescued."

Autumn looked at Mai-Lee. "The Black Knight?"

When the slightly older woman nodded, Autumn said, "I know of him. When I was alone and about to be set upon by some men, he came along like a strong wind and saved both my life and honor. Mai-Lee?" She touched the woman's arm, "Is he really Russ—"

"Look!" Song cried. "The big sparkles are here!"

"Saved," breathed Mai-Lee.

Thirty

Sutherland's castle tower, an old fortification built in the eleventh century, stood alone, apart from the manor house; both were surrounded by a new wall that had replaced the crumbled and old broken one. The manor house was an informal group of buildings all constructed of timber and stone. The windows, like the eyes of many dragons, shone like jewels in the sunset.

A woman with long dark hair, braided into thick swirls either side of her head, rushed out of the manor house; her high squeals of pleasure could be heard by everyone present in the courtyard.

Elizabeth Sutherland was a very beautiful woman, and very pregnant.

Autumn had watched as they rode up, as the sun glistened through a tall, leaded window, sending a bright shaft from one side to the other. An omen?

"I saw it," Elizabeth said breathlessly. "The bright shaft of sunlight." She hugged Autumn as the younger woman came down off the huge war-horse she'd been riding double with a lovely fair-haired girl. "It is a good omen, for it happened once following a victorious battle, and then when Maryse Nicole was born. Oh, Autumn, where have you been? And who do you have with you?" She placed a hand over her mouth then, as Autumn shook her head slowly, her expression saying, *"Not now. I do not know yet."*

The others came into the courtyard and Elizabeth rushed to Song, cooing over her. "Come here, angel, you must be so weary and hungry, too. We will get you all baths and then after you have eaten something you can meet my daughter. She, Maryse, must be the same age as you." Elizabeth hugged the child once more before letting her go back to the lovely Oriental woman, waiting for her charge.

Autumn followed Elizabeth inside, smiling gently over her shoulder at Gwen who was coming along at a slower pace. After all, she'd never been to Sutherland and just the manor itself was a delightful adventure to walk into, with all its new woodwork, bright tapestries, cheerful stone hearths lighted even in summertime. Orion Sutherland always kept low fires going, windows flung wide. The manor glowed like a wonderful cathedral, all year round, especially in winter when the fires blazed a cheery welcome.

"We have so much to talk about," said Elizabeth. "Orion is with King Henry and will not be back for another week. We have hundreds of knights, and many more than that who can, at a word, come posthaste. But I do not think we will have any more trouble from Stephan and his robber knights. Howell Armstrong sent word to us, reporting there was no fight and that Stephan was in such a hurry to flee, he left all his prisoners behind in his dust. He said he would come to fight in the tourney." She laughed. "Odd, but is this not the way it went?"

Autumn could only think of one thing as she looked at Elizabeth. "You did say Howell Armstrong, did you not?"

"Why yes," Elizabeth said, laughing. "Yes I did. You remember him. He is Orion's best knight."

"I never knew his last name," Autumn said. "Curious . . ."

"Come, let us get you some rooms." Elizabeth led the way and the women and Song followed. They took in everything, the gleaming stairs, the open rooms, tapestries, carpets, and Song's eyes were very big.

Autumn blurted, "Is he related to Tyrian Armstrong?"

"Who?" Elizabeth said, tossing over her shoulder as they made their way to the third landing smelling of new wood and lemon wax.

"Howell," Autumn said. "Is he related to Tyrian Armstrong?"

"He could be." Elizabeth gave Mai-Lee and Song a lovely, airy apartment, then swooped on her way with Gwen and Autumn trailing behind. "Here. Would you like to share?" She looked at Gwen and Autumn. "You could get to know each other—" Her eyes twinkled happily and she didn't add "again," though she'd very much like to. "There are two beds in your bedchamber."

"I know." Autumn laughed, touching Elizabeth's arm.

With a kiss on Autumn's cheek, Elizabeth excused herself. "We will talk later."

Autumn's head was whirling as she sat on the edge of the bed. So much had happened. They had been rescued . . . and she hadn't known that Howell had been one of them. All knights looked alike with all their armor donned. She did not remember Howell all that much, for he'd always been training in the field with his men and Orion Sutherland. Tyrian's brother? Cousin? Were they even related? What? Why hadn't Raine told her this?

And the Black Knight had disappeared after the rescue.

Autumn shook her head and looked around for Gwen, finding her fast asleep in the middle of one of the huge beds that occupied her old sleeping chamber. Everything looked different and yet, actually, it was not all that unfamiliar to her; she'd slept here for the past six years before going on her adventure.

And before that, she'd lived with her sisters and parents at Windrush.

Walking over to the bed—the one standing below the dais—Autumn placed her hand gently upon Gwen's cheek. She brushed back a strand of silver-blond hair, now dull from lack of washing. She is so lovely, so pale, so gentle of countenance. Having seen her with Song, Autumn knew that Gwen loved children and it was in her eyes that she wished to have some of her own one day. She looked at the tattered clothing, the dirt smudges on her flawless skin of extraordinary texture like a white rose and fine, long lashes. Gwen's arms were slim and finely muscled as her own. There were no birthmarks she could see. Autumn did not recall that any of the Seasons had any such marks on their skin anywhere. Her own was unmarked also, but for a few freckles across her nose and upper cheeks. Gwen had none. She was flawless. She touched the tattered cloak, sighed and looked away, tears stinging her eyes.

I will let Gwen sleep, Autumn told herself.

She glanced at Gwen over her shoulder once before going into the bathing room down the hall. There was a question or two molded on her lips before she turned back toward the door:

Are you my sister? When will I know for sure? Dear God, if only this were true.

"Dawn and Jay are not here," Elizabeth was saying as she arranged her daughter's hair into neat braids. "They are visiting my cousin Clytie who now has holdings north of here. Clytie still has not wed. Oh, listen to me, rambling." Elizabeth patted Maryse and sent her off to play with her toys, and Song who was already happily occupied in a corner of the room piled with the playthings.

"Song and Maryse have much fun together, it is good to see," Mai-Lee was saying, running off again to chat with Orion's man, Rajahr, an Oriental like herself. However, Mai-Lee was never far away, and always returned quickly to check on Song wherever she was presently occupied at the time in the huge manor. "Autumn, you watch Song," Mai-Lee asked, popping her head back in the solar.

"Yes," Autumn said with a laugh. "I am watching Song. It is a delight to watch them play. Go on, Mai-Lee, visit your friend and do not worry. Song will be fine."

Elizabeth still tilted her head in the direction Mai-Lee had taken. "What a wonderful woman. I should be so lucky to find such a guardian for Maryse. Dawn is good with her, but she goes visiting a lot with her husband Jay."

"She is not with child yet?" Autumn asked, sipping her juice. Dawn and Jay had been trying to have a child for many years, but nothing came of their exhaustive lovemaking.

"No. Dawn is often inconsolable over it. Jay takes her visiting often. Too bad she does not have family of her own."

"Dawn and I talked about that a lot," Autumn said. "Jay is her family."

"And of course—all of us. I just meant it's too bad she does not have blood relations. Someday perhaps someone will arrive to say they have found Dawn's relatives, or at least one, that would be nice. She's always been a forlorn but lovely orphan, this is what my brother calls her, His lovely orphan."

"It is sad to think of it," said Autumn, with a fine mist in her eyes.

"Do you think she is Winter?" Elizabeth could ask, now that Gwen was out of the solar, off in the stables looking over the fine horseflesh there.

"I truly hope to God this is so," Autumn said, breaking off a bit of chicken from a leg and nibbling. "It would be so nice to find just one of my sisters. I believe that that in itself would bring luck and thereafter one would appear after the other."

"You know," Elizabeth began, "God gives us back what we once lost. In one way or another, when we've lost a special love, He will bring us someone else, be it a small furry creature or a human. When I lost all that had been dear to me, I said to myself: A new love will come into my life. I will find a sense of courage

361

and a center of calm relief, hope, and peace that I never knew existed before."

"You have it now," Autumn said to Elizabeth. "When I first came here you were not sure you had found love. Then I watched it grow between you and Orion. It is a beautiful thing you and he have together. And look, now you are expecting your second babe. How grand."

"How about you, Autumn? Have you met someone special yet?" Elizabeth tilted her head, her dark hair shining like precious gemstones surrounding her gorgeous face.

"I have severed him from mind and heart," Autumn said, watching the children play with the creative wooden toys Rajahr had fashioned right before Maryse's birth.

Elizabeth leaned forward. "No you haven't. The yearning is there in your eyes, your face, your motions. You walk across the room like a woman who has lost that love and longs for its return."

"No, really?" Autumn said, hugging her slim shoulders and then letting her hands drop back to her lap. "I—I didn't know that it showed."

"It does. You are different from when you left here." She smiled. "The Sutherland knights brought a new female back to us." Across the room, she looked at the beautiful child. "Who is she?" Elizabeth swung her gaze back to Autumn, waiting.

"Song . . . she belongs to a very special man."

"Her father then."

Autumn nodded.

"We will have a tourney here soon. It will be a splendid day of games and jousts, and knights will arrive from every corner of the country. Henry will return with Orion from France. That is, if the king is not ill as rumors would have him be."

Of the tourney, Autumn merely said, "That will be nice."

Elizabeth looked away and smiled.

Silence fell, as together they watched Song and Maryse Nicole play.

Thirty-one

Songs were being sung about the Seasons by traveling minstrels and people on the streets of Herst stopped what they were doing while others would rush out of houses and shops to watch the entertainers as they walked and rode through the village. They were dressed in colorful costumes and along with them came the jugglers and acrobats, fortune-tellers, and the two-wheeled carts.

The troupe would wind in and out of streets, laughing and shouting, banging on drums, jugglers tossing bright balls high in the air, while other players were doing cartwheels.

These players lived on sufferance alone, since they lightened the lives of those they entertained, but no law protected their lives or possessions. Laws were only for those who had an accepted place in society; men, and women alike, were unequal before the law. Outlaws did not have masters, neither did the players, who were considered by many to be little better.

A beautiful, chestnut-haired woman traveling with the troupe, had come to be with them six years before. She had wanted to travel, to find her missing sisters if she could. Quite by accident, the traveling musicians had discovered her beautiful singing voice.

Her name was Spring; she had realized for some time now that the musicians of the troupe had been singing about her and her sisters. She had begun to sing right along with them, never telling them she was one of the Seasons.

There was a rumor that had begun to spread like wildfire between this village and the last, that the first two of the Meaux sisters were to be found at Sutherland. Young women from all over were coming to claim title to the missing legacy: two more females were yet to be found.

Spring had to see the two at Sutherland for herself. So many had come and gone in the past year, claiming the same. She'd know them once she looked them over, Spring knew. At least she thought she might be able to. Time had passed, true, but what could be so difficult about realizing one's own flesh and blood?

She had been searching for a long time and her friends in the troupe weren't aware that she'd been singing about her own family. It was quite exciting to keep the mystery to oneself.

Spring had heard the name of Autumn being bandied about in the streets, and through the swirling dust she found her gaze now going to the tall tower rising far into the hills above the village. They were going there to entertain at the celebration following the huge tourney to be held in just a week's time. The lord of the castle was returning from France and King Henry; no one knew if Henry himself was coming. Also, the young woman calling herself Autumn Meaux, had just returned from a journey in which she supposedly had been searching for her long lost sisters.

Could this Autumn be an impostor, a liar? For six years?

Sutherland. What secrets would be revealed to her there? Spring wondered.

As the tourney drew near, some of the townsfolk and others from afar pushed at the gates of Sutherland. Young women threw themselves at the guards, screaming and claiming to be Autumn Meaux's lost sisters. Some guards would laugh out loud, asking, "Which sister?" to which there was most times a blank look following. Some were very persuasive, so much that guards begged Autumn Meaux to come and see for herself. Could any of them be her kin?

Shaking her head, Autumn would walk away, exhausted, time after time, as women with blond, red, brown, and curiously streaked shades of hair would parade in front of her, each proclaiming Meaux blood as their own.

One woman had thrown herself so forcefully at Autumn that she'd been knocked down. Thereafter she looked down from the high wall. But this ritual was taking its toll. Autumn was becoming weary and depressed.

Elizabeth paced in the solar. "What has brought this thing about? How can so many women be so stupid and ill-advised. Do these young females not know that there are those who've seen them come into this world, walked with them, talked, worked beside even—that their names are not that of Meaux, their features not even closely resembling Autumn's kin?" She spread her hands.

"Do not be so hard on them," Autumn said with a sigh heard all the way across the room. "To be a Meaux would be quite exciting, wouldn't it? To have a large, loving family?"

"That is very kind of you, Autumn. Love is quite desirable. Orion has the credit for helping me to love more deeply."

"I heard it was you who helped him. He was a mess before you came along. He was called the Dragon of Herstmonceaux. He was a drunkard and an evil-tempered man." Her laugh tinkled in the air. "They said he ate children for his dinner."

"Orion?" Elizabeth laughed, and then her expression sobered, her eyes moist, her voice tenderly loving. "Was he like that?" she whispered. "I can hardly recall all that; he is such a different person now."

"All because of love," Autumn said wistfully, smoothing the chemise sleeve ending in lace ruffles. "Perfect love must make a woman and a man kind toward each other, gently caring for the welfare of others along with that special love."

Elizabeth's eyebrows lifted. "Is this how you have felt?"

"Yes. I truly have. And I miss the feeling that is something so wonderful it makes your eyes mist. You do not have to pretend anything. Everything seems to fall into place. The world is a wonderful place to be, no matter what happens. Even the exhaustive arguments are exciting."

A laugh erupted from Elizabeth. "You know love then, Autumn. You have found it."

"Yes."

"He will come to you."

"When?" Autumn said, feeling her heart jump.

"Love will find a way." Elizabeth grinned. "You will see. Just believe."

Oh, she did, she *did!*

He waited, his breath merging with the soft rhythms of the hot August air around him and his skin with the dappled shade. Out in the training field the vivid sunset struck sparks from the steel weapons.

And still he waited.

Stealthily, he moved from the trees flanking the training field toward the old wall, climbed the thick ropes of vines to the top and looked across into the courtyard.

Then he saw her. She was there, just having stepped outside. Laughing, she flung back her head. Her beauty was unmistakable; she was wearing a royal blue gown with sleeves ending in lace ruffles. Her hair was like a living flame spread about her shoulders. Beside her walked Elizabeth and a fair-haired woman he did not know.

She drew him, like a moth to flame. Even so, he stayed where he was, did not make a move toward her, only observing her as she walked with Elizabeth and the other young woman.

Then he saw Song come rushing outside, Mai-Lee following close behind.

* * *

Autumn had neither seen nor heard anything to suggest to her that she was being observed. But she could feel it; there were a pair of eyes on her. The feeling was unbelievably strong and she had to catch her breath.

Moving aside from the others, she moaned slightly, drew a couple of deep, sighing breaths, and looked round her. She lifted her eyes, shielded them from the sun, and kept walking.

"Where are you going?" Elizabeth called to Autumn, taking Song's hand, while Mai-Lee laughed and took Maryse's hand. "Don't you want to come with us and see the men training in the jousting field for the tourney?"

"I'm going for a walk," Autumn answered. "I won't be long."

Autumn stared up at the old wall and kept walking, holding tight to the Windrush jewel clutched in her hand.

She was alone now, but the sensation of being watched was leaving her. Back against the old garden grew tall trees, as tall as the wall where heavy vines climbed upward and in some places made a canopy across to the tallest trees.

It was shady and cool beneath the leaves and vines. Wild roses grew here, their delicate pink lovely, their slight perfume sweet. Autumn heard a sound and walked toward it, thinking perhaps some children might be playing there. She was surprised to hear the whinnying of a horse, a very familiar whinny.

She drew closer to the spot where she knew a horse waited. She stepped around the thickets and green growth.

Autumn gasped.

There stood her horse. She merely whispered, "Ghost." And he came to her.

"Dear God," she exclaimed, "where did you come from?"

Autumn was just returning from bringing Ghost to the stables. She walked across the outer bailey . . . and stopped. Something drew her to the small wooden doors in the old section of the castle yet standing, and her feet led her up the stone stairs to the chapel above.

The chapel was hushed, not even a mouse making a sound as Autumn stepped inside and walked slowly round the room. A few candles had been lit and she went toward them, her face illuminated in the soft yellow light.

"Autumn," said the soft voice.

"What?"

"Here, over here." The voice was so familiar . . .

Rushing toward the low ceiling behind the pillars, Autumn stepped around the screens, and came face to face with Raine.

He pulled her into his arms, nearly crushing her in his embrace. He kissed her, all over her face, taking her hands into his. Then he stopped, looking down at her in a most romantically stirring way.

"God, I've missed you," he said in a choked voice. He kissed her again and again, running his hands all over her body.

"Cease!"

Raine pulled back to look at her. "Why do you say that? Haven't you missed me?" he asked Autumn.

She looked up at him. "Ah, the man with the secrets has returned. What are you up to now? Did you bring Ghost to me?"

"Of course," Raine said with a shrug, his handsome mouth curling up in a generous grin. "You have kept my daughter safe. I am indebted to you."

"Why, thank you, m'lord rogue," she said flippantly. "You can also thank Mai-Lee, she had much to do with caring for Song. *Now,* what are you doing here? I've asked you."

He grinned, even wider. "That, my love, is a secret."

"Oh!" Autumn said, fuming, walking away. "We are done, Raine. Over. No more."

Autumn did not even look back, she just kept walking, sputtering, fuming, talking, all the way down the stairs, across the courtyard and over to the manor.

Raine laughed, a deep-throated, low laugh. He tossed the Windrush jewel up into the air, clutched it once again, then walked away, chuckling all the way over to the stables.

He ducked under the low beam and walked into a spacious room, bragging, "Tyrian, wait until you hear *this* one."

Thirty-two

"The Windrush jewel!"

Autumn glanced down at her hand, again and again. He took it! Raine took the jewel from her! How had he gotten it from her? She'd held it tightly in her fist and when he'd . . . ah, when his hands roved her body, that is when she must have . . . could she have . . . dropped it?

Autumn raced back to the chapel, searching frantically the spot she'd last been standing with him. There was no sign of it, not here, not anywhere in the room, she discovered as she walked here, there, everywhere she'd stepped.

Her eyes turned dark and angry. Raine, damn him, he had taken her jewel!

"I will find him," she said out loud as she almost ran to the stables. She collided with the strong frame of a tall, light-haired man.

"Here!" he cried. "Where are you going in such a hurry?"

She looked up and gaped. "You. What are you doing here?" she asked Tyrian.

He laughed. "Visiting my cousin, Howell Armstrong."

"I knew he was a relative of yours!" she shouted up at him as he released the hold he'd had on her slim arms.

"I never said otherwise." Tyrian laughed again. He had been thrilled to discover that Gwen had not been hurt, and now he wanted to see her. Raine had made it clear that he must wait until the right time to let it be known to her that he was here. "Where were you going in such a hurry?"

"You are all related, every last damn one of you!" Autumn screeched at his head.

He stood nonchalantly with hands on his slim hips. He was dressed in chain mail; he must have returned just now from the jousting field, Autumn told herself. "Where is your other cousin? You do know who I mean, do you not?"

"Hmm." Tyrian thought for a moment, tapping his chin with a forefinger.

"You men!" Autumn fumed. "Raine . . . or does he go by some other name again?"

Pressing the button of Autumn's nose, Tyrian cryptically said as he walked away from her, "You needs discover that for yourself, dear lady."

About to turn away from the bales of hay she'd been glaring at for several minutes, Autumn cocked her head, quite certain she'd heard a rustling coming from behind that huge pile of straw.

"Who is there?"

No answer.

"I ask again: I know there is someone there. 'Tis not the horses; they are at the other end. Come out, right now, whoever you are!" She walked closer, meaning to jump around the hay pile and catch who was hiding there.

Suddenly she was staring into a pair of huge blue eyes. They blinked as Gwen came around the pile, grinned, shrugged her shoulders, and swallowed.

"Gwen," Autumn said, astonished at finding her there. "Whatever are you hiding for?" She glanced the way Tyrian had gone. "Not him . . . and you?" Her eyes darkened. "He did not . . . he was not. Did he touch you?"

Vigorously Gwen shook her head.

"Then what?"

This time Gwen appeared embarrassed.

"He must have done something. Come, Gwen, do not be afraid to tell me. I will have Orion's men whip him, or worse, if Tyrian has touched you . . ."

Autumn leaned forward at the misty light in Gwen's eyes, the soft tilt of her mouth, the dreamy expression that bordered on silly. "No," Autumn said. "You are not in love with that big rogue. Tell me you are not."

Gwen looked even sillier.

"You are." Autumn gaped. "Indeed you are."

Gwen nodded and clasped her hands together in front of her.

"Come," Autumn said. "Let's go tell Tyrian you are in love with him. He should know."

It was like trying to pull a stubborn mule. Gwen balked and shook her head violently, her lips saying No, no, no!

Autumn stopped, reading the truth in Gwen's eyes.

"My God, he did not know you were spying on him, did he?"

Again the vigorous shake of Gwen's head.

"Oh my. You poor girl. You do have it bad, don't you?"

Very definitely, Gwen's four-time nod stated.

Gwen was feeling sick, very very sick.

"What is wrong?" Autumn asked as she put the young woman to bed. "I have just returned from Elizabeth and she filled me in on the gossip that is going about the old castle. You and Tyrian were on the road a lot together . . . he did not make you with child, did he?"

Gwen started to shake her head in the negative when she found Autumn catching her when she almost fell over. She groaned and put her head in her hands while Autumn rushed over to the washbowl to rinse a cloth in cool water.

"Here, this will help." Autumn was about to place the cloth in Gwen's hands when the blonde looked up at her with red-rimmed eyes. And her face! "There are dots all over your face, Gwen. Here"—Autumn said, picking up a slim arm, then looking at her neck—"Oh my, these dots, they are all over you. Was it something you ate?"

All of a sudden Gwen's eyes lit up. She nodded, her lips forming, Yes, yes, yes!

Autumn grabbed for a chair. "It—" Autumn faltered. "They weren't strawberries, were they?"

Gwen looked at Autumn, seeing the wildly hopeful look. Then: *Yes.*

Suddenly Autumn jumped up from her chair and whirled round and round the room, cheering, jumping for joy. She ran over and pulled Gwen up, hugging her as if to break her bones.

Gwen blinked as Autumn pulled back to look at her, tears of joy coursing down her cheeks. She held both Gwen's shoulders then, looking her straight in the eyes.

"Winter always breaks out from strawberries!"

What? Gwen's look asked.

"Winter . . . Gwen," Autumn said with a heavy gulp. "You are my . . . *we are sisters!*"

Thirty-three

Autumn was so excited that she forgot all about the Windrush jewel.

Her sister!

She still couldn't believe it, but believe it she must, for it was true.

The strawberries!

Gwen—she still called her that for now—was seated beside her now in the stands that had been set up in the big meadow; the festivities for afterward were being readied even now. The musicians had come. Jousts were being prepared. Tents had already been set up in the meadow. There were sweet buns and mugs of ale for the knights. The goldenrod and bluebells were blooming in the hedgerows. Everywhere the air was full of the buzzing of bees in the still heat of late summer.

Sounds rippled across the meadow and the brown dust of the jousting field. Elizabeth looked none too happy, for Orion had not yet returned from King Henry. She was worried; he should have been home early the evening before. Something must have gone wrong, she fretted. Then again, when matters needed attention,

Orion would be the first and last to stay around and right things.

Elizabeth leaned to Autumn. "I have grown used to the peculiar haze that hangs over the land even when the sun is high."

"What is it?" Autumn asked. "I have seen it, too."

"I'd thought no one else seemed to see it. I thought perhaps there was something the matter with my eyes."

"There is also a feel to it," Autumn added. "Like a rumbling so low it cannot be heard, just felt, like distant thunder."

"It is a premonition perhaps?" Elizabeth said with a nervous little laugh.

"At times I have the feeling it has to do with King Henry."

"Where is Orion?" Autumn asked. "And wasn't he supposed to come with King Henry?"

"Orion is with him, or was, at Bois de Vincennes. I hope he is on his way home."

"Is the king well?"

"Rumor would have it that he is not. His health, they say, has grown worse since the sieges of Melun and Meaux, and he might have come down with camp fever."

"I hope and pray all goes well here before his return."

Appearing anxious, Gwen nodded vigorously, her thoughts running along the same lines perhaps. Autumn looked at her sister, hugged her, and then they weaved their fingers together, leaning their shoulders close. Orion's mother Julia came to join them, and Mai-Lee stayed back at the manor with Song who was in bed with a slight fever.

"The child rests and feels better," said Julia, easing Autumn's worried mind as she patted her hand.

Autumn had not only had Song for a worry. She had not been able to find out where the mysterious Raine Guardian had taken himself off to. For all she knew, he had left the castle compound. But she didn't think so. There was something afoot and she had a feeling it would not be long for the waiting of the scene to unfold. It made her think of the strange dream the night before:

He was so wealthy, he should have come with a groomsman. But he had come alone. He must have been riding hard because his horse was lathered with sweat, and his clothes were dark, black with silver, and perfectly fitted to the tight muscles of his legs and shoulders. She remembered how her body had burst into flame when he touched her. They'd been standing near a window, looking out over the meadow, when he kissed her. Incredibly, in her dream, she had been glad to kiss this stranger, melting against him, hungry, thrilling in the desire that consumed her. They had stood like that for a long time, locked together with a blinding intensity, before the torrent eased and their straining bodies had softened to each other. Tense moments had flowed away. She remembered the sweetness she'd tasted, anticipating a climax that seemed to be inevitable. He had held her in his arms and her head rested easily on his shoulder against the warmth of his neck.

And then he had spoken to her, his voice thick with desire, "Come with me."

And she had—they had been inside of each other, wonderfully, magically, so thoroughly that she had awakened with the smell and taste of him surrounding her for only brief moments, and then she'd known the feeling of being so damnably alone.

She could smile now, hours later. But who in the name of God was he, this man of her dreams?

"Autumn, look, the jousting is about to begin," Elizabeth said, smiling as if she knew what had given Autumn such a warm, melting expression.

"Have you heard any more news of your husband this day?"

"I only received word that my husband was supposed to arrive late last night." A delicate line furrowed her brow. "Of course, he never showed. It must be this strange heat has slowed them down. I believe we will get a huge thunderstorm soon."

"That must be what it is," Autumn said, switching her regard to Gwen on the other side of her. Gwen was eagerly looking forward to the games. Autumn could guess why.

"Is that not Tyrian?" Elizabeth asked. "Howell's cousin?"

"Yes, it is he," Autumn answered, nudging Elizabeth, to which Elizabeth leaned forward a little to see Gwen.

Elizabeth smiled at Autumn and leaned back to watch the competition begin. Her belly stuck way out in front, but she did not appear to be uncomfortable in any way. She just folded her hands across her stomach and let herself be entertained.

The preliminaries were brief, since this was no formal contest to be judged upon gentle points. No rules applied, no graceful pennants of bright colors. Stephan's arms and surcoat were travel-stained, and knights' shields were so battered with hard wear that the devices were almost blotted out. The combatants' own strength and skill would be judge and jury. They would fight until one of them yielded, was incapable of battling any longer, or was dead.

The field was dead silent but for the soft sound of the horses' hooves on the turf as Armstrong and the Duc drew apart and an occasional creak of harness as one of the watchers' horses shifted position.

Gwen's heart was pounding. She was watching Tyrian, her neck frozen in one position, only her huge blue eyes moving slightly, glued to the tall blond man of *her* dreams.

The women in the stands looked gorgeous in their beautiful finery. Mai-Lee had fashioned new gowns for them all, with the help of Elizabeth's talented needle and that of her mother-in-law's.

Autumn was just rising from her seat. Elizabeth's hand touched Autumn's arm. "Where are you going? The games are about to begin."

"I forgot to give Song some medicine powders I'd made up for her earlier."

"Sit down," Elizabeth ordered firmly. "I've already given your powders to Mai-Lee. She will administer them to the child when she awakens from her nap."

Autumn smiled gratefully but Elizabeth could see there was something weighing on her mind. Elizabeth had a strong suspicion that Autumn was looking around the meadow and the stands of tents for someone.

Could that someone be Fulcan of Salisbury? Elizabeth wondered and kept her mouth sealed on the man in question. Only time would tell what was going to happen here.

The men faced each other and slowly hoisted their lances, each watching the other. Tyrian settled his lance firmly between his arm and his body, then raised his legs and drove his spurs into his war-horse's sides. The horse leapt forward into full gallop. Only a second later Stephan was also moving. Clods of turf flew upward.

There was the thunder of pounding hooves and the loud grunts as the air was forced out of their lungs by the first impact. Tyrian's lance had caught Stephan's shield near the center. Stephan, a little too sure of himself, had been careless. His point, landing off-center above the embossed metal of Tyrian's shield, had slipped harmlessly over Tyrian's shoulder.

Gwen would have gasped if she could have made herself heard. As it was, her fingers had been biting into Autumn's arm. Autumn, unwinding Gwen's fingers, took her sister's hand and clasped it in her own.

When Gwen looked up at her sister, her look said she was sorry for having hurt her.

"I understand," Autumn said, patting Gwen's hand, then clasping it again. "Hold my hand and don't let go."

Elizabeth, almost as knowledgeable as a man-in-arms, having learned from Orion, her husband, was seeing for the first time the kind of man Tyrian fought. She became frightened for Gwen's love and began to pray he'd not be killed.

Both of the knights took fresh lances from their squires and returned to their starting points. The horses thundered across the turf again. In the instant before they met, Tyrian took a desperate chance and threw his shield against his body. Stephan's lance never wavered toward Tyrian's naked heart. It hit his shield's edge and slid off once more without damage. The noise of the crowd behind the ladies settled down once again to a low roar.

By this time Gwen was standing and, as promised, Autumn had stood with her sister. Two passes were over and Tyrian was still alive.

Stephan, thoroughly angry, whirled his horse at the end of the field and started back without taking a fresh lance. Now the lance caught the inner edge of Tyrian's shield with the full power of two galloping beasts and Stephan's own huge strength thrusting behind it. The shield turned inward and the point slipped between to slide against Tyrian's chest.

"No!" Gwen cried, clutching Autumn's hand as if to tear it off.

The women in the stands turned to look at Gwen. They knew she could not speak; she had no voice. Autumn gasped. Elizabeth now stood. Julia stared. Everything went still.

Tyrian looked up, staring into the stands, lifting his helm. He had felt the point pierce his mail, felt the pain of tearing flesh. Yet, he had felt Gwen's cry more than anything else and there was no time to think further of pain. She, Gwen, was the only thing on his mind at this time. His left arm was immobilized by the heavy shield that dragged against the stirrup, and he could do nothing to ease his fall or to protect himself.

Gwen saw Stephan's horse thundering down upon Tyrian again as he turned to face his enemy.

Tyrian shook his head as if to clear it from the mists that fogged his brain. *Gwen, Gwen, you cried out,* was all he could think.

Tears flowed down Gwen's cheeks unfelt as she watched Tyrian stand to be ridden down. She was capable of no feeling at all except the desire to close her eyes and her mind and blot out the sight and knowledge of what was happening.

She would not watch every moment of Tyrian's death.

Thirty-four

The duchess also watched the joust . . . from where no one could see her. She sat her horse atop a hill, in a stand of shadowy oaks. Her lips curled and her long nails bit into the palms of her hands.

Damn them, Rowena thought, damn them. They have foiled me again. The child was not at Castle Salisbury as she'd thought, but her spies had informed her that Song had been taken from Salisbury, along with Autumn Meaux. Now she would never get her hands on the jewel. Nor the child. Nor the sisters who were called the Seasons.

Her eyes narrowed in on Autumn Meaux . . . and who was that seated with her? Was it? Could it be?

Or would she get her hands on the jewel? Perhaps there was *one* strategy left that she could take. Two sisters were better than one. There was always ransom. She licked her lips and rolled her eyes and laughed.

Tears poured down Gwen's cheeks as she watched Tyrian stand to be ridden down. Tyrian was frozen to the spot, the only moving thing on him was the blood that dripped down his chin; it stained his surcoat from the gashes as he bit his lower lip.

"No!" she cried again. "No!"

Autumn held on to Gwen's arm, trying to steady the poor woman. Dear God, she prayed, spare him.

Just then a mounted knight charged over to help Tyrian. It was a common tactic on the battlefield to help a friend in need. And Autumn stared, seeing the man in black and silver, mounted on a huge black war-horse. Who is this man? Wasn't he the one she'd seen in her dreams?

Autumn was just as tense as Gwen was, as she watched the scene unfold.

With a grin of sheer pleasure, Stephan raised his sword to strike. He had not killed his opponent; he'd only stunned Tyrian. He wanted to bring Tyrian to his knees, to plead for mercy and promise anything to buy his life.

With a twist of her head, Autumn looked at Gwen. No, she thought, *no,* he would not ask Tyrian to give up the woman he loved, to give her over to Stephan. Or would he? Stephan was after them, and once he had Gwen, he would stop at nothing to get her, too. She just knew this was what Stephan was after. Them, and the Windrush jewel.

But who was this man in silver and black?

"The Fulcan," Elizabeth breathed.

"Who?" Autumn asked. "The Fulcan of Salisbury?"

"Yes. It is he. One of the greatest knights in the realm."

Autumn was waiting, but just then there was the scream of Stephan's horse, and the crash as the beast fell. The man in silver and black was nearby and Autumn could only stare now. Had he, the Fulcan, caused the beast to fall?

The Fulcan launched a blow that could have cut Stephan in half, but Stephan was too experienced to be caught by that. He was up and after Tyrian again. He knew he had to make this blow good. He had to win the one woman first, and then slay the other knight, in order to request the bonus of both women.

Tyrian leapt aside to avoid Stephan's blow, but he was injured and bleeding from two minor wounds. Fulcan's helm was up, his eyes were alight with blood lust, and his mouth was curved in the hard, merciless, fixed smile of the victor.

On the ground now, the men fought. From the rear of the stands came the shout, "The prize will go to Stephan—two of the Meaux sisters!"

"We?" Gwen managed to croak out, clutching Autumn's arm again. "No," she breathed, her gaze going to Tyrian over and over.

"Who said that we, the sisters, are the rewards of this game?" Autumn wanted to know.

Elizabeth gasped. "Indeed: Who has said this?"

Just then, Baron Drogo stepped out from the crowd. "Why, I have, m'lady."

"You!" Autumn shouted. "How can you have any say over this matter?"

"I do," said Drogo, reaching behind to pull a woman out from behind him. "I—and the Duchess Rowena."

Now it was Autumn's turn to inhale sharply. "You—and *her?*" Autumn slowly nodded her head toward the duchess with the curling lip and shrewd eyes.

"Yes," Rowena sneered. "I. We, and Raine Guardian,

are all related to Catherine of Aragon, all of us cousins, some of greater blood, some of lesser to the French king's daughter." Her laughter was deep and full of spite. "Catherine's husband Henry is dead!"

"Dead?" Elizabeth said, knowing it had been coming.

"How?" Autumn followed.

"Camp fever," said Drogo.

"So," Elizabeth began, beginning to feel the heat of the late August day, "Catherine has given you leave to do as you wish?" Where was her husband? Why had Orion not arrived home by now? Of course, she thought, he would wish to remain with his king for a time—his, *their* dead king.

"The king is dead!!" shouted a man from the fringes of the crowd.

At once the games ground to a halt. The knights who had been fighting stood as if transfixed in time.

Just then Duc Stephan swung his sword at the Fulcan and missed. His breathing was uneven, his timing off. The Fulcan's blade slipped under Stephan's shield and nicked his chest.

Stephan's fear grew. The crowd was going crazy again. Gwen was standing. Autumn and Elizabeth exchanged eye contact. The strange mist. Indeed, a premonition. The king was dead. The Valois curse had been the beginning. The French king had been mad. War and pestilence would empty the land in the coming years; especially in France. There would be a prolonged struggle for power between the crown.

Raine Guardian, Autumn thought angrily. Related to Catherine of Aragon. Her eyes swung back to the jousting field.

Never had Stephan jousted against an opponent such

as the Fulcan of Salisbury. He was still determined to win. He raised his sword over his head and brought it down hard. He'd hoped to cleave the head or arm of the Fulcan, he with glittering eyes who smiled so tauntingly and surely into his face. He twisted aside, gasping and crying out. Fulcan's leg was behind his.

With a shout of fear, Stephan went down. Fulcan leaned his weight against his sword that was pointed at Stephan's throat.

"Yield, Duc Stephan. I know there is mail at your throat and I've not opened it. I need only lean my body against the point. You'll choke, Stephan, even if your mail holds."

Fulcan turned his head and gave a low, sharp order. Seven men set spurs to their mounts and galloped off toward the rise behind which Fulcan's army waited word. Now the whole group moved down the field, not toward the combatants but to block the entrance to the gate in the stone wall. There was no other method, to Fulcan's way of thinking, of preventing Stephan's—and now Drogo's—men from making a dash for the old castle. He must prevent Stephan's men from carrying the women with them and bringing the battle Fulcan had fought to naught.

Stephan's and Drogo's men were many now. Over a thousand strong.

Elizabeth told the women, "They only have to hold their ground for a little while. Soon Orion's entire army will be pouring over the ridge to reinforce the Fulcan."

Where was Raine Guardian keeping himself? Autumn asked herself as her searching eyes went over the crowd of men and women. And whose side was he on? How had this battle gotten started without their knowledge?

Her eyes swept behind her. And where had Drogo and his witchy duchess taken themselves off to?

Like most men who were as nearly irreligious as a man could be in the year 1422, Duc Stephan was deeply superstitious. The Fulcan was the first man to ever defeat him in hand-to-hand combat. They were related. But how much of Raine Guardian's blood really flowed in *his* veins?

As Stephan cried aloud the formal words of yielding, Stephan vowed revenge and sought an escape route. Although Fulcan had spared him, Rowena's assassins would not. She hated men who lost the game she had set for him to fight. He had lost.

"Look!" Autumn cried. "Stephan shakes his shield loose so that he is totally without armor or weapon other than his mail."

Now Stephan caught at Fulcan's ankle as he was about to step back. "My lord," Stephan whispered as Fulcan raised his sword again, "heed my words. Baron Drogo has instructed his men to carry your lady off if I should fail."

"My lady," said Fulcan with eyes of anger.

"The flame-haired one." His lips curled covetously as Fulcan's gaze scanned the crowd for an instant and came to rest. "She—the season that comes between summer and winter."

Stephan's voice died as Fulcan's expression did not change. Stephan did not know that Fulcan had seen his men move in to guard the gate.

"You have spared my life," Stephan said, his eyes dark evil. "You are accountable for seeing that I receive mercy. Drogo and that bitch Rowena will kill me. I've lost their wicked game."

"You've more of their blood than I."

Stephan appeared not to have heard; he clutched the Fulcan's leg. "Spare me. Make me your prisoner."

Fulcan wrenched his leg free and stepped back just as Tyrian came up leading his black horse. He did not glance back at the man still lying on the ground.

"You took my fight from me," Tyrian said gently into Fulcan's ear.

"You are no match for the likes of that bastard. He would have flayed you alive. You are younger than I and have not fought with his kind."

"And you have fought with good King Henry." Tyrian bowed his head, tears misting his great golden eyes. "You are right." Tyrian bent to kiss Fulcan's massive ring. "The king is at peace."

Fulcan's green eyes twinkled. "Tyrian, you'll have to give me a leg up onto my horse. My shoulder is in bad shape, I'm afraid." He sheathed his sword without wiping it and put his left foot into Tyrian's hands to be thrown up into the saddle.

"You've had fighting enough for one day." Tyrian's voice was angry, since he'd still not had time to readjust his emotions.

"My lord!" Stephan cried aloud.

Distaste came and went across the Fulcan's face. "Tyrian, if there are men to spare, let them take that— that thing prisoner."

Tyrian was surprised. "One does not usually make a prisoner of one's opponent." It was held that Fulcan was ordinarily a stickler for rules. "Why do you?"

Fulcan looked back at Tyrian. He rubbed his thigh. "Yes, why do I." Now he looked back at Stephan, every inch the coward as his gaze scanned the crowds for his crazed Rowena and her baron. "Let him go." He grinned. "He'll be well taken care of."

And now Fulcan removed his helm and cap.

Tyrian gasped, amazed.

Fulcan laughed. "Who did you expect? Did you think fairies or elves had carried my body from Salisbury? After all, it was you who urged me to it."

Tyrian's eyes gleamed as he followed after the greatest knight that had lived thus far. He was also the richest in all of England.

Thirty-five

The women in the solar whispered and giggled and laughed to one another while slipping dresses of gorgeous silks and velvets over their heads.

All of a sudden the room went quite still. The man who'd stepped into the space near the door, the many fat candles burnishing his hair, was dressed in silver and black. He wore a full mask.

Lute music trickled up the stairs and filled the empty spaces of the corridors outside the room and, gently, gently, entered the solar.

Autumn suddenly came to her feet.

Gwen swallowed.

The giggles broke out again, this time nervous ones, as the young maidens fled around the stranger in the mask and ran out the door, dressed in their beautiful ruby and gold gowns.

"Fulcan," Autumn ventured at last in a voice that trembled slightly.

"Yes." He eyed Gwen for so long that she dropped the gown she'd been trying on to her ankles, gasped, and snatched it back up to cover herself.

"What do you wish, Lord Fulcan?" Autumn said, coming around a heavy, huge table.

"You."

There was a long pause, which the Fulcan made no effort to ease.

"Go ahead, Gwen, to the screen, and dress yourself," Autumn finally said. "Elizabeth awaits to speak to you."

"Yes," said Gwen in a still shaky voice. "Then . . . I shall . . . join the others . . . in the festivities below."

After Gwen had gone out and left Autumn alone with the Fulcan, the solar was more silent than ever. Even the sound of the lutes, the singing, the laughing, seemed very distant, almost angelic. It grew even fainter as the man and the woman stared at each other. He drew nearer and could smell the pungent scent of herbs rising from her hair. Hair the color of berries in the autumn.

"You smell of lavender also," he said in a deep, thrilling voice. "Are you ready for the festivities?"

"No. The king is dead. I believe it should have been postponed until the time when Orion would arrive from France. Even a year should be set for mourning."

He shrugged. "Does not eating and chatter follow most funerals?"

"But they should not get drunk and have fun."

The Fulcan said, "Life goes on. Death and laughter and renewal."

Autumn softly laughed. "Why don't you remove your mask? I'd like to see what the Fulcan of Salisbury looks like. Are you handsome or is your face scarred and ugly? Are you the same who hid yourself in silver helm and suit at Salisbury? You, who meant to keep me prisoner and toss me into the dungeon, and you said, I quote 'where you'll be tortured in more ways than you can imagine'? Come out from the mask, Lord Fulcan." She faced away from him to stare at the painted screen. "Go ahead. Take it off and surprise me."

When she turned to have a look, he was gone.

Gwen left Elizabeth's apartments and walked downstairs. Elizabeth was feeling tired and would not join the party. She'd promised the knights and the castlefolk some fun following the jousting that had almost turned into a tragedy; the people needed something relaxing after so much tension. Julia and Elizabeth's father had joined the merrymaking along with the newly arrived Jay and Dawn Reynaude; it was toned down, however, since the king had passed away and a measure of good form should be practiced. Song and Mai-Lee had retired early, the child still feeling poorly from her fever.

After Gwen had entered the hall, looked around at all the entertainers, the women in colorful costumes, she turned and ran. A few of the bold knights had seen her, smiled, grinned, and waved her over. That was it. Gwen was sailing out the door and to her own apartments across the bailey.

Tyrian had caught sight of Gwen. He wasn't about to let her get away, not this quickly and easily. He'd been looking for her ever since the games had ended.

He was faster than she.

Across the inner bailey, Gwen ran, feet flying in the golden slippers. Some kind soul had brought, bought and paid for all the beautiful gowns for the ladies of the castle. Some of the "ladies" were orphans that the wonderful lady Elizabeth had adopted years before when they'd only been young maidens still in their teens. "Lord" Geoffrey was a squire, training to be a knight. He was one of Elizabeth's favorite young males. She had so many favorites that actually, Gwen was thinking, they were all special and beautiful in the kind lady's sight. And now Elizabeth had treated her as if she were also family.

Gwen hurried. She did not wish to be seen with any knight other than Tyrian. If it got back to him that she had been speaking with another man, he might never come to her at all. As it was, she was beginning to wonder why he'd not looked for her after the games.

She could speak now! After a few moments of that elation, thinking that now she could converse with Tyrian, she hung her head as she walked, feeling like a coward. The only thing she could *not* do was go and seek him out and pour out her heart.

Gwen was walking with her head down, watching the golden slippers, yearning to be seen by Tyrian in the beautiful clothes, when she bumped right into a solid hunk of man.

At once strong hands were being clamped round her shoulders, then one came away to lift her chin. Gwen looked up into the golden eyes and believed she might swoon with unspeakable joy.

"Tyrian," she whispered.

"The voice of an angel," he said just as softly back to her.

Her heart was pounding so hard that Gwen thought it would shake her asunder. Now that she could speak and tell him what she felt, she had gone and gotten tongue-tied. She could only stare down at the toes of her slippers after he'd released the gentle hold on her chin and stepped back a little.

"Would you like to walk?" Tyrian asked, sliding his hand down to feather-brush with her trembly fingers and then hold fast.

"Yes," she told him, feeling remarkably shy now that she had voice.

The merrymakers of the castle created a background music as Gwen and Tyrian passed through the courtyard and through the trees. The August moon reached through the trees with slim fingers and graced every shrub, branch, stone, and human with a magical light. Even so, deep patches spread before them and shadows abounded. Especially where lovers would go to be hidden from view.

And Tyrian took Gwen under the spreading branches of an old tree, begging, "Say my name again, sweet Gwen . . . Winter."

"Tyrian," she again whispered. Then, "Kiss me. Please, do kiss me."

His lips brushed, then molded, settled, suckled, began searching again restlessly, over and over, until Gwen began to moan softly. He stopped to look down at her and his smile was a fierce fissure of victory. His lips came to hers again. When his tongue slipped inside, penetrated, retreated, she felt the strange yearning begin. One that was foreign to her. Straps of heat were whipping her insides.

"Gwen. Kiss me back. Give me your tongue."

She did. And almost swooned in Tyrian's battle-hardened arms.

"You know so much," she told him when he pulled back for a short breather. "I know nothing of this."

His laugh was like a gentle wind, stirring her tendrils of hair. "You need do nothing different from what you already are doing, sweet Gwen."

"Truly?"

"Truly," Tyrian said.

"I could kiss and kiss all night," Gwen told him, then blushed hotly.

"Ho." Tyrian looked down into her eyes. "If we did that you would not be a maiden come morning."

"I want you, Tyrian."

He swallowed tightly. "Gwen," he said, taking both her hands in his huge palms, "I want you for my wife. First I would wed you before making you my own with my body."

"Marry me then, Tyrian."

Tyrian tossed back his head, then looked down at her. "You do take charge now that you've found your voice, don't you." It was no question. "I love you, Gwen, everything about you."

"I love you, Tyrian Armstrong." Her shoulders suddenly drooped. "Oh no. We will have to wait. The king is dead, Tyrian. Being a knight, do you not have to ask permission?"

He took her hand. "Sit down, Gwen," he said as he brought her over to a stone bench.

"What is it, my love? You look suddenly grim and desperate," Gwen told him.

"I have nothing, Gwen. My manor was confiscated by the king's men. Drogo had much to do with the taking of Golden Valley. My home. Or used to be. I was much younger than I am now at twenty and five. I went to live with the Woo'folk, remember I told you, brought you there. Now that the king is dead I shall never regain the rights to my estates."

"Surely someone, like his wife Catherine, can give us permission to wed."

Her voice was so soft, like velvet roses twining round his heart and soul. Like heaven. He'd known beforehand if she could but speak he'd hear the voices of angels singing in his heart; especially her voice.

"Marry we might be able to; still I'd not have but a simple cottage to put you in and have you call it home. You'd have no castle, only a hearth."

Tenderly stroking his arm, she murmured, "I had but a tiny dark room and shared halls and gardens with so many novices and nuns. 'Twould be heaven to live in a humble dwelling and have you all to myself." She ducked her head and slid in against his throat, placing her fingers over the soft material of his vest. She looked up at him. "Where then do you find such good clothes to wear?"

He gave a crack of laughter. "You've not looked close enough. If you would have you'd see the tiny holes in my clothes."

"I shall mend them all."

"You would?"

"Of course. I'm very talented with needle and thread. I can make everything for us. Elizabeth will help us out. She and Orion are very rich."

Tyrian dropped his chin to his chest. "As I was." Suddenly he was up off the stone bench. "I go immediately to speak with the Fulcan of Salisbury."

"Why?" Gwen stood along with him.

"We will go to see who has taken over my holdings.

Someone must be living there. No doubt some of Stephan's or Drogo's men."

"How can there be so many of the devils?" Gwen asked, stroking his chest.

"Because that is just what they are. Devils. They overrun the land." He pressed her hand to his heart. "We will marry, Gwen. If this is your wish, then I promise, we will become man and wife."

"When?" Her eyes were huge and silver-blue in the moonlight. Her slippers brushed the thick carpet of creeping thyme beneath their feet as she tried to move even closer.

"When you say, my angel." He drew her to him.

She climbed into his lap and he encircled her in his arms. "Soon," she whispered, feeling his manly heat. "Soon."

"I want you, Gwen."

"Take me. I am yours."

They slipped to the creeping thyme and each entered the other's soul.

"I love you, my angel. I will love you forever and ever, and nothing shall part us save death."

"And I," she said, crying with joy at the magnificence of him. "Yesterday; today; now; tomorrow; I will always love you. You are my golden knight." The thyme was carpet-soft.

Neither Gwen nor Tyrian saw the Duchess Rowena and her hideous assassins sneak into the garden like slithering snakes. Gwen gasped and cried out with the hot ecstasy pouring through her as Tyrian thrust deeply, kissing her full on the mouth. He stiffened and arched his back. He now pulled away and looked down at her with surprise, pain, and joy in his eyes. She could feel a sharp pain upon her chest as he lowered himself slowly, putting his full weight on her. She stared straight into his eyes as the sparkle died. She pushed his weight to one side, now throwing the back of her hand to her mouth and screamed as everything grew black.

The man with milky skin, light hair, and pink eyes, withdrew the long dagger from Tyrian's back and picked the young woman up who was still flushed from love-making. He cradled her in his arms as he looked down and watched the blood trickle down the slope of her stomach. After placing the gunnysack over her, he trailed after the quickly moving form of the duchess, her mercenaries spread out to protect their passage down the tree-dotted hill.

The group led by Rowena never stopped to look back, not even at the naked man who lay on the creeping thyme with his blood spilling onto the carpet of herbs. Only the moon's rays found the crimson stain as the men moved on with the wariness of wild animals.

Gwen came out of her swoon into a dark lonely world of horror. The bag she was inside felt scratchy. Her clothes were gone, only her chemise and inner skirt remained on her cold cruel flesh. She remembered, but the memory was fading swiftly. She hurt, hurt so bad inside with the grief and torment that was like an evil creature devouring her very soul. She tried to scream again.

She had no voice.

Thirty-six

"He died with a smile on his mouth."

"Who would have killed him?"

"Could have been the one he'd been jousting with on the field yesterday—that devil Duc Stephan."

"Stephan's gone. Long gone; he rode out like all the devils in hell were after him."

"He could've come back for Tyrian Armstrong and slain him."

"Look—his cousin Howell's coming to the manor. He looks fit to be tied in chains."

The gossipy speculations filtered from the kitchens to the stables, the storehouses, and the stone walls, down into the village of Herst. It wasn't long before the news reached Autumn where she sat in the solar having a somewhat quiet conversation with Elizabeth.

"I'm so worried," Autumn told Elizabeth. "We've searched everywhere. No one can find Winter . . . I mean Gwen. She's used to that name; I was going to ease into using her real name and not push it with her all at once."

"I know." Elizabeth leaned over—as much as she

could with her huge belly—and patted Autumn's hand. "We'll find—"

Suddenly the doors burst open and Howell stepped inside the solar, Elizabeth's men-at-arms close behind trying to stop the man. "Sorry, m'lady, but he—"

"That is enough, Pierce. I'll hear what Howell has to say."

"Have you not heard?" Howell asked, frustrated when two girls interrupted his speech. "My cousin has been stabbed to death."

Elizabeth reached for her belly, wrapping her arms about herself protectively. "Tyrian. No," she whispered.

"Gwen!" Autumn shot to her feet, dropping the embroidery frame to the floor. "Where is Gwen—my sister?"

The huge man seemed to grow smaller before their eyes as his shoulders slumped with grief. "Your sister," he said in a daze. "Gwen. Told me he loved her, was going to marry her. She was his life." He glowered at Autumn. "And she ended it for him. That bastard Stephan was after her—and you—wasn't he." No question. "Seems the whole country is after your blasted inheritance. Where do you women hide that damn jewel, anyway? How many more will perish because of the Seasons?"

"Howell!" Elizabeth exclaimed.

He kept on, looking at Autumn, "Do you know, little witch, that another of your sisters has turned up; she sang with that wild troupe that entertained last eve."

"What?" Autumn cried.

"Enough," Raine said, walking into the solar.

Autumn blinked at him. She shook her head. Blinked again. Raine . . . he was wearing silver and black . . .

just like the Fulcan of Salisbury. *If he was* . . . he better not have lied to her. She swallowed as his glance found her and burned, staring for several instants.

Slowly Autumn backed up. Then she came forward, boldly. "It is my sister we speak of here. Keep your eyes off me, Lord Fulcan."

Raine made no indication that he'd acknowledge the title as Lord Fulcan. "We shall find your sister," was all he said as he turned to go. "By the way," he said at the door. "The king has ordered us to wed and join our lands."

"To become man and wife?" Autumn gasped. "That is outrageous. Our king is dead. How can he—"

Just then Orion Sutherland's voice was heard behind them. "I'm afraid this is so, Autumn. The king entered the final edicts only hours before he drew his last."

"Orion!" Elizabeth shouted coming out of her daze, running into her husband's open arms.

They kissed on the lips and pressed each other tight by the arms, her skirts brushing his mail-clad legs. Autumn looked from one to the other, her glance coming to rest with a snap of violet-blue upon Raine Guardian.

"Ah," murmured Orion, watching Autumn as she drifted to the windows, "The Fulcan has joined us. You did take care of Stephan the Bastard, did you not?"

"Of course," Raine answered with a bark of laughter, endeavoring to keep calm, desiring most to murder the ones who'd ended his friend Tyrian's life. "He, Stephan, almost wet his hose, too. He's so afraid of his loose-shirt cousins. Namely one: Rowena."

"I have seen her," Orion informed. "She and her

hideous mercenaries were on the road . . . the albino was there, too."

"Albino," Autumn said as she whirled from the window with an audible intake of breath. "Gwen had a bad dream of the albino . . . just three nights past."

"He's got her!" Howell snarled. "The bitch and the albino."

Autumn turned to Orion. "*They* must've stabbed Tyrian. He's dead."

"I know," Orion said. "I'd heard the news upon arrival. It's the news of the day, I'm afraid."

"I shall go get her," Raine said of Gwen, walking over to Autumn, touching her arm briefly. She flinched away. "Sorry to have dared touch you, Maiden."

"Don't call me that, you sarcastic bastard," Autumn whispered. "Save my sister and then let's see the last of you."

"I cannot allow you that, Autumn," Orion announced in a conciliatory tone. "You and the Fulcan of Salisbury must wed to join your lands and stop the covetous battle over the Windrush jewel and the Seasons' inheritance. You are very wealthy, you know. Almost as rich as the Fulcan here. But not quite." He grinned at the Fulcan, seeing the jewel of Jeraux on his finger.

Ignoring the men, Autumn directed her question to Elizabeth. "Who is the Fulcan of Salisbury, pray tell."

"Why," Elizabeth began with a look of chagrin, "he's Raine Guardian."

"Yes," Orion said with a laugh. "Even the Fulcan of Salisbury must have a *real* name."

"See," Raine said to Autumn as he stepped out into the corridor, turned to face the room. "I never lied." He bowed deeply from the waist.

"You could have told me," she yelled after him in a most unladylike voice as he turned to walk away from the door.

"You never asked."

"The bastard," Autumn ground out, plopping into a deep scarlet chair.

Elizabeth blinked. Orion put his hand over his mouth to stifle a crack of laughter.

"The *stinking,* deceitful bastard."

Now Orion put his hand over Elizabeth's huge belly. "This is much too harsh for such tender ears."

Elizabeth laughed softly. "Silly."

Autumn continued to spout mild expletives. Orion and Elizabeth looked at the girls standing frozen near the toys; they were grinning at *Aunt* Autumn's strange language and pointing chubby fingers at her. The adults rushed over, took Maryse and Song by the hand, one apiece, and fled the solar with babes in tow.

Autumn fumed alone.

She sat there for a long while.

All of a sudden she sprang to her feet. "Gwen," she whispered, disgusted at herself for having fumed so long. "I must find Gwen. My sister needs me."

Below in the hall Autumn bumped into a beautiful young woman, then held her aside in order to pass. "I'm sorry but I'm in a hurry," said Autumn to the woman wearing a colorful costume. "Please, move your friends, too."

The chestnut-haired woman stared at the beautiful, red-haired Autumn. "I have come to sing for you," said Spring. "You must hear what I have to—"

"No. Excuse me. I must go."

Passing the first set of stairs, speeding up the second set, Autumn wrenched open the door to her bedchamber and bent to search her trunks. She found what she'd been searching for: Drogo's jeweled hunting knife, the one she'd taken from him long ago. Hiding it in the folds of her plain green gown, then snatching a coarse brown cloak, she ran to the stables and rode swiftly from the castle grounds.

Halfway across the meadow, she was caught by strange men galloping their horses from out of the trees. They encircled her like a deadly force and propelled her along, to ride among them all the way to Drogo's most recent hideaway.

Autumn was certain these were Drogo's men; she'd seen the handsome scarred one among them outside the hills of Salisbury Castle. He was a traitor to Howell and the Sutherland knights. His name was De'Beau.

He rode close beside her now. "Do you know who would have been your assassin years ago, pretty lady?"

She glared at him. "No. Pray tell me. It does not seem to matter at the time, does it? I've one too many enemies it seems. What can one more hurt?"

"Raine Guardian, the Fulcan of Salisbury. Rowena's assassin." He grinned maliciously. "Think on it, m'lady. When will he try again?"

"Why say you this now, when you bring me to your leader Drogo, to no doubt be ravished and slain at his hands?"

"Ah. Drogo wants more than your gorgeous body, pretty lady. You have a jewel that is coveted more than any in the land. The Windrush jewel." His eyes gleamed greedily. "A chunk off the Star of Africa. So beautiful.

So priceless. No wonder men and women would kill for it."

"It is nothing but a sparkling rock."

"A gem, like you, lovely Flame, for your hair is like a living flame burning in a world of darkness."

Raine? Autumn thought to herself. He'd been the one tracking her in the woods that day? Dear God, Raine, one of Rowena's assassins. She thought she remembered his face, a flash of memory, but had put it away. Now, this knight had pulled it back to the front. Her heart beat faster. Was he still trying to kill her? She looked to the oak branches above as though imagining she'd find help in the gentle green fans that exploded at the tip of each twig.

For the jewel.

For the lands.

The king was dead. Would Raine try even harder now?

Suddenly, he was not the man she loved more with each breath. He was the one who would see her dead. And Drogo. They could all fight over the jewel, the lands, when she was gone. Blast them, let them have it all. *I am weary, so damn weary.*

Why should I give up? she asked herself. She still had her sisters to live for. Thinking *that,* the world did not appear so black to Autumn. Sighing, she clenched her fists and looked straight ahead. Have to keep going, have to keep strong, have to keep fighting.

De'Beau gave Autumn a glittering glance before turning back to the mounted men surrounding them. She looked away also; he'd not seen the fierce look in her eyes that were the color of shadows of evening. Her horse, fretting as it was under the tight rein while it sensed the excitement of its rider, leapt forward eagerly. "Easy there," she whispered to the black stallion. "First things first."

First she would take care of Drogo. And then would come Raine. She would be meticulous and unsympathetic in her dealings with them.

She considered that for a moment. And something else. This had all been a wicked game among Stephan and Drogo and the duchess to see who could gain the most with their rich relative, by stealing, coveting, whatever method suited their evil scheme at the time. She wondered now if Richard and Dalenna had made a secret pact with the Fulcan's parents. Why else would the king be so eager for them to wed? Was this what her own parents had meant when they'd been worried, said they must locate the jewel else all would be lost? Raine had not been given the jewel. He'd *stolen* it. Yet, how could he steal something that had possibly belonged in the Guardian family long ago? Secret pact. Both families.

Perhaps Raine had *not* been lying.

Thirty-seven

London, a day and a half later.

"And now, Autumn—now we are alone at long last."

"The Fulcan will kill you, Drogo," she said forcefully, "Surely one night with me is not worth your life."

"But your fierce lover does not know where you are. We have the entire night before us, and I'm sure you will prove worth the waiting."

"And then—you will send me back?"

"If he wants you. Although, you will be, I regret to say, not as you are now."

"What do you mean?" Autumn felt the blood drain from her face. "I knew you were steeped in corruption, but—"

"Shall we wait and see? Who knows? You will be amazed at some of the things I have learned in these past years."

Autumn's voice was flat, compassionless, "From what I've heard, you already were a master of the unsavory."

"Ah, but my talents have been refined. My men and

myself have sampled some of the night life, the parties the duchess Rowena throws. You would be delighted to see all the manner of things that go on there."

Nausea rocked through Autumn. "God help you— you are vile!"

"Perhaps so. You are a woman of passion, I believe, and not averse to dalliance with a man not your husband."

"I have no husband."

He went on as if he'd not heard. "You might even learn to like some of these things I have in mind. The most delicate sensations, the pain so fleeting that you will hardly notice it, I promise you."

Autumn's voice came in quickly, "You will never see the day I would like anything *you* have in mind!"

"I do not mind a little resistance," he said, a smile touching his lips, but not reaching his eyes.

Drogo made a sudden movement and there was a knife in his hand.

Autumn caressed her own blade beneath the folds of blue. "What will you take to let me go free? You are greedy for jewels, I know. How many gems will it take?"

"Gems?" He laughed. "This night is not for sale at any price. The first thing—" he murmured, tapping his palm with the blade, looking deep in thought.

"The first thing," she said, with an air of calculation, "is food. I've had nothing to eat all day." She eyed him warily, to see whether her ploy might work. "Now, you would not want me to faint dead away. Would you?"

Drogo stopped to consider. "I think not. There are some interesting things we might try together—but perhaps later. There is wine here, and I urge you to drink of it."

He handed her a small glass of pale yellow liquid.

"Drugged wine?" she said. "Although I suppose you'd not tell me if it were."

Drogo watched her with blunt animal lust. "Ah, but drugs would only veil the exquisite sensations you shall feel, very soon. Drink the wine, Autumn. I become impatient."

With misgivings she dared not show, she swallowed the drink. Dear God, she hoped he was truthful about the wine. Pale logic told her he probably was. He would want to extract every ounce of pleasure from her.

Suffering or ecstasy, either one, he wanted to relish and savor it all.

He came to take her glass away and set it on the table. He came close, but his eyes were too watchful for her to make any move away from him. He set the glass down, and the knife beyond it.

"You'll have no chance at the knife, Autumn. I remember too well your expert handling of even a small dagger."

The lamp flickered, tossing its flame high when Drogo moved toward her. In the sudden light she could see his odd eyes, tiny pupils startlingly dark in the glazy pale iris, flashing like an animal's with reflected firelight. Cruel, thin pink lips made a slash across an otherwise handsome face, along with black, peaked eyebrows. She could see the devil's lights in his eyes grow harder with animal lust now, just as she had the day he had come upon her in the wood's clearing.

"Where is Winter?" she demanded.

"Winter? You mean Gwen of course. I didn't know

she was here. Enough," he said with an alarming change in his voice. "I believe 'tis time."

He stood stock-still, arrested in motion. "Oh yes," he said, still in that strange eerie tone, "it is time. I should like to tell you, Autumn, just what I shall plan to do to you."

"What?"

"Or perhaps it will come better as a constant series of ambrosial surprises? Yet I feel that delay may defeat my purpose, dear Autumn."

"You are the worst of beasts, Drogo."

"I think not. That was your dear uncle. He did rut on every female in the castle. Your father's castle. He even lay with your mother."

"That is not true! You and Stephan share the same lie!"

Drogo cast his glance to the window. "It is moonrise," he said.

Beneath the cloak her hands went spontaneously to her dagger. *His* dagger. The one he'd lost to her.

With a sudden movement of his shoulders, the flowing robe fell to the floor around his feet. He stood naked before her, and she could see that, as he'd said, it was indubitably time.

He came toward her.

All the notions of torture he'd mentioned were forgotten as he flung her back on the cushions, unable to subdue the rising urgency of his lust. He did not raise her skirts above her waist, or remove her breasts from the bodice. He simply shook a few seconds before he suddenly toppled his body upon her and he lay heavily, as though unable to lift his arms. He choked and gasped out her name.

413

Autumn lay shaking as a warm liquid sensation ran down the length of her thigh. Oh my. Dear God, had he—?

Of course he had, the repugnant bastard lord. For now he lay spent, shuddering great breaths, his weight pinning her. Autumn was unable to move.

What manner of man—? Again she did not finish the repulsive thought. Slaked, he rolled to one side, one hand heavy on her waist.

"Get away from me, you pig," Autumn said flatly.

His laugh was self-condemning. "You see why you must die?"

"No. I do not see."

"If an heir is born, the Windrush inheritance would be lost to us."

"It will be anyway. Don't you see? You must have all four sisters to claim anything. How can you, or any-one, wed four women at once?" she asked, smiling at her own lie with satisfaction. She saw his nasty smile had not wavered. "What are you thinking now? Surely not—"

"Oh, that now I shall have more leisure to arouse an equal delight in you. Something, I confess, I'd not planned."

He loosed her to wipe his beaded face with his free hand. Instantly, she slid from the cushion and was on her feet facing him.

"You stinking bastard!"

"Witch—come back!" he said, scrambling to his feet. "You'll not escape me, don't you know? There's no place for you to go! I have a greater idea! We shall ransom you! First you, and then all your other sisters to follow!"

"Hah! Just try and find them all!"

"The duchess, even now, has your sister Winter." He snickered. "She's very chilly where she's at at the moment."

A dungeon!

Her wild, violet eyes staring at him, she backed away, step by step, as he stalked her. "Leave me be!" she shouted, holding the hilt of the dagger beneath the brown cloak.

She skirted the smaller of the cushions on the floor, and he kept following, his eyes on her like a hawk's on his prey.

She had no plan, but fear drove her.

She kept backing until she could get the cushion on the floor between them at the right angle. Then, with a quick thrust of her foot, the cushion shot out into the path of the wicked baron and he could not avoid it.

Suddenly, he fell, and his arm doubled beneath him. She kicked him downward to place pressure on him in his awkward position and then gasped . . . She could hear a bone crack and he cursed her to high heaven or deepest hell.

He employed a milder curse then. "Damn you, I'm hurt . . . bleeding, too! This is the second time you've hurt me. Get help before I bleed to death!" He looked down. In all his battles this pain had never befallen him . . . He screeched like a banshee. "The bone, bitch, right through my flesh!"

Bile rose in Autumn's throat as she rushed to the door, but just outside, barring her escape, was the ugliest guard she'd ever seen. He was scarred, his mouth crookedly grotesque. *Another scarred beast.* Swifter than thought, she gestured toward the baron who was holding his arm and shouting curses at her head. He could not rise from the floor. The guard looked at her, and then at the baron; he couldn't believe his eyes. He rushed to his master.

And the jeweled dagger lay unwatched on the cushion behind him.

Now she had it in her hand!

Armed with the dagger, Autumn fled the room, closing the door behind her; the noise might alert guards or others in the manor.

Had he taken other captives from Sutherland? She ran down one hall after another, peering into room after room, alcoves, curtains, through screens in the gallery.

She found a young woman tied to a chair, waiting the further pleasure of the man who had taken her this far. He had already torn the chestnut-haired beauty's tunic, and ropes cut cruelly into her white flesh.

The dagger served its purpose swiftly, and the ropes were severed, falling away.

"Where is the other guard?" Autumn quickly questioned.

"He's gone for more drink," said the beauty.

"Where is the scarred one, the ugliest one?"

She knew who Autumn meant. "He, too, for drink."

Out into the night they sped, through the back door, through the shadowed grass and trees toward the sound of the river, praying to find a gate surrounding the manor, one that would be unguarded.

"We'll go this way. Hurry, we have to find a way out before they discover our absence."

"No doubt they have already," said Autumn's companion urgently.

They found the gate, a small door in the stone wall

416

surrounding the manor. Autumn stopped, gasping for breath. She still held the other's wrist in a tight grip, and the sharp dagger in her other hand.

She loosed her hold and her companion in stealth rubbed her wrist. "What are we going to do now? We have to get away from them. Next they will kill us."

Autumn looked back at the manor they'd just left. Torches were springing up at various windows. The guard was summoning help. For Drogo, of course, and then, no doubt, to search for the woman who had felled their master and made her escape, taking another prisoner along.

"We're going to leave here," said Autumn, praying she was right. She found the latch to the gate. Surprised at the ease of its turning, she lifted it and the gate swung inward.

"Oh no," the brown-haired beauty said to the redhead, "it will not budge."

It stuck fast, not open enough to let them through. She dropped the dagger, somewhat surprised to find that she still carried it, and used both hands to tug at the gate.

It was no use.

"We cannot get through an opening only a handspan wide," Autumn said.

"Move the gate closed again and then pull it toward you—hard, Autumn, hard!"

This time it opened easily and she nearly fell to the ground. "How did you know?" she asked, looking up. "And how did you know my name?"

"Many gates as this one gave us trouble at the abbey. A twig underneath the bottom," Autumn's new friend guessed, bending to show it to her sister, for she truly knew this was her kin. "Come, Autumn, you go through first."

"It may be a trap."

"Do you have any other ideas?"

The sisters stared at each other for a long moment. The one said they would simply have to trust in their prayers and the Lord, in His hand that had guided her escape from the horrible fate Baron Drogo had prepared for them.

"Look!" cried the young woman. "They're coming!"

Torches were bobbing in the darkness along the manor, spreading out into the dark trees. There was no more time. Without hesitation, Autumn watched her companion as she slipped through the gate. She was slim enough!

There was no one in the London streets beyond. Drogo had felt secure enough that he had not bothered to set guards at the gate.

"I am Spring."

"What?"

"Yes."

Autumn turned to face the beautiful young woman next to her. "You said you are Spring? My sister?" For a moment she felt elated and then she recalled all the young women who had come to her declaring to be her lost kin. "I'm afraid I do not believe you."

Spring looked her straight in the eyes. "One day you will."

"I—"

"We must go," said Spring, her colorful costume peeping out as she lifted herself straight.

Autumn stared. The young woman at the castle, the one who'd wished a word with her before she'd been taken by Drogo's men. Had they known about her sister? Oh Jesus, if this were true, there was only one sister left to be discovered.

Autumn grinned to herself. Like she'd thought before: who could marry four sisters at once? Four brothers? Four cousins?

The river lay on their left. Therefore, the way out of London town must lie to the right, and southward. Now it was Spring who pulled her sister along with her. There must be streets that rose upward away from the waterfront. They must make their way ever upward, until at last they were on level streets that led out of town.

"Come—I see three of the horses belonging to the baron's nasty knights. We will take two." Autumn crept along, with her sister close behind. The horses were tame, easy to catch, both being saddled and ready to ride. "Let's go!"

Autumn was not surprised at how expertly her sister handled a horse. The past had been coming back to her swiftly these days, piece by piece, day by day, hour by hour, moment by moment. Memories blurred together sometimes and then arighted themselves, falling into place, more carefully and wonderfully—and sometimes horribly. She could see things in her mind that she really did not wish to see; but had to. Life was sometimes full of heartache, misery, and pain, but to grow, she knew, she and Winter had to take things as they came, one step at a time. And perhaps this young woman beside her, also, was her sister. Maybe. 'Twould be so wonderful.

At last, the two of them stood the horses side by side at the crossroads, at the sign leading out of town. "We must go south, my sister. To Sutherland."

Autumn blinked at the boldness of the young woman. "Do you think they will follow anymore?"

"I believe we are safe. Drogo is a coward. We never realized that. Now we know. He and his robber knights killed our parents." She could not tell Autumn the rest, what they'd done to her once they had gotten her and Summer alone.

Autumn blinked then leaned to hug the woman with the chestnut hair; they stared into each other's beautiful countenances, and stood their mounts that way for several more minutes before breaking away to ride.

And then they began the long, dangerous ride home.

Thirty-eight

After hours of riding, Gwen was permitted to dismount. She was sore and stiff from the grueling ride where the mercenaries had not allowed her to come down from her horse to walk a bit and get some exercise. She ached all over, especially in her backsides. She couldn't remember ever having ridden for such a long stretch of time without some form of activity after several miles. Even a walk into the woods for some privacy would have been nice. Now she did that, for she'd had to hold it for such a long time. She emerged from the stand of trees and almost bumped into the two guards who had posted themselves right outside her momentary sanctuary.

Now, furtively, she glanced around to see where they had brought her. There was a manor in the clearing and the men walking around it looked like knights, but they wore tattered battle gear; it came to her that they were little more than bandits, just like the rough knights who had brought her here.

Guards near the old manor leered at her as the albino walked her to the manor, and they kept watching her as she stepped inside and glanced them over her shoulder. Her heart was aching. Nothing seemed to matter, for her beloved was gone from this earth. The sun had ceased to shine. The flowers had wilted and the grass had lost its green color. All was dull and she felt like the walking dead. Her eyes gazed and saw nothing. Swallowing hard, feeling the acute pain of loneliness in her breast, Tyrian's words came back to her in a waking dream.

I will love you forever and ever, and nothing save death shall part us.

Death. She would welcome her demise just now. There was nothing more to live for. How could there be? She had found love, first love, and they had had such short moments of joy and bliss together. He was lost to her now, her splendid golden knight.

The albino led her into a dungeonlike room where food had been laid out beforehand. He left her alone and she stared at the small feast of bread, cheese, small pasties containing spiced chopped meat, and tall flagons of wine.

Gwen stared at the protruding stones of a big hearth as if an enormous fire burned there. The stones gave out a steady heat, even though there was no fire in the hearth at this time of year.

Still, Gwen felt the heat move toward her like a living, breathing thing. Her heart ached badly, but something was happening. Something . . .

Something warm moved within her just then. The sensation was so fleeting, almost golden, so brief she could have cried out when it had vanished. She felt strength and an odd sort of pleasure coursing through her, a power enhanced by the thought of perhaps . . .

just perhaps Tyrian had left her with child the night before.

Oh Tyrian, how will I live without you? My golden shining knight? Where are you? Why can't you come to me, be with me, as you said, forever and ever?

It was meant to be . . . meant to be. Gwen, it was his time to go.

Listen to the voice-laden winds outside. Hear them.

I will be with you, sweet Gwen. I love you, and I am yours, for now and for all time.

Her eyes filled with tears. She would live. For the babe. For Tyrian's child. Let it be a son with eyes of gold, Dear God.

Thirty-nine

"Tell me more about what has happened these past six years we've been away from each other," Spring begged her sister.

They had left London behind long ago and were riding south, always south, following the sun to Sutherland.

"I have told you much. Why don't you tell me about yourself?" Autumn asked right back, riding atop the huge Percheron Norman.

Spring's borrowed horse was huge, also. "I cannot. Not yet; the past is still too painful. I will have to tread softly. Else I shall have the nightmares again . . . about the killing of our beloved parents. The nuns taught me this, to not run the horror through my mind over and over."

"You were at the nunnery in Kirklees, yet you never knew that your sister, Winter, was there?"

"No. I was not there that long. Summer disappeared and I broke free of the nunnery to join the troupe."

"I must hear you sing soon." Autumn did not want to worry about Summer just now. Too much had happened.

Spring shook her head. "Not until our sister is rescued. You say this Duchess Rowena and her assassins have taken her?"

"Yes. I wish I could remember the way to the duchess's home. She has a house in London, but I do not believe she would have taken Gwen there; I believe De'Beau did not say this correctly. Drogo is also a liar, besides being everything else under the sun in the lousy rotten book of thieves, felons, murderers. I believe the duchess took our sister to the manor in the Greenwood."

"Gwen—Winter—fell in love with the golden knight Tyrian; what a wonderful true story you have shared with me." She shook her head. "How sad that he was taken from her so soon. I wonder if they had made love. You said at Sutherland they discovered Tyrian's body and he wore a smile. I pray that they loved before his soul was taken to be with the Lord Jesus. There might come a child, which Gwen can hold and love."

"That would be nice," Autumn said. "Now, we only have to hope and pray Raine and his knights will find her."

"They must do away with this Duchess Rowena and her assassins," Spring declared.

Autumn nodded. "The only problem with that is, Raine and Rowena are cousins. Distantly related, perhaps. Drogo and Stephan have said that Raine would have been my assassin if—"

"If?" Spring shook her head, making her long fine hair sparkle in the sunlight. The strands had less red than Autumn's own locks, and her skin was slightly paler. "If what, Autumn? What were you going to say?"

"If he'd gotten the chance, I suppose. Something made him halt the stabbing of my person." Autumn stared, as if back in time. "He must have heard the dogs, the baying sounds. I had been running, peering into the shadows, hearing something, knowing not what. And he moved closer, I could feel him coming closer all the time to me. I had no idea if he be man or beast. But I knew, knew something was there, tracking me, wanting and needing to get to me. I could almost hear his breaths being fed from his lungs like bellows before a hearth."

"Why did you never tell us this, Autumn? What did happen next?"

"I'd dropped the flowers. Dogs leapt into the clearing and then . . . then the assassin's prey was lost."

"You."

"Yes," Autumn said. *"Me.* Raine Guardian had almost become my executioner."

"How could you love him?" Spring almost shouted, causing her mount to jerk at the harshness of her voice.

"He made me love him," Autumn told her sister. "I did not wish to fall in love. I had a mission and a dream to fulfill."

"To see your sisters all together again," Spring said, staring at her sister in admiration and love.

Autumn nodded. "Yes. That was my dream. And Raine Guardian became a part of it."

"Guardian?" Spring asked.

"Yes. He was the Guardian of the Thieves in Sherwood forest. Something like the Robin Hood of several centuries back, taking care of his wretched fold of scoundrels. He was my guardian especially, Raine was."

"Tell me everything," Spring begged. "The whole story of your love. Perhaps then I shall understand why

I see love and adoration in your eyes for this man who might have killed you."

Autumn told the story, holding nothing back. By the time she'd finished, Spring was almost in a swoon. "How very romantic. Now you must discover why he wants our jewel so badly. Why he must marry you."

"I do not believe he desires to possess the jewel all that much anymore, not really; he wants something more, I have no idea what just yet but I know he holds the key to gain my holdings, perhaps some long lost parchments," Autumn told her, wondering if she should reveal that Raine had the jewel in his possession at this very moment! "And King Henry made the edict that we must marry and join our lands, in the same name."

Suddenly it was growing darker over their heads, but the two women did not take notice, so engrossed in conversation were they.

"Guardian," Spring murmured. Her eyes were the color of new grass in May. "What a perfectly romantic name. Does he have brothers?" she asked hopefully.

"He has a sister. Her name is Tiercel. And he has many many cousins. They are rumored to be related to Catherine of Aragon." Suddenly Autumn held her head. "So someone has said." Had it been Stephan who had said this?

"Autumn, look." Spring pointed to a huge manor house in the middle of the woods. "Where have you brought us?"

"I?" Autumn asked, looking around. She sucked in her breath. "Dear God, we are at the Duchess Rowena's manor. How—" She twisted to look behind them. "How in the world have we come here?"

"Look!" Spring breathed. "Who is that in the duchess's garden, there, where it is full of weeds?"

"Praise God," Autumn whispered. "It is our sister. We have ridden right into the den of Rowena's assassins!"

Spring looked at Autumn's horse. "I might have something here: Perhaps you have ridden a horse belonging to one of Drogo's or Stephan's men . . . I mean, maybe the master is one who has frequented the duchess's manor?"

"A lover?" said Autumn, watching her sister's eyebrows lift higher as their excitement grew.

"Precisely."

Autumn glanced down at the horse she'd been riding. "De'Beau's . . . the devil's own."

De'Beau emerged from the bedchamber where he'd just frolicked with Rowena. He was sweaty, frustrated, angry. He'd wanted the Meaux sister, the blond one, but Rowena had not given her to him. That, and the fact that he'd left his favorite mount in London, like a stupid fool, made his blood shoot almost to boiling point.

Rowena, still wearing her silken dressing gown, trailed after De'Beau, finally catching up and, reaching around his hard, lean body, fondled him boldly.

"Enough, Rowena!" De'Beau thrust her hand aside. "Don't you ever get enough?" he hissed.

"Nay!" she shouted, reaching for him again.

"*Nay* is out, 'tis timeworn, Rowena." He thrust her hand aside again. "You are drunk. Do you not know when to stop?"

She giggled, shouting, "Nay! Nay! Nay!"

De'Beau shuddered. Rowena was becoming more unsightly, repulsive, and overweight, with every day that passed. Strange marks were suddenly appearing on her flesh. Her eyes were always watery and red. Her hair was dry and thinning. Her lips were too moist and sticky. Her teeth were loose and her breath was foul.

De'Beau realized it was time to be rid of the woman. She was just going to get in the way. Snatching up a bottle of wine, he walked up to the turret room—there was one on either side of the manor house—and walked directly to the open window. He sat there on the stone ledge, waiting for her, knowing she would come tripping after him, her body seeping with the juice of her desire.

"Ah—there you are. You naughty boy. You cannot get away from the duchess."

"Come here, Rowena." De'Beau looked below, seeing the guarded, beautiful blond Gwen in the weedy garden. "Come, sit on my lap."

Rowena hurried. Up this high the wind howled demonically through wide cracks and crevices. She walked faster, not knowing what was in store for her.

Instantaneously, De'Beau's boot shot out, catching Rowena's foot. She tripped, and fell against him lightly. De'Beau reached out and helped propel her out the window. She fell, going all the way to the stone flags below. De'Beau watched, emotionless as the cold stone that ended Rowena's life. At last, he said, "Poor Rowena. You were of no use or amusement to anyone at this point in the game."

A muttering ran through the afternoon and several intakes of breath from the robber knights.

Gwen looked up, seeing the woman falling down, down, quickly, and then the dull thud as the duchess's body hit the uneven stones. Staring down for several moments, she tried to keep the awful bile from spilling from her throat. She blinked, looked up, thinking *Oh no, not him,* and then crumpled to the weedy beds of pathetic red and white roses.

"Look—Gwen has fainted," Autumn said, spurring her mount closer to see between gnarled trees and wild hedges.

"Someone has fallen from that tower," Spring told her. "Did you not see?"

"I was looking behind to make certain none of the terrible knights crept up on us."

"Autumn—how can we help Gwen? There are so many men in the area. And look, up in that tower, there is a man looking down with a wicked grin on his face."

"De' Beau. We must hurry. He will murder our sister next."

"I don't think so," Autumn said quickly. "Come, let us go to the other side of the woods where there was another clearing as we rode toward the manor. I want to see what is on the other side."

"That is far," Spring argued.

Suddenly they were surrounded by men. But they were not Rowena's assassins nor were they De'Beau's nasty followers.

"It is the Fulcan," Autumn whispered. "He has come to rescue Gwen. Now we will all be taken back to Sutherland and I will have to wed Raine Guardian."

"Is that so bad?" Spring's eyes twinkled merrily.

Autumn sighed. "I think not. After all, he has the jewel. We will be safe. I love his daughter Song."

"And?"

"And? What do you mean?" Autumn asked her sister, watching as the Fulcan and his many knights quickly dispatched Rowena's assassins, searched for Gwen, and took prisoners of the servants remaining that had not put up a fight.

Autumn and her sister gasped as De'Beau went flying through the tower window, joining the duchess's body below. Momentarily Raine's face showed at the window, then was gone.

"Why do you not say it?" Spring urged, her hand over her heart to still its wild pounding.

Autumn shrugged. "Well, I suppose you are right. I do love Raine Guardian—the Fulcan of Salisbury."

"I know what is beyond the duchess's manor." Spring nodded. "An hour's ride will take us to Windrush."

"Good Lord, sister, how did you know?"

"I just remembered the way. It is all coming back to me. I am not as bad off as you and Gwen—or Winter—seem to be in regaining your memories. I recall much but I do not say so. Some things are too painful to remember fully. Some day I shall, however, and then perhaps we will be able to find our last sister—Summer."

The fight was over. The Fulcan was gathering them together, coming to ride beside Autumn to make certain she did not try to escape.

Where could she go? Autumn asked herself. Wherever she went, Raine would always be right behind her. "It's just as well," she whispered. "He wants everything

431

that is mine. And I am ready to give it—and hold nothing back."

Was this not the way love should be? What could be so bad about a love that seemed so right? She would no doubt travel the wrong path if she did not have her "Guardian" to rescue her.

Raine was a magnificent knight, and he was sworn to avenge wrongs. She knew, as surely as the sun was dying and would be born again in the morn, that he would slay the demons in her life and keep her and her beloved sisters safe.

"I have the jewel," he murmured, leaning over to her as he rode his war-horse beside De'Beau's black; De'Beau was dead and he'd give the beautiful spoils of battle to his bride.

Autumn looked up at Raine. "You stole it from me; I know this."

"You should thank me for that. If you would have had it on your person, it would have been snatched from you and you might have not recovered it for years." He did not say he had important ancient documents of the Meaux and Guardian holdings in his possession, taken back from Duc Stephan who'd been caught rifling the coffers of Windrush, documents now safe at Castle Salisbury. "The jewel is ancient, rare."

"No one searched me. Drogo almost had his way with me, but I left him with a broken arm and a wounded pride."

"Your sister is with you." He grinned handsomely, looking splendid in his black-and-silver trappings. "Both of them. Now you have only one more to go."

"Spring will not speak of it. I believe something terrible happened to our last sister. She is lost forever, I think."

"Never say never, my love."

She looked into his gray eyes. "We will be wed. I trust you, Raine. You are my guardian and you will always keep us safe. Even as you kept the jewel safe, with Song."

"I am sorry your sister Gwen lost Tyrian. He was a good friend and cousin; I shall miss him very much. He was like a brother who stuck by me through strong and lean days . . . and what more can I say?"

"Silver knight," Autumn whispered, leaning closer to his face. "You would have tied me up in your castle." Her eyes spoke volumes. "And then what? Were you planning to keep me prisoner all the days of my life?"

"Of course. If you did not accommodate me and comply to my wishes to keep you with me always, yes, I would have chained you to the bed," he'd whispered right back.

"You are arrogant."

"As always." He kissed her cheek. "We will be wed come next Saturday. Everything is being prepared at Sutherland even now as we speak."

"Sure of yourself, are you not?"

"I am the Fulcan of Salisbury. The blood of great knights flows through my veins, as royalty flows through yours. Your great-great-grandmother was a princess."

She breathed in. "How do you know?"

"Pardon me," Spring broke in, coming closer with her mount. "I heard that."

"Hush," Raine teased.

The chestnut-haired beauty laughed. "My songs, Autumn. I sang about our ancestors. True, we are descended from nobility. Our distant grandmother was a princess and she lived in the days of the Crusades. She was rumored to be very beautiful."

Raine put in, "Your sisters and yourself derive your great beauty from her, Orlena, the Swan Princess, with hair as yellow as the sun."

"How very exciting." She turned to her sister. "Do you not think so?"

"Indeed," said Spring. "I will sing you the song at your wedding feast. The runes tell about the jewel, how it has been in our family and"—she looked to Raine—"in the Guardian family. They had been feuding with each other, the Meauxs and the Guardians, and the priceless diamond with a blue-white cast, was passed back and forth," she said, laughing, "more like stolen in that manner. Orlena, the Swan Princess, had something to do with it. It was said that Merlin the great magician gave it to the princess. Whoever would possess the jewel would become immensely wealthy, have love, health, happiness as long as it remained in their possession."

"No wonder people like the duchess, Drogo, and Stephan would kill, kidnap, and ransom for it." Autumn blinked at Raine in a new light, then said, "Wonderfully exciting."

Raine chuckled, murmuring in Autumn's ear, "I will show you wildly exciting, my dear betrothed, once we are wed and in our bed."

Nudging her horse into a trot, Autumn called over her shoulder, "Do not be so eager and certain of yourself, Sir Knight and Poet. I could always change my mind."

"I think not."

Forty

As the door closed, Autumn was back in her husband's arms, sighing reproachfully. "Could you not have waited ten minutes more, my lord? I would have found reason to send them all away."

"They are only servants, my lady wife, come to draw our bath."

"Gentle-bred servants you have brought from your village to your castle. I like them all, have found no fault with any," she told him, glancing at the cold joint of mutton they'd hardly touched, and sweet breads, mugs of unfinished ale. She sighed. "None at all."

Whatever Raine would have replied to that was lost when Autumn looked up at him. And there was such love and desire in her face that he forgot completely everything but their nearness.

"Every night," he whispered, "every night I dreamed of us like this before we'd finally wed at Sutherland," and fastened his lips to hers.

When they finally came up for air, she muttered, "Will you put me away after we've been married so long, my love?"

"Put you away?" he snarled. "For other women?" He sneered at the thought, crushing her tightly against him. "How could I put you away when you burn in my heart and my brain every minute of the day and night? I need you, my wonderful, wild Autumn wind. I must have you—you and only you. I care for no other woman or naught else."

"Why would you have been my assassin? For the Duchess Rowena? Did you love her so much?"

"She was beautiful in my youth. The temptress. I loved her. I would have died for her. The sun rose and set for Rowena."

"Just a short time ago? You still loved her then?" She watched him go to a chair, lower himself into a slump.

Raine's shoulders lifted; fell hard. His hands dangled between his thighs. "I was a young fool. I admit I was her assassin for a time. She had so many male enemies I had lost count."

"Ghastly," was all Autumn said. "And you would have murdered me in cold blood."

Raine turned anguished eyes to her. "I could not murder a child. This was when I had begun to know the witch with a comely face, to hate her, to the very depths of my soul."

"You did not complete your mission to slay the Windrush daughter. Why, indeed, me? Why not slay one of my sisters?"

"You, it was rumored, were the first to arrive at the birthing. This meant the jewel would come into your possession, as the eldest of four girls born at a single birth, born during the season after which you were named."

Autumn smiled wistfully. "Autumn was my mother's favorite time of year also," Autumn said, a poignant twist in her heart. "I remember her face. And she had most red in her hair, as I."

"Rowena's hold on me is gone, the chains have been broken, have been since the first time we loved."

"No. When you had Song, the beautiful child who wore the secret of the Windrush jewel. She is the deliverer of us all, as the Holy Christ is of our souls."

Autumn looked down and away.

With great reverence, Raine lifted her head and kissed her mouth. "You are my secret jewel, my love. I did not know it. I almost took your life. If I would have kissed your lips in death, I would have perished because you would have sealed my heart, even as you were, without life. Alive, you've shown me the greatest love, a simple and pure love, it outshines all others. Rowena was like dust in my soul when I came to you and made myself your secret guardian."

Although there was a tight sad core deep inside her, Autumn smiled. Whatever reason Raine had for not wanting another child, there did not seem to be lack of love for her. She would think no more of it. She would accept the joy of loving him and being loved and let all else happen as it would.

Only . . . even as Raine pushed her face up to kiss her again hungrily it occurred to Autumn that, if he did not intend to make her with child, almost as if afraid to do so, then his wife must have died birthing Song. She yielded her lips willingly and savored the embrace.

"You will have jewels of silver, jewels of gold, jewels of every color in the rainbow. You will wish for no

437

more," he murmured against her mouth, then sucked at the bud of her upper lip.

Autumn glanced over to where the Windrush jewel sparkled on its bed of soft silk tangled with blue-and-gold brocade.

Now, Raine flung his tunic away and began to unlace his shirt, saying, "I've been hungry for you for near a two-month." But he knew that she was as eager for him as he was for her. There was a mischievous glow in his eyes. "Come, let's bathe."

"Come into the bath with you?" Autumn eyed the bath with consternation. It was a large tub, a long oval, about thirty inches high smoothed and polished and oiled to prevent splinters; an old tub. However, Raine was a very large man and the tub, she looked down again, was rather full of water that was not steaming but lukewarm.

"Come in with me," he urged, standing back almost naked.

Autumn doubted the tub would hold the both of them. She was absolutely certain that, if they did what Raine obviously intended, most of that water would end up splashed all over the floor.

She looked up from her slightly startled perusal of her fate to see Raine, free of his clothing, laughing at her.

"But, Raine," she protested feebly, "I do not see how we could manage . . ."

Nonetheless, Autumn had her clothes off before she finished the sentence; the only bit of cloth that remained was her chemise. The idea was rather appealing. And there'd been no time for a wedding night, since they had traveled at first light after falling exhausted into bed following the wedding festivities.

She had always taken a sensuous pleasure in the sensations of the warm water of a bath lapping round her body. The idea of that pleasure added to the delight Raine was offering interested her greatly.

"Come."

She began to laugh, "You'll not drown me, will you?" She looked at the underdress and shift already on the floor and hesitated with the taking off of her chemise.

"Only in love," replied Raine, getting into the tub.

Autumn slid off her shoes and stockings without further argument. Trustfully, she put her hand into the hand Raine held out to her. His eyes were alight.

Raine was sitting upright somewhat forward in the tub and directed her to slide her legs around his chest under his arms and place her feet behind him.

"This will be entirely impossible," Autumn told him, aware that no person could stand at such an angle.

"Easy. I've a firm grip on your hands. It will work. Get ready. Now. Come."

Now, as Autumn swung free, she was supported by Raine's powerful grasp on her hands. He leaned forward suddenly and buried his mouth in the mass of glossy curls that hid her Venus-mound. Autumn gasped with surprise and pleasure at his tongue's invasion. Then the pang of joy undid her. Her knees buckled, sending her down upon Raine with a tremendous splash.

Autumn was not hurt because she landed on the flat of his thighs above the knees; and from there slid down slowly. Both Raine and Autumn were laughing helplessly, but the laughter did not quench the passion.

Quite the opposite; it added its own stimulus, so that when their mouths met, a flame leaped between them.

A flame that even oceans could not quench.

They played with Song for hours and then Mai-Lee took her away to a room far to the other side of the castle.

Then there was the big bed, freshly made, sweetly scented, and more slow caresses. Sweet, idle words. Kisses that wandered from fingertip to breast tip, steel-hard hands so light, so gentle, as they fondled a beloved body.

There was time for Autumn to touch also, to sigh and have her laughter broken by passion and sigh again at Raine's reaction to kisses that did not aim at his mouth.

Excitement grew and deepened.

There was neither anxiety nor weeks nor months of deprivation to drive it into a flashing explosion. The half-day's abstinence had built appetite but had not pushed it out of control. The need Autumn felt for Raine and he for her was hot and steady. Like the bright red core of a long-burning hearth-fire.

This time there were no sparks and flashes. No jolt of sensation that was over too soon. When Raine mounted Autumn, he arched above her, his lips gently on hers, his shaft touching, entering slowly. So slowly. Both pairs of eyes shut languidly to hold in the exquisite relief and fulfillment.

He withdrew as slowly as possible, Autumn sighing softly at the loss of his pulsing warmth and simultaneously thrilling with joy at the knowledge that her satisfaction would be renewed. Withdrawn, renewed, each time the core of heat grew hotter. Still, there was no urge to rush it, no need to find culmination before they might be interrupted. Each time Raine thrust a little harder, a little quicker, sighing and then moaning softly with each movement. The image of heat was growing intense.

Behind her closed lids, Autumn could imagine her whole body deep coral with lust, then scarlet as her excitement heightened. At last then, a sharper pleasure stabbed her, as if a tongue of bright flame found a fissure in her smoldering body. That stab of fiercer joy, much like resurrection, broke Autumn's quiescence.

"Raine!"

She cried aloud, arched herself upward under Raine's weight. The single tongue of flame changed to a rampart of fire, flashed over her whole body, enfolded her in an agony of white-hot delight. She heard Raine groaning above her, a monotony of sound at one level, until his voice broke and lifted higher.

Aware of his weight, Raine turned on his side, lifting Autumn with him and supporting her on a powerful thigh so that their bodies remained joined, his shaft high inside her.

When eventually they slipped apart, they still lay nestled together. There was an easy silence. A gentle kiss. Seconds ticked away. Then minutes. A dead silence in relief. She looked at him. He looked at her. She sighed. He waited. A sigh again.

A languidly dropped arm to the bed. Autumn reminded Raine that she had been cleaning out the lowest level of the keep. The servants had discovered some arms and armor in a dark corner. Likely, they were too rotted to be of use, but would Raine look and please see if any could be salvaged? Both thought passionately that this was what marriage should be. Hot and sweet, passion and pledges, mingled with the small tasks of every day and with time enough for everything.

The idea—like the Windrush diamond—lay heavy and cold in Raine's mind: He did not want to force Autumn into anything. He did not want a wife who would watch him fearfully for a change of heart or a desire to steal her heritage.

Raine left the bed and returned shortly. Autumn gasped as a document was pressed into her hand. "What is this? A piece of paper?"

"Read it, and you will see you have lost nothing," Raine murmured. "Beloved mine, you have only gained a willing slave to serve you forever."

"You are very kind, my husband," Autumn whispered, pushing the parchments back at him. "But I do not need any contracts."

He lifted his eyebrow and one corner of his mouth.

"Take it; sign it. You do not need it to protect you from me, but it will protect our children—"

"Our . . . But I thought you did not want them."

"Song's mother died in childbirth. Before we wed," he confessed.

Autumn was speechless.

"Sign. To protect them—a second son or daughter. I believe you never mistrusted me. I took the "family" diamond. I wished to possess you. Not your land. Not you and your sisters. Not your already old rundown castle that knaves and robbers have all but destroyed."

She stiffened her shoulders. "Windrush will be beautiful again one day. The place is a stronghold, of French design. My sisters can live safely there."

"If you wish. But sign."

"Wait. I have more questions, Raine. Or should I say Fulcan." As she said this he shrugged as if it mattered not either way. "Who could marry off four sisters at once?"

"Four brothers; four cousins."

"As I thought." Autumn picked up an orange, then put it back into the bowl. "Not enough to go around. Gwen is in mourning; who knows if she'll ever wed. Spring, the songstress, may not ever settle down. And Summer is still gone."

"Someday she'll return, my love."

"Spring has said that Windrush borders the deceased duchess's lands."

"No. Beyond the boundary line of Windrush lay the old Baron Drogo's holdings. Quite ruined now these past seven years. Rowena never owned anything much of value. She coveted more lands, more jewels, always. And . . .," he said with a smile, "more men."

"I see."

"Castle Salisbury borders Rowena's lands, the lands she stole from her murdered husband. A murder with her consent."

"Did she?" Autumn's eyebrow lifted. "Or did someone else?" She looked at him significantly.

"Speak no more, Autumn, not of that. As for Castle Salisbury and Windrush, our ancestors lived very close to one another. The Meauxs and the Guardians and the Jerauxs." He looked back at her after he'd glanced aside. "Know that your uncle Robert had been there with Drogo the day your parents had been slain. Robert's jealousy lured him to steal back the jewel, break the secret pact between the Guardians and the Meauxs."

"Where is my uncle Robert?"

He shrugged. "Dead perhaps."

"I don't want him returning to our lives."

"We'll keep watch for him. No worry; we've very much protection. Many of the king's knights have come this way." He smiled. "Now. Sign."

She stared at his hand, the finger on which he wore the beautiful jewel of Jeraux. "First I will don my robe. Then sign your document, husband."

Mai-Lee and the seneschal Dominic—a powerful official in the household of a noble, one who was in charge of administering justice and managing the domestic affairs of the estate—were summoned. Dominic and Mai-Lee brought the newer contract. It was signed and witnessed, along with the ancient documents. Later it would be signed by Baron Orion Sutherland and Sir Jay Reynaude, and Raine intended to have it witnessed also by the Bishop of Hungerford.

"By the way, husband," Autumn said. "Who was the kind soul who bestowed the beautiful gowns to the ladies of the castle?"

Mai-Lee and Dominic looked at a loss.

Raine shrugged. "I've no idea." In his eyes shone a definite glimmer of mischief.

Mai-Lee and Dominic left the room and the newly-weds were once again alone. Raine kissed Autumn and caressed her, his eyes promising unhurried caresses later on as he pulled back from her.

"Later on, my lord?" Her fingers paused at the waist of her robe.

"My God, but you're a bold woman, aren't you?"

444

She only smiled as she removed her silken robe and thought about the child they would make together. If they tried. Very, very hard.

Epilogue

Gwen/Winter Meaux stood at the top of the hill to the side of Castle Sutherland, a lonely solitary figure in lace and creamy white at throat and wrists. She wore the aqua gown Tyrian had purchased for her without her knowledge; the gown had been discovered among Tyrian's belongings. A gift.

It makes no sense just now, his death, but God has a hand in everything.

Her face was to the sun and her blue eyes glittered with moisture. She gazed mournfully down at the grave where her lost love lay beneath the mound of dirt.

Ashes to ashes . . .

In the name of the Father, the Son, and the Holy Spirit . . .

May you rest in Peace, Beloved . . . till we meet again in Paradise. . . .

She turned away from the grave, couldn't look at the heavy wooden cross any longer, the name Tyrian, My Beloved Golden Knight—that was all, and the date—and she faced the ancient grounds of Sutherland to the east.

446

She began to move away.

Her smile was lost and sad as she caressed the small bulge beneath her dress, and looked back over her shoulder one last time and made the sign of the cross . . . achingly aware that she would never love again nor look into those wondrous golden eyes.

Yet . . . she caressed her belly . . . *one could never tell.*